RODINA

RODINA

Alla Crone

Authors Choice Press
San Jose New York Lincoln Shanghai

RODINA

All Rights Reserved © 2001 by Alla Crone

Authors Choice Press
an imprint of iUniverse.com, Inc.

For information address:
iUniverse.com, Inc.
5220 S 16th, Ste. 200
Lincoln, NE 68512
www.iuniverse.com

ISBN: 0-595-17521-X

Printed in the United States of America

To my husband, Bob Hayden, whose faith in this work never wavered

Where liberty dwells, there is my country. (John Milton)

Prologue

Leningrad, U.S.S.R.
Summer of 1957

On a warm sunny day, the young American woman walked along the Neva embankment pausing occasionally to close her eyes and lift her face toward the cool breeze coming from the Gulf of Finland. Two men walking past looked at her with interest. "*Interesnaya baba*," one of them said; the other, "*Da, no ne Russkaya.*"

The woman suppressed a smile. What would their reaction be if she turned around and thanked them for the compliment in flawless Russian and told them that she too was Russian? They would probably stop and want to know who she was and where she came from.

She didn't want to talk. Not now. She hurried past her admirers, then stopped for a moment. Another three blocks and she would reach *his* street.

Near the railing of the Dvortzovy Bridge that connected the main part of Leningrad with Vassilievsky Island, she paused to look down at the river. A hydrofoil flew by, skimming the surface of the Neva; the plaintive horn of a steamer hooted in the distance. A rush of wind picked up a stray leaf, veined and dry, and carried it over the railing to settle on the rippling waves. It floated, reminding her of the toy sailboats on the pond in Shanghai's Jessfield Park, where she had walked arm-in-arm with him, talking about their lives, and planning their future.

She leaned over, watching the leaf as it bobbed up and down, aimless and helpless, a toy for the breeze. Then she straightened and gripped the cold iron railing with both hands until her knuckles turned white.

Across the river, she could see the famous landmark of this beautiful city: Peter and Paul Fortress, a place harboring centuries of pain and tears. On this side, there rose the stately needle of the Admiralty Building, the golden dome of St.Isaac's Cathedral, and the somber palaces of St. Petersburg's past that stood like pastel sentinels along the blue Neva. Leningrad. She shuddered. How incongruous to have this graceful Venice of the North renamed after that hard-fisted, balding man responsible for the death of millions. Pedestrians hurried past her, busy with their thoughts. She could stand here as long as she wished or she could go on. But what was to be gained except more pain and the opening of old wounds?

His sister had begged her to see him: *You can tell me how he is, how he lives.* And she had agreed. After all, no one else would know about it. She would visit the Hermitage to see its western art, and the Government Museum to enjoy the Russian paintings. She would tour the Pavlovsk, the Pushkin, the Summer Palaces, and she would slip in a visit to him...

But now that she was here, and had done all those things, a heavy weight filled her limbs. Her thoughts were only about him.

Was he well?

How did he live? What did he look like now? Was he happy here? Had he made peace with himself?

They nagged, those questions filled with memories that darted like hummingbirds, vibrant, elusive, a hum of energy remaining in the air.

Memories. All of the happy times, and none of those that happened later, except the final one. But that was in another park, and in another country.

She looked down at her hand, still resting on the black railing. A ladybug had landed on it and was embarked on a tickling journey to her wrist. She watched the ladybug a moment, blew it off and saw it settle in the dust…then she turned and headed toward his street.

Once she found the number on the house, she stood across the street studying the drab apartment building. The sun and the rains had faded the paint, leaving an uneven yellow hue. Along its front, ran a huge drainpipe; its corroded opening leered at her across the wide sidewalk like an obscene and gaping mouth.

What if the door opened and he walked out? He would misunderstand, think she had finally given in. It would be cruel to mislead him.

Anger flared again. And what about *her?* She pressed her purse against her chest. She would see him. She must.

There was no one on the street. No one had seen her come here and no one would see her leave.

Her head ached. She rubbed her temple, pushed her hair back, then crossed the street and rang the bell.

PART I

SHANGHAI, CHINA

1937-1947

CHAPTER ONE

14 August, 1937

That Saturday the city was heavy with humidity that clung to the body like a steaming sheet. No one suspected the muggy day would turn into a carnage.

At a 100 degree temperature, pedestrians, both Chinese and European moved at a lethargic pace, careful to avoid sinking their heels in the softened asphalt. Even rickshaw coolies sat on the curbs cooling themselves with straw fans instead of running along sidewalks soliciting customers.

Two women and a teenage girl came off the tramcar at the corner of Nanking Road and the Bund. They walked slowly avoiding huge wooden wheelbarrows filled with loads of food and chickens, and a row of one-wheeled carts that nosed their way among pedestrians. The coolies, bent under their bamboo poles with buckets of hot water, singsonged 'hey-ho, hey-ho' to clear their way, and the high-pitched voices of hawkers shouted bargain prices on wares piled high in doorways and alleys.

The women stopped. One was fair with short blond hair and gray eyes. Dressed in a white linen dress and white high-heeled shoes, Lydia Muravina at 38, still had a shapely figure. The other woman had dark, wispy hair tied in a knot at the nape of her neck. A straight print dress that covered her rather plump figure made Sara Rosen look older than her 42 years. Vickie, the young girl, was Lydia Muravina's daughter and although she had dark chestnut hair and brown eyes, she bore a striking resemblance to her mother.

Suddenly, Lydia frowned. "Aren't we near the area Jacob warned us about?" she asked, nodding toward Nantao and Pootung.

Sara shrugged. "My brother is a worrier, Lydia. The Chinese sectors are close, but we're still in the International Settlement."

When Lydia hesitated, Sara touched her arm. "You asked me for the best place to buy a watch for your husband's birthday, didn't you?" And when Lydia nodded, Sara went on: "It would be a shame to turn back now when we're only a block away from the Palace Hotel's jewelry shop." She looked toward the river and squinted. "Down there, the Japanese flagship *Idzumo* is anchored right off the Japanese consulate. It's nothing but an aggravation to the Chinese. I don't know how long this war will go on, but they drive each other from one Chinese sector to another with a frightful loss of life. Sooner or later the Japanese will take over, and we might as well get used to the idea now."

They stood on the Bund along Whangpoo River that was crowded with moored junks and small boats. Farther down, a steady stream of Chinese refugees poured across the Garden Bridge that spanned the foul-smelling Soochow Creek filled with dozens of sampans. Women carried baskets full of howling babies and squawking chickens; some men dragged their possessions piled high on two-wheel carts; others carried their elderly parents on their backs. Trotting, pushing, shoving, they fanned out on the Bund like a spilling sack of grain.

Into this din of human misery, another sound intruded...a distant drone of planes. Vickie and her mother looked up. Four Chinese planes emerged from the dark clouds and headed downriver toward the flagship *Idzumo*.

A rapid ra-ta-ta of gunfire came from the ship. Without a word, Sara grabbed Vickie and Lydia by the arms, and rushed away from the Bund. She passed the Palace Hotel entrance without stopping, and hurried them on until she rounded the corner and pressed herself against the wall of the Chase Bank, motioning to Lydia and Vickie to do the same.

"We'll wait here until the planes are gone," Sara said. "Sometimes there's more danger from the falling shrapnel than from the…" Her words were strangled in the shrill whistle of a falling bomb. Seconds later, as Vickie peeked around the corner, a huge wall of water rose from the Whangpoo and spilled over the banks, sweeping the grassy promenades and washing over the parked cars. In the next instant a splintering explosion sounded so near that Sara pulled Lydia and Vickie down to the ground. Vickie covered her head with her arms. Two more explosions shattered the air before the drone of the planes faded in the distance.

Sara was the first to rise. The women looked at each other. "My God, what did they hit?" Lydia cried. "Let's go home!"

Vickie was too stunned to speak.

"People are hurt," Sara said. "We must see if we can help."

Lydia put her arm around Vickie's shoulders. "I don't want to expose you to it."

Vickie stiffened. She threw her mother's arm away. "Mama, I'm fifteen, not a child anymore."

Without a word, Lydia turned and followed Sara. Once around the corner, they all stopped and Vickie stared. The street where they walked minutes earlier, was thick with black smoke and flames. Two hotels facing each other across Nanking Road, had been hit. One bomb had gone through the roof of the Palace Hotel, the other had struck the street, creating an immense crater and damaging the Cathay Hotel.

Twisted coils of steel and iron protruded from the buildings like fractured bones, and the hotels' splendid façades lay on the ground in huge slabs. Bodies, pinned under heavy debris, lay in grotesque positions, and for a few seconds, there was utter stillness…a moment frozen in time. Then, a swaying window broke loose and crashed to the pavement already thick with shattered glass.

The gigantic hole that filled the street between the two hotels came alive with people clawing, slipping, scampering to get out. Screams and cries for help rose into the sky as if hell itself had been recreated. Vickie's heart pounded and she trembled all over. She saw her mother, dizzy and perspiring, lean against the wall of a building. She reached out and touched Lydia's cheek.

Sara looked at her too. "Don't you dare faint, Lydia," she said.

Vickie put her arm around her mother's waist and held her, until Sara took her by the arm and tried to pull her toward the injured. But Lydia stood immobilized and seemed disoriented. Vickie looked at her mother's shocked face and wondered if memories of the Siberian horrors she had faced in her youth returned to haunt her.

Another explosion shook the ground. Seconds later a cloud of black smoke rose in the distance.

"Another bomb," came a shout behind them. "Looks like it hit near the French Concession this time."

Lydia started to shake and cried out: "Sara, did you hear that? We must go home!"

Sara, who by then was helping someone tie a tourniquet around the hemorrhaging arm of an unconscious man, said: "I can't leave now." She raised her head to the sky. "The smoke is far from here, but go home if you want."

Vickie bent over a small boy in a sailor suit. The child was crying in great gasps and calling for his mother in French.

Lydia grabbed Vickie's arm. "Come with me!"

Vickie shook her head.

"Vickie! Did you hear? We're going home."

Vickie freed her arm and bent over the child again. "I'm not going. I'm staying with Aunt Sara."

She heard her mother hesitate for a few seconds, then say: "If Sara wants to stay, it's her business. But you must come with me."

Vickie tightened her lips but didn't move.

Her mother raised her voice. "You're headstrong, that's all! Your father and Nina…they may need us! We have to go home!"

Sara straightened. "Don't worry Lydia. For goodness sake, Kiril is a doctor, he would know what to do if need be."

Lydia looked at both of them with frightened eyes, then turned and fled. Vickie watched her mother go and for a few moments was tempted to go with her to safety.

A child's scream pierced the air behind Vickie. She whirled around and saw a Chinese girl trapped under a piece of masonry. All fear forgotten, Vickie rushed toward the child. Sara knelt beside her and together they tried to lift the slab. The sharp edges scraped Vickie's hands as she pushed up but it was too heavy. A man appeared by their side and as he and Sara barely raised the slab, Vickie managed to pull the child out. She couldn't have been more than five or six years old. Her mangled legs were covered with blood and as Vickie lifted her, the girl fainted in her arms.

Her vision blurred, Vickie swallowed tears trying to control a rising sob. Gently, she pulled back a few strands of hair off the child's face and stroked her forehead with a trembling hand.

"Give her to me, Mademoiselle," the man said in French and Vickie handed the child to him. He carried the little girl to his car which already held two other wounded people. After lowering the girl to the car floor, he got in and drove away.

Sara rose and glanced at Vickie's bloodied hands. "We'll have to get some iodine to put on those scratches," she said, wiping them with a handkerchief. Unable to control her trembling, Vickie leaned against Sara.

Sara. A dear, selfless friend. When Vickie and her family fled to Shanghai from Harbin two months ago, Sara and her brother, Dr. Jacob Rosen, found them a temporary place to stay and did everything they could to make their adjustment easier.

Vickie took Sara's hand. Together they picked their way among shards of glass, plaster, and bent metal, circling a burning automobile parked at the curb. Unharmed civilians, who moments earlier huddled in shock at hotel entrances, now rushed to help the injured who had been thrown into the entrance of the Cathay Hotel by the force of the explosion.

A small Chinese boy whimpered on the ground near the entrance to the Palace Hotel, and two stories above him, a woman clung to the partially demolished wall. The piece of masonry broke loose, crashing to the ground through the glass awning of the hotel entrance. The woman's shrill scream reverberated in Vickie's ears. She made a move toward her but Sara held her back. "No, Vickie. This time we must wait for help."

A few minutes went by. Vickie's stomach churned until the Municipal Police, the Volunteer Corps, and rescue workers arrived on the scene.

Their arms and clothes now covered with blood and dirt, Vickie and Sara helped the rescue teams wherever they could until Sara finally said: "It's time to go home. We've done all we can here."

Dazed, Vickie felt a sudden cramp in her jaws. She touched her face and the pain worsened.

"Your teeth are clenched," Sara said. "Open your mouth and take a deep breath."

Afraid to relax, Vickie stood rigid.

Sara placed her hand on Vickie's shoulder. It was a gentle touch, and Vickie looked at Sara's hand.

"It's all right to let go, Vickie. It's all right."

Hiding her face against the older woman's chest, Vickie wept.

*　　　　　　　*　　　　　　　*

The next morning the North China Daily News, the English language paper, described the bombing in detail. The Chinese pilots had missed their target, the *Idzumo*. As a result of the Japanese anti-aircraft guns, the planes' bomb racks had been damaged, which accidently discharged bombs on the International Settlement and on the refugee center set up in the Amusement World at the edge of the French Concession. The paper reported that close to twelve hundred people had been killed and hundreds more wounded.

Vickie translated the article into Russian and when she finished, her stepfather rose from the dining chair and paced the room. Tall, with patrician bearing and slow, deliberate movements, he looked every inch the aristocrat that he was. A physician by profession, but a Prince Muravin by birth. His reddish-brown hair framed a high forehead, and his gray eyes looked at the world with confidence. Right now he faced Vickie's mother with a frown. "Stay away from the Bund. We can get everything we need right here in the French Concession," he said. "Please don't take any foolish chances."

"I tried to tell that to Vickie," Lydia said, "but she disobeyed and stayed behind with Sara."

Vickie waited for a reprimand but instead, Kiril put his arm around her mother's shoulders and kissed her cheek. "Vickie hadn't gone through the Siberian horror as you did, my dear. She wanted to help. Be patient with her. We're all under stress now. Yesterday's bombing is a reminder that we're not yet safe."

Lydia didn't answer and without looking at Vickie started setting the table for dinner.

How painful yesterday's experience was for Mama, Vickie thought. Her mother was only eighteen when the Bolsheviks overran her home in Krasnoyarsk and killed her parents. When Vickie asked how it happened, her mother said that someday she would tell her about it but until then she didn't need to know more. How terrifying it must have been to flee alone from Siberia, leaving her dead parents behind. Vickie shuddered.

She went over to her mother and tried to hug her, but Lydia turned away and busied herself over the table.

That night Vickie could not go to sleep. The night before, she had nightmares about the bombing and tonight she could still see the bloodied legs of the child she had held in her arms. She and her family had to flee Harbin because of the Japanese, and now the Japanese were in Shanghai. What would happen to them? She had lost count how many times her Mother had said what a tragedy it was that they were refugees—no embassy, no consulate to protect them, no *rodina*—their motherland, they could return to if the going got rough.

The moon was out. She climbed out of bed and ran to the window, the moist soles of her feet sticking to the polished floor as soon as she stepped off the rug. Pulling the curtain aside, she leaned out the open window. The full moon cast long, hazy shafts of light into the room. I am fifteen years old, she thought. Dreadful to be fifteen. Not a child anymore, but not an adult either. What did the future hold? Security was vital, and security meant citizenship and a safe place to live. Eerie shadows surrounded her. Padding back to her bed, she climbed in and curled up, burrowing her face into the pillow.

CHAPTER TWO

Vickie's stepfather was right in keeping the family away from the International Settlement for in the weeks that followed, there was a succession of bombings by both sides. The Japanese hit two of the largest department stores in the downtown area, killing over six hundred more people.

The French Concession was safe from bombings, and with Sara's help, Vickie's mother found a suitable place in the Berne Apartment House on Avenue Joffre. It was perfect for their needs. Divided into two sections by a long corridor, it afforded total privacy between the living quarters and what would be Kiril's waiting room and office. The 'key money' however, was three thousand dollars, which, at the rate of current exchange, came to forty five thousand Shanghai dollars.

Vickie was in the kitchen peeling potatoes, when her mother came home and told her stepfather about the key money.

"My God, I had no idea it would be so high," Vickie heard him say. "That's out of the question for us. Once we get the apartment, I'll have to equip my office and our savings won't stretch…"

"We'll manage," her mother interrupted. "Your office has to be in a good location. People are influenced by things like that. You're not yet known in Shanghai. First impressions are important. Remember the proverb, 'at first you're judged by your clothes, and only later by your intellect.'"

Kiril shook his head. "You and your proverbs. I'm sorry, dear. But the price is unrealistic for us. We'll have to find something less expensive."

Her mother walked into Vickie's room and took her by the hand. "Come, let's go for a walk, I need some air."

Something in the tone of her mother's voice made Vickie follow her without question although she was surprised at the strange time Lydia chose for a walk, it was mid-afternoon and still too warm for a pleasant stroll.

Once on the street and without looking at Vickie, Lydia said: "We're not going for a walk. I didn't want your father to know where I'm really going, so I pretended you and I are going for a stroll."

Vickie knew better than to ask questions, and soon enough she knew where they were headed. The Rosens lived only a few blocks away.

Jacob opened the door. "Come in! Sara and Joseph have gone to buy shoes," he said, pushing his disheveled black hair off his forehead and stuffing a stethoscope into the side pocket of his doctor's white coat.

"That boy's feet grow by the day," he added, his craggy face settling into an indulgent smile whenever his nephew was mentioned. His shoulders were stooped, making him appear shorter than average. He lumbered ahead of them leading the way into his office.

The apartment was light and airy. In the entry hall chairs were lined up against both walls. Newspapers and magazines were neatly stacked on two low tables and Vickie guessed that the hall served as a waiting room for Jacob's patients.

"My afternoon patients aren't due to come in for another hour, so we can talk."

When they sat down, Jacob behind his desk in a swivel chair, and Vickie and her mother on leather armchairs facing him, Vickie noticed that Jacob saw her mother clutching her purse nervously. He leaned forward, pushing aside a journal on dermatology, his dark eyes studying Lydia kindly. "Are you or Vickie sick?" And when Lydia shook her head, he raised one brow: "Is everything all right at home?"

Her mother nodded and dabbed her upper lip with a handkerchief. Jacob's ink-stained fingers twirled a pencil. "Still hot. It will take a while for you all to adjust to this climate."

"It was hot in Harbin, too," Lydia said. "I remember the dust storms and the hot air but when we used to go across the Sungari to picnic and swim, the air was dry and my dress never clung to my skin like this." She pulled the collar of her beige print dress away from her neck.

"It's the humidity that makes the difference. Unfortunately the Whangpoo is no Sungari, so you'll have to settle for cool showers instead."

Her mother put the handkerchief back in her purse, snapped the flap closed, and leaned forward. "Jacob, I came to ask your advice."

Jacob waited.

Vickie watched her mother interlace her fingers tightly on her lap and wondered what made her so ill-at-ease.

"I found this nice apartment and it is absolutely perfect for us," Lydia said, rushing on. "It's made to order for us. There are two large rooms that could be Kiril's office and waiting room, and they're set quite apart from the rest of the apartment. The place is in good location, sunny and cheerful. The trouble is Kiril says the key money is too high and he wants me to find something more modest, but I feel we should start out in a place that is large enough and…and *nice* enough for his office. So, I wonder—I mean—could you recommend a bank where we could get a loan? We don't have anything to offer as collateral right now, but what with Kiril's future practice and his past reputation, it shouldn't be too difficult, should it?"

A note of such desperate plea sounded in her mother's voice, that Vickie squirmed in her seat. How embarrassing.

"How much is the key money?" Jacob asked.

"Three thousand dollars."

Jacob put down his pencil and pushed his chair back. "Let me loan you the money," he said. "This way you won't have to worry about meeting monthly payments at the bank. With me, you pay back at your convenience."

"That's most generous of you, but I..." Lydia's voice trailed off lamely. "We shouldn't be taking advantage of our friendship, Jacob."

"No advantage. What are friends for? It's not a gift, only a loan, so what's the big deal?"

"How can we ever thank you?"

"Forget it. There's give and take in every friendship. Who knows? Someday I may need a favor from you."

*   *   *

On the way home, Vickie's heart filled with tenderness toward her mother. She saw how difficult this visit had been and now she didn't know just how to express her feelings to her. Instead, she ran her hand gently over her mother's forearm as they walked in silence. Lydia looked at her, eyes filled with tears and said: "You see, Vickie, our Russian proverb is right when it says that it's better to have a hundred friends than a hundred dollars."

At home, Kiril glared at her mother. "You *what?* How could you..."

"Jacob *offered* it. He insisted. We'll repay. He knows that."

Kiril slammed his fist on the table. "That's not the point."

Vickie had never seen him so angry. "Then please tell me what is," her mother said, her head high.

"It's demeaning to me that you accepted it from..."

"From another doctor?" Lydia interrupted. "But there's a difference. He's already established here. He's been here for ten years and you've just arrived. There's nothing shameful in that. He was very tactful about it, said we needn't pay back right away."

"How magnanimous for a Jewish moneylender."

Vickie stifled a gasp. How could Papa say such a thing? Her mother's eyes narrowed. "So that's what's bothering you—the Jewish part."

Kiril's frowned. "That's not true! How can you say that? Why, in Russia my family was always courteous to Jewish merchants and moneylenders. We never believed rumors about pogroms. I remember that every time such vicious gossip surfaced, my mother went to talk to the Jewish owner of her favorite millinery shop." His voice rose. "You don't know it, but I referred patients to Rosen. He is a fine dermatologist and was highly thought of in Harbin."

Vickie was trained never to interrupt adult conversation and certainly not when there was an argument, but now with fingers crossed behind her back, she said: "Papa, I was there, I heard everything. Mama only asked Uncle Jacob to recommend a bank but he insisted on loaning the money."

"Kiril, Jacob is not only a good physician," Mother said, "but he and Sara have been good friends, they made it easy for us. If not for them, we wouldn't be where we are now."

Kiril went over to the window, put his hands behind his back and hit one hand against the other. "The whole idea is humiliating," he said in a more conciliatory tone. "I'll write him a promissory note right away."

*   *   *

They got the apartment. The rooms were large and sunny and the furniture they were able to ship from Harbin fit in so well that there was very little they had to buy besides her stepfather's office equipment. The piano, however, had to be sold in Harbin and Vickie's and Nina's lessons came to a stop. Nina hated practising, but Vickie missed the piano and hoped that some day she'd be able to play again. She turned to poetry and wrote poems at night when everyone was asleep.

The girls were enrolled in the Sacred Heart French Convent on Route Bourgeat. The transition from Russian to English and French was easy for Vickie who had a natural facility for languages.

"It's easy for you," Vickie's nine-year old half-sister, Nina, pouted, her copper curls tied in the back with a ribbon. She was still flat-chested and skinny, but her hazel eyes, inherited from her father, often flashed defiance. "But I hate the new school! English spelling is terrible and the French speak through their noses."

Vickie couldn't resist hugging her sister and kissing her on the cheek. "You'll catch on soon enough, Ninochka. Shanghai is not Russian like Harbin was, so we have to learn to speak English and French."

Nina stamped her foot. "I hate Shanghai. I hate this apartment. I want to go back. Everybody spoke Russian in Harbin. Our streets had Russian names. And we had our own rooms there. Here I have to sleep with you."

Vickie looked at her sister with affection. "What's wrong with sleeping with me in the same room?"

"I don't have enough space. I have to share the drawers with you. Why did we have to leave Harbin, anyway?"

"It's complicated, Sis. Mama and Papa didn't want to leave either, so there must have been a good reason for us to come here." Vickie picked up the Berlioz English textbook and handed it to Nina. "You better concentrate on this right now." Nina pursed her lips but took the book.

LaFontaine's French fables lay on the table and Vickie started to read. She didn't want to talk about the reasons for her family's displacement. How could a nine-year-old understand the complexity of political upheaval in Harbin, when she, at fifteen, could comprehend only a part of it?

'A Russian enclave outside of Russia', her mother used to call Harbin, and it truly was. When Russia wanted to shorten the Trans-Siberian railway by some 300 miles, China gave her the right to build and govern the railway through Manchuria. Russian engineers built Harbin and by the time Vickie was born, there were over one hundred fifty thousand Russians living in the city with shops, theaters, churches, and medical facilities to serve them.

Life was wonderful for them even after the Japanese took over Manchuria in 1932. Nothing changed in Vickie's and Nina's routines. They still had governesses and piano teachers and yearly vacations. When she was fourteen, Vickie heard her parents discussing rumors of Japanese abuses. "Nothing but gossipmongers," her mother had said and the subject was dropped.

But then one day something happened to her stepfather. He came home upset and talked to her mother behind closed doors for a long time. Shortly thereafter his busy medical practice was no longer busy and after a few months, he announced that they were leaving Harbin.

Once in Shanghai, the Prince Muravin family became known among the nobility and the intellectual members of the Russian community. Vickie's stepfather's medical practice, although not as prosperous as he had enjoyed in Harbin, nonetheless afforded them comfort and relative affluence. It piqued him, Vickie overheard him say to her mother, that although he was a prince, he could not become a member of the Officers' Club because he had never served in the military. Still, his company was sought after by those who belonged, and he and her mother frequented the club as guests. On the other hand, Vickie could see how pleased he was to be able to secure membership in the Cèrcle Sportif Français for he enjoyed speaking French—the language of his childhood and his peers in Russia.

Then, on November 8th, Shanghai fell, and the fighting ceased. On December 13th Nanking fell too, and Chiang Kai-shek took his government to Chungking. The Japanese set up their forces in the Chinese sectors of Shanghai, and although the Chinese municipalities were now under Japanese control, the French Concession by agreement was still under the French, guarded by a large garrison of soldiers. The foreigners found to their relief, that not that much changed after all, and gradually, life resumed its normal pace. At the exclusive British Shanghai Club at #3 The Bund, men still leaned against the longest bar in the world, sipping their gin and tonics and inviting no one into their inner sanctum but a select few friends; in the French Concession, tennis matches still continued at the Cèrcle Sportif Français, followed by dances at the club's reputedly most elegant ballroom in town; the Russians still dined and danced at the Officers' Club on Rue Lafayette, where you couldn't be a member unless someone in the family had been an officer in the Russian Imperial Army. Others danced and attended plays at the Russian Community Center, favored by Russian youth. The Soviets had their own club and kept to themselves.

*   *   *

Vickie's school days were full. In the evenings, after her homework was done, her stepfather took it upon himself to continue her education in Russian. "You've only finished the elementary grades of Russian school, and you should study more of our history and literature," he insisted.

"Do you know," he once told her, "that Dostoyevsky was a spendthrift and gambler? His family called him the *executioner of money*. His children adored shopping with him for he always bought extravagant presents for them."

Vickie enjoyed Russian history, too, and listened attentively to her stepfather's interpretation of major events during the reign of the Romanov dynasty and the subsequent tragedy of the Revolution.

Sometimes when Kiril gesticulated, her gaze followed his hands as he pointed to a paragraph in the history book. Such graceful, refined hands for a man to have…long, tapered fingers with blue veins barely visible beneath the smooth wrinkle-free skin. The kind of hands that never had seen hard labor yet cared for the sick, her kind, loving stepfather. She loved him so. How smart he was, how much he knew. Yet he and her mother were without a country, tossed about and humiliated by circumstances beyond their control. So unfair. One day on an impulse, she bent over and kissed his hand.

Startled, Kiril's face reddened. "My dear child, I'm touched, but please remember that a lady should never kiss a man's hand, no matter how close the relationship."

"I'm sorry," Vickie whispered, her face hot with embarrassment. "What was it you were telling me about the Revolution?"

She listened to the reverence with which he spoke of the Tsars, blaming their subordinates and military leaders for any bad judgments.

"Didn't the Tsars themselves ever make mistakes?" she once asked, but when Kiril began to explain the complicated Imperial government's structure, her mind drifted.

She missed her friend, Zoya Letina. They were good friends before Zoya's father sold his brewery and left Harbin. When the Muravins first arrived in Shanghai, her stepfather forbade her to contact the Letin family. "I don't want tongues wagging about this awful flat," he said. "Until we find a decent place, we're not going to make any social contacts. Plenty of time for that later."

When Kiril finally told her she could see Zoya, Vickie telephoned her and then took a tramcar to the corner of Avenue Joffre and Route de Say-Zoong. In an alley at the back of a long apartment building facing Avenue Joffre, there was a row of three-storied garden apartments. Zoya and her family lived in the middle one. The front of the house was freshly painted in white and the brass bell by the side of the varnished door brightly polished.

Before Vickie could ring the bell, the door was flung open and there was Zoya. The same Zoya she remembered from Harbin, only taller and wearing lipstick. Her blond, wavy hair was braided and arranged in a crown around her head giving her a grown up appearance. But the voice and the smile were the same.

"I've been watching from the living room window, waiting for you. When did you come to Shanghai? You didn't say anything on the phone, and I was so surprised. Well, don't just stand there, come in, come in!"

The same dear breathless Zoya, rushing on with questions, hugging and kissing and laughing.

Vickie followed her into a small living room crowded with blond wood chairs, a round table covered with ecru linen cloth, and a sofa with an oversized armchair slipcovered in a floral print fabric. Lace curtains filtered the daylight, throwing intricate shade-patterns on the sideboard where a decanter and colored crystal liqueur glasses sparkled in the waning afternoon light.

Zoya plopped down on the sofa, kicked off her low-heeled pumps and curling her feet, dug them between the cushions.

"Here, sit by me, Vickie, and tell me all about yourself. Papa is at work and Mama is out shopping. We have the whole afternoon to ourselves."

Vickie sat down and leaned against the back pillows, her legs crossed and tense. "I miss Harbin, Zoya. Shanghai is so…" she waved her hand searching for the right word, "so foreign, so strange."

Zoya laughed. "Of course it's foreign, silly. What did you expect, Russian street names? All the streets here are in French, because we live in the French Concession. They even have their own police force."

"It's just that in Harbin I felt like we were living in Russia. Everything was Russian, and it was home."

Zoya rolled her eyes. "You know why."

"Of course I know." Vickie felt color rise to her face. "I feel like a refugee here."

Zoya leaned over and hugged her. "You'll enjoy Shanghai more, I promise you. You'll see more Chinese and foreigners on the streets, but there are a lot of Russians here just the same. About thirty-five thousand. We have a Russian daily newspaper, *The Shanghai Zarya,* and a Russian school. You'll get used to it. There are so many things to do that are fun. I love Jessfield Park on Yu-Yuen Road. It's beautiful. Lots of magnolia trees and flower beds. We often picnic there by the pond, or sit in a sidewalk cafe.

"Oh, you wouldn't believe how many theaters there are here, Vickie. Just a few blocks from your apartment is the Cathay Theater on the corner of Avenue Joffre and Rue Cardinal Mercier, and a block down from there is the Lyceum Theater where my parents take me to the concerts and even opera and operettas. In the International Settlement on Bubbling Well Road, there are theaters too, but the Cathay Theatre is closer to us."

"What kind of movies do you see?"

"Oh, different ones. The last one I saw was *The Charge Of The Light Brigade* with Olivia De Havilland and Errol Flynn." Zoya rolled her eyes again, this time with a dreamy smile. "He's so romantic!"

Vickie clapped her hands in delight. "Can we go together sometime?"

"Of course! The movie is about half way between us; we can meet in front and go in together." Zoya shifted on the sofa and moved closed to Vickie. "Now tell me," she lowered her voice, "why did you leave Harbin? What's going on there?"

Vickie sighed. "The Japanese put pressure on Papa to do something he didn't want to do. He never told me. At first he must have refused, because two Japanese from the gendarmerie came over one day and terrorized us by waving pistols at us while Papa was away." Vickie shuddered, remembering the sight of a shouting man waving a gun at Mother. "Anyway," she went on, "we heard rumors of arrests, people disappearing," Vickie lowered her voice to a whisper, "even...rape."

Zoya's eyes opened wide. "Oh, I'm so glad you're here now! We'll see a lot of each other from now on."

"What school do you go to?" Vickie asked.

"The English School in the Settlement."

"Oh, and I'm going to the Sacred Heart Convent. I guess Papa wants me to perfect my French."

"That's all right. We'll see each other on weekends."

The girls chatted for another hour over cookies and tea. Then Vickie reluctantly said goodbye and went home.

*　　　　　　*　　　　　　*

During the next year, Vickie's figure began to fill out, and as she walked to and from school, she was aware of admiring glances from passing young men. In the mornings, she lingered longer in front of the mirror combing her long, chestnut hair and scrutinizing her skin for any signs of pimples or blemishes, fearful of infections that were rampant during the humid months. She shuddered remembering the crusty sores Zoya had had on her cheekbone and chin, and the indignity her friend had suffered walking around town with zinc ointment on her face.

One summer day, the two girls were sitting in a small park, talking about their future. Zoya reached up and pulled a magnolia tree branch toward her, brushing it against her cheek and smiling. "I can't wait to finish school," she said. "I'll be allowed to go to the Arcadia night club with my parents, and maybe I'll meet someone…" she giggled, "someone handsome."

"And what kind of man do you want to marry?" Vickie asked.

"Oh, a good man, but he has to be good-looking and rich. Well, not necessarily rich, but one with a profession, so he can always earn a living."

"Do you have someone in mind?"

Zoya smiled dreamily. "Sort of. I've seen him a few times at ROS Club. Oh, Vickie, he is so handsome."

Vickie threw her a sidelong glance. "Is he Russian?"

"Of course. I wouldn't have anything in common with anyone but a Russian." She glanced at Vickie. "And what about you? Who do you want to marry?"

Vickie scraped the sandy ground with the toe of her shoe, drawing circles and eights. "A foreigner…a European, or maybe an American." When she saw Zoya's surprised look, she added: "A man with a country."

"A country?" Zoya repeated. "Everyone has a country. Ours is Russia."

"You don't understand. I mean someone who has a passport, who is a citizen of some country. We're not Russian subjects. We are…nothing."

"I see," Zoya said slowly. "You don't want to be called a Russian emigré, is that it?"

Vickie avoided a direct answer. "Look what happened to many of our parents. They fled from the revolution and the Bolsheviks, lost their country and found what they thought was their haven in Harbin. For a while, everything was wonderful. Schools, businesses, theaters…all flourished and all were Russian."

Vickie paused, her throat tight, eyes stinging with tears. "And then what happened? The Japanese came. Your father had foresight. He sold his brewery and left, but we stayed and suffered. The foreigners had their countries, their consulates to protect them. The Japanese wouldn't dare touch them, but we had no one to help us. No. I want security."

"And what makes you think you'll have security with a passport? What if the man is unreliable, and has no money in his pocket?"

"Of course, I'd look for a decent man."

"What about love?"

Vickie flushed. "I hope for that too, but love alone won't keep you from going hungry or protect you from enemies."

"A passport without love won't guarantee you happiness," Zoya said.

"And love without a passport, won't guarantee you happiness either," Vickie countered. "Natuarally, it would be ideal to have both."

"Tell that to someone else. You're a romantic underneath all that talk. I've seen you dreamy-eyed many times after a Nelson Eddy movie."

Vickie raised an eyebrow and winked. "I can't fool you, can I? I know what kind of man I would like to marry."

Zoya giggled. "Let me guess. He has to be tall and handsome. He has to like poetry and music. Right?"

"Only partly true. He doesn't have to be handsome, but I want him to be kind and caring. He has to be a gentleman, someone I can respect. Most of all, he has to be fun to be with." Vickie closed her eyes and thought for a moment, then added sheepishly: "And of course it wouldn't hurt if I were madly in love with him."

"I knew it!" Zoya cried, clapping her hands. "You really are a dreamer."

"What's wrong with that?" Vickie lowered her eyes and was silent for a moment. "But dreams don't always come true," she said quietly. "My mother suffered a lot when she fled from Russia, and then again when we all had to leave Harbin. Even here, Mother and I were nearly killed in that terrible bombing last year. The French and the British Consulates protested the raid, but who spoke up for the Russians who were killed or wounded? No. I want to leave here…go to a safe place." She nodded with each word. "Yes! A safe place."

Zoya looked around. "Shhh. You never know if someone is listening. You're too outspoken, Vickie. Watch that it doesn't get you into trouble. The Japanese seem to materialize right out of the ground."

Vickie fell silent. The summer humidity sapped one's energy, filled the body with oppressive lassitude. People in the park, mostly Chinese, moved slowly, their faces glistening with sweat, the thin fabric of their white shirts damp and clinging to their skin. Vickie looked up into a sycamore tree where birds dozed, loath to fly or even chirp.

Her cotton blouse was limp with perspiration, and she pulled it away from her skin.

Zoya tugged at her. "You've been miles away, Vickie. What are you thinking about?"

Vickie turned and studied her friend. "I don't know. Day-dreaming I guess. About our future and what it holds for us," Vickie said at length.

"You shouldn't look at people with such scrutiny," Zoya said with a nervous laugh. "If I didn't know you so well, I'd be afraid of you. It's your eyes. Dark, shiny. They're…" she shrugged. "I swear sometimes I think you see right into my soul." She paused then said: "I'm a year older than you are, so listen to me, don't look too far ahead."

"Why?"

"I hate disappointments. As soon as I graduate from high school, I'm going to take secretarial courses. University costs too much. Then, when I marry, it'll be only for love. I hope that your goal won't backfire on you."

"Don't be such a prophet of doom, Zoechka," Vickie said, trying to make light of the conversation, but Zoya was not to be put off.

"I'm only saying this because you're my friend, and I don't want you to be hurt. Don't think so much of security."

Vickie jumped up, whirled around and flipped her hips. "You wait and see. I'll get what I want."

CHAPTER THREE

Over the next two years Vickie studied hard, concentrating on perfecting her languages. In June of 1941, after she was graduated from the Sacred Heart Convent with both French and English high school certificates, she signed up for a business course at the League of Russian Women School, on Rue Cardinal Mercier, to study secretarial skills.

To celebrate her graduation and her coming nineteenth birthday, her parents announced that they would take her to her first ball at the *Cèrcle Sportif Français*.

"You'll love the dance floor at the Club. It's on springs and you feel like you're floating," her mother told her. "We'll ask Zhenia Bagarov to be your escort. Hasn't he been walking you to school for the past three months? I like the young man, and we know his parents…they're fine people."

There was no use arguing. In her parents' eyes, Zhenia was eminently suitable. A student at the St.John University, a year older than she, and, most important of all, he was the son of a former officer in the Imperial army. But he didn't interest her. He was too serious. How could one survive without a sense of humor? Vickie rolled her eyes, visualizing him whirling her stiffly around the dance floor while quoting Schopenhauer and Nietsche.

In the Rue Cardinal Mercier arcade, between Avenue Joffre and Route Bourgeat, a number of couturier salons, mostly owned by

Russian seamstresses, displayed the latest in fashions. Lydia took Vickie there to select her first formal. A peach-colored silk taffeta with tiny bows scattered over a bouffant skirt caught Vickie's eye. Off-the shoulders, with small puffed sleeves it had a narrow roped belt that tied in front. The bodice was ruched and fitted snugly around the mannequin. When she tried it on, it fit as if it had been made for her and only the hem needed a bit of shortening. The soft fabric caressed her legs as she turned this way and that in front of the long mirror.

"Your daughter looks lovely, *Princess* Muravina," the saleslady said, emphasizing the title. "All she needs now is a coronet on her head."

Just the right kind of compliment, Vickie thought, and was not surprised when her mother bought the dress without haggling over the price.

*   *   *

The night of the ball came at last. Her mother looked regal in a sapphire blue silk gown that draped around her body, the vivid color enhancing the gold of her hair. She was beautiful, and Papa, too, looked dashing in a tuxedo, his patent leather shoes new and spotless. Vickie stood fingering her peach taffeta, smoothing the little bows that now seemed childish next to her mother's elegant dress.

Vickie had been allowed to cut her long tresses off and get her first permanent wave. For the ball, she had piled her hair on top of her head into a crown of curls—a homemade coronet all her own. She smiled, remembering the obsequious saleslady's comment. With her long slender neck exposed, she appeared taller than five-foot-five.

Nina pouted through the preparations, complaining about being left at home. At twelve, her lean figure was still gawky, but her hazel eyes and her curly, bronze-colored hair were beautiful.

Lydia stroked Nina's hair. "I'm sorry to leave you home Ninochka, but the next time there's a family evening at the Officers' Club, we'll all go together. If you'd like, we'll take Joseph along."

Nina brightened. "Joseph! He can do a polka without stumbling all over the place like some other boys."

Zhenia Bagarov's mother had called earlier in the day to say that her son had come down with a fever. She apologized that Vickie would be left without an escort at the last minute.

"Too bad, Vickie," Lydia had said, but Vickie shrugged. "That's O.K., Mama. Papa is a good dancer. Anyway, Zhenia was your idea, not mine."

"Don't be testy. I was only trying to make it more fun for you."

"I'm sorry. I didn't mean it the way it sounded." Vickie reached out to touch Mother's arm, but Lydia turned away as if she hadn't noticed the gesture.

At the entrance to the French Club, Vickie held on to her stepfather's arm and concentrated on the hem of her dress as they climbed the broad steps. It wouldn't do at all to stumble and embarrass herself!

Inside, she gaped at the grand ballroom, which surely was the largest and the longest she had ever seen. Men and women in formal clothes chatted around the dance floor. Kiril introduced Vickie to acquaintances in his flawless French. She smiled politely, murmuring "*merci*" or "*enchanté,*" surreptitiously scanning the crowd to see how many young people there were beside herself. She had spied a few, when a gasp made her turn around. Her mother had her hand clasped over her mouth and was staring at a plump, dark-haired woman. The two looked at each other for a few seconds, and then the woman asked hesitantly: "Lida…Lida Zamovskaya?"

Small, giggling sounds escaped Lydia's throat as she cried: "Yes, yes, I'm Lida. And you—you are Katya Borisova!"

The woman threw her arms around Lydia, hugging and kissing her. "Lida! My friend from Krasnoyarsk. All this time…oh, miracles do happen. Come, come, meet my husband and my son…but tell me…tell me where you've been all these years?"

But Lydia pulled her toward Kiril. "Let me first introduce you to my husband…Prince Kiril Muravin."

So careful was the enunciation of his title and such pride in her mother's voice that Vickie stepped back in embarrassment.

Her stepfather clicked his heels and bent over the woman's hand.

"Katya, my dear, here's my older daughter, Victoria," her mother said. "She has just graduated from the Sacred Heart Convent. This is her first ball. We have another daughter, Nina, but she's only twelve. Wait till you see her. She's beautiful…" Lydia turned and looked at Kiril, "and looks just like her father."

Vickie wanted to melt into the floor and vanish.

Katya offered Vickie her small, soft hand and said: "I'm so pleased to meet you…so pleased, my dear. You look lovely in that pastel dress. It complements your dark hair and brown eyes…beautiful eyes!" Then she turned to Kiril with a smile: "This daughter of yours is enchanting…truly enchanting. Any young man who sees her eyes will soon be lost."

Kiril glanced at Vickie fondly, and inclined his head to Katya. "Thank you, Madame."

"And now," Katya said, "you must come and meet my family." She led them around the dance floor to the other side of the ballroom where several men were engaged in an animated conversation.

She stopped in front of two men, the older large and heavy-set, the younger tall and muscular. Katya switched effortlessly into French: "*Monsieur le Prince et Madame la Princesse Muravine,* may I present my husband, Monsieur Jacques Jobert, and my son, Henri. We also have a daughter, Claudette, who's twelve, like your younger one."

While Katya was introducing her, Vickie was amused at her mother being called *Madame la Princesse.* Clearly, Mother's friend was impressed by the title. When her turn came to be introduced, Vickie bowed to the senior Jobert who nodded rather stiffly and shook her hand without kissing it. The younger man, however, bent low over her hand, and Vickie studied him shyly. He had his mother's blue-green eyes, so light they seemed translucent, his father's firm jaw and dark, wavy hair which was brushed off his forehead. There was nothing shy in the way he held his head high, making him seem taller than he was.

The senior Jobert turned his attention to Kiril whose immaculate French seemed to have charmed the Frenchman.

Her mother slipped her arm through Katya's. "I'm so thrilled to find you, Katyusha. Tell me about yourself…everything starting with the last day I saw you in Krasnoyarsk." They moved away leaving Vickie and the men behind, but Katya hesitated and turned to her son.

"Henri, this is such a special moment for me. We're going to sit over there in the corner and talk, so do take care of Victoria."

Henri put his arm around his mother and gave her a gentle kiss on the forehead. Vickie was impressed. What a loving son.

As the two women moved on, engrossed in their conversation, Vickie stood looking at the handsome young man before her. She could not take her eyes off him. *He must have half a dozen beautiful girls chasing after him.*

She wanted to say something clever and sophisticated, but all the elegant phrases she had planned to use if she ever had such an opportunity, now deserted her.

When Henri smiled, a deep crease on the side of his mouth, half-wrinkle, half-dimple, gave him a mischievous look.

"Our parents are chatting away," he said, "and I predict that our mothers will be catching up on all the years for quite some time. How about this tango?"

Vickie gave him her hand. "I'd love to."

As she stepped down on the dance floor, it bounced under her feet. Mother was right, it did give a floating sensation with each step. Henri slipped his arm around her waist, put his cheek against her forehead, and guided her forward. Her skin tingled where his hand pressed against the thin fabric of her dress, and her face burned where his smoothly shaven cheek touched it.

It was a dream, this tango, this lovely melody of *Jalousie*. As they executed the intricate patterns of the dance in perfect rhythm, she wondered if he would try the most dramatic of the tango steps and in a moment had her answer.

He lowered her arm, then swung her out and held her at arm's length. Taut with anticipation, she waited. When he tugged, she whirled toward him, the momentum propelling her against his chest. He caught and held her for a few moments in his embrace before falling into step again.

Close against him, she felt new and intoxicating stirrings within her which aroused a frenzied desire to press her body even tighter against his.

He hadn't spoken throughout the dance. To enjoy it, to fully submit to its magic, one never spoke while dancing a tango. So! He loved it too.

The music stopped. For an infinitesimal moment they stood embraced, not yet ready to end the dance. Her heart fluttered like a caged bird. Mortified at the thought that he might feel it, she stepped back. Henri turned and offered her his arm. Still filled with the rhythm of the tango, vainly trying to control her racing pulse, Vickie moved in a daze.

They strolled into an adjoining room, where they sipped champagne and talked. "You're a great dancer," he said. "Where did you learn the tango? You knew all the fancy steps…never missed one."

He sounded surprised, and Vickie thought: he assumed I couldn't follow his lead, that I haven't been out before. Do I look that immature?

Color rose to her face but she managed to raise one brow and give him, what she hoped, a sophisticated half-smile. "I often dance at the Russian Officers' Club," she said, "and that's where I learned the tango. It happens to be my favorite."

"Mine too," Henri responded. "The only problem is that sometimes I get carried away and my feet take on a life of their own. "He paused for a moment, took a sip of champagne and suddenly burst out laughing.

"One night I took a wide step and one of my feet began to slip on this slick floor and if it weren't for my dance partner, a girl with hefty arms who held me up, I would have fallen flat on my face." His laugh was unrestrained and warm.

Vicky pictured the scene and laughed with him.

When their laughter subsided, Henri changed the subject. "Do you work somewhere?" he asked, watching her over the rim of his glass.

Vickie didn't want to tell him that she was just out of high school. "I'm going to a business school right now," she said. "I'll be through in six months. After that, I'll look for a job."

"What kind of work would you like to do?"

"I'd like to be an interpreter or a translator," she said, and added: "I'm good at languages."

"Why haven't I seen you here before?" He studied her for a while, then said: "I would have noticed you."

Vickie's champagne glass had tilted and she concentrated on straightening it in her hand.

"This is my first time at the *Cèrcle Sportif*," she said. "I don't play tennis, and we usually go to the Russian Officers' Club. I'm surprised that our mothers haven't run into each other before this."

"My mother doesn't like balls. It's only because my father insisted we come here tonight that she agreed. And how lucky it turned out for her."

"Hasn't it. Just imagine, they haven't seen each other since Krasnoyarsk!"

"Well over twenty years. A lot to catch up on."

Acutely aware of his nearness, Vickie twirled the stem of her glass. "And what do *you* do, Henri?" she asked.

"Well, I took political science at th Aurora University and this autumn I'm thinking of going to Paris to attend the Sorbonne. I want to go on with my studies in international affairs."

Their eyes met. "Are you planning a diplomatic career?"

"Yes, I am. I'll come back to Shanghai after I'm through at the Sorbonne. As you can see, I speak Russian well, thanks to my dear mother. It seems to me that with my qualifications, I would be needed here more than in France."

"How long will you be at the Sorbonne?"

"Probably a couple of years. I'm not sure."

Trying to conceal her disappointment, Vickie asked:

"What do you do for fun?"

"I play tennis, and I read."

"I love to read too. What kind of books do you like?"

"Mostly Russian. I'm not afraid of forgetting my French since I'll be living in Paris, but I don't want to lose my fluency in Russian. I've been steeping myself in all kinds of Russian literature, from Dostoyevsky and Tolstoy to Aldanov and Maxim Gorky."

Vickie looked at him curiously. "Maxim Gorky? You read a Bolshevik writer?"

"I wouldn't call him that," Henri said with an amused smile. "Gorky was a socialist, not a Bolshevik. He was the conscience of the people. He championed the poor and the suffering. So, I take it you prefer nine-teenth century literature?"

"Not really. I admire many contemporary writers: Remarque, Kafka, Hemingway."

"Rather heavy stuff for a young and pretty girl." His eyes were dancing and Vickie flushed. "I don't think so at all," she said rather testily.

He touched her hand, and it ingnited a spark in her that took her breath away. "I'm sorry," he said, "I didn't mean to offend you. Do you read any contemporary Russian authors?"

"Not if they are *Soviet* authors," Vickie said, taking hold of herself. "I always wonder how sincere they are…do they want to tell a story or just spread propaganda to the world?"

When they finished their champagne, Henri said: "I'd like to carry on our discussion. Perhaps you and your mother will visit us soon. We live on Rue Delastre. While our mothers talk to each other, you and I can argue about Soviet writers."

Vickie laughed and said: "I'd love it," and thought: *Rue Delastre, a street of many mansions.*

"Is your father in the diplomatic service too?" she asked.

"No. Papà's business is foreign trade. He exports silks to France and imports French perfume into China, among other goods. But tell me about you. Your father is a physician. I've seen his name listed in the Russian newspaper."

Vickie placed her empty champagne glass carefully on the table. "Prince Muravin is my stepfather. Mother married him when I was four. His parents wanted him to serve at the Court of the Tsar, but Papa wanted to be a doctor, so he went to Kazan's medical school."

"I admire him for that. It must have taken a lot of courage for a prince of the blood to defy the family tradition," Henri said and then asked: "So he fled to Harbin during the revolution?"

"Oh no, long before that. Papa heard about Harbin's terrible plague of 1911, and felt that he would be needed far more in the Tsar's new territory than at home, so he moved to Harbin."

"And his family? What happened to them after the revolution?"

"His parents and two sisters were killed and he knows nothing about his cousins or other relatives."

"How tragic," Henri said softly. "And now you've left Harbin and moved to Shanghai. Was it because of the Japanese?"

Vickie pursed her lips and nodded.

For a few moments they were both silent. Then Henri asked: "May I call on you soon?"

"Yes, of course," Vickie said.

He had invited her to his home, and now was asking to call on her. A dream come true.

CHAPTER FOUR

-

For the next two months, Vickie lived for Henri's phone calls; waited for his soft baritone to caress her ear as he asked her to a cinema, or a concert, or a walk in the park.

On their first date, he had invited her to the Renaissance Restaurant on Avenue Joffre. It would be her first time at that restaurant, famous for its gourmet Russian food. Although her stepfather was doing well in his practice, the family continued to limit their outings to the Russian Officers Club where prices were considerably less costly than at the Renaissance.

She put on her best batiste dress of white and blue print with a bolero jacket, and high-heeled platform shoes with ankle straps. In front of the bedroom mirror she swept her hair up and pinned it into a small crown of curls. A dusting of powder on her nose, a touch of lipstick to add color to her mouth, and she was ready.

When Henri came to get her, his gaze swept over her with unconcealed amazement. "You're beautiful!" he said, bent over to kiss her hand, and then pulled it through his arm. "I'm sure you won't mind that I didn't reserve a pedicab," he said with a mischievous twinkle in his eye.

"People would think we're really crazy," Vickie said, "to use a pedicab for half a block." They both laughed and walked arm-in-arm to the restaurant.

They were greeted with great deference and it was clear to Vickie that Henri was a frequent customer there. He ordered dinner of zakuski, consisting of slices of sturgeon, smoked eel, beluga caviar, and cucumber salad, to be followed by chicken Kiev. For dessert he specified Napoleon cake, and then asked the waiter to bring a bottle of demi-sec Veuve Cliquot champagne.

"I hope you don't mind my ordering a sweeter champagne. The Brut is too tart for me." He crossed his eyes, and sucked in his cheeks.

Vickie laughed. He must have guessed that it was her first time there and tried to put her at ease. She was touched.

After the bowing and hovering waiter poured the champagne, Henri raised his glass. "Well, Vickie, here's to our first date. And let's make sure it won't be the last."

"What do you mean?" Vickie asked, taking a sip from her glass.

"Well, if you won't mind my silly antics, we'll get along just fine."

"I won't mind at all. I like your sense of humor, but I don't know much about you," Vickie said. "Tell me about yourself. Who *are* you?"

Henri raised his brows. "Who am I? I don't understand. You know who my parents are and what I plan to do in the future. What else do you want to know?"

"I guess I didn't say it right. I want to know about your childhood, who influenced you the most, what your ideas are, that sort of thing." When she saw him hesitate, she added quickly: "I don't mean to pry into your private life, I just want to know what kind of person you really are."

Henri twisted the stem of his glass for a few seconds. "I guess I'll have to begin with my mother," he said. He seemed suddenly shy and flustered. "As soon as I was old enough, she told me Russian fairy tales, sang Russian folk songs to me, and gave me Russian poetry to read. In short, she gave me insight into the Russian soul. And so, I fell in love with Russia."

Vickie leaned forward on her elbows. "Define Russian soul," she said. "What does it mean to you?"

Henri thought for a moment, then said: "It means endurance when the going is tough, it means ability to laugh and cry freely. It also means the exuberance, the generosity of spirit."

Pleasantly surprised, Vickie said: "And, don't forget the great enthusiasm for music, poetry, food, and life itself."

Henri grabbed her hand and shook it. "We agree."

"But on the other hand," Vickie went on, acutely conscious of his holding her hand, "it can also be melancholy. I think the Russian soul goes to extremes on everything."

"Well, then, I'd like to claim the Russian soul as mine." He paused, released her hand while the waiter served them zakuski, then said: "Anyway, you asked what my ideas are. My dream is to be involved in rebuilding the Russians' lives after this war is over. They've come a long way since the Revolution, but now their leadership will need help in many fields."

"Their leadership?" Vickie repeated. "Are you saying that you want to strengthen the Soviet rule?"

Henri's mouth twitched. "How can I, a single person, strengthen any rule? I just want to help the people."

Vickie looked at him with admiration. He was educated and spoke with spirit about things that were close to his heart, yet he was careful not to force his love for Russia upon her. She waited for him to go on but when he didn't, she said: "So far you've talked about your mother's country. What about your father, your French heritage?"

Henri passed her a plate of sturgeon and Vickie took a piece. He helped himself, then said: "My father. What can I tell you about him? We are fond of each other, but I don't see much of him. He was born in Tours, got a degree in business and economics and came to Shanghai to seek his fortune. He married my mother when she came here from Mongolia."

Vickie was startled. "Why Mongolia?"

"She and her parents fled Siberia through Mongolia."

"And from there to Shanghai?" Vickie asked.

"No. In Mongolia, they ran into the Cossack detachment of Baron von-Ungern." Henri's voice took on a sharp edge. "The Cossacks questioned my grandparents, and when they admitted to being Socialists, they killed them." Impulsively Vickie reached over to touch his hand but checked herself in time, and picked up the saltsellar instead.

Henri's eyes were full of deep pain. "They hacked my grandparents with sabers," he said.

Vickie was horrified. "My God! The White Army Cossacks did that?"

"Why are you so surprised? Baron von-Ungern was not the only one who was brutal. Ataman Semenov in Chita threw countless Bolshevik soldiers into his train's furnace."

Shocked, Vickie countered: "My stepfather told me that Bolshevik soldiers drove as many nails into White Army officers' shoulders as there were stars in their epaulettes."

"Vengeance can be savage when the mob rises against the privileged class," Henri said. "Atrocities also happened during the French revolution of 1789."

Vickie shuddered. "And now Stalin is in control of Russia. All those purges we hear about."

"Mother Russia will survive," Henri said, and waved the waiter over. "We're ready for the next course," he told him and then offered Vickie a plate of sliced smoked eel. "Have some of this. It's my favorite."

"How did your mother escape?" Vickie asked.

"One of the officers took pity on her and put her on the train that eventually brought her to Shanghai." He looked pensive and Vickie changed the subject.

"Tell me about your sister. Does she speak Russian as well as you do?"

Henri's face softened. "Claudette went to a French boarding school in Tsingtao for a few years, so her Russian is not as good as mine. You'll have to meet her. She is quite an independent spirit, bright and popular among her friends. And now that I've told you about myself and my family, what about you? What are your pursuits in life?"

Vickie told him about her desire to leave China. "I want to have children, but it's important to me that they be born as citizens of whatever country I live in. I also want to have a profession, something aside from being a wife and mother."

"Like what?" Henri asked, looking at her with open admiration.

Stirred, Vickie stumbled on: "I suppose I'd like to do something with languages. Interpreters are needed all over the world."

"And on a personal level?"

"I guess I'd like to play the piano. Music means so much to me. And maybe…" she hesitated, then fell silent.

"Yes?" Henri prodded, "Go on!"

"Maybe someday I could have my poems published."

"I didn't know you wrote poetry," Henri said with surprise. "Listen, on Wednesdays, my mother hosts a group of young poets at literary meetings at our house.

We'd love to have you come."

The plural 'we' did not escape Vickie. "Thank you," she said, "I'd love to."

"You're not drinking your champagne," he said with a spark of amusement in his eyes.

Over the rest of the dinner Henri asked her to recite some of her poems and she did softly, afraid that the neighboring diners might hear her.

Henri had the capacity not merely to listen, but to focus all of his attention on her and she was immensely flattered. When he spoke, he offered no criticism, only praise.

After they finished their dinner and champagne Henri repeated his invitation to his mother's literary meetings.

When he took her home, she walked on air, or so it seemed to her.

*   *   *

Vickie went to the Jobert's on Wednesdays, and although Henri encouraged her to read her poems at the meetings, she told him that she was not yet ready to do that. She saw another quality in Henri that she liked: his respect and sensitivity in keeping her confidence and not betraying it to his mother.

While she tried to summon courage to share her work with the group, she developed her skill to spot an uneven meter or a false rhyme in a stanza. What pleased her most of all, however, was her ability to catch the inner meaning of the most obscure lines in a poem and comment on it.

Henri was always present at these soirées. He sat in a corner on a Louis the XVI chair, clad in white linen slacks, his legs casually crossed, his eyes following Vickie's movements. He would listen to her comments with a raised brow as though she surprised him each time she voiced an opinion. Finally, she asked him why he seemed to doubt her judgment. He was quick to deny it.

"Not at all, Vickie," he said. "You misunderstand. Far from doubting, I'm impressed. For one so young, you possess an amazing sense of what is good and what is not."

She was enormously pleased. "What if I become a twentieth century female Belinsky?" she asked.

Henri raised his hands in mock horror. "Heaven protect us from another acerbic-tongued literary critic. Surely you don't want to be feared by every writer?"

Vickie continued to offer her thoughtful opinions, not so much because she was still too shy to read her poetry, but because she was in the same room with Henri.

One evening Katya asked her why she didn't write poetry herself. Vickie hedged for a moment, then confessed: "I've written poems but I do it as a hobby and I don't think they're very good."

"My goodness, dear girl, my goodness! Why don't you let the group be the judge of that?"

And so Vickie read two of her best creations and was overwhelmed by the positive reaction from everyone.

One day Katya said to Vickie: "You're an unusual girl. You are so young and delicate, yet you are not only talented, yes, talented, but are a mature critic." She tilted her head, studying Vickie. "Your mother told me you want to be an interpreter or a translator after you finish your business courses. Would you like me to ask Mr.Jobert if he knows of an opening at the French Consulate?"

"Oh, yes," Vickie replied eagerly, "I'd be so grateful."

*　　　　　*　　　　　*

As the summer drew to an end, and with it, Henri's imminent departure for France, Vickie accepted all his invitations. She changed her schedule to fit his, and did her homework late at night, cherishing every hour she spent with him. That she was falling in love was obvious not only to her, but to her mother as well. Vickie caught her mother's speculative looks, but was relieved that she asked no questions.

It was Sara Rosen, dear Sara, to whom Vickie went to share her thoughts and her heart. Sara never once chided her for falling for a man who was soon to go out of her life for several years, never once gave her a critical or speculative look, the way her mother had on occasion. No, when Sara did express a different point of view, she did it kindly, as a loving friend. Sara was on her side, Vickie thought, and the closer she felt to her old friend, the more she was saddened by her stepfather's reticence to invite the Rosens to visit them, and his stiff courtesy to Sara. Vickie was aware of Kiril's anti-semitic sentiments and for the first time, was disappointed in him.

"Enjoy this summer, Vickie," Sara said one Saturday afternoon when Vickie dropped by for a chat. A poppy seed roll, Vickie's favorite, appeared on the table and soon the samovar was steaming. Joseph was in another room doing his homework, and Jacob was in his office. So

Sara and Vickie were alone at the dining room table. Familiar tune of Debussy's *Claire de Lune* sounded behind his closed door.

"Jacob always has his record player on when he does his paperwork," Sara said. "I could never understand how he can listen to the music and go over his patients' charts at the same time." She poured Vickie and herself a cup of tea, then stirred a teaspoon of raspberry jam into her cup. As long as Vickie had known her, Sara had worn her hair parted in the middle and pulled back in a severe knot. Now, the gray streaks at her temples had broadened, paling her dark eyes and giving them a washed out apperance. Vickie waited for Sara to speak. The older woman's conversation was often punctuated by short silences, as if she were loath to express her thoughts until she'd found the exact words.

"Yes, enjoy yourself while you can," Sara repeated, and continued to stir her tea absent-mindedly. "You see, I know what it's like to love. You never know how long such happiness will last. Mine was short, but I have my memories. Forever." She paused, and Vickie waited.

"I want to tell you about my David, my husband." A thread of love and longing shone in Sara's words. "He was so good looking yet he chose me, a plain girl." She smiled in wonder, her eyes gazing into some distant past. "David had a degree in forestry and spent a great deal of time in the taiga. We didn't know at first that the forest was infested by Chinese bandits who raided the outlying areas." Something flashed in Sara's eyes. "In one of the skirmishes between the outlaws and the local police, my husband was killed. We were married for only a year and a half. I was eight months pregnant at the time." She paused, braiding and unbraiding the tassels of the table cloth. When she raised her head, Sara's eyes were glistening with tears. "Jacob never married, so, I came back to live with my brother. I knew he would raise my child, so I took my maiden name back. Jacob loves Joseph as his own son." At the mention of her son, Sara's face shone with radiance. "Tell me, Henri is leaving soon, isn't he?"

Vickie's throat tightened. "Yes," she whispered.

"Will you keep going to the Wednesday night poetry meetings after he is gone?"

"I'm not sure. I haven't given it much thought."

Sara toyed with her spoon. "I think it's a good idea to continue. They'd miss you if you stopped going. I know, my dear, because I've heard what a good critic you are."

How typical of Sara to avoid saying 'you should' or 'you must' because if she stopped going, it would be obvious that the only reason she had been attending those meetings was to be with Henri.

Impulsively, Vickie threw her arms around Sara and hugged her. "What would I do without you, Aunt Sara? You're my dearest friend."

Sara gave Vickie one of her rare smiles. "Friendship must always be nourished, my little friend. To me, you're the daughter I never had. That's why sometimes I give you advice." She cocked her head and listened, then sighed. "That brother of mine...I scold him for forgetting his tea time. Jacob never listens."

"*I* listen to you, Aunt Sara."

"What's this that I never listen?" Jacob said, shuffling into the room with a stack of papers in his hand. He had on wrinkled searsucker gray slacks and white short-sleeved shirt that hung over his pants.

"Your tea time," Sara said. "You're always late."

"And you're always early. I hear your alarm clock going off several times a day," he said, leaning over and kissing the top of her head.

Sara poured tea into a glass with a silver holder engraved with Jacob's initials, put two cubes of sugar in and a thick slice of lemon which she crushed with a spoon. "At least I'm never late," she said handing him the glass.

"My sister is so well organized," Jacob said, passing a plate of poppy seed bread to Vickie, "that she even checks my daily appointment schedule to make sure it's not overloaded. I don't know what I'd do without her."

"Nor I, Aunt Sara," Vickie said.

Sara patted her hand. "It's time you stopped calling me Aunt Sara. It makes me feel old. You're a grown young lady. Just call me Sara."

*   *   *

Two days later, Vickie sat with Henri on a bench near the marble pavilion in Jessfield Park, watching children sail their toy boats on the little pond in the distance. The tots' happy voices were carried toward them by a lazy summer breeze. Vickie was conscious of Henri's proximity, his touch, his voice, remembering what Sara said about happiness not lasting.

Henri's mother had telephoned that morning. "Oh Vickie," she said, "I have such good news for you. Good news! Mr. Jobert told me that, though they have no opening for you at the French Consulate, he himself needs both an interpreter and a translator. Tomorrow morning they will give you a test in his office."

If only Henri could stay in Shanghai, life would be perfect.

"You haven't told me how long you're going to be at the Sorbonne," Vickie said, now.

Henri gave her a sidelong glance. "Haven't I? I guess I'm not sure myself. It all depends…" He mopped his forehead with a handkerchief. "This beastly heat…anyway, with the Germans now in Paris and Maréchal Pétain 83 years old…who knows how long he'll last, and what the situation is going to be. I plan to be at the Sorbonne for two years, but if I need additional courses, I may stay for four."

In spite of the heat, a shiver rippled down Vickie's back. "Will you come home for vacations?"

"I don't know. What with the war on…It's a long way home…" his voice trailed off.

After a brief pause, she said: "A lot can happen in four years."

Henri studied her face, his lips twitching. "You mean that by the time I finish school, you may be a married lady with a child or two?"

Vickie flushed. Was he mocking her or was he sincere? "That's not what I meant. If you go into the diplomatic corps, and the war is still on, you may be sent away for a long time."

"I hope the war will be over by then."

A gentle wind rippled the magnolia tree above them. They sat in silence for a few moments, enjoying the breeze, then Vickie said: "You told me how much you love Russia. How do you feel about the German invasion last June?"

Henri jumped up and started to pace the gravel path in front of her. "I'm outraged. Ever since then, everyone but we Russians thought it would be over in a few weeks. Look what's happening now."

"You mean the siege of Leningrad?" Vickie asked. It hadn't escaped her that he said 'we Russians'. She studied him closely. His features and coloring were French and there was nothing typically Russian about him, except perhaps his eyes, open and curious like his mother's, now flashing with a mixture of anger and pain. But then, Vickie thought, what was typically Russian? There were so many ethnic groups in Russia...

"Yes, Leningrad," Henri said with passion. "The Russians will fight to the death and never surrender. I hope it won't last too long. So many people could die."

Vickie nodded. Russian endurance of the spirit. Two hundred years under the Tartar yoke; The horrors of the Napoleonic war; Yes, they would endure this too, but at what cost? A thought struck her. "You said 'we Russians' a while ago. Your father is French, how do you feel about France?"

"How do I feel?" His face clouded. "I'll tell you. The French in me is a pure accident of birth. As I told you before, my mother has spent a lot of time teaching me to read and write Russian, and to love Russia. As for my father, I respect him, but when we're together, we have little to say to each other. He...he's distant. A kind of remote stranger providing for us. Beyond that..." Henri shrugged, smiled, and took Vickie's hand. "Such a small hand, so delicate. Why are we talking about deep subjects today? We both love Russia. I know you do, and I envy you your undivided ethnic background. We both want Russia to win, don't we?"

"I'm glad you always call it Russia and not the Soviet Union."

"It's the people who are defending Leningrad, and yet, how far can we separate them from their government? Think about that, Vickie." His voice was soft. "Anyway, we're being serious again. Let's enjoy the time we have left. It's already the end of August. I can hardly believe that in a couple of weeks I'll be sailing for France."

Two weeks. In two weeks he'd be gone and she'd be left with memories. Like Sara. She shifted on the bench and watched the frolicking children. The sun was shimmering through the top of a sycamore tree, sending slanted rays toward her, burning her neck and shoulders with a searing touch.

A rivulet of perspiration tickled her spine. How she hated the Shanghai climate. Humid heat in the summer, penetrating winds in the winter with mud and slush all over the streets.

She stood up.

"Where are you going?"

Henri's voice. The soft baritone that feathered her ear, sang to her in her sleep. "I have to get away from this humidity," she said. "Besides, with only two weeks left, I'm sure you have better things to do than sit here in the heat. It's cooler on your terrace, and your mother could give us some cold cider."

Henri looked at her with surprise. "You're a veritable chameleon. What did I say to make your mood change so suddenly?"

"Nothing. I'm simply tired of sitting in this heat, that's all."

"I don't believe you." He sounded disappointed. "Your eyes give you away, did you know that?" and when Vickie shook her head, he added: "Well, they do."

After a brief pause, he said: "You should smile more often. Do you know what a penetrating look you have at times? It's positively disconcerting.

Sometimes you retreat into your own world and I can only guess that something has upset you."

Vickie laughed. "I'm amazed that in so short a time—what, wee've known each other two months?—you can analyze me so thoroughly."

"I'm very fond of you, Vickie, in case you haven't guessed. It wouldn't be fair for me to say anything more now, but when I return, and if you're still free…" he didn't finish the sentence, took her hand and squeezed it. She glanced at him. Didn't he think things were serious between them? He expected her to get married to someone else while he was away. When he returned, she would be twenty-one or so. Well, there was something about her he didn't know. She wanted him, not someone else. She would still be free. She could wait.

They walked toward the exit, not speaking, his unfinished promise floating in the air, gathering energy. Was it wrong to hope, to read significance in lightly spoken words?

As they drew near the gate, Henri stopped and pulled her off the path into the shrubbery. There, he took her in his arms, raised her chin with his finger and kissed her, opening her lips with a firm pressure of his mouth.

There flowed into her body such delicious weakness, such great sweetness, she wanted it to last and last.

But it was brief, their first kiss, and as he pulled her back onto the path, she was silent. Why break the magic with her voice, when he would surely clothe his kiss with words and leave them in her safekeeping?

He did not.

CHAPTER FIVE

Autumn 1941

Late Autumn in Shanghai was a dismal time, foreshadowing the cold winter which would bring rain and sleet to the streets, and misery to the poor. The skies were hidden behind pewter clouds that pressed down on the city with chill and gloom. Often, walking along Yu-yuen Road, Vickie found herself pausing at the entrance to Jessfield Park, gazing inside where the grass had grown around the flagstones and yellow and brown leaves covered the pond, once populated by children's sailboats. The leaden weather matched Vickie's mood.

She had completed her basic secretarial course by studying at night, and had passed her language test without difficulty. The examiners at Mr. Jobert's Trading Company were impressed by the fluent ease with which she moved from French to Russian to English. She had stumbled a few times over unfamiliar textile terms, but her examiners waved her embarrassment away with a shrug, giving her a few pages of printed terminology to study at home. She was hired on the spot and given a desk in a room with other secretaries.

Although she had a job, she followed her mother's advice and took an advanced secretarial course in the evenings.

"Who knows what the future will bring, and whether you'll be able to continue as an interpreter," her mother had said. "Just be careful when you walk home at night. Look around you and stay away from dark alleys and open doors."

"Aren't we safe in the French Concession?"

"Yes, but one can't be too careful. We hear rumors. Things go on in the Japanese occupied areas that don't bear repeating." Her mother gave a quick shudder and changed the subject.

The distance between them had grown with the years. Lydia's life seemed to revolve entirely around Kiril and his needs. Then too, she devoted a lot of time to Nina, who at the age of thirteen needed guidance and 'gentle reins,' as Lydia termed her vigilance over her younger daughter. Vickie was now nineteen, an adult of marriageable age and no longer required her mother's attention, but sometimes yearned for it.

Only once in recent months had Vickie tried to talk to her mother about Henri, but Lydia brushed past her and reached for her apron. "What's on your mind, Vickie? I'm busy today, can't it wait?"

"It's   it's something personal, Mama. You're always in a hurry when I try to talk to you, and—"

"Well," Lydia interrupted, "if it's something important, I'll listen, but make it short." She sat down, folded her hands, and looked at Vickie with impatience.

Vickie's words stuck in her throat.

"Well?" Lydia said testily, but before Vickie could say anything, Nina burst into the room, bubbling with excitement, and Lydia's attention was immediately distracted. "What is it, Ninochka?" she asked.

"Joseph asked me to the movies on Sunday, is that all right?" Nina asked.

"Of course," Lydia said.

Vickie picked up her books and headed toward the door. "I'm going to the library, Mama. I won't be long."

What was the use? Nina was always the center of attention. Vickie was six years older, and she cared about her little sister. Once in a while, though, she wished some of the attention showered on Nina would come her way. She swallowed hard, hugged her books and left.

So again, it was Sara, to whom she took her troubles and her doubts. Vickie was aware that her mother resented her closeness to the Jewish woman, but she had adopted Sara as her surrogate mother, and visited her several times a week. She found warmth and a soothing peace under the Rosens' roof.

In their homey atmosphere, Vickie relaxed. Jacob, with his tousled hair and ready smile was always busy in his office, and Joseph usually had his nose in school books. This left Sara at Vickie's disposal.

"There's something that really bothers me, Sara," Vickie said during one of her visits.

"What is it, dear?" Sara asked, and as usual, placed a cup of tea and jam before Vickie.

"It's the way Henri said goodbye to me. So casually, and in front of my whole family. You'd think he was going away for just a month or two. I hoped that he would say something special, but he avoided being alone with me."

"My dear Vickie, how could Henri promise anything? He'll be away for years. Don't forget, he'll be facing Paris—a formidable temptress. And there's the war. Who knows what will happen?"

"Are you saying that I shouldn't hope at all?"

"I didn't say that. Where would we be without hope? Our souls would shrivel." Sara patted her arm. "But hope comes in different sizes. If too big, it can burst like a bubble, but a number of smaller ones can fit nicely in your heart. If one dies, another will fill its place."

"But I love him, Sara. And I don't even know if he cares for me," Vickie blurted out. She couldn't assume that he loved her from that one kiss in Jessfield Park. How many other girls would he kiss in Paris? She didn't tell Sara about the kiss because it seemed to her that putting it into words would reduce the loveliness of the memory.

Sara tucked a strand of loosened hair behind her ear. "I don't know the answer to that, Vickie. I know it's hard to wait and hope when there are no guarantees, but remember, we're stronger than we think. Keep busy and the time will pass faster." She let her hand fall back on her lap. "Your work is interesting, is it not? Tell me about it."

"I don't do much interpreting right now," Vickie said, "but there's quite a bit of translating. I do the dispatches that come in. The contents are often quite a challenge, but it's good practice for me. I enjoy pulling idiomatic expressions out of one language to fit another. It's exciting to get just the right nuance of meaning."

"I guess interpreting is more difficult. You don't have time to search for the exact word," Sara mused, leaning back in her chair.

Vickie nodded. "Exactly. That's why I don't mind translating. Some day, though, after this war is over I'd like to become a simultaneous interpreter. Right now most of my work is secretarial anyway. I'm glad I learned to type."

"How are things at home?" Sara asked after a moment's silence. "I haven't seen much of your mother lately. How wonderful that she has found her old friend after so many years."

There was no sign of resentment in Sara's face, but Vickie avoided her gaze. She studied the tiny forget-me-nots painted on her teacup instead, rubbing her thumb over its smooth surface. After she'd found Katya Borisova-Jobert, her mother had neglected Sara, and Vickie felt embarrassed.

The late afternoon sun shone through the window bouncing its light off the gleaming china. Vickie's face grew warm, even though Sara couldn't possibly read her thoughts. She had come to accept the fact that her stepfather was bigoted, although it still disturbed her. But her mother? They had been good friends, Lydia and Sara, ever since they met. Still, now that a friend she'd known since childhood had come back into her life, it was natural for her mother to spend more time with Katya.

On her way home, Vickie realized that she hadn't answered Sara's question about how things were at home. What could she have told her? That Kiril's practice had grown steadily and they were well off again? Yet, there were tense lines around his mouth, his face had become pale and had lost its robust, healthy look. Often her mother was nervous, and lost her temper with Vickie, even with Nina, over trifles.

"Japan is gaining in this war," Vickie heard Kiril say to her mother one evening. "I'm worried. How long will it be before their arrogance is felt in the French Concession? Most of the Russians live here, and we are defenseless."

"Don't be an alarmist, Kiril," her mother snapped. "We have no dealings with them."

"Remember Harbin? Over there, I had no dealings with them either. Yet they found me, and wanted me to work for them in their hospital, with their medicines, and their equipment." Kiril's voice rose with each phrase.

"O.K., O.K.," Lydia said, "I know all that, but they didn't hurt you or our family in any way."

"You surprise me. You really have a blind spot, don't you? They *did* hurt me. They took my patients away, don't you remember? In a cunning way, they cut my practice in half and would have done more had we not left town. Besides, there's something I have never told you. I heard they were conducting bacteriological experiments on human beings in some secret compound outside Harbin. I'm sure that sooner or later they would have sent me there to treat those unfortunate victims. That made the decision to leave easy."

Horrified, Vickie slipped away into her room, closed the door, and leaned against it. So, that's why we left Harbin, she thought. God! Using human beings as guinea pigs! Monsters!

She pressed her elbows into her sides to control her trambling. Mama always said that fear had huge eyes, but Papa was right to bring us to Shanghai. We're safe here. No use dwelling on the bad days in Harbin…

*　　　　　　　　　　*　　　　　　　　　　*

Vickie continued to attend the Wednesday night literary meetings at the Jobert mansion and found it a bittersweet experience. On one hand, she felt close to Henri when she sat in his parents' living room; on the other, it reminded her how long it might be before they met again.

He wrote regularly, telling her about his progress at the Sorbonne, but never mentioned any of his other activities.

> ...It is a venerable old university, he wrote, and I am glad to be here.
> My studies keep me busy, but once in a while, my mind wanders and I catch myself thinking of Shanghai, my family and everyone I know.
> Tell me everything about our city, anything exciting.

There was never any personal remark to her, but that he wrote at all was enough to keep her hope from fading.

She answered his letters with care, agonizing over each sentence, trying to match his light tone. Her activities must seem dull to him, a young student living in Paris, that graceful city full of thrilling and romantic settings. What could she tell him about her life in war-torn Shanghai? That the Japanese were tightening their noose around the city? That fear shadowed everyone? France's Vichy government was an ally of Japan, and she had to weigh every word she put on paper. She spent hours conjuring up interesting things to tell him.

> ...We went to the Lyceum Theater to hear Madame Zorich, she wrote.
> I agree with you, she has a wonderful soprano voice...Your mother's poetry group is growing...My translating work is interesting and I enjoy working for your father..."

Rereading her letters filled her with despair. So shallow, so boring. One question haunted her. Were Henri's ties to her stretching too thin across time and space? She dreamed of him at night, and his image was never far from her mind. She longed for him, reliving over and over, the times they had spent together.

It was stupid to think about him all the time. There were other things that should occupy her mind, her work, the war, her family. But Henri dominated her waking hours and the last thought before she fell asleep was about him.

On Monday, December 8, she was so immersed in translating a stack of dispatches she'd found on her desk, that for a long time she ignored the unusual amount of traffic going through her office. Finally she became aware of the excited, hushed voices of the other two secretaries, and began to listen.

"I didn't hear the shots, did you?" one of them asked.

Vickie raised her head. "What shots?"

"On the Whangpoo. A British gunboat opened fire on a Japanese vessel and the Japanese sank it."

"Why would the British do that?" Vickie asked.

Françoise Gilain, a slender Eurasian girl, turned to her. "We've just heard that the Japanese bombed Pearl Harbor in Hawaii, and they're now at war with the United States and Britain."

Vickie dropped the sheaf of papers she had been holding. An attack on Honolulu? And here in China, what was going to happen now? The Japanese already controlled Shanghai. Would Henri be able to return? Would the British and the Americans be interned?

Later, at home, she sensed the tense atmosphere the moment she entered the apartment. She hurried into her stepfather's office where he was putting away his otoscope in the glass cabinet.

"What does all this mean, Papa?" Vickie asked, noticing his trembling hands as he fumbled with the cabinet key.

"Papa?" she said, stepping forward, but Kiril waved her aside.

"What are you talking about?" he asked without looking at her.

"Haven't you heard? The Japanese bombed Pearl Harbor in Hawaii. America and England are at war with the Japanese."

"I heard. We can only hope that the Japanese will be defeated soon. In the meantime, we're more than ever at their mercy. God knows how they'll treat foreigners from now on."

"But we're neutrals, Papa. They wouldn't harm us, would they?"

Kiril removed the key from the lock before he turned to face Vickie. "History may repeat itself. We Russians felt trapped in Harbin soon after the Japanese took over Manchuria." He hesitated, as if he were trying to decide whether to go on, then motioned for her to sit down.

"I've never told this to your mother," he said, lowering himself into his armchair behind his desk, "and I don't want to worry her now, but I think I'd better tell you something to make you understand why I'm concerned. From now on I want you to be doubly careful when you"re out on the streets alone."

As she listened, Vickie was struck by the pallor of her stepfather's face and the dark circles under his eyes. "Do you feel all right, Papochka?" she asked, leaning forward to touch his hand. He frowned, and said, "Yes, of course." So, she waited for him to go on.

"You know already why we left Harbin in a hurry. But that is only part of the whole story. Remember all the kidnappings of the wealthy businessmen by the Chinese bandits? They were orchestrated by the Japanese gendarmerie, who employed Russian thugs with criminal records to torture their victims. Then the Japanese pocketed the ransom money, while professing indignation and vowing to prosecute the culprits."

"How do you know all this, Papa?"

"Because I was asked by the Japanese gendarmerie to tend to their victims after they'd been worked over. It was a painful task, and what made it worse, was to know who was really to blame. The Japanese implied that I shouldn't be squeamish about it, because, as they put it, the work was done by my own compatriots."

Stunned, Vickie rose, went around the desk and put her arms around her stepfather. "Oh, Papochka, I had no idea. How dreadful!"

Kiril rubbed his forehead. "So you see why I dread the growing Japanese power. With it comes arrogance, cruelty, atrocities. Rumors of the things they did to the women when they occupied Nanking in 1937 are indescribable. With the British and the Americans now at war, I'm sure the International Settlement will be taken over by the Japanese. We're lucky to be living in the French Concession. Still, I warn you again, be doubly careful on the streets."

He glanced at the medicine cabinet, then ran his hand through his graying hair. Vickie couldn't help noticing that its lustre was gone and it had thinned. She sat there watching the dust particles float in a shaft of the sun. When she was a little girl, she had clasped the motes out of the air, grateful for the moving things to keep her company when she was alone in her room. Now, in the presence of her stepfather's strained face and heavy silence, it was comforting again to watch them float between them, a multitude of light and tranquil specks.

The door flew open and her mother came in. "I don't know what's gotten into that child of yours, Kiril," she said, panting. "She's already thirteen, but acts as if she's still in kindergarten."

Kiril smiled wearily. "When she annoys you, she becomes my daughter. What has Nina done now?"

Lydia's anger evaporated. "I'm sorry, Kiril, I don't know what's the matter with me lately," she said, running her hand across her eyes. Then she looked from Kiril to Vickie. "What are you two talking about?"

Kiril glanced at Vickie, narrowing his eyes in warning. "We were talking about today's news," he said.

Lydia thrust her chin forward. "I think it's a good thing for all of us. With the Americans and the British in the war now, the Japanese should be driven out of China that much sooner."

"We can only hope," Kiril said. "It's much too early to speculate on the outcome."

"Why are you such a pessimist today, Kiril? Why not see an encouraging sign in this? Japan will be too busy fighting from now on to bother with us."

Kiril rose. "Let's not talk about it now." He forced a smile. "Why don't I take you all out to dinner for a change?"

Going out to a restaurant for dinner *en famille* was a rare occurrence in the Muravin family; for most of their outings Kiril preferred the Officers' Club. Vickie guessed that her stepfather wanted to avoid the discussion of the war that he knew would follow over dinner at home. Inevitably there would be mention of food shortages and rampant theft in the city. For once, the prospect of the Russian custom of prolonged table talk didn't seem appealing.

Lydia turned and hurried out of the room. Alone again, father and daughter exchanged glances. "Your mother will never forget the horrors she lived through in Siberia," Kiril said. "You must be patient with her. She lives in mortal fear of something like that happening again, so she has created a mental block against anything bad happening to us. Let's forget the war tonight and enjoy our dinner out, shall we?"

CHAPTER SIX

Soon Allied nationals were required to wear armbands identifying them as Americans or British. If the Japanese hoped to humiliate them, the effect was quite the opposite. Vickie, for one, eyed the armbands with deep envy. These people were citizens of their own country and had passports to prove it. And what did the White Russians have? A registration identifying them as White Russian émigrés. A mere statistic among the other displaced persons without a country. Someday, somehow, she too would become a citizen with a passport.

Early in 1942 the armbands disappeared from the streets of Shanghai and all citizens of Allied countries at war with Japan were interned in the Chinese sectors of the city. Commercial businesses run by the Allies were either closed or taken over, and their automobiles confiscated by the Japanese. A strict curfew was put into effect that allowed only those holding permits to be seen outdoors after nine o'clock in the evening, and those who had to be out, no longer strolled but hurried along, casting furtive glances over their shoulders. Streets, once teeming with pedestrians, now lay deserted and dark. The elegant, spirited city, like a cowed lioness retreated into her cage. The Russians employed by British and American companies lost their jobs, and either found less lucrative positions or subsisted on selling their jewelry, furs, and other valuable possessions. Some chose to work for the Japanese in the naïve hope of gaining their protection, but rumors of abuse and beatings spread a miasma of fear over the Russian community.

One evening as the family was sitting in the living room, Kiril lowered the newspaper he was reading and looked at Lydia. "One of my patients who lives on Avenue Joffre told me today that a rumbling noise woke him up the other night, and when he raised the blackout curtain, he saw truck after truck racing at high speed. Something was piled high in the back of the open trucks but it was covered with tarpaulin and he couldn't tell what it was."

"So?"

"Don't you see? Why race so fast and hide whatever it was? Guns? Bodies? What?"

Lydia frowned and closed her eyes. "Oh, darling, please don't frighten us more than we already are. The mood in the city is tense and everyone is nervous. At the bakery, and delicatessen, people used to smile and chat, but now they mumble brief greetings and hurry away. People are afraid to be denounced for a careless word, and it's getting worse as time goes on."

"I'm sorry, my dear, but it's better to be cautious than to get into trouble. Actually, I'm more worried right now about our finances."

In the brief silence that followed, Vickie watched her mother carefully fold Kiril's socks she was mending, pick up the sewing basket and leave the room. The question of finances had become an added worry. Although the number of her stepfather's patients remained the same, their incomes had dwindled and payments became erratic. People resisted seeing their doctor for checkups and minor ailments, and waited until more serious physical problems arose. Some offered goods in lieu of money, others paid with foreign banknotes that were highly devalued.

"I should have chosen a sub-specialty," Kiril said with a crooked smile when Lydia returned to the room. "Roentgenology, dermatology, obstetrics, they're all more lucrative than being an internist. We've been too extravagant buying unnecessary furniture and spending money on luxuries. We've saved so little since our arrival in Shanghai."

"The war will be over soon, and until then we'll manage," Lydia insisted, a bit too brightly.

Vickie, who was reading the current issue of the *Roubezh* magazine, looked up. Her mother turned to Nina. "Ninochka, take your book and go study in your room. You can't concentrate while we are talking."

Nina, picked up her geography book, rose without a word and walked out. Vickie watched her go. Her sister's figure was filling out and she moved with grace and assurance, aware of her blossoming beauty, not the least of which was her thick hair, unbraided and falling in waves to below her shoulders. Her beautiful sister. What an awful time to be young! Vickie fought the urge to run after her, smooth her rebellious silken hair and hug her. Instead, she pushed a loose strand of her own hair off her forehead.

Her mother's optimism sounded so false. Poor Mama. Vickie knew of course, how could she not know, that they needed hard cash to buy food and pay rent, not the jewelry and furs that the patients offered. Jacob Rosen had fewer problems. He had had a busy practice in Shanghai for many years and must have saved enough to fall back on now. Besides, skin diseases in Shanghai were an ongoing problem; furuncles and carbuncles attacked victims with regularity and needed treatment.

Sara, aware of their problems, had been asking them to dinner more often. Strange, that Lydia accepted Sara's invitations far more often than those of Katya Jobert.

When Vickie had questioned her about it, her mother's answer had been evasive. "I could never keep up with the Joberts' style of entertaining. Besides, her husband is a total stranger to us and I find it difficult to carry on a conversation with him."

"But Papa enjoys speaking French with Mr. Jobert," Vickie said.

Lydia averted her gaze. "Well, our kitchen isn't all that big and you know how I hate to cook."

Vickie looked at her mother. That wasn't true. Vickie remembered only too well the care and love her mother had put into the elaborate preparations for holidays in Harbin, doing the work herself in spite of the full time cook they once had. It was the money. They didn't have enough to reciprocate the Joberts on an equal scale. But then, they seldom invited the Rosens back either, yet she continued to accept their invitations.

"Papa doesn't enjoy going to the Rosens for dinner, yet we go there often enough," Vickie said looking pointedly at her mother.

"That's different," Lydia snapped, "and watch your tongue, young lady."

"Well, Mama, it's all right to accept Jewish hospitality without reciprocating, but not proper with the Joberts, is that it?"

"How dare you, Victoria? Just because you have a job and bring home your salary, doesn't give you the right to say these things to your mother!"

"I'm speaking the truth, Mama. I hate this kind of double standard."

"The Rosens must enjoy our company or they wouldn't ask us. Don't forget, it's a feather in their cap to say that they entertain the Prince Muravin family."

"I don't believe that for a minute. Sara is a kind person, and keeps inviting us because she knows we are short on cash." Vickie turned on her heel and stalked out of the room.

*   *   *

Letters from Henri had become infrequent, but Vickie was grateful that he continued to write at all. One day in the late spring of 1942, he wrote:

> ...It seemed wise to extend my studies to three years. One cannot get enough education when future success is involved. Here in Paris, I'm comfortable and busy. From what my parents tell

me, it is a poor time to return to Shanghai. It is almost a year since I left. Time will pass quickly enough and then I shall be seeing you again, Vickie...

Vickie folded the letter with infinite care, joining the corners evenly and replacing it in the envelope. She kept the letters hidden inside a leather diary that had a strap with a brass lock. She had torn out some pages to make room for his letters, and hid the diary among Russian grammar books on the shelf. She didn't trust her inquisitive sister, who seemed to poke her nose into everyone's business. But Nina, a reluctant student, hated studying Russian, so Vickie was reasonably sure she would never look for Henri's letters on that particular shelf.

Vickie sat down in an armchair, thinking about the last year. It had not gone by quickly for her, and another two would drag even more. Fortunately, she was still working full time at the Jobert office, and was in no danger of losing her job. Her work load had even increased, because the British secretaries had been interned.

Summer, with its stifling heat and humidity, came and went, easing everyone's short tempers; when another winter came, Vickie welcomed the passage of time, in spite of shortages of coal and foodstuffs. Next July she would be twenty-one years old. Her friend, Zoya had met the Russian man she had dreamed about, a nice enough young man on the French Police Force, five years her senior, and they'd been married last May at the Russian Orthodox Cathedral. Vickie, who had been a brides-maid took part in the ceremony without envy.

These days, however, she found little in common with her old friend, who was now engrossed in her new-found bliss. There was a certain air about her, perhaps because she was now a married woman. Vickie had stopped dating young Russian men—she was waiting for Henri. Once in a great while she went to a party at Zoya's home, where she danced to gramophone records and felt safe in the company of married couples. In between, weeks went by and she stayed home in the evenings. The curfew was too early for her to attend Madame Jobert's salon.

She loved to read. In her room, she was surrounded by friends: her books, Henri's letters, the matted Mishka—her stuffed bear from childhood, a few red carnations on the table; they were all her friends and she was never alone...

She had become a frequent visitor to the Russian library on Rue Paul Henry run by a scholarly middle-aged couple who welcomed her as a steady customer and sometimes suggested books for her to read. She loved romantic novels, immersing herself in Tolstoy's *Anna Karenina,* shedding tears over Anna's tragic love affair, and dreaming of Henri as Count Vronsky, who appeared in her dreams dressed in a dashing uniform.

In another year and a half, Henri would be back. But what if he doesn't fall in love with me? she thought. What then? I couldn't stand to be shamed again.

She caught her breath. What made her think that? She had buried the memory all these years, and now it came to her in its painful detail.

She was three years old when her father, Peter Sokolov, left them. He was a loving father, who spoiled her with toys, and she could not understand why one day he came home angry and screamed at her mother: "Don't you call her *my* daughter!"

Scared, and hiding behind a sofa, Vickie couldn't figure out what she had done to anger her father. After he left, her mother cried and wouldn't tell her what happened. In a few weeks, she and her mother moved from their large apartment on Turemnaya Street to the rooming house on Vagonnaya. It was very small and money was tight.

Then, on her fourth birthday, her mother told her that they were going to see her father at his office. Lydia instructed her what to say and sent her in to see him alone.

Once inside, Vickie stopped, wide-eyed at the sheer size of the room and the number of women who filled it. The clicking of abacuses and the pounding of typewriter keys were all around her. One of the women directed her to the partition at the far end of the big room where her father's desk was.

At the sound of her father's voice, Vickie ran toward the partition and stopped in the doorway.

"What are you doing here?" her father said, and because his voice was rough and angry, she forgot the carefully memorized words and said instead: "I want my birthday present!"

Her father frowned. "You better go now. I'm busy. Who brought you here?" Vickie remembered what her mother told her to say and blurted out in one breath: "Mama-says-we-have-no-more-money-and-nothing-to-eat."

Her father's face turned red. He half-rose from his chair and pointed at the door. "Get out of here, you little bastard!"

Shivering in terror, Vickie turned and fled through the large room where the women had stopped clicking the abacuses and were watching her run, her white socks roping around her ankles, tears running, face burning with shame.

No matter how many times Vickie had asked her mother to tell her what happened, Lydia put it off with the same answer: "I'll tell you when you are old enough to understand."

Vickie had suppressed this bitter rejection and knew that she would go to great lengths to avoid such a painful experience again. She tried to shake off the scene now. What's the matter with me? she thought, angry with herself. Stupid. My imagination is out of control. Why bring up the past? The future will be good. I know it.

∗   ∗   ∗

The curfew was changed from nine to eleven o'clock, and Vickie was able to attend the Wednesday evening meetings at the Jobert mansion again, but over Lydia's and Kiril's objections.

"Please don't worry," she told them, "we never walk alone anymore." And it was true. Before the curfew went into effect, everyone used to go their separate ways after the meeting broke up, but now, without discussing it with one another, the group waited until everyone was ready to leave, then walked the dark streets together.

One evening, to bolster their courage as they walked along the deserted Route Delastre, they burst into an old Russian song: *Vzveytes sokoly orlami*—Soar falcons, like eagles.

Singing together, arms linked, they did not hear the rumble of a truck until its headlights blinded them from a side street.

Uniformed Japanese jumped off the truck and blocked their way with bayonets. One soldier stepped forward and aimed his flashlight at the nearest Russian, his cleated boots making the only sound on the asphalt beside the idling engine of the truck. Slowly, he moved the light from face to face. He stopped in front of Igor Sevich, one of the poets, and pulled him out, barking in broken Russian:

"You! Come!"

The young man resisted, jerking his arm free. "What's the meaning of this?" he shouted. "I'm a Soviet citizen. My consul will hear of this tomorrow!"

Vickie looked at Igor with surprise. She had no idea that he was a Soviet citizen, but then she remembered Katya Jobert saying once that she sought out talent regardless of the person's political affiliations.

The Japanese soldier stepped back and stretched out his hand.

"Papers!"

Igor fumbled in his pocket and pulled out his passport. The Japanese took time examining it, then gave it back to Igor with a grunt.

The flashlight moved again. The heavy darkness hung around them, the narrow beam of light teasing each face, playing a cat and mouse game. Vickie stood rigid, afraid to attract attention by the slightest movement. Who were they looking for? Her father's words rang in her ears: kidnappings were orchestrated by the Japanese gendarmerie... they tortured their victims...

Terror, sharp, numbing terror seized her. A crippling cold flowed down to her fingertips and immobilized her. Yet her heart knocked in her chest with such force, she was sure it moved the fabric of her blouse.

She watched the flashlight get closer and closer. In a few seconds the light was on her, its beam blinding. The unseen man behind it was studying her face, and she imagined that his eyes were stripping her naked. She stood before him, fighting a shiver, squinting against the fierce intensity of the light that seemed to be piercing her eyes, probing her brain.

When she thought she could stand it no longer and would scream, no matter what the consequences, the light moved on and she was enfolded in the soothing comfort of the moonless night.

The beam from the soldier's flashlight stopped on Misha Sharkov's face next. Misha was a reporter on the staff of the *Shanghai Zarya* newspaper. Short and stocky with a freckled face and an easy grin, he was liked by everyone. The soldier grabbed his arm and pulled him forward. Misha did not struggle, only looked back at his friends with a desperate plea on his face.

It wasn't real. It couldn't be happening in the middle of a quiet street. There was safety in numbers. There had to be. Suddenly, Vickie rushed at the shadowy figure of the soldier, and pushed him away from Misha.

"Leave him alone! He hasn't done anything wrong. Leave him alone!"

The soldier lunged forward. A swishing sound in the air and the cold steel of the bayonet slammed sideways against her temple, breaking skin, sending a spurt of blood down her face.

As Vickie staggered and fell backwards, someone cushioned her fall. She sank to the ground, pressing her hand against her temple to staunch the bleeding.

The soldiers prodded Misha with their bayonets, and shoved him into the truck. No one moved to stop them.

Damn it, Vickie thought, forgetting her pain for the moment, *Misha is a Russian emigré with no consul to protect him.*

After the truck had roared away, everyone rushed to help her. Bile rose in her throat, bitter, sickening. She fought hysteria, weakness seeping into her legs. Someone took a large handkerchief and tied it around her head. They all talked at once.

"There's only one place they'd take Misha, to the Bridge House...*the Kempetai*...We must see what we can do to get him out...There must be some mistake...We'll talk to the head of the Emigrants' Committee... He ought to be able to clear this up..."

Igor Sevich, who had ridden his bicycle to the meeting, insisted that he take Vickie home. "Are you strong enough to sit on the bar in front of me?" he asked, and when she nodded, he helped her onto the bicycle and pedalled to her apartment. By the time Vickie got to her front door, she was dizzy, her teeth chattering.

Nina took one look at her, shrieked, and ran after her father.

"Papa! Papa! Quick! Vickie is hurt!"

Kiril and Lydia ran out of their room and together helped Vickie into the examining room.

"What happened? Who did it?" her mother asked, her voice shaking, but Kiril silenced her with a raised hand.

"We'll talk later. Let me take care of the wound first."

Lips pressed in a thin line, Lydia watched as Kiril, pale and frowning, examined Vickie's temple, then swabbed it with iodine and bandaged her head. That done, he helped her into a chair. "Now tell us what happened."

After Vickie told them, Kiril took her hands in his. "Vickie," he said, "fortunately the cut is superficial, but do you realize how much worse things could have been tonight?"

Vickie's lips quivered, as Kiril lifted her chin. "I know you enjoy these literary meetings, but you're a sensible girl and you're not to attend them again. Do you understand?"

Vickie nodded, and as the reaction set in, she fought to hold back tears. Her mother left the room, and returned with a glass of milk. "Drink this," she said in a trembling voice, "and go to bed." As Vickie took the glass gratefully from her mother's hand, their eyes met. She had never seen such fear and pain in her mother's eyes, as if Lydia were seeing a ghost from a forgotten past.

Vickie was about to ask her mother if she was all right, when Lydia turned to Nina, who stood aside, watching Vickie. "Help your sister undress."

Nina put her arm around Vickie and helped her up. "Were you terribly scared?" she asked, kissing her on the cheek, and leading her out of the examining room.

Vickie leaned her head on Nina's shoulder, and said in shaky voice: "Yes, but I had to do *something!*"

Nina studied her sister and shook her head. "You look awful. Come on, I'll get you into bed."

Unable to control her shivering, Vickie curled up under the blanket. In a few minutes, she heard Nina's even breathing as her sister fell asleep. Her mother's and Kiril's agitated voices were muffled behind the closed door, and Vickie could not hear what they were saying. The door opened quietly and her mother tiptoed in. "I see you're still awake," she whispered, leaning over Vickie. "Get your slippers on and come to our bedroom. There's something I want to tell you."

Vickie got out of bed and followed her mother. Kiril was in his office, so mother and daughter were alone.

"Sit by me, Vickie," her mother said, patting the blanket next to her. Vickie obeyed.

"What happened to you today brought painful memories back," her mother said in an unsteady voice, and gently touched Vickie's bandaged temple. "I realize now, how wrong I was not to tell you about my past. You would have been more careful. You would have known what a cruel world it is out there."

Lydia paused and took a couple of deep breaths. "It's not going to be easy to tell you what needs to be said. Do you remember how many times you've asked me in the past about Peter Sokolov and what happened to us when you were four years old?"

Vickie nodded, eager to learn about it.

"You were born seven months after I married Peter," her mother said. "Rumors started that you were not his daughter. When Peter heard that, he refused to support us until the court settled on a minimal alimony."

"My God, Mama, how could my father turn against us because of some rumors?" Vickie asked.

"Because it was true. Peter Sokolov is not your father."

Vickie gasped. "Then who is, Mama?"

Lydia's gaze was unfocused and staring into some distant, terrible past. Her hand found Vickie's and squeezed it hard. "Listen to me, child, and listen carefully. Although my father, Arkady Zamovsky, was born into landed gentry, he was a liberal, and I was allowed to mix with the peasants and play with their children. One of them was the son of our overseer, Mitrofan Ivanov. I went to school with him and he was my friend."

Lydia paused, and Vickie watched her mother's face with compassion. There were deep lines of stress on either side of her mouth and her eyes filled. "When the Bolsheviks came," she went on, "the world turned upside down. They overran our estate and stormed the manor house. I hid in my mother's wardrobe. I can still smell the naphthalene as I crouched among my mother's dresses. The soldiers broke into the bedroom." Lydia's breath quickened. "I heard broken glass. Shouts. Screams. Oh God, terrible screams. And then...then the shots and laughter."

Vickie frowned. "Laughter? What do you mean, Mama, laughter?"

Her mother closed her eyes. "Can you imagine?" she said, lowering her voice to almost a whisper, "the soldiers actually laughed! When they left, my whole world had shrunk into the dark wardrobe and I could not bring myself to come out."

Lydia grasped both of Vickie's hands and held them, tears streaming down her face. "Oh, Vickie, when I did come out, I—I saw my parents— on the bed. They were dead, Vickie—shot and stabbed." Lydia covered her eyes with her hand. "There was blood everywhere. In shock, I ran out into the courtyard, straight into Mitrofan's arms. He was dressed in the Bolshevik uniform with a red star on his cap, but I was so distraught, I didn't think about it. All I wanted was to be comforted."

Vickie held her breath and looked at her mother through tear-filled eyes.

"He took me into the barn," Lydia said, "and when I realized what he wanted, I clawed his face and fought him, but he swung his fist at my jaw and I fainted. When I came to, he was gone." Lydia stared at some point above Vickie's head. "When I realized what he had done to me, I ran to the house of my best friend, Katya Borisova…that same dear Katya who is now Henri's mother. Her parents took me in, but I was scared to stay there…" Lydia sighed deeply. "A few days later I fled from Krasnoyarsk.

"I worked my way through Siberia. I scrubbed floors for a train ticket, a warm place to sleep, and I stole bread to keep from starving. It took me a year and a half to reach Manchuria, but I had no papers to cross the border. To my horror, the commissar who was checking papers, was Mitrofan. He agreed to give me the papers but at what a price!" Lydia shuddered, and began to cry.

Vickie put her arms around her mother and held her tightly. "Oh, Mama, dear, dear Mama. What awful things you had to suffer!"

Her mother pulled back. "I was two months pregnant with you when I married Peter Sokolov. You have Mitrofan's eyes, and sometimes when you look at me a certain way, I can see him." She frowned, then patted Vickie's hand. "But you must think of yourself as Kiril's daughter. Remember, he adopted you when you were only four years old. You are now *his* daughter."

Vickie heard an emphatic tone in her mother's voice and clung to her. They stayed that way for a few moments, and then Lydia said: "Now, go back to bed. Your wound will heal soon, and I know that from now on you'll be more careful out on the streets."

Vickie kissed her mother and tiptoed back to her room. Her heart hammered painfully as she lay in bed.

My father is a Bolshevik commissar who raped my mother, Vickie thought in shock. Poor Mama. That's why she seems to favor Nina at times. How can she love me at all? It must be wrenching for her to see a certain look in my eyes and be reminded of Mitrofan.

Vickie turned and tossed in bed. Kiril is my father now, she whispered through clenched teeth, and I am a princess by adoption, but it is Nina who is the *real* princess.

I'm the Bolshevik's daughter.

A knot was in her throat, and burrowing her face in the pillow, Vickie let go a flood of tears.

*   *   *

It took a week to negotiate Misha Sharkov's release from the Bridge House. The Kempetai let him go without apology, stating that it was a case of mistaken identity, but by then he had been beaten so badly, he needed to be hospitalized. News of the incident spread fast among the Russian community and the streets at night became even more deserted than before.

We are defenseless, Vickie thought, remembering her stepfather's words. We're cowards by necessity—realists in the face of danger. She even envied Igor Sevich his Soviet passport. It was shameful, even unthinkable to covet Soviet citizenship, but…the Soviet government, such as it was, protected its citizens.

Given the choice, however, would she take it? Of course not. How could she even think about it after what her mother had told her? Even now, years after the Revolution, stories of arbitrary arrests, of innocent people disappearing into the labor camps never to be heard from again, continued to come through. That dreaded knock on the door at night, the enormity of a sudden wrenching separation from a loved one. Stalin's purges of the thirties…and if not Stalin, there would be another, equally paranoid leader. Igor Sevich may have escaped arrest by the Japanese, but how safe would he be in his own country?

Vickie sighed. A while longer, and Henri would return. Hen-ri…She repeated his name softly, the sounds in her mouth sweet with music.

CHAPTER SEVEN

By the spring of 1943 Shanghai, Queen of the East, as she was called by some, had become a frightened shadow of her former self. Gone was the thrilling atmosphere of a port city where foreign currency bought unimaginable bargains and exotic pleasures, where sailors on shore leave and tourists on a shopping spree eagerly dropped a token into the turnstile of the famous *Wing On* Department Store on Nanking Road, looking for embroidered silks and linens, or browsed in gift shops on Yates Road for jade and carved ivory pieces.

Subdued, too, was the night life. Only well-heeled neutrals and members of the Axis countries enjoyed the elegant nightclubs, *Ciro's, Lido's, Roxy's*. Only they could spend freely or dance throughout the night with enchanting girls, Chinese, Eurasian, Russian.

For the less affluent however, there still existed the seamy gambling and opium dens in Nantao, where one could try his luck at a game of mah-jongg, or escape from life's adversities by reclining on a *k'ang* with an opium pipe.

But freedom was gone. Shanghailanders were restricted to the city limits. In May of that year the Japanese, as an Axis nation in agreement with German policy, forced all Jewish refugees from Nazi-occupied Europe into a ghetto in the Hongkew district. That area, north of the International Settlement across the Soochow Creek, had long been inhabited by poor working class Chinese and Japanese. There the Ward

Road Prison and the infamous Bridge House, the headquarters of the
Kempetai, the Japanese secret police, were located.

All Jewish refugees were confined to living in Hongkew. Required to
carry monthly passes for work outside of that district, these denizens of
the ghetto trudged daily to work in different parts of town, and
returned to their crowded lodgings at night. Only those Jews who were
not refugees from Europe, were allowed to remain outside the ghetto.

Shortly after the order was announced, Dr. Rosen came to see
Vickie's stepfather on a Saturday morning. With his freckled face clean-
shaven, his usually dishevelled hair neatly parted on the side and
pomaded, Jacob looked very much a prosperous gentleman. When
Vickie's mother had asked him once why he had never married, Jacob,
spread his arms. "I already have a family," he said. "My dear Sara takes
good care of me and, widowed as she is, she needs my protection. Her
Joseph is my joy. So who needs a wife? Someone who might bring dis-
cord into my home?"

He must have read Lydia's next silent question because his eyes had
twinkled with mischief. "I have no shortage of lady-friends when I want
them, if that's what you're wondering about," he had said, watching
Lydia flush with embarrassment.

Today, dressed in a dark gray pinstriped suit and vest, a starched
white shirt with a gray and red tie, he exuded prosperity. As Vickie
opened the door, Nina ran out in the corridor to greet him.

"My goodness, young lady, every time I see you, you've grown
another centimeter or two." He tilted her chin. "I suppose your pretty
little nose is not going to get any higher if I tell you how beautiful you
are. Woe to your future suitors!"

He patted her on the cheek, and Nina, tossing her fluffy curls off her
shoulders, gave him a hug. "Uncle Jacob, you always have something
nice to say." Then she asked, "How's Joseph?"

"He's fine. Told me he'll be asking you to the movies again."

Nina ran out of the room, brushing past Vickie.

Jacob turned to Vickie. "My dear, every time I see you, you grow more stunning."

"Not nearly as stunning as my sister," Vickie replied.

"Not at all. Nina is entirely different. Your sister may be pert and pretty, but there is something about you…" Jacob shrugged with a smile, "Something elusive. Your disarming smile, your eyes. Yes, it's your eyes. Are you sure you can't read people's minds?"

Vickie laughed. "Uncle Jacob, you're too kind. I'm glad I can't read minds."

Her stepfather walked in. "What brings you over this time of the day, Jacob?" he asked, shaking hands and motioning him into the living room. "Lydia has gone out to shop and should be back soon."

Vickie studied Jacob's face. There was weariness behind those smiling eyes. She followed the men into the living room. For a few seconds they sat stiffly: Jacob, head bent, massaging the fingers of his left hand, and her stepfather, watching him with a raised brow. The only sounds came from Nina's room where she was humming and putting her school books away.

Jacob ran his finger along the collar of his white shirt, pulled his chin up and said: "I'm sure you know that the Japanese have ordered all Jewish refugees from Europe to move to a ghetto in the Hongkew district. The rest of us who lived in the Far East long before the war started are exempt, but I'm concerned just the same. There could be a mixup in identities, that sort of thing. I wonder if you'd vouch for us in a letter? It could state that Sara and I have lived in China for many years, and that Joseph was born in Manchuria."

When Kiril didn't say anything, Jacob cleared his throat and went on: "One never knows what proof the Japanese may demand. I'm sorry to have to ask you this. The letter need not be long—just a few lines saying that youu've known us for a long time—brief and to the point."

Vickie averted her gaze. He sounded as if he were asking a tremendous favor. She waited for her stepfather to say something to reassure him, but when Kiril didn't, she said quickly: "Why, of course, Uncle Jacob, there's nothing to writing such a letter. I'll be glad to type it up."

"I've never been to Hongkew," Kiril said. "Are living conditions bad there?"

The skin on Jacob's face pulled taut. "We wouldn't get as nice an apartment as we have here, if we got one at all. Most of my patients live in the French Concession and I'd like to be sure that I stay here. To tell the truth," Jacob added with a glance at Kiril, "we would find less in common with the Jews from Europe than with the Russians here. We don't even speak their language."

"Wouldn't that be proof enough that you're not from any of the Nazi occupied countries?" Her stepfather said.

"You'd think so, but the Japanese are unpredictable."

Vickie rose. "You don't have to explain, Uncle Jacob. I'm going in the kitchen, would you like a cup of tea and some biscuits?"

Kiril glanced at his watch and rose. "I'm sorry, Jacob, but I still have to see two of my patients today. I'll get in touch with you soon."

Jacob's lips pulled into a tight little smile. "Thank you, Kiril. I need not tell you how important it is for me to have that letter."

With a nod to Vickie, Jacob hurried out.

After the door closed softly behind him, so softly that Vickie barely heard the click of the lock, she whirled to face her stepfather. "Papa there are no more patients scheduled today. Why did you say that?"

"Isn't that rather obvious? I didn't know how to make him leave without hurting his feelings."

"What do you mean?"

"I'm not going to write that letter. I don't want my signature to find its way into the Japanese files."

Vickie stared at him hard. "Is that the only reason, Papa?" she asked.

"That's reason enough."

"But the other—" her voice rose, "the real reason is that you don't want to vouch for a Jew, isn't that so?"

"A Prince Muravin has never been placed in such a position."

"I can't believe I'm hearing this."

"What is it that you can't believe?" Her mother said, walking into the flat. She put down her packages and joined them in the living room.

Vickie told her about Jacob's visit.

"They've lived in Shanghai longer than we have," Kiril said. "Surely there are other friends who can vouch for them. Why us?"

"Because you're a physician and a colleague, Papa," Vickie said.

"I don't think so," her mother said drily. "I think it means more to Jacob to have *Prince* Muravin's signature on that letter than any colleague's."

"So what's wrong with that even if it were true?" Vickie cried. "Anyway, I don't believe it for a minute. It's only natural that he doesn't want to live in a ghetto. All he wants is a short letter from us in case there's any trouble in the future. Is that too much to ask?"

"I'm not going to sign that letter," Kiril said and headed for the door. "Let's all think of an excuse I can give him."

Vickie turned to her mother. "How can Papa do this to the Rosens after they've been so good to us?"

Lydia went into the hall and picked up the rest of her packages. Vickie followed.

"All they did was find us a temporary place to stay and show us around a bit," her mother said without looking at Vickie.

"How can you say that? What about the loan for the key money?"

"We would have done the same for them if the situation had been reversed."

"What about feeding us lately?" Vickie said angrily.

Lydia brought in her packages and sat down in a chair. "Watch your choice of words, Victoria. They don't feed us, they invite us for dinner because they enjoy our company."

"Come on, Mama, why can't you admit that Sara asks us over more often now because she knows that we don't always have money to buy extra food. And yet, when they ask us a small favor, Papa refuses."

"It's not a small favor in Papa's eyes. He doesn't want the Japanese to know that he's close to a Jewish family. I can't ask him to do something that's against his principles."

"But it isn't against his principles to go to the Jewish family's home and eat their food?"

"Don't raise your voice. I don't want Papa or Nina to hear you."

Vickie stared at her mother. "Mama, Russian Jews are stateless and so are we." She paused, then added softly: "What if it happened to us?"

Lydia, who had risen out of her chair, sank back. "All right," she said with a sigh. "Type up a short statement To Whom It May Concern—no need to address it directly to the *Kempetai*—and I'll sign it. We'll think of something to tell Jacob why Papa didn't sign it."

"No matter what we tell Uncle Jacob, he'll guess the truth. How can Papa do this to his friend? It's shameful and…"

"Impertinent girl!" Lydia's eyes blazed. "He told you he doesn't want his name in the *Kempetai files*. That's the main reason for his refusal. The Jewish business is secondary."

Two days later, her mother was on her way out to take the form letter to Sara, when Vickie stopped her. "What are you going to say to them, Mama?" she asked.

"I'll say that I signed it because Kiril was not home when you brought it from the office, and I thought they would like to have it right away." Her mother shrugged. "A lame excuse, but I can't think of a better one."

When her mother came home, Vickie insisted that she tell Kiril right away what they had done, threatening to tell him herself if Lydia refused.

Kiril's face turned ashen and he jumped up from his chair, knocking it over. "I told you that I didn't want my name in the Japanese files. Up till now I've felt safe in Shanghai. Now if the Jewish situation changes…" Kiril paused to catch his breath. "Connected to a Jew, no less. How dare you go behind my back!"

"Why are you so afraid of the *Kempetai?*" Lydia asked.

Kiril shot Vickie a warning glance, but she ignored it. "Papa, don't you think Mama has a right to know the real reason we left Harbin?" and before Kiril could stop her, she told her mother what he had described about the kidnap victims.

Lydia paled. "Oh, my dear, I wish I had known. I thought it was mostly your…your feelings about the Rosens."

"That's part of it. The Japanese have ordered the Jews to a ghetto, and a German Jew or a Russian Jew is still a Jew."

"But dear, what harm could the *Kempetai* do us now? You're not involved with them in any way."

Kiril started to say something but instead, clutched at his chest, gasped, then ran his hand over his left arm, grasping his wrist. They both rushed toward him as he collapsed into his armchair.

Nina, who had just entered the room, let out a cry and dropped to her knees by the side of his chair. "Papa, Papochka, talk to me, what's the matter with you?"

Vickie pulled her away and gently pushed her toward the door. "Go to our room and stay there."

Eyes full of terror, Nina whimpered. "What's wrong with Papa?"

"We don't know. Now go!"

"Vickie!" Her mother cried, hysteria rising in her voice. "Call the ambulance!"

*   *   *

Kiril had had a heart attack, and he remained in the Rue Maresca Hospital for three weeks. When he was allowed to go home, he had strict orders from his doctor to recuperate for several weeks before resuming his practice, and then only on a part-time basis. The cardiologist called in Lydia and Vickie and told them that Kiril's heart had been damaged. While he could live for many years, he had to be protected from undue stress, and the daily pressures of a heavy patient load.

Mother and daughter walked home slowly. Both knew that they could no longer afford the rent for their large apartment. Part of their savings had gone to pay the hospital bill, and the rest would be needed to live on while Kiril recuperated at home. Since they had no "key money" for a smaller flat, they would have to move into a rooming house. Vickie realized how devastating that would be for her parents and felt genuinely sorry for her mother.

"Mamochka," she said, "We'll manage, don't worry. I still have my job."

"I wish he didn't have to practice at all," Lydia said. "I wish I could go to work. I learned a little bookkeeping when I worked for Kiril, but who'd hire me at my age? As it is, there are so many well-trained younger women who are out of work."

"It wouldn't help anyway, Mamochka. We must think of Papa's ego. His pride would be hurt. We'll have to let him work, even if only a little. My salary will help."

"You're right, it would kill Kiril if I took some menial job. God, why did it have to happen right now while the war is still on?"

Vickie didn't answer. She had accused her stepfather of bigotry and prejudice, and had shamed her mother into signing the statement for the Rosens, all of which indirectly precipitated Kiril's attack. But she wouldn't tell her mother how guilty she felt. Why add to her anguish? And this time, Vickie couldn't even talk about it with Sara. Especially not Sara. There were some things one had to cope with alone. Her stepfather was coming home and she must help her mother to protect him from daily annoyances, money worries above all.

They found a rooming house in a quiet section of Rue Cardinal Mercier between Rue Lafayette and Route Vallon, a block and a half from the main Avenue Joffre. Her mother wanted to be closer to where they had lived, but the places she and Vickie looked at were dark and depressing, permeated with stale odors of human habitation and seasoned dirt kneaded into the hall runners by the tenant traffic. The ones on Rue Cardinal Mercier were different. No luxuries, but at least they were airy, rows of two-storied, cream-colored buildings perpendicular to the street, their symmetrical fronts separated from one another by high bamboo fences that created an illusion of tiny gardens. The alleys between buildings were wide and kept clean by the owners, the fronts of one complex facing the back entrances of the next, the garbage cans and kitchen debris hidden inside wooden sheds.

Her mother had chosen the first building whose rear faced the garden of a Chinese *taipan*. His mansion was hidden behind elms and tall poplars.

The inside of the rooming house was narrow and consisted of five rooms: three on the ground floor and two upstairs. The landlady, Klavdia Urova, a muscular woman of uncertain origin, occupied the largest room on the ground floor. A small kitchen with a four-burner stove and one oven was to be shared with the landlady and two other families who occupied the rooms on the main floor. Upstairs were two other rooms and a full bathroom.

When Lydia saw these, so separated from the hub of the downstairs occupants, she rented both rooms on the spot. The landlady assured them that they would have a modicum of privacy except for the bathroom of course, for it would have to be shared with others.

"You have the advantage," she said, "of having it close to you. For this, and the fact that there is an additional sun room, the rent is naturally the highest, payable in advance. I make no exceptions for anyone."

"What about utilities?" Lydia asked, ignoring the woman's abrasive tone.

"The electricity and cold water are included, as well as the telephone in the hallway, but coal is getting scarce and too expensive, so I don't provide hot water or heat."

Dismayed, Vickie saw a small potbellied iron stove in one corner. She turned to Madame Urova.

"But how are we to heat water for the bath?"

"On the corner of Route Père Robert and Route Vallon, there's a Chinese boiler room. You or your sister can buy two buckets of boiling water which the coolie will bring." On seeing Lydia's distressed face, she added, "It's only a block and a half from here and it's still hot when the coolie pours it into the bathtub."

The smaller of the two rooms would be Kiril's office, and could be converted into her parents' bedroom at night by pulling out the fold-away sofa. The larger room with its adjoining sun porch was to be the family room, waiting room for the patients, and Vickie's and Nina's bedroom at night. A large sofa, covered with a tapestry coverlet was wide enough for Vickie and Nina to sleep on.

Since the rooming house was furnished, Lydia sold their furniture, glad to have a small amount of cash for the 'black day' as she said to Vickie, using her favorite Russian expression.

There was no way of course to protect Kiril from what had happened. Weakened by illness and deprived of half of his practice, a perpetual frown had settled on her stepfather's face; sadness and shame clouded his eyes.

"This is not the life I had planned for you," he told her mother as he watched their furniture being hauled away from their apartment. "I can't believe that my heart has been so damaged that I can't return to work full time. When the war is over and the economy stabilizes, my patient load will improve and we'll get another apartment…"

"Of course, our situation is temporary, darling. In the meantime you must obey the doctor's orders. We don't want a relapse."

Vickie hugged her stepfather and kissed him. "We'll all manage very well, Papa. Please don't worry."

*   *   *

The move was accomplished mostly through Lydia's and Vickie's efforts. Nina was no good at organizing things. She helped carry assorted small bags up the stairs of the rooming house, but was careless even with her own belongings.

Vickie stood by the door and pointed to Nina's bundle of clothes on the floor. "Please remember, Ninochka, that this is not a bedroom, but an all-purpose room. We have to share this wardrobe, too, so let's have a rule that we'll stay out of each other's shelves. O.K.?"

"I won't have you ordering me around."

"I'm not ordering you," Vickie said and was suddenly aware of her sister's wrinkled blouse, her scrawny adolescent neck, her dishevelled hair. She reached out to push Nina's unruly curls off her brow, but Nina pulled back.

"Leave me alone, will you?" she cried. "Just because you're six years older, doesn't give you the right to—"

Her mother raised her hand. "Stop it, Nina," she said, her voice weary. "We're all testy, but let's try to get along while we're here. It's temporary, you know. And remember Papa's health. We mustn't upset him."

Vickie picked up her own bundle and studied the room. It was large and cluttered with shoddy, dark wood furniture. A round table with four hard-backed chairs stood in the middle of the varnished oak floor. On her right, a mirrored wardrobe concealed most of the sand-colored wall, badly in need of paint, and near the door to the sun room was a small closet with a flimsy rod for hanging clothes. Lydia stacked Kiril's guns in one corner, behind her dresses. Vickie pretended not to notice what her mother was doing. Space in the rooming house was at a premium. How long would it be before her stepfather could afford to hunt deer and boar again as he had done in Harbin? Not once since they arrived in Shanghai did he mention hunting. So why save the guns? Better to sell them and put the money to good use. But her mother would never suggest it to her stepfather.

Vickie studied the rest of the room. Next to an armchair, slip-covered in a faded olive-green fabric, stood a small end table with a stained top. Her mother covered it with a white crocheted doily.

"Now, then, it looks much cozier, don't you think?" she said survey-
ing it critically from a distance, and Vickie marvelled at her mother's
ability to embroider reality. True, the doily on the end table and the tas-
seled cloth Lydia was spreading on the big table made the place look less
grim, but cozy?

Vickie eyed a wide sofa in the far corner against the wall. She knew
that Nina was a restless sleeper. In the absence of a headboard, they
would have to push two chairs against the sofa every night to prevent
the pillows from slipping to the floor. Out in the sun room, however, a
long wicker table hugged the outer wall and could serve as a bed in
emergencies, or she could sleep on a cot they used sometimes on hot
summer nights when the soft mattress was unbearable to sleep on.
Could be worse.

The smaller room was cozier and better furnished. Her mother
brought her own bed, which she covered with a Turkish woven bedspread
to match the smaller rug on the floor. Near the window that overlooked
the *taipan's* garden, Lydia arranged a desk, a glass cabinet with Kiril's
medical instruments, and placed a Chinese screen to separate his tiny
office from the rest of the living area.

Nina checked out the rooms, and said: "The best view of the garden
is from the toilet seat."

Vickie laughed. "Could be the best seat in the house."

Kiril worried that their tight living conditions might put off new
patients. But, in fact, his load increased. Although his patients still paid
erratically and often brought foodstuffs instead of money, they seemed
to feel more comfortable now that their physician had descended to
their own economic level.

That first summer in the rooming house, the Muravins endured the
heat in their poorly ventilated quarters with difficulty. Humidity permeated the air, invaded the house, clung to their skin which erupted in
prickly heat, draining energy and straining nerves. Tension hung in the
rooms like a frayed electric cord ready to ignite.

In this time of torpor with no comfort to the body or mind, her mother moved in with them, sleeping on the cot with only a sheet over the brown canvas, so Kiril could have the bed to himself. Kept awake by Nina's restlessness, Vickie found that sleeping on a folded flannel blanket on top of the wicker table was much cooler than sharing the bed with her sister. Nina complained of the soft mattress too, waking up in the morning with the sheet and pillow soaked with perspiration, but Vickie stood her ground.

"I need to be alert in the office," she said. "By the time I walk the three miles to work, I'm sweaty as it is, so at least I need to start out from the house fresh."

Nina continued to pout, and Vickie finally relented. "All right," she said with a sigh. "Let's compromise. We'll take turns sleeping in the sun room."

Quick to change moods, Nina waved her hand. "Never mind. I guess you do need it more than I do."

Vickie insisted on taking turns.

Although Vickie's monthly salary was only eighteen thousand Chinese National Currency, or CNC as it was called, it covered the rent and most of the food, and with the income from Kiril's practice, they managed to stretch their money from month to month.

Foodstuffs such as canned vegetables, fruits, coffee, became scarce and black market prices skyrocketed. Milk was prohibitive and three grades appeared on the market: 100% pure, 25% water, and half-and-half. A wooden box hanging on the inside of the rooming house bamboo fence kept the milk under lock and key. Every day Vickie or her mother replaced the delivered milk with an empty bottle and locked the box, for theft was rampant and even empty bottles were stolen and resold.

A Chinese grocery store was half a block from the rooming house and a wiry Chinese man sold them food on credit, payable on the first of each month. Sometimes the debts were more pressing elsewhere, and needed to be paid first. Kiril's pharmacy bills had to be paid on time and on occasion they were late with grocery payments. When the Chinese butcher pressed, her mother would disappear for a few hours, and return with the necessary sum.

One day Kiril asked Lydia why she no longer wore the diamond rings he had given her in Harbin.

Vickie held her breath.

"My knuckles have swollen in this climate," her mother explained. "We all have prickly heat in the summer and chilblains in the winter. I can no longer wear the rings. As soon as the war is over, I'll have them enlarged."

Kiril didn't ask why she had to wait for the end of the war, and accepted her explanation without comment.

At the end of the first summer in the rooming house, Vickie decided that tight as the family finances were, she needed to start putting aside small amounts of cash out of her salary to buy a bicycle to ride the three miles to work. When winter came, it would be more difficult to walk the distance in the cold wind, and she ran the risk of catching bronchitis, so rampant during the Shanghai winters. It didn't make sense to fight two crowded tramcars to make connections and then still walk several blocks to her office. Besides, pennies for the fare mounted up.

Across the street from the grocery store was a converted garage where Chinese peddlers sold used bicycles. She had already priced them and chosen the one she wanted to buy.

Rather than argue with her mother over it, she took a few bills and waited until everyone was asleep, then hid them under her underwear on the wardrobe shelf. Every payday, she stashed away small amounts of money keeping track of the sum by the number of months since she started to save.

On the first of December, Mr. Jobert raised her salary, saying that he should have done it earlier when her work load had increased, but he wanted to see if she could cope with the added responsibilities first. A flimsy excuse to be sure, and Vickie guessed that this was Katya's way of helping the Muravins. Kind, friendly Katya, trying to help, without stripping Lydia and Kiril of their pride.

Vickie hardly felt the ground under her feet as she walked along the sidewalk, clutching her pocket-book with the fattened check in it. Mr. Jobert had also told her that Katya was planning a Christmas party on December 25. He hoped that since the Orthodox Christmas was not celebrated until two weeks later, the Prince Muravin family would be free to honor them with their presence.

What formal words. But a sincere welcome was there, and Vickie was determined to win the fight this time and make her mother accept the invitation. Papa would be so pleased to get away from the shabbiness of their rooming house. How he would enjoy chatting with Mr. Jobert in French, sipping a glass of French brandy in Mr. Jobert's mahogany-panelled library, and forgetting their circumstances for a while.

And she—she would hear more about Henri's life in Paris, more news of him. She missed him so.

CHAPTER EIGHT

"You don't happen to have some extra money, do you?" Lydia asked Vickie soon after the Jobert's invitation came. Vickie looked at her mother sharply. Lydia's voice was too casual, too light.

"Why do you ask, Mama?"

"Nina needs a new dress for the holidays, especially since we're going to the Joberts on their Christmas Day. I checked in Madame Sophie's salon yesterday and found just the one for her. It's pale green crepe de Chine and would suit her red hair beautifully. But if I bought it, we wouldn't have enough money left till the end of the month. I thought maybe you…" Lydia raised a questioning brow and let the sentence hang. Vickie turned the page of the Turgenev novel she was reading. "No. I don't have any spare cash. I'm sorry."

The money hidden in the wardrobe was for her bicycle, and that bicycle was a must.

A dress for Nina, indeed. And what about my own old burgundy crepe dress? Vickie thought. It had been cleaned over and over and was beginning to show wear. Why was it so important to have Nina in a new dress, and not me? Was it because Nina would look shabby next to Claudette, while I would have no competition? No matter. Mama could freshen Nina's old dress with a new belt and perhaps a satin bow around her neck.

On her way home from work the next day, Vickie stopped at the converted garage on Route Vallon to check on the bicycle she had chosen. It was still there. She asked the Chinese clerk to pull it out, then inspected it again. Freshly painted in black, its chrome polished, it was sturdy and serviceable. She bargained over the price, finally settling for 1,000 CNC, the exact amount she had already saved. She told the man to put it away for her until the following day.

At home, she found her mother alone, dusting the furniture. "Where's Papa? And Nina?" she asked, taking off her coat and hanging it in the closet.

"They've gone out for a walk," Lydia answered without stopping to look up.

Impatient to get her money, Vickie opened the wardrobe in front of her mother, since there was no reason to keep her hiding place secret any longer. She reached deep into the far right corner of the shelf, sliding her hand over the smooth paper lining. Her fingers found only the back wall of the wardrobe. She moved her hand to the left corner, then back and forth in circles.

The money was gone.

Her stomach contracted. Who?

She wheeled to see her mother watching her with a dust cloth in her hand.

"Don't look. It's not there," Lydia said. "I was rearranging your clothes this morning and found the money. I must say, it was sneaky of you to hide it from your family when you know how every penny counts. I took it for Nina's dress."

For a second Vickie was so stunned, she couldn't talk.

"A...dress...for Nina?"

Rage, so bitter she could taste it, rose to her throat. "How could you do this? It's my money. Do you know...do you have..."she was choking, "do you have any idea how long it took me to save that money?"

"For what?"

"For a bicycle. I have just enough for a used one."

"A bicycle? What do you need a bicycle for? It's good for you to walk."

"There is a cold, damp wind, Mama. I'm afraid to catch bronchitis. I'd be out of work."

"Everyone I know walks. A bicycle is a luxury."

"And a new dress for Nina is not?" Vickie was aware that her voice shook. She cleared her throat. "I want that money back, Mama."

Lydia shook the dust cloth out the window, folded it and put it away. Then she turned to face Vickie, her hands on her hips, and studied her daughter with narrowed eyes.

"Your salary has gone to your head, hasn't it? You don't know what real hardships are. Do you have any idea what I had to go through crossing Siberia in winter? And what about some Russian girls less fortunate than you who had to go to work as waitresses or become dancing girls in nightclubs? You know what kind of reputation that work has. But you complain about walking in the cold wind. And what's worse, you were stashing money away on the sly."

"With good reason, as it turned out."

"Where did you learn to steal?"

"It's a matter of opinion who stole from whom."

"To think that I've lived long enough to be insulted by my own daughter."

Vickie swallowed hard. "Mama, give me my money back."

"And I said that I took it to buy Nina a new dress."

Vickie's hands closed into fists at her sides. "That money is mine."

"Don't you raise your voice to me."

Vickie grabbed a chair. She mustn't cry. She must be strong. With all her might, she threw the chair down on the floor. "Give it back to me right now, do you hear?"

"How dare you!" Lydia screamed. "I have a right to take something that belongs to the family."

Through the closed door, they heard the landlady shouting from downstairs: "Stop the dog fight up there!"

"What do you think Papa would say if he heard you speak to me like that?" Lydia asked lowering her voice.

Vickie grasped the edge of the table and stared into her mother's face. "Why don't we both tell Papa the whole story and see what he has to say about it?"

Lydia's face reddened. "Leave Papa out of this, Victoria. You know his heart. He gets upset over arguments."

"Then give the money back to me, and I mean now."

Lydia hesitated, then opened the dresser drawer, took out the stack of bills and threw them at Vickie's feet.

"Here's your filthy money, you selfish, impertinent creature."

The bills fluttered through the air and scattered. Some landed on top of the table, some around it.

On her hands and knees, blinded by tears, Vickie crawled around, scooping a handful under the table, bumping her head, then moving to the door to pick up more bills, and back again under the chairs.

Lydia stood over her and watched.

Eyes stinging, humiliated, Vickie rushed out of the room and locked herself in the bathroom. There she sat down on the toilet lid, and let the tears flow. After a while, she took a terrycloth towel off the rack, blew several hot breaths into it and pressed the warm cloth against her burning eyes.

Nothing was said over dinner, but afterwards, as Kiril rose from his chair, he peered down at the floor. Then he stooped to pick up two bills from under the table.

"What are these doing on the floor?" he asked, turning to Lydia.

Vickie put her hand out. "Those are mine, Papa."

Kiril raised his brow and placed the bills in her hand.

Vickie glanced at her mother. Lips pressed tightly, eyes downcast, Lydia sat stirring her cup of tea.

"I was in a hurry and must have dropped them, Papa," Vickie said. And that's the truth, she thought, putting the money in her purse.

That night, she slipped the money under her pillow and slept with her hand over the bills.

The next day, she paid for the bicycle and stored it in a breezeway behind a locked gate near the rooming house, securing it with a lock and chain attached to the wall.

She told her stepfather about the bicycle when she got back to their rooms.

"I've been worried about you walking all that distance, Vickie," he said with a pleased smile. "I'm so glad you were able to buy it. Bring it over tomorrow and let us see it."

Tight-lipped, Lydia added: "I guess it will make life a little easier for you."

Their eyes locked and Vickie watched as her mother's filled.

"Thank you," Vickie said softly.

"May I ride your bicycle sometime, Vickie?" Nina asked, happily unaware of the undercurrent.

Vickie hugged her sister. "Of course, Ninochka."

*   *   *

The next morning, when Vickie woke up, she saw her mother warming up the coffee on a hibachi stove. The supply of coal that had been delivered and dumped in one corner of the porch had been used up and there was none to buy. Now every scrap of wrapping paper and newspapers was saved to be used in the small pot-bellied stove. It burned fast of course and barely took the chill and dampness out of the room, so the family ate their meals wearing overcoats. Vickie had become adept at pulling on her underwear and stockings while still under the blanket, stretching what few seconds of body warmth still lingered under the covers, and this morning was no exception.

For a few minutes, she watched her mother. They had decided that the purchase of a hibachi would save the wait in the communal kitchen where the other families cooked breakfast, and Lydia had become an expert at fanning the fire and getting Vickie's breakfast in a hurry. This morning in her own way, Lydia was trying to make amends; perhaps even show her older daughter that she did love her. She was dressed in a gray wool dress, heavy black sweater and thick cotton stockings. She also wore gloves with tips cut off to allow finger mobility yet provide enough warmth to protect her hands from chilblains.

Vickie pulled on her underwear, reached for her sweater, slipped her feet into slippers and looked at her mother again. There was more gray in her hair. To save money, Lydia no longer went to the beauty parlor, but washed it at home once a week. The healthy shine was gone, and the hair, neatly combed behind her ears looked drab. She was not old yet, in the middle of Balzakian age, yet what future could she hope for with a sick husband, even if the war were to end soon?

Vickie rose. Thank God she was young and could hope for a better future. She reached over and kissed her mother's cheek. It was warm from the heat of the hibachi.

Taking her hand off the chipped wooden handle of the aluminum coffee pot, Lydia wiped the perspiration off her forehead. "Breakfast is ready," she said setting the pot on the table. "Here," she added, pushing sesame bread and jam toward her daughter. Vickie ate hungrily. Bread had been rationed to half a pound a week per person, but because of Kiril's illness, his ration was increased to three quarters of a pound, and it helped.

In a hurry to get away, Vickie thanked her mother and tiptoed out of the room while Nina was still asleep.

The bicycle proved to be all she had hoped for. On her way to work, she rode through Nantao as fast as she could pedal. She dreaded this Chinese sector of town where she had to pass the daily yield of frozen beggars. Sprawled on the pavement naked, they were stripped of their rags at the moment of death by other beggars struggling to survive in the freezing temperatures. Bluish-gray, as if powdered with ash, the dead lay on their backs with mouths open, eyes half-closed, pubic hair glistening with tiny crystalline icicles.

Filled with pity for those unfortunate beggars, Vickie nevertheless shivered from the ghoulish sight, and tried not to look at the corpses, but she could not block out her peripheral vision.

A rat squealed and scurried from under her wheels into an alley, further unnerving her.

*　　　　　*　　　　　*

As the Jobert Christmas party approached, Vickie bought a green satin scarf for Nina's yellow dress and watched with amusement as her mother fussed with it, wrapping and rewrapping it around Nina's waist.

On the day of the party, Vickie was surprised to find her own dress cleaned and pressed. A new white lace collar threaded with a black velvet ribbon had been attached to the neckline, and matching lace cuffs added. The dress appeared fresh and pretty. Vickie stared in the wardrobe mirror with eyes blurred by tears.

"Like it?" Lydia asked, glancing over her shoulder as she was smoothing her own dark blue velvet dress.

Vickie whirled around and threw her arms around her mother. "Oh, thank you, Mama. It's so dressy. I love it."

Lydia pushed Vickie back to survey her outfit. "I must say, I'm rather pleased with the results. Now let's see what Papa is going to wear today."

Kiril looked elegant in his charcoal gray, pin-striped suit and vest, maroon tie with pearl stickpin gracing an immaculately starched shirt.

How long had it been since they had all gone to a party together? Lydia had accepted the Jobert's invitation easily and Vickie guessed that she too wanted to escape from drudgery for a while. And what better time than the Christmas holidays?

They were invited for four o'clock in the afternoon, and it was still daylight when they arrived. It had been several months since Vickie's last meeting at the Jobert's. As they walked up to the mansion, she was able to admire the house anew. The heavy iron gate opened smoothly on well-oiled hinges as they entered the grounds. Deep in the garden, beyond a well-manicured lawn, the house stood so far from the street that city noises barely reached its white columned front and open patio. Doric pillars supported the second story French doors leading onto a gallery balcony that ran the full width of the house. Recessed farther from the front, the third story mansard with its dormer windows gave the mansion an elegant façade.

Vickie felt a twinge of envy. So much space for a family of four. The affluence of the people who owned it spelled security, but more than that, oh, so much more than that, their citizenship meant safety.

The Joberts met them at the door, Katya in a long mandarin hostess gown of gold embossed silk and Jacques in a burgundy velvet smoking jacket with quilted satin lapels. A portly man with horn-rimmed glasses and balding head, he was formal and reserved, but greeted the Muravins with a courteous smile. Claudette ran down the stairs, a vivacious dark-haired girl in pink dress and black patent shoes. Her curly chestnut hair bounced off her shoulders as she threw her arms around Nina and hugged her. Moments later, the two girls were at the other end of the large living room, huddled in the corner, whispering in each other's ear and giggling into their hands.

Katya smiled. "Girls. Teenage girls. And you have two of them, Lydia. I'm glad I have only one to cope with."

Kiril and Jacques exchanged pleasantries in their impeccable French, Jacques courteous, friendly; Kiril with his patrician bearing every inch the aristocrat. In spite of many ersatz titles that Russians in Shanghai had suddenly acquired after the Revolution, Vickie knew there was no doubt in anyone's mind that Prince Kiril was the genuine article.

Vickie was proud of her parents, especially tonight in the Joberts' palatial mansion, where her stepfather blended into the luxurious surroundings as if they were his own. Her mother looked beautiful with her hair parted and waved, her delicate skin still young; and pert Nina so at ease with her friend, Claudette, so unselfconscious. So where did this leave her, the older sister, not so beautiful, not so self-assured? Vickie pulled her sleeves down, smoothed her collar, made sure her belt was in place.

There were no other guests. "Just the two families," Katya explained, "*en famille* so we can catch up." She turned to Vickie and put her arm around her. "I've missed you at our poetry meetings, my dear," she said, "but I do understand your parents' concern. The incident with the Japanese was a dreadful…dreadful experience for you."

The lavishly decorated tree was the tallest Vickie had ever seen, but then of course the twelve-foot parlor ceiling could accommodate such magnificence. She could hardly see the tree itself, it was so covered with ornaments and lighted candles. The dinner, too, was sumptuous, reminding Vickie of their holiday receptions in Harbin. Ham, suckling pig, leg of lamb, and her favorite smoked goose. She had to hold back not to embarrass herself by eating too much or too fast.

And through it all, she thought, one presence hovered nearby. Henri. She felt him everywhere.

Katya's voice, warm with laughter, startled her. "Vickie, dear, you've left us, where are you?"

She blushed. "I'm sorry, I guess I was daydreaming for a moment."

"I was just saying how happy I am this Christmas. We've just heard from Henri. He's coming home in May to join the French Consulate here. Isn't that wonderful?"

The room grew suddenly warm. Her heart raced. Afraid to betray herself, she only nodded.

Next May. Five months. How should she make the time pass quickly? May. A beautiful month in Shanghai. Magnolia trees would still be in bloom in Jessfield Park, filling the air with sweetness. The days would not be cold but soft and tender, as yet untouched by summer heat. A good month. A gentle month for lovers.

CHAPTER NINE

They stood in the middle of the room without moving, and looked at each other. Of such moments, eternities are made. Vickie wanted to say something meaningful, something intelligent, but all she said was: "So you've come back," and was immediately furious at her inane words.

When he had first entered the room, Henri had kissed Lydia's hand and handed her a bouquet of carnations. Then, he shook hands with Kiril, and smiled at Nina, marveling at how she had grown. When, at last, he gave his full attention to Vickie, she was afraid that he would glance around their drab room, and turn to her with pity in his eyes.

Instead, he stared at her without a smile, never taking his eyes off her, never once sweeping his glance around the place.

Finally, he took her hand. "You're lovelier than I remembered."

"Thank you, Henri," she said and felt a blush rise to her face. He looked just as she remembered him, in his immaculate palm beach slacks, a casual short-sleeved sport shirt open at the throat.

"I'd like to take Vickie to my house to show her the books and pictures I brought back from Paris," Henri said to Kiril and then added, hastily, "if you don't mind."

"Of course not," Kiril said in French.

"I'd like to see pictures of Paris, too," Nina chimed in, echoing her father in French.

"I'll be glad to show them to you soon," Henri replied in Russian.

His abrupt return to Russian did not escape Vickie. The years in Paris had not destroyed his love for his mother-tongue. She was relieved. And now, the most wonderful thing of all, he wanted to be alone with her.

But Lydia, already pulling cups and saucers out of the cupboard and placing them on the table, nodded at the chair. "First, you'll sit down and have tea and tell us about France. I know Kiril would love to hear all about Paris. Vickie, get the *krendel* from the porch. I baked it just this morning, and you Nina, go down to the kitchen and bring the kettle up."

Henri glanced at Vickie, made a small helpless gesture, smiled, and sat down.

As Vickie turned toward the porch, she noticed that one of the crocheted doilies Lydia had placed on the green armchair had fallen off and lay on the seat. The exposed arm showed shining threadbare fabric. Stepping sideways, Vickie swooped down without bending over and pulled the doily over the arm, before going to the porch.

When the tea was served, Nina put her elbows on the table and resting her chin in the palms of her hands, stared at Henri. Vickie cringed. How many times had Lydia admonished them: "A lady never places her elbows on the table."

"Did you go up the Eiffel Tower? Does it sway at the top? Is there an outside balcony to go around and see Paris from above? Did you see Mona Lisa at the Louvre?" Nina bombarded Henri.

Vickie lowered her gaze to conceal a flash of anger at her sister for monopolizing Henri's attention.

"Slow down, Nina," Kiril said, "one question at a time."

"Have a piece of my *krendel,* I bet they don't make them like that even in Paris." Lydia cut a generous piece of the cake and slid it onto Henri's plate. Vickie noticed she was using their silver spatula with engraved initials on the handle. It was the first time she had used it since they moved into the rooming house.

Vickie couldn't swallow her piece of *krendel.* Her heart was in her throat. She was only conscious of Henri's hands with long tapered fingers, masculine, strong hands resting on the table or handling his glass of tea as he answered their questions with his natural charm. He dominated the room which seemed grayer and more drab than before.

Those interminable questions. And at last, when she thought she couldn't contain herself any longer and would say something silly, Henri rose and after thanking Lydia for the tea and *krendel,* took Vickie's hand.

"I promise not to keep her late," he said, as they left. Vickie, glad to be out of the room and away from her family's scrutiny, wondered what Henri's reaction was to the way they now lived.

"My mother told me that your stepfather had a heart attack. I'm so sorry," Henri said as they walked along Avenue Joffre toward Rue Delastre. Vickie glanced at him and thought: he is tactful. He's telling me that he knows why we live in a rooming house. Aloud she said: "Yes, it left his heart damaged. He has to rest a lot."

"I hope I didn't tire him by my visit. It was nice of your mother to prepare tea, but what I really wanted was to be alone with you." He reached for her hand.

They were on a crowded street, and Vickie pulled her hand away self-consciously. He looked down at her with a smile that was irresistible. "I'd like to guess what you're thinking right now."

Vickie gave him a questioning glance.

"You're thinking that I have my nerve trying to hold your hand on the street where a lot of your friends could see us."

Vickie blushed, for that was exactly what she was thinking, in spite of the delicious thrill that spread through her body at the touch of his hand. "Are you a mind reader?" She asked playfully.

"Just a lucky guess," Henri said. They reached Rue Delastre and he guided her to his family's mansion, where he took her upstairs to the study.

"This is my mother's private world of Russia," Henri said, sweeping his hand around the room. "Will you excuse me while I go get the pictures?"

"Yes, of course."

Left alone, Vickie studied the room. A blue velvet loveseat was piled high with cross-stitched pillows. Behind the loveseat, a wall hanging bordered in blue velvet was also cross-stitched in vivid colors, and matched the diamond-shaped pattern on the pillows. The parquet floor was covered with oriental rugs and at the window overlooking the garden, stood a rolltop desk of Karelian wood.

Vickie sighed. The room brought memories back of her childhood in Harbin when life was secure and free of worries. She looked at the ceiling to floor bookshelves that were filled with Russian books: Tolstoy, Chekhov, Maxim Gorky. Poetry by Anna Akhmatova, Sergei Esenin, Osip Mandelstam and, surprisingly, Alexander Blok's revolutionary *The Twelve.* But no Pushkin. The incomparable Pushkin whose poems were required reading in Russian schools and on whose works Tchaikovsky based his operas, this greatest Russian poet was missing from Katya's shelves.

Vickie was even more surprised to see works of Marx and Engels and a pamphlet on Lenin tucked in one corner of the highest shelf, but then she remembered Henri telling her on their first date that his grandparents were socialists.

Henri returned with an armful of books and albums.

Vickie pointed at the bookshelves. "There is no Pushkin," she said. Henri glanced at the books and laughed. "Mother can quote whole passages. She keeps his complete works by her bedside. These," he nodded toward the poetry books, "are some of her favorite twentieth century poets."

He opened one of the albums and showed her the snapshots of Paris. Then he picked up a French volume. "Here's Simone de Beauvoir's novel, *L'Invité.* It's a fictionalized story about Jean-Paul Sartre. I think you'll find it interesting."

"Thank you. I'm familiar with Sartre and some of his works."

As he passed the book to her, their hands touched. Vickie's was trembling. He stroked it. "I hadn't realized how much I've missed you. I'm so glad to see you again, Vickie," he said softly.

"So am I," she whispered and turned away, afraid that he would see her flushed face. She put the book down beside her purse. "The time crept while you were away," she said, looking down at her hands, then added: "And yet so much has happened in the meantime."

"You mean your stepfather."

"Yes. He can't work full time anymore."

"I'm so sorry. Must be hard for him. Maybe with time he'll improve."

"I hope so."

Henri changed the subject: "So, tell me, do you like working for my father?"

Vickie brightened up. "Oh, yes! He's very kind, and I enjoy doing something I love. I'm so grateful to your mother for recommending me for the job."

Henri smiled. "That's my mother." He picked up the French book and handed it to her. "I just had an idea. I'd like to take you to a movie. There's a good one at the Cathay Theater. How about it? Let me call your parents, so they won't worry."

*   *   *

She couldn't see enough of him. All during the day in his father's office, she couldn't get him out of her mind. At home she talked about him, quoted him. "Henri spends a lot of time in the library, we talk about books…He has so many flowers in his garden…I love flowers…"

She was also enormously pleased that Henri shared with her the news bulletins that came into the French Consulate where he worked. Allied troops had landed in Normandy in June, and France would soon be liberated from the Nazis.

Over sixty thousand Germans had been killed in Sevastopol last May. Vickie found herself pitying the enemy soldiers who followed orders from the high command and died in the process. When she shared her feelings with Henri, he looked at her with obvious admiration. "You have an inner grace, Vickie. It shines through!"

On her twenty-second birthday in July he brought her two dozen long-stemmed roses. Vickie flushed as she thanked him, his confession of love surely implied by the language of flowers. The thrill softened her disappointment in his reading taste after she had read Simone de Beauvoir's *L'Invité*, which she found very leftist. "It was interesting," Vickie said, and handed the book back to him with a polite smile. "The roses are beautiful." She leaned over and smelled them. "They are so fragrant."

Henri took the book and gave her an enigmatic look. "Perhaps we can talk about the book later."

That evening, bathed in the blue light of the moon, they strolled under the bright stars. Along their path, silvered trees slept in the still night air. As they neared the edge of the park, Henri mentioned that a few blocks away, a statue of Pushkin graced a small square hidden among tree-shrouded homes. He suggested they go there, and taking her hand, he walked faster.

"Why so fast, Henri? Is this a bad area?"

He laughed a happy laugh. "Not at all. We're safe here. If we walk long enough, we'll run into night patrols. I'm just anxious to get to the Pushkin square. It's lovely there."

He hurried on, and Vickie ran along, caught up in his mood and giggling without knowing why.

At the square, just below the statue, he pulled her down on a bench beside him. Here, cross-currents moved the air, wrapping them in soft coolness. Henri took Vickie's hand in both of his. He caressed its surface with care. Then he took her face in his hand, and Vickie read such love in his eyes, such deep emotion, that for a moment it took her breath away.

"I want to…" he began, but suddenly dropped her hand and turned around toward the sound of scratching footsteps.

A Chinese beggar moved toward them, limping, unsteady on his feet. He stopped and looked at them as if deciding whether to beg or not, then turned and shuffled away.

"There's no escape from them anywhere," Henri said, his voice tinged with annoyance.

Disappointed as she was by the interruption, Vickie felt only pity for the beggar. But the mood of the evening, the fragile, intangible mood had folded upon itself and vanished.

At the bamboo gate to the rooming house, Vickie turned and gave Henri her hand. The moon was bright. The windows, wide open like curious eyes, denied them any privacy at all. He wouldn't touch her, wouldn't kiss her now.

"We've been invited to a dinner dance at the Officers' Club this Saturday, and Papa would like you to join us," she said, holding her breath for his answer, convinced that if he turned her down, she would die on the spot.

"I'd love to, Vickie. It has been a long time since we danced that tango, remember?"

He hadn't forgotten. After all the distraction of Paris, he hadn't forgotten.

Today was only Wednesday. How many minutes to Saturday night?

*   *   *

One of Kiril's patients, a former White Army officer who paid erratically, had given Kiril carte blanche to be his permanent guest at the Officers' Club. It was understood of course, that Kiril would pay for his meals even though he could hardly afford it, but the privilege of using the Officers' Club at will was something he valued more than money, in fact, he treasured it.

The Club was serving *pelmeni* in bouillon that night, and Kiril had ordered vodka for Henri and himself and a bottle of white wine for the women. A three-piece orchestra played modern dance music as well as the old-world dances of Pas de Quatre, Pas d'Espagne, the Hungarian, the Polka. Vickie knew these intricate dances well, dances her stepfather had taught her because they were part of his heritage, a bygone era of elegance and finesse, he had said. She was prepared to see Henri stumble over the complex steps, and so was delighted when he led her easily into the polka.

"Why do you look surprised?" Henri asked, holding her hands high above her head and leading her forward.

"I didn't think you knew these dances."

"I too have an old-world mother, remember?"

Vickie laughed. "I'm so glad that she taught you. I adore them."

They circled the dance floor, caught up in the exuberant tempo of the polka. At the end of the dance, the orchestra paused only briefly, then started a Viennese waltz. When it ended, Vickie was breathless from the delicious sensation of being in his arms for the first time in three years.

After dinner, Henri danced with Nina who had been disappointed earlier when the rest of the Jobert family declined the Muravins' invitation to join them. Vickie felt sorry for her sister, because she knew that Nina enjoyed Claudette's company. Diplomatic as the refusal seemed, the real reason was obvious: the considerate Katya was once again protecting the Muravins' budget.

When the orchestra took a break and the dining area was relatively quiet, Kiril leaned over to ask Henri in French: "What does the Vichy Government think about Stalin? Do the Parisians fear Soviet influence in their future?"

Henri glanced at Vickie, then replied: "I was only a student in Paris, mon prince, so I can't tell you what the government thought except what I read in the censored newspapers. As for the Parisians, they've been rejoicing ever since the American and French troops liberated Paris in August."

Kiril drummed the table with his fingers. "I had hoped that early in the war the invasion of Russia would turn the tide against communism. Instead, it seems to have strengthened the Soviet's hold."

"Your people, mon prince," Henri said, "will always fight fiercely to protect their motherland from invaders. The Swedes, the Turks, the Poles, all tried. Even the Mongols didn't last. Didn't Santayana say that those who do not learn from history are condemned to relive it?"

"And for just that reason," Kiril said, "foreign occupation of Russia could be tolerated temporarily. It is Bolshevism that mutilates my country. In the past, our Church played a major role in our history. And what do they have now? Hammer and sickle, Five-year plans, tractors, kolkhoz…Materialism is in the forefront, the spirit is crushed, and our beautiful estates are desecrated."

Lydia cleared her throat. "What do you think of our dances here, Henri?" she asked in Russian.

"They're fun, and I love them."

Vickie, who sat stiffly, listening to her stepfather embark on his favorite subject, relaxed and gave her mother a grateful smile.

"You two dance well together," Lydia said, picking up her purse. "You must join us again, Henri, but right now it's time for us to go home. I don't want Kiril to get overtired."

She rose and gave her hand to Henri. "You and Vickie enjoy the rest of the evening—" then turning to Nina, "Come, my dear."

Nina pouted, but Lydia gave her a long stare and Nina followed her parents without comment.

Vickie watched them leave, then turned to Henri and realized that he had been watching her. Her face grew warm. "You have to forgive Papa for talking about politics, and always in French. You see, it's only in a place like this…" Vickie swept her arm around the room, "where he can pretend his world hasn't changed, and he is still Prince Muravin."

"I understand," Henri said. "The prince lives in the past, and why shouldn't he speak French when he wants to?" He paused for a moment, then added: "Habits of youth are hard to break."

"Papa can't accept," Vickie said, "that the old way of life is never coming back."

"So you accept the status quo?"

"Oh no! I hope communism won't last, but it's unrealistic to hope that the old regime will return."

"Then what would you like to see happen?"

"I don't really know." Vickie hesitated, trying to formulate her thoughts. "I suppose I'd like Russia to have a constitutional monarchy, or even better, a democratic republic."

Henri averted his glance, then clasped her wrist. "The music is going to start in a moment. Let's forget the politics and dance, shall we?"

As the orchestra started the *La Cumparsita* tango, he rose and pulled her close against him, so close, that his forearm pressed her against his chest and her face was buried in the hollow of his neck. His breath warmed her skin, and as they moved in rhythm with the sensuous music, Vickie moulded her body against his.

She smelled his delicious masculine fragrance, so familiar now that she identified it only with him. So close was his cheek, so near her mouth, that it was all she could do not to turn and brush her lips against his skin. She resented the bright lights in the room, was annoyed by the crowded dance floor, impatient to leave and be alone with him somewhere.

The dance ended. Henri's breathing came fast. Vickie looked up at him and was caught in his excitement, oblivious of people around them. His hand trembled as he took her arm and kept her from going back to the table. "Vickie, we never seem to be alone. Always surrounded by people, at your house, in the club, or even on the streets. Let's go."

Vickie followed him without a word. They walked out of the club and Henri turned toward Rue Delastre.

"Where are you taking me?" Vickie asked and immediately regretted her question.

He said: "I'm taking you to my house."

"But there's no privacy in your home either."

"Yes, there is. I have my own apartment on the third floor."

Vickie flushed. "It wouldn't be right, Henri. What would your parents think if I came to your apartment so late at night?"

"They won't see us. Originally, the third floor was intended for the live-in help with a separate entrance in the back to give the tenants privacy." Henri smiled mischievously. "It now gives *me* privacy."

"What about the curfew?"

"I have a diplomatic pass." His smile faded. "Don't worry, Vickie," he said quietly, "I'll get you home safely."

The dark night sheathed them in anonymity as they walked toward his home. At the gate to the Jobert mansion, Vickie slowed down.

Henri stopped and squeezed her hand. "I'm sorry, Vickie. I forgot. This darkness, this street…It must remind you of that dreadful night when the Japanese terrorized you."

Before Vickie could answer, he went on: "You said it was Igor Sevich who took you home that night. I've met him. He seems an honest fellow." After a brief pause, Henri added: "He told me how relieved he was that his Soviet passport worked a miracle that night."

"Any passport would have worked a miracle," Vickie said.

"True enough, but a Soviet passport is the most available one to a Russian. Anyway, I'm grateful to him for taking care of you that night."

Vickie sighed. "Yes, I was glad to get away from that street and, I must admit, a little envious of Igor's passport even though a Soviet one." She smiled apologetically, then followed him across the dark garden to the back of the house.

She trembled as she waited for him to turn on the lights. This was a forbidden adventure to be alone with a man in his apartment, especially so late at night. But the energy between them was powerful, and the anticipation of something momentous to happen lulled her conscience.

The green lamp shade on his desk filled the room with soft light. Opposite the desk and bookshelves that stood near the dormer windows, a green leather sofa and two arm chairs were grouped against the inner wall. Thick Chinese rugs covered most of the oak wood floor.

Henri switched on another lamp on the end table, then sat down and pulled her beside him, taking both her hands in his.

Her heart thumped, echoing so loudly in her ears, she thought Henri could hear it.

"Pushkin's statue in the moonlight was a far more romantic setting than this room, Vickie," Henri said, "but at least we needn't worry about any beggar disturbing us." He smiled, then said: "Vickie, all those years in France—I thought about you all the time. I had fallen in love with you long before I realized it. But I didn't know how you felt about me." He paused and shook his head. "I've rehearsed this speech so many times I knew exactly what I was going to say, but now—itt's gone." He tightened his grip on her hands. "What I want to tell you is that I am madly in love with you, and that I want to spend the rest of my life with you."

He searched her face. "Darling Vickie, will you marry me?"

Vickie took his face into her hands, blinked away her tears, and murmured: "Yes, oh Yes! If only you knew how long I have waited to hear those words!"

When their eyes met, his look held such raw, undisguised emotion, that she caught her breath. In the next instant, his arms slid around her and held her close. Kisses feathered her face, moved down her neck, then stole back up to her mouth to fill it with sweetness.

Overcome by sudden longing for more, she ached for his hands and his lips, her fear and guilt melting away. It no longer mattered to save herself for marriage.

He led her to the bedroom and turned the light out. When she heard him begin to undress, she slipped off her own clothing with trembling hands and got under the covers. Before he joined her, he turned on the night light and she saw his lean and muscular body above her.

Desire filled her with abandon. Love filled her with a sense of magic and provided her with the skill and yearning to give pleasure as well as to submit to pleasure. In total trust, without hesitation, her body arched to meet his as he leaned over her, passion clouding his eyes. The delicate caresses of his hands and lips made her skin tingle with anticipation, until his mouth found her breasts and she gasped from the shock of electricity that surged through her.

The erotic touch of his fingers, sensuous and insistent in search of her secret place, drove her wildly to open to him like a budding flower, swelling and throbbing with impatience. Her mind soared to the brink of unconsciousness, when in a fugue of pain and pleasure, she felt him as one with her. He moved against her tender flesh, slowly at first, then faster, and her body rose into an explosion of spasms and ecstasy. She felt him shudder and give an inchoate scream of passion.

She never knew, had never dreamed that passion could cause such intense sensations. Now, he was a part of her. They were forever bonded as one. At that moment nothing mattered but to be together in the same place, and needing only each other.

Henri possessed more than her body, her soul, her mind, her heart, and she knew that for her, there would never be another.

The gentle breeze played with the curtain, letting the opal moonlight slip into the room. The sounds were tender, a gentle murmur, a gasp, a sigh. Vickie lay in the crook of Henri's arm, face pressed into his shoulder, lips moving gently with murmured endearments. Under the light sheet draped over them, she marvelled at the beauty of his body, the smoothness of his skin, the passion of his response.

Vickie looked at him with tenderness. His flushed and dewy face glowed near her, his warm breath kissing her cheek.

The clock on Henri's desk chimed and Vickie started. "My God! It's after midnight, what will I tell my parents?"

Henri gathered her in his arms again and kissed her on the forehead, then buried his face in her hair. "Darling, remember I told you I have diplomatic pass? You can tell your parents that we walked and talked, enjoying the balmy air outside." His eyes twinkling, he added, "And that I have asked you to marry me."

"They will ask me when—"

"Tell them that we're not rushing into this," Henri said. "Tell them that we must wait until I am well established in my career. A year from now we shall still love each other as much."

Vickie gasped. "A—year? A whole year?" Her eyes were wide with disappointment and fear.

"Yes, my love," Henri said, gently. "I'll be here and we'll see each other all the time. Our love will only grow. Time will pass quickly, I promise."

CHAPTER TEN

When Henri made a formal call on Kiril to ask for Vickie's hand in marriage, the Muravins celebrated with a bottle of Russian red wine. "An occasion like this calls for champagne," Kiril sighed, "but with no refrigerator in the rooming house, where would we chill it?" As he raised his glass to toast Vickie, he added, beaming: "I couldn't have made a better choice for my daughter myself."

Although her mother was disappointed that Katya insisted on delaying the formal announcement, Kiril agreed that since the date of the wedding had not been set, it would be better to wait.

Pleased that both families approved of their love, Vickie was resigned to wait. She was too proud to ask how long it would be before Henri would set the date, yet happy with the hours she spent in his apartment.

Her mother trusted her, and as for Katya, whatever she knew or suspected, she kept to herself. Although Vickie felt little guilt at the loss of her virginity, she could not bring herself to confide in her mother. It was equally impossible to confide in Sara, but Sara could not be fooled.

"You've changed, my little friend," she said to Vickie one day over their usual afternoon tea. "Your face is glowing, your eyes are shining with love. Do you spend a lot of time with him?"

Vickie couldn't hold her gaze, and reached for an extra spoonful of sugar. Sara watched her.

"I don't know what you'd consider often," Vickie said, "But I see him only in the evenings, after work."

This time Sara held her gaze and Vickie wondered if she could ever keep a secret from her wise friend.

Speaking casually, Sara referred to a hypothetical woman who, through ignorance, became pregnant out of wedlock with its accompanying disgrace, and how important it was for a young girl to learn about such matters. "We mothers tend to idealize our children and refuse to admit that they are adults and all too human," Sara went on. "Whatever past we may have had ourselves, we want our children to have a better life, to grow up as near perfect human beings. Some day when you're a mother yourself, you'll remember my words."

Vickie yearned to tell Sara that she had told Henri about her fears soon after their first lovemaking, and Henri had assured her that he had taken care of the matter and she should not worry about it anymore. Vickie did not want to question him further. There was something plebeian and unromantic in discussing such details. It infringed upon the unrestrained passion between them, so she trusted him to know what was necessary to do to prevent her from getting pregnant. He was a sophisticated man, and such men should know of these matters, she reasoned.

Still, Vickie could not talk about her affair with Henri. As long as it was secret between them, it was beautiful and unmarred by anyone's disapproval, even her dear Sara's. Instead, Vickie avoided meeting Sara's glance and in doing so, realized that she had confirmed what Sara must have guessed all along.

Vickie and Henri spent hours together walking in Jessfield Park on weekends, talking about everything that occurred to them. He respected the Russian language, venerated the same poets, shared ideas that came to his agile mind. In turn, she confided her eagerness for a home of their own, their future life that held such radiant promise. For Christmas he gave her a pin of apple green carved jade mounted on a gold oval. It depicted a bird soaring over a branch of a tree.

"I want you to be always carefree like this bird," he said kissing her on the lips and stroking her hair.

The tenderness in his words, the love that flowed between them, the enthusiasm he projected made the waiting less trying. It was enough to be with him, to enjoy a sense of belonging, to breathe the same air.

Sometimes, they went to the Lyceum Theatre to hear a Lehar operetta or a Tchaikovsky opera with Kudinov and Zorich in the leads, or danced the evening away at the French Club. There were dinners at the Renaissance or the Kavkaz restaurants or an occasional sumptuous meal at the elegant Sun-Yah's on Bubbling Well Road in the International Settlement, where he introduced her to Chinese delicacies she had never tasted before. Those were heady experiences, forerunners of what she could expect of her life with this man she loved. He lifted her out of the drab world she lived in and the magic hours they spent together made her feel a real princess. As time went on, it became harder and harder for her to leave the enchantment he created and return to the rooming house where stale cooking odors permeated the hallway and the aging walls seemed to shrink their rooms a little more each time she came home.

"You know something?" Henri said to her one evening as they sat in his cozy apartment, "I resent every hour we are apart. I want to be with you all the time, I want to know what you are doing every minute of the day."

Vickie laughed. "But darling, even after we're married, you can't do that. We both work in different places, remember?"

"After we're married, you won't have to."

"But that still won't keep us together all the time, silly. You have your work."

"I love you. I want to have you by my side every waking minute."

In spite of what he said, she wondered if he felt as bonded to her as she did to him. Her love was irrational and extravagant and it had no bounds. She wanted her thoughts to be his thoughts, her feelings to be his feelings, but he had his own life quite apart from hers, and she had no control over it.

"Thank God," he said, breaking into her thoughts, "the war won't last too long now."

From his words, she inferred that as soon as the war ended they would be married, and although she could not understand what the war had to do with it, she followed the news with mounting excitement.

In November of 1944 Allied bombing of Shanghai intensified. Although their targets were the outlying Japanese-occupied sectors of town, it became dangerous to be caught outdoors during an air raid even in the foreign sectors because of the falling shrapnel from the Japanese anti-aircraft guns that were strategically placed atop various apartment buildings, one of which was only half a block from where the Muravins lived.

During the winter and spring of 1945, the Allies made steady progress toward victory in the Far East. After Germany surrendered on May 7th, the mood in Shanghai changed. Smiles of anticipation appeared on Russian faces. Hope was palpable in the air in spite of increasing shortages of food. In recent months, milk had become pro-hibitively expensive and Lydia started buying a substitute soybean milk, a thick yellowish liquid with a strong smell that made their coffee barely palatable. But no one complained in the Muravin family.

The White Russian newspaper, *The Shanghai Zarya*, aware of Japanese censorship, reported Japanese victories, mentioning the pre-cise number of enemy planes shot down and ships sunk, but never the Japanese losses.

Vickie, however, read the paper between the lines, for the battle-ground shifted from one island in the Pacific to another with no final outcome reported and only a brief silence between battles. It was simple to study the map and follow the Allied progress from Mindanao to Luzon, from Iwo Jima to Okinawa and see that the Allies were moving closer and closer to Shanghai.

Although the Nanking Kuomintang Government, pressured by the Japanese, curtailed the Soviet radio station's blatant propaganda in Shanghai, the Soviet news agency, TASS, intensified its campaign, and after the war ended in Europe, Soviet newspapers and bulletins actively solicited White Russians to return to the motherland to help rebuild their country. They reported that the all-suffering *rodina*, having emerged victorious from the war, now invited every one of her sons and daughters, even those who were born abroad, to return to their country and be a part of its glorious future. Offers of citizenship, housing, full repatriation expenses and work according to individual qualifications were guaranteed. With their penchant for statistics, the Soviets were soon quoting numbers, boasting seven hundred full members of the Soviet Club in Shanghai and over two thousand of what they called 'permanent guests' who had applied for Soviet citizenship but were not yet granted the coveted passport.

Kiril was incensed. "The fools, those young ones. They're afraid to face their future abroad. They think that Soviet citizenship would solve all their problems. What clever propaganda with promises of work and security. Some security! They'll be sent to Siberia to work in the mines. And the older ones, they don't want to return to Russia. Still, they think: why not kill two birds with one stone? Get Soviet citizenship for protection here in China, yet avoid being repatriated to the motherland. Bah!"

"What amazes me," Lydia said, "is the way this young man, Igor Sevich, was able to expand his news bulletin. A few months ago he started a small pamphlet, and it has now grown into a full-fledged newspaper. I picked up a copy the other day out of curiosity and was amazed to read detailed accounts of agricultural expansion in Siberia and, of course, one-sided reports on foreign relations. What worries me is his paper's subtle attack on us, the White Russians. He hints that our community leaders are passive, and he's openly wooing young Russians to sign up for Soviet citizenship."

Kiril looked at Vickie. "Isn't that the young man who brought you home the night you were stopped by the Japanese?"

"Yes, it is," Vickie said, and was about to leave the room, when her mother asked: "Do you know anything about this Igor Sevich? Doesn't he attend Katya's poetry sessions?"

"He used to, but not anymore."

Igor. Enterprising young man, Vickie thought. A full-fledged newspaper, no less. Too bad he's working for the Soviet side, and tempting White Russians with the protection of a Soviet passport.

       *   *   *

On a July afternoon, the air hung leaden over Shanghai. Motionless, humid, with no respite even at night, it drained energy, shortened tempers. The sun's merciless light blinded the eye, burned the skin. Shopkeepers, slumped in doorways, cooled themselves with parchment fans; beggars sought shady spots on sidewalks, clinging to stone walls, their ar_____hed, rattling tin cans in front of passersby. Above _____ swarming over their filthy rags. Rickshaw coolies _____ hiding under their wide-brimmed straw hats, too _____ stening rivulets of sweat trickling down their bare _____ listless in the elms' leafy shade, eyes closed, dozing. _____ ped their bicycles over the softened asphalt with _____ of the wide street's center rails where tramcars _____ rating on everyone's already taut nerves.

_____ reached one hundred, with humidity not far _____ stifling atmosphere there came the now familiar _____ an air raid siren. Pedestrians ran for shelter more _____ appreciable fear, for in spite of almost daily raids _____ ral months, no Allied bombs had fallen on either _____ lement or the French Concession.

Shortly after the siren sounded, Japanese anti-aircraft guns, posi-tioned atop the Astrid Apartments on the corner of Rue Cardinal Mercier and Route Vallon, opened fire.

Vickie was walking on Avenue Joffre, nearing Avenue Roi Albert when the gunfire started. Perhaps she should run home. She clutched her purse. No. Not now. She had had enough of arguments with Nina for one day. Her sister had been quarrelsome of late. Nina had skipped a year of school, and graduated from Sacred Heart Convent ahead of her classmates, so she was at loose ends. College education was deemed too expensive, and Nina reluctantly enrolled in shorthand and typing classes at the League of Russian Women Business School, but was not happy about it. Then too, Nina was probably a little jealous of Vickie. Otherwise why did she needle her about Henri?

This morning's argument had been particularly ugly, especially because their mother was involved. It began when her mother warned her younger daughter not to get too attached to Joseph Rosen.

"I've seen him look at you with puppy love eyes," Lydia said.

"I like him. He's fun to be with," Nina retorted.

"You should be meeting young men who are a little older, instead of running around with Joseph and Claudette. And I don't understand why you devote so much time to the children at the League of Russian Women. They have enough teachers as it is."

"What's wrong with that? I love little girls. They're so sweet. Besides, I help the teachers with games. They appreciate it."

"You're not going to meet anyone worthwhile if you keep on playing with kindergarten girls. And as for Joseph, don't ever forget that you're a born aristocrat, and a Russian princess shouldn't encourage the atten-tions of a Jewish man."

"I have more fun with Joseph than anyone else." Nina paused for effect, then added: "Don't worry, Mama, if you're thinking of marriage, I'm not ready yet."

Lydia frowned. "You seem to shun Russian friends. It isn't good. Remember your heritage."

"What good is our title when we're stateless? Papa is a prince but he's still pitied and looked down upon by all the foreigners."

Vickie, who was ready to leave for work, stopped. "Shame on you, Nina. How can you say that about Papa?"

An odd smile twisted Nina's mouth. "You should talk. You've picked yourself a rich Frenchman so you can get a passport. He's conveniently handsome of course, but then all men with passports are handsome to us Russian girls."

Vickie held back a sharp retort. Instead, she picked up her purse and ran out on the street.

Now, the siren's plaintive whine scraped at her nerves, and in a reflex reaction, she stopped and pressed her back against the window of the Josepho Photo Studio. High above her, she saw the steel glitter of American planes flying in formation, majestic and unperturbed by the frantic spurt of guns.

She watched them without fear. What was America like? An Eden on another planet?

"Silver birds," she whispered, "when are you going to come down to us?"

A passerby stopped and stared at her.

"The worst thing you can do is to stand against a glass window," he said, shaking his head, then hurried on.

True. Not only that, but she shouldn't linger on the streets during an air raid, for one never knew where the shrapnel and debris would fall.

She was headed toward the Jobert mansion to see Henri, to talk to him, to…She felt her face grow warm. Opening her purse, she pulled out a handkerchief and fanned herself. This ghastly, humid weather. She could hardly wait to reach Henri's home. Its spacious rooms with high ceilings were always cool, and its French doors opened onto the wide green lawn, whose bordering stately trees shaded the house and refreshed the eye. Well, she did know what she was doing. She was twenty-three and perfectly able to take care of herself.

Was she now? a small voice needled. Vickie moved. She glanced over her shoulder and edged away from the center of the photo studio's window. The stranger who had admonished her was right. She admired the displayed photos from the side. Josepho's was one of the best studios in Shanghai. Everyone who could afford its prices had their portraits done there. A huge black and white portrait of Miss Shanghai dominated the window. The girl was beautiful with her dreamy eyes and soft flowing hair.

Vickie refocused her gaze and stared at herself in the glass; she couldn't compete with this lovely Miss Shanghai. Yet Henri kept telling her that there was something classical in the straight line of her nose and the oval shape of her face. She reminded him of Raphael's madonnas, he said, and he liked to run his fingers through her hair, pushing it off her forehead.

Henri. Her beloved. Her passionate lover. Vickie closed her eyes bringing his image to mind. He often watched her through half-closed lids when she least expected it. He was in love with her, he'd told her so many times, and she—she was mad, hopelessly mad about him…

What a stunning discovery to realize how passionate a nature she possessed. Occasionally, she had orgasmic dreams about him, waking up with a shock, appalled at her own sexuality. And the hours she spent with him in his apartment were charged with such passion, she sometimes wondered if their mutual ecstasy were not too overpowering to allow a more subtle, more enduring emotion to develop, but she quickly dismissed such thoughts. They were in love, and theirs was the ardor of youth.

She dabbed beads of perspiration off her upper lip with a handkerchief, careful not to smear her lipstick. The shade was soft, just enough to give her lips a natural blush. None of the bright reds that some Russian girls wore; those others who, before the war, walked on the arms of American sailors, or paraded now up and down Avenue Joffre with wealthy foreign escorts, their flashy clothes and heavy makeup setting them apart. Her strong-willed mother would never allow her to paint her face that way, and she herself wouldn't think of doing it. Besides, she would never embarrass her stepfather; her adored, wonderful stepfather. How could she ever repay him for his loving care, for treating her as if she were his own daughter? She tried never to think about the Bolshevik peasant who fathered her, or about Peter Sokolov who rejected her in such a cruel way. She could not forget the fear and shame she felt as a four-year old when he threw her out of his office.

Deep in thought, she was startled when the sirens whined again. The raid was over. No shrapnel this time. Ever since last spring when she had seen a five-year old boy cut by falling debris and heard him scream in terror at the sight of his bleeding arms, she trembled at the sound of anti-aircraft guns. If she ever had a child, she would protect him with her life, and if that little boy had been hers, she would never have allowed him to be on the sidewalk during an air raid.

She started to walk. Another few blocks, and she'd be at the Jobert mansion.

Henri would be waiting this afternoon. He had told her that his mother would be gone for the day and his father was checking his merchandise at the godown. It was Friday, and, claiming a headache, she had asked to leave the office early. She felt no pangs of conscience. She worked hard, sometimes after hours, and had been given another raise in the past year. She had earned an occasional afternoon off.

Trying not to let her high heels sink into the heat-softened asphalt, she crossed the street. Avenue Joffre teemed with pedestrians. Besides the foreigners, there were crowds of scurrying Chinese, most of them in black cotton pants and white shirts, or gray and faded blue gowns—what had Henri told her, that there were six million of them in Shanghai? It would have been much faster had she chosen to walk on the quiet Rue Lafayette, but she had to stop at a pharmacy on Avenue

Joffre. She needed to pick up a bottle of pyramidon for Kiril, to ease the pain that he had developed in his leg…

When she left the noisy thoroughfare and walked along the quiet streets, she wondered whether it was her imagination that the air had become cooler. She chuckled. Of course not. She was close to Henri's home and that's what had given her a feeling of coolness. The quiet servants who shuffled silently past her at a respectful distance, the absence of noise, all seemed a world apart from the outside hub of the Shanghai humanity.

As she walked up the sandy path to the house, Katya Jobert walked out onto the patio, surprise and genuine pleasure glowing on her face.

Taken aback, Vickie hesitated, but Katya threw her arms wide and hugged her.

"Vickie, dear child, what a pleasant surprise. Come in, come in. How did you know I'd be home? Henri isn't home yet, not yet, and I've been sipping ice tea, trying to beat this blasted heat."

Vickie was genuinely fond of Henri's mother. Right now she was glad that Katya often asked questions more from habit than real curiosity.

To hide her disappointment at not finding Henri home, Vickie said: "I just took a chance, Ekaterina Ivanovna. I developed a headache and left the office early, but I feel better now and decided to come by."

Katya patted her on the shoulder. "Let's have a glass of ice tea. It'll help."

Vickie followed the older woman in, comparing her labored gait, her heavy figure and aging face with her own mother. The two women were contemporaries, but Katya looked years older than Lydia. Vickie had heard her mother say that Jacques Jobert was married to his business and paid little attention to Katya. Could it be that her mother's happy marriage and the love that Kiril showered on her kept her looking younger, while marital neglect that Katya endured added aging lines to her forty-seven years?

"You are so lovely, my child, so lovely," Katya said with a meaningful smile. "I'm so happy that you will be my daughter-in-law. I love you like my own daughter. I can't say it often enough. Truly, I can't."

Embarrassed by Katya's exuberant outpouring of affection, Vickie said: "Thank you. Mama told me how wonderful you are. I already feel that you're my second mother."

Katya's face glowed with pleasure. "Oh, dear Vickie, how nice to hear you call me that...Please call me Mother in the future."

After she finished her glass of tea, Vickie realized that Henri must have been delayed somewhere. But where? She thanked Katya for the tea, declined to stay any longer, saying that she was needed at home, and left.

CHAPTER ELEVEN

Vickie closed the gate behind her and walked slowly along Rue Delastre, hoping to intercept Henri on his way home. How disappointing not to have found him waiting for her at the door. She lived for the hours she spent with him. Why was he late? An empty crushed can lay in her path and she kicked it. It rolled to the edge of the sidewalk and fell on the pavement with a clanking sound, jarring her nerves.

As she turned the corner, she suddenly stopped. A block away, Henri was talking to Igor Sevich. She remembered Henri once saying that Igor Sevich was an honest man; she also remembered that he gave no answer when Katya asked why Igor stopped coming to their house.

Vickie clutched her purse to her chest, and stared. The scene she was watching made no sense. What was Henri, a Frenchman and a diplomat doing, passing an envelope to Igor Sevich, a Soviet citizen and an avowed communist who published Soviet propaganda? And why hadn't Henri ever mentioned seeing Igor to her?

She waited. Henri shook hands with Igor and came toward her. He kissed her lightly on the cheek and chatted casually as they walked back to his apartment. Inside, he took a bottle of orange squash from the small refrigerator in his tiny kitchen, and poured two glasses. After he handed her the cold drink, he sat next to her on the sofa.

"I didn't expect you quite so early, darling," he said. "Is everything all right at the office? And where were you when the sirens sounded?"

Vickie took a sip of the orange squash, then put the glass down on the little table in front of her. Her hands trembled.

"Henri, I saw you talking to Igor Sevich. I didn't know he was a friend of yours." There was a bronze vase on his desk across the room and she focused on it carefully. It became imperative not to look at Henri's reaction to her words.

"I don't know all your friends either, darling. I'd say Igor is more of an acquaintance than a friend."

"But this man is different, Henri. He's a dedicated communist. His newspaper praises the Soviets, and what's more, there are rumors that he solicits Russian emigrants to repatriate to Russia."

"Oh, my! I hear your father speaking. You're echoing his words."

"It's not just my stepfather. We all hate the Bolsheviks and what they stand for."

"What makes you think Igor's description of life in Russia is not true? Have you ever thought that the White Guard newspapers may be using their own propaganda to turn young Russians against the Soviet Union?"

Vickie stared at Henri with widened eyes. White Guard. He had used that deprecating Soviet term.

"Are you trying to tell me that you favor the Bolsheviks?"

"I think we should update our terminology, darling. The people in Russia are not Bolsheviks anymore. They're Soviets. It's the Soviet Government that rules Russia. The days when Bolsheviks, Mensheviks, and Social Democrats fought the Imperial Government are long gone."

"You haven't answered my question, Henri."

"Let's say I'm objective in this matter. The Soviets have done a lot to improve the lives of the working class. They eliminated illiteracy, bridged the gap between the wealthy and the poor. I'm convinced that socialism is the hope of the future."

Vickie took a deep breath. "Henri, what was in that envelope you passed to Igor?" For the first time Vickie saw anger flash in Henri's eyes. It lasted only a second and then his expression softened. "I don't like you questioning me, Vickie, but if you have to know, I had a little money in that envelope. Igor's newspaper is a good cause, so I help him once in a while."

Incredulous, Vickie leaned forward. "Worthy cause? You call his propaganda-filled paper a worthy cause?"

"It's all in one's point of view, darling. I see nothing wrong in educating the White Russians." Henri paused and a shadow crossed his face. "All I have to remember," he went on, "is what Baron von-Ungern's men did to my grandparents."

"And I'm reminded," she retorted, "of what the Bolsheviks did to *my* grandparents."

As she told him again about the murder of her grandparents, she remembered her mother's distress when she talked about sex and violence. Suddenly, Vickie knew how her grandmother died. She stopped talking and shivered.

"Those were the extremes of the revolution," Henri said. "You mustn't forget that after centuries of oppression, soldiers and workers unleashed their vengeance. But what Baron von-Ungern did to my grandparents was not out of revenge but out of sport." He looked at Vickie. "That makes a big difference, don't you see?"

"Betrayal still goes on," she said and told him about a family friend who went back to Russia after she was promised a job as an accountant in Moscow. Instead, she ended up in Siberia working in a mine and writing her family for warm clothing.

Henri shrugged. "It's hearsay. Distorted rumors, that's all."

Vickie stared at Henri as if she had never seen him before. A gentle smile replaced tension on his face as he moved toward her, took her hand and kissed it.

"Darling, let's not argue over politics," he said, "Our love is the most important thing. Nothing must spoil it."

He pulled her toward him, and Vickie, safe in his embrace, clung to his last words.

"But I'm so shocked," she said. "How can I rationalize it away?"

"You've been listening to your parents for so many years that these ideas are naturally new to you. We must not let them interfere with our happiness."

His arms tightened around her. "I love you, I adore you," he whispered, kissing her eyelids.

Vickie wriggled out of his embrace. "Henri, I've got to know. How long have you been involved with Igor's newspaper?"

His eyes darkened as he pulled her back against him, his hands moving up and down her back. "Shhh! I love you, do you hear? I want you."

The familiar sweet weakness coursed through Vickie, robbing her of her will. "Henri...please...I need to know."

Henri caught her ear lobe between his lips, sucking it in. Vickie closed her eyes and gasped. "Ohhh! What are you doing to me..." She felt his hands unbuttoning her blouse and pulling it off, the touch of his fingers sliding to the hollow of her shoulders and then farther down, setting her skin on fire and making her quiver. Moments later she was lost in a dazzling ascent into ecstasy.

Afterward, when she lay soothed by the caress of his fingers as they traced her profile, Vickie pretended to doze. A few more minutes and she would leave, as she had done on so many previous occasions during the past year.

Only this time it would not be the same. She had discovered a side to him that disturbed her more than she was willing to admit.

It wasn't just a matter of political disagreement. The Soviet form of government was, to her, a reign of terror, abuse of human rights, corruption of everything honorable and decent in an individual. She could not understand how Henri, who was a gentleman and an educated man, could sympathize with it. But that wasn't all. The real shock was the discovery that Henri was devious.

On her way home, she chose a longer way through the quiet residential streets, walking along the bamboo fences that concealed the mansions of Chinese and foreign tycoons. Tall, shady trees guarded their seclusion. In these quiet streets, unanswered questions shadowed her. Why was Henri reluctant to tell her what was in that envelope? How could she trust the man she loved after what had happened today?

She slowed her pace. This blasted heat. Perhaps she was overreacting. Perhaps in due time Henri would have told her about his friendship with Igor. Just because Igor was a Soviet citizen didn't mean one had to treat him as a pariah.

*   *   *

A week later, she saw Henri talking to Igor again on the corner of Rue Lafayette and Route Père Robert. Some sixth sense prompted her to stop and watch the two men, but they didn't linger and soon turned into a nearby alley. Vickie hurried after them, stopped at the corner building to conceal herself, and watched. She saw Henri look around furtively, reach inside his breast pocket, pull out an envelope and hand it to Igor. It was the reenactment of the same scene she had witnessed on Route Pichon, only this time, the envelope was much too large for a few bills.

For a few moments she stood still, her stomach sick. She turned and fled in the opposite direction.

The next day Igor's newspaper carried reports of the new French government's policies abroad. Perhaps it was nothing that one could not have read in another paper, but where did Igor get his information?

She couldn't wait for the evening to come, hoping that Henri would explain everything.

But he didn't explain; he only repeated what he had already told her about his relationship with Igor Sevich. When she accused him of giving Igor political information, he shook his head.

"I didn't give anything to him. You saw us talking on the street corner. There's no law against that."

"But I saw you pass a large envelope to him in the alley, Henri," she said.

For a second, Henri narrowed his eyes, then said: "A few more bills for his expenses, that's all."

"Are you spying for him, Henri?"

Henri laughed. "What strong words we Russians use."

"We? You're French, remember?"

"At heart I'm Russian, and you know it, but that doesn't make me a spy."

"Then where did Igor get his information about the new French Government? And why France in particular?"

"I resent your cross-examining me, Vickie. I won't justify every action I take. Love is based on trust, and when certain things are impossible to prove, we must accept each other's word on faith."

He reached for her, but she backed away, grabbed her purse and rushed toward the door. He caught her and swung her around, locking her in his arms. "I love you. Doesn't that matter? I love you!"

She struggled to free herself. Nothing mattered just then but to get away, to leave his apartment and think. She had to think.

He must have seen the anger and determination in her face for suddenly he released her, dropped his arms and made no attempt to stop her as she ran out.

Dusk had darkened the sky and was wrapping the city in a gray shroud. She found her way to the little square by the Pushkin statue, where she was glad to be alone.

Crippling anxiety ripped her. Shadows. Shadows under the trees, below Pushkin, shadows on the bench beside her. Henri had neither denied nor confirmed her suspicions.

How to go about finding out more? She thought of a number of ways, only to eliminate them by simple logic. Then slowly, a plan formed in her mind. She would have to be secretive, scheming. How shameful to resort to an underhanded thing. But she had to learn the truth.

The day darkened around her. She shouldn't be sitting there alone. She rose and went home.

It was suppertime, and she was surprised to find Lydia and Kiril weren't sitting around the dining table, but were in their room. Nina sat in the armchair, her nose in a book. Before Vickie could ask what was going on, Lydia threw the door open and motioned for her to come into the other room, where Kiril was lying on the bed in his robe.

"Papa! What's wrong?"

"Papa has a couple of boils on his body that are very painful," Lydia answered for Kiril. "Remember you picked up the pyramidon at the pharmacy for a pain in his leg?" and when Vickie nodded, she went on: "Well, that pain developed into a boil and now there's another one on his buttocks."

"They're furuncles, Vickie," Kiril explained. "I guess there's no way to avoid dirt in this city. I must have picked up an infection somewhere."

"My God, Papa," Vickie said, "why haven't you gone to Uncle Jacob? He's a dermatologist. What better help could you get?"

Kiril turned his head away and stared into the wall. Lydia sighed. "He won't go to Jacob."

"Why not, Papa?"

"We've asked for enough favors from the Rosens. The furuncles have drained, and I don't know what Jacob can do that I haven't done already."

The next morning was Saturday and free, so Vickie went to see Jacob Rosen.

After she explained why she had come, stumbling over invented reasons for Kiril not seeking help himself, Jacob cut her off with a nod.

"I can understand why Kiril didn't come to me," he said. "We physicians are a stubborn lot and think we have all the answers ourselves. I've seen these furuncles many times and I have just the stuff for it."

Jacob reached behind him, opened his medicine cabinet and took out a small jar. "Here, take this and make him use the ointment every day. Let me know how he's doing."

"Thank you very much," Vickie said, taking the jar. Before she realized what she was doing, she threw her arms around Jacob and burst into tears. Jacob held her for a few moments stroking her hair, and when she pulled back, embarrassed by her outburst, he put his arm around her waist and led her out of the room.

"Sara overslept this morning and is only now fixing some breakfast. Why don't you stay and have jam and bagels and a cup of hot tea?" he said, opening the door into the dining room where Sara was already seated. "Joseph left to meet some school chums of his. So you and Sara can have a good visit," he added. "You'll have to excuse me if I don't join you right now. I have some pressing work to do in my office."

Sara leaned back in her chair. "I put the folders in your left drawer, Jacob," she called after him. "That scatterbrain," she muttered, handing Vickie a cup of tea and a pitcher of hot milk. Vickie pulled a handkerchief out of her purse and blew her nose. Hot milk. The Rosens had real milk. Reverently she picked up the pitcher and poured some into her cup. After whispering "thank you," she gulped the hot liquid. She had forgotten how delicious pure milk tasted in tea. She put down her cup and fought to hold back tears.

Sara lowered the teapot and moved her chair closer to Vickie. "Now what's this all about?"

Hesitantly, Vickie related how Kiril refused to come to Jacob for help. Sara heard her out, then tilted her chin and made Vickie look into her eyes.

"I know you, dear girl. You wouldn't cry over such a thing. That was only the crumb of the whole story that triggered the tears. Now what's underneath those stormy waters? Out with it, tell your friend Sara."

How could she tell anyone of her fears and suspicions about Henri? Lips pressed, eyes downcast once again, Vickie shook her head.

Sara sighed. "Well, at least you can cry in my presence."

As Vickie rose to leave, Sara hugged her. "Remember, when you're ready to talk, I'm here to listen."

"Thank you," Vickie whispered, and hurried out.

*   *   *

Anemic moonlight wrapped around Vickie as she walked to Igor's printing office that evening.

His address took her in the direction of Rue du Consulat to a back alley that branched off the main thoroughfare. It was narrow and dark with one light at the end. She headed toward it, only to find the open door led to a Chinese bakery kitchen. Several men were milling about the small room. One of them was swaying, and Vickie drew closer to look. A long vat with a low wooden border, buried deep into the floor, was filled with dough. A tall Chinese, his black pants rolled up above his knees, was walking up and down the container, kneading the dough with his bare feet. Back and forth he moved, working his toes, and rolling his feet from heel to toe and from side to side.

With a shudder, she turned to the other side of the alley and rang the bell by the door to Igor's office.

The look of surprise on Igor's face as he opened the door was so great, that it almost made her laugh. His shirttail was hanging out and he had thongs on his feet. For a few seconds there was an impasse and then Vickie said: "Please, may I come in?"

Igor backed away, waving her in. "What a surprise, Vickie. To what do I owe this honor?"

Vickie gave him a token smile and walked inside. The room was large. Newspapers were strewn everywhere, on the tables, on the chairs, even on the floor, each carrying the imprint of the hammer and sickle and the title, *RETURN*, in bold letters. An old Underwood typewriter and a half-full tin cup of coffee vied for space on a small table near the wall. A broken cookie lay on top of one of the papers, and the stale odor of fried food mixed with the pungent smell of ink hung in the air.

Following her gaze, Igor scooped the crumbs into his palm and threw them in a wicker waste basket.

"Sorry for the mess, but I didn't expect anyone this evening."

"That's all right. I came by to see your setup. Where is your printing press?" Vickie asked.

Igor pointed toward the door at the far wall. "It's in the back room under lock and key." He spread his arms and lifted his shoulders. "One can never be sure, thieves will steal anything nowadays. This front room is a kind of reception office."

Vickie picked up one of the newspapers and without looking at Igor, said: "I saw Henri pass an envelope to you on Rue Lafayette. Yesterday he told me what was in it."

She waited, but Igor was silent. Vickie opened the newspaper and pretended to read. "You've done a good job on that article about the new French policies."

This time Igor reacted. "Aha! I'm glad you thought so. Henri doubted that what he gave me would be of much value, but I guess I worded it well enough to impress my readers."

The newspaper in her hands shook so violently, she put it down, but Igor did not seem to notice.

Keeping her face down as if she were looking through the papers, Vickie said: "I'd like to get a copy of yesterday's paper, if you have one to spare."

Igor handed her a copy and added the current issue as well.

Vickie thanked him and asked: "What do I owe you?"

Igor waved it away. "Nothing at all. Consider it a gift."

She was relieved. She felt there was something immoral in giving up even a fraction of her money to contribute to Stalin's gulags and a system that had killed millions.

"It appears that I won the bet," Igor said.

"What bet?"

He laughed and clapped his hands. "Henri told me that he would have a hard time converting you to our cause, and I bet him that he could do it. I see that I won. Now his decision to immigrate to Russia doesn't have to be a secret anymore."

A ringing started in her ears. She mumbled something and walked out, fighting an overwhelming urge to run.

Once outside, she ran stumbling, fighting nausea. At the corner, where the alley opened onto the street, a garbage can stood open. Aware that she would disgrace herself if she went out on the street, she stopped and bent over the garbage can. Mice or rats, rummaged inside. What did it matter? They were somewhere deep in the can, feasting on man's refuse. She emptied her stomach, holding onto the can's tin edges, then tore off a corner of the newspaper, wiped her mouth and threw the two papers into the garbage.

She roamed the streets until the curfew hour, stopping occasionally to lean against bamboo fences to control her trembling. Had Henri really decided to immigrate to Russia without telling her of his monumental decision? She recalled the way he sometimes looked at her as if he was gauging her reaction to what he said, a look she had not recognized until now.

She looked up at the sky, blinking away tears that blurred the stars. The same sky as on the night he told her he loved her. She wanted that hour back, she wanted things to be like they were then. She wanted to walk with him again and plan their future. She wanted him to hold her and tell her it was all a bad dream and that nothing had changed.

Had he planned to marry her and then tell her the truth, expecting her to follow him to the Soviet Union? Was he blinded to the real possibility that he could become yet another statistic in one of Stalin's labor camps? She could have tried to cope with their ideological differences, but *live* in the Soviet Union? Did he expect her to abandon everything she believed in, suppress her convictions and live a life of hypocrisy? Dear God. She could not do that.

The streets were quiet, and all around her the trees stood still. She envied them. Only man was burdened with a conscience.

It was late. She must go home, crawl into bed and pretend that all was well.

It was her turn to sleep on the soft bed tonight while Nina rested on the long table by the porch window. There was a certain measure of comfort in the unavoidable routine of nightly ritual: In pushing the chairs against the bed to hold the pillows, in taking off the baptismal cross hanging around her neck on the gold chain under her clothes, in undressing, and finally, in crawling under the covers.

And then the nightly sounds: The darkened room with the rhythmic breathing of the sleeping women; the muffled meowing of someone's cat; the slow footsteps of the street patrol checking blackouts. Vickie slipped out of bed, tiptoed to the bathroom, and locked herself in. There she sat down on the toilet seat lid and pressed her forehead against the cool porcelain of the washbasin.

The enormity of Henri's deceit. His betrayal. Vickie shook in a flow of tears.

I had thought him so perfect, so honest and sincere. How could I have been so wrong? I can never trust him again. But oh, dear God, I still love him…I love him, but I can never marry him.

As she thought that, she clamped her hand over her mouth to stifle a groan at the vision of her tarnished tomorrows without Henri, and all that she had lost.

*   *   *

For days she avoided Henri under the pretext of having a cold. She could not bring herself to face him, to look into his eyes and argue. Some things bear no debate, for they are so ingrained into the soul, they are a part of the soul. Not for a single moment did she consider the possibility of going with him to Russia. She would never support a government of murderers. In that she was determined. But she wasn't strong enough to tell this to his face. So, she decided to call him.

Half a block away, in the converted garage where she had bought her bicycle, she had seen a wall telephone. The Chinese salesman spoke only pidgin English, so she could speak freely.

"I lied because I didn't want to lose you," Henri pleaded. "You don't need to know everything about my work."

"But what about immigrating to Russia? Did you really believe I would go with you?"

"Yes. I believed you would."

"Does your mother know about this?"

"No. She'll know when the time comes."

"Why do you want to waste your life? One man's effort, is that going to change the world?"

"Every man needs a vision, a goal to pursue. Mine is to return to my mother's native land. It's in my blood, and it has now become my motherland, my *rodina*."

"And what if this *rodina* turns out to be a cruel stepmother? What then?"

"You mean the current government, of course. Well, stepmothers come and go, but the land and the people don't change. It is the country of my heart."

It wasn't so much what he was saying but the way he said it that angered her again.

"My God, you're reciting a well-rehearsed speech. How brainwashed you are. You're confusing your mother's childhood memories of something that no longer exists with Igor Sevich's propaganda. You can't be that blind. It's a false vision."

"And what hope do you have without a land you can call your own? Even if you do go to another country, you'll never feel at home."

"So what? I'd rather be a foreigner in a free country than live in my motherland without freedom."

"Vickie, you're upset. I beg you, please think it over."

"I have thought it over. For days I've thought it over. There's no way I'd agree to immigrate to Russia. I'm ashamed to even talk about it."

"Then you don't love me enough."

"And you? If **you** love me enough, give up the idea."

"I can't. I'm committed."

He kept her on the phone for almost an hour, alternately pleading and accusing her of lack of understanding. Finally, the Chinese owner of the shop made signs that she could not hold up the phone any longer.

Embarrassed and angry, she hung up and walked out of the shop into the noisy, busy street where people hurried past, paying no attention to her. As she walked around the block, her legs trembled so hard, she stopped and leaned against the bamboo fence. It took all her strength to make a choice, to reject the man she loved, to deprive herself of security, and face an uncertain future. But oh, how it hurt! Never to be in his arms again, never to feel his body against hers, never to thrill to his love-making. Never.

Another thought wormed itself in. Henri was betraying his country. The French Government should be informed. That meant exposing Henri and with it, ruining his career, shaming his family.

A persistent fly buzzed near her ear. With a sharp flip of her hand, she waved the fly away and with it, the alarming thought.

CHAPTER TWELVE

The next day Vickie returned to work, and after dinner that night, stony-faced and dry-eyed, she announced that she and Henri were no longer engaged. Lydia pressed for reasons, but Kiril raised his hand to silence her.

"You must forgive us, my dear," he said to Vickie, "for being so disappointed. The match seemed so perfect. Of course, we would like to know what happened." He paused, studied Vickie for a few moments, then said: "But we won't press."

Afraid to trust her voice, Vickie was only able to nod and look at her stepfather with eyes blurred by tears. Her mother, however, was not so easily put off. When Kiril was out of the room, she accused Vickie of throwing away an enviable match.

"You're headstrong. Always have been. Was your pride hurt?" When Vickie didn't answer, Lydia went on. "So what? You can't afford to be choosy. Swallow your pride and makeup with him. He's such a catch. He is a man of good breeding, a charismatic, handsome man, and he's crazy about you. It's stupid to give him up."

Nina had listened to her mother's nagging, and the next night, when the lights were out and she and Vickie were getting ready for bed, she whispered: "You fooled Mama and Papa but I knew you were sleeping with him, and I can guess why you broke up. I bet he cheated on you."

When Vickie did not answer, Nina went on: "Mama is right. You don't have to be that proud. So he strayed a little. That doesn't mean he stopped loving you. Imagine, giving up a passport because of that. If I ever get the chance, I'll grab at it, and sponsor Mama and Papa to whatever country I'll go. You're not only stupid but selfish as well not to think of your family."

Nina waited for a response, but when it didn't come, she turned to the wall and was soon asleep.

Fists clenched, arms rigid at her sides, Vickie lay still and made no sound, though she was swallowing tears as fast as they filled her throat. Where had such cynicism come from in a seventeen-year old? She was so angry, it took all her will power not to tell her sister that if she married Henri, it wouldn't be to France they would go.

Only Sara sympathized and accepted Vickie's decision without asking for reasons. Vickie desperately wanted to share her heartache, but how could she without revealing the truth?

"You're young, Vickie," Sara said. "The young heal faster. Besides, the war is almost over and the Americans will soon be here. You'll meet many young men."

Vickie remembered her friend Zoya saying that she could only relate to a Russian man, and hadn't she Vickie, fallen in love with Henri mostly because he had a Russian soul?

Henri telephoned, left messages with the landlady, but Vickie did not return his calls. One saving grace was that Henri's father was rarely around her office, and on those occasions when he did pass through, he continued to greet her politely.

The hardest thing of all was facing Henri's mother when she came to the office one day, and took her to a nearby Chinese restaurant for lunch. She told her how heartbroken Henri was, and asked for an explanation. Flushed, choking on her food, Vickie stumbled over words.

"Please," she said, her voice trembling, "don't ask me why."

Katya toyed with her fork for a while. "Henri is very distraught. Very. When I question him, all he says is that the differences between you are too great. A long time ago I had advised him to talk things out with you more. What happened to change your mind? Is there anything, anything at all that I can do to straighten things out between you?"

Vickie shook her head. "No, thank you. My decision is final. It's…it's very painful for me to talk about it. I love you and your family very much." Her voice broke. "That has not changed."

In the ensuing days, Henri waited for her on street corners, walked her home pleading with her. One day, as she was riding her bicycle home, he stepped off the curb and made her stop. Afraid to create a scene, she followed him into an alley.

"Vickie," he said, holding her by the shoulders, "listen to me. Life in Russia is better now than it was under the Tsars. Remember the Decembrists? They were members of the privileged class and still *they* rebelled. Way back in 1825!"

His touch seemed to burn her, and she freed herself. "Please, Henri, we're getting nowhere with this. I told you, I won't live in Russia."

"Then your love is not deep enough."

And she thought: I'll never love anyone like this again. You are my love for life. Aloud she said: "I can say the same to you."

She waited, still hoping, but after a moment's pause, he only said: "Then this is final?"

Blinded by tears, she nodded and ran out on the street. Without looking back, she mounted her bicycle, and rode away.

At night, in the hush of the room asleep, memories haunted her. She heard again the Jessfield Park band playing a Strauss Waltz as she walked with Henri among magnolia trees. She smelled again the flowers and the freshly cut grass, sensed the cooling night breezes and felt his clear, smooth skin. She longed to touch him, to feel his mouth and hands upon her. Her body throbbed with yearning for his lovemaking. The images crowded, pressed upon her chest, mocked. Never again…

During the days she spoke little as she helped her mother with the cooking, or washed dishes in the crowded communal kitchen. Glad for the chance to reduce her leisure time, when thoughts of Henri were impossible to avoid, she did more than her share of work. She knew she was indulging Nina who was only too happy to escape housework.

Through all these painful days, Vickie watched with a mixture of affection and alarm Joseph Rosen's budding love for her sister. The starry-eyed, young man had become a frequent visitor at the Muravins. If Nina were to return his love, Kiril and Lydia would oppose the match. How painful it would be for Sara and Jacob, and especially for Joseph.

"I brought you your favorite chocolates," he told Nina one evening, handing her a large box. "These are all dark, your favorite," he repeated nodding in emphasis, and pointing at the box with a self-effacing gesture.

Vickie watched him. He was tall, about six feet. His dark brown eyes glowed with affection as he looked at Nina from under thick brows. His curly hair, usually unruly, was combed back neatly, and he wore a pressed white shirt that hung loosely on his thin, and slightly stooped frame.

Nina took the box, hesitated a moment, then put it on the table. "Thank you," she said, throwing the words over her shoulder. "Everyone in our family likes dark chocolates."

Vickie glanced at Joseph. He didn't seem to notice Nina's lack of enthusiasm, but she knew that as soon as Joseph left, Nina would open the box and dig into the chocolates. Just as she thought that, Nina however, slipped her arm through Joseph's and gave him a peck on the cheek. "You're always so thoughtful. What do you say we go to a movie?"

Joseph's face lit up with a grin. "Why not?"

He waved goodbye to Vickie and ushered Nina out of the room.

*   *   *

Early in August they learned that the Americans had dropped a new bomb, called the atomic bomb, on Hiroshima and Nagasaki in Japan with devastating results. Details were sketchy but rumors abound: The Japanese were packing up, preparing to leave the city. They were burning official papers and covering up everything they didn't want the Allies to find. In the last frenzy of their power they were arresting and beating people...

On August 14th, 1945, Japan surrendered. Thousands of people roamed the streets waving Allied flags and carrying long hidden posters of Chiang-Kai-shek, Roosevelt and Churchill. "But Roosevelt died last April," Vickie mused after she told her stepfather what she had witnessed on the way home from the office.

Kiril smiled. "I think we still associate the victory with him rather than with President Truman. What else did you see?"

"Boats are blowing whistles on the Whangpoo and I'm sure you all heard church bells toll. Stores are closed and I saw vendors dancing around with passersby. It's wild out there. The talk in the office is that Chiang Kai-shek's Nationalist forces are due to take over the city and that the Allies are close by."

"I too have heard that," Kiril said, "but I also heard that the Japanese are still guarding the key posts and there are rumors of mobs on the rampage looting shops on Nanking Road. As long as the occupation forces are not yet in Shanghai we better stay off the streets."

On August 23, Zoya telephoned Vickie. "I'm so excited," she said, "I just learned that the American marines have entered the city and will be marching up Avenue Joffre." She paused to catch her breath, then rushed on: "I'm going out to watch!"

Vickie and Nina, caught up in the excitement, ran the block and a half to Avenue Joffre, the main thoroughfare of the French Concession. The streetcars and all vehicles were cleared from the street and in the unaccustomed eerie silence, Vickie and Nina stood on the corner of Rue Cardinal Mercier and waited for the Americans.

Americans! Vickie thought with a smile. At last! And as she thought that, a distant, rhythmic sound of marching men, faint at first, grew louder and closer. A few more minutes and there they were. Weary but smiling at the exuberant crowds lining the sidewalks, they filled the street. Here and there young girls threw flowers in their paths and shouted in English: "Welcome to Shanghai! We've been waiting for you a long time!"

How improper, Vickie thought, to gawk at the marching marines, no matter how happy one was to see the Americans. Yet she was curious, and watched covertly from around the corner as the men marched past. The enthusiasm was palpable and the crowd's joy so infectious that Vickie and Nina forgot all decorum and rushed out to wave and cheer with everyone else.

The American Army Air Corps established their headquarters in the Chase Manhattan Bank Building near the Bund, and the Army occupied the Hamilton House around the corner. Funny-looking vehicles called 'jeeps' appeared on the streets, and because of the increased traffic and ever careless pedestrians, the speed limit was reduced to fifteen miles an hour.

The mood of the city was giddy as everyone celebrated the end of the war. The euphoria, despite the Chinese currency losing value by the day and inflation escalating wildly, would not abate. Each U.S. dollar brought twenty thousand Chinese yuan, and as the months went by, it climbed to fifty thousand with no end in sight. Americans carried suitcases of money to pay restaurant bills, tipping generously and offering their girlfriends boxes of K-rations in their ingenuous and sometimes tactless manner. But all was forgiven because they were Americans, the victors, the liberators, and they meant well. So the Russians swallowed their pride and accepted the gifts gratefully.

At home, discussions as to which country to apply for an immigration visa lasted late into the night.

"I want to live in France," Kiril said one evening. "So many of our own kind have gone to live in Paris. I may find relatives or family friends. I'd be at home with the French language. Besides," he added after a pause, "France is closer to Russia than the Americas or Australia. When the monarchy is restored, we would be near our *rodina*."

Lydia was in favor of America. "It's the land of opportunity, Kiril, of great security."

And as the discussion continued, Vickie saw that her stepfather was taken aback and not a little miffed at Lydia's refusal to agree with him. In the end, they put the decision aside for the time being, 'into a far drawer' as Lydia put it. There seemed to be no immediate hurry since life in Shanghai was returning to its prewar prosperity. They knew that Jacob Rosen's practice was busier than ever and that he and Sara were content to stay in Shanghai. Why rush into such an important decision, her mother argued, a decision that would influence the course of all their lives? And so they waited.

Winter passed with its usual dampness and cold. Driven by wind, storm clouds raced across the sky, dumping rain and sleet on the city. Vickie continued to work, ignoring the delirious exuberance of others her age. The young celebrated holidays late into the night, dancing the Lambeth Walk down Nanking Road.

One Saturday afternoon, Vickie decided to visit her friend, Zoya. She wondered if Zoya and her Russian husband planned to stay in Shanghai or immigrate somewhere. Zoya was so very Russian, it would be difficult for her to adjust to a foreign country. Vickie remembered Zoya's reaction to an incident at a party she and her husband attended in an army officer's apartment at the Hamilton House. By error, they arrived fifteen minutes early and found the host's Russian girlfriend, Lara, ironing her dress in the bedroom.

She showed no embarrassment at Zoya's startled look, and pointing to the closet, said: "Do me a favor Zoya, will you? Get me my slip from the hanger."

Zoya opened the closet door and found it half full of the girl's clothes hanging next to the officer's uniforms. She handed the slip to Lara and asked: "Are you living here?"

Lara laughed. "No, of course not. This is bachelor quarters and no women are allowed." She winked at Zoya and added, "but I do sneak in on occasion."

When Zoya's glance wandered to the night table and the picture of a beautiful woman and child, Lara flushed.

"It's not what you think," she said, slipping on her dress. "We're very much in love and Tom will send for me as soon as he returns to the States and divorces his wife."

Vickie could still hear Zoya's indignant voice: "What I can't understand, Vickie, is how can Lara be so naive as to think that her boyfriend is serious about her? It's obviously a mere fling for an officer of the victorious army. When Lara was out of the room, I asked him who was in the photo on his table—I admit it was devious of me—and he picked the picture up and said with pride that it was his wife and child."

Vickie argued that it was not fair to judge all American military men abroad by the example of one, but Zoya was implacable.

That was several weeks ago, and she wondered if Zoya had had any more contacts with the Americans that perhaps had changed her opinion.

Passing a jewelry shop, Vickie stopped to look at the display of jade rings and bracelets. As she studied them without much interest, for jade was so commonplace in Shanghai one tended to underestimate its value, she became aware of someone standing beside her. As she looked up into the reflection of the window, an American officer tipped his cap and smiled.

"Excuse me," he said in English, "I wonder if you could help me?"

Vickie turned around. He was not much taller than she, his sandy hair short beneath his cap, the clear gray eyes anxious as he said: "I'm afraid I'm lost."

"Where do you want to go?" Vickie asked, fascinated by his American accent and disarmed by his friendly manner.

"I was told there are a lot of gift shops on Yates Road. How do I get there?"

"Go back three blocks to Route des Soeurs, turn right, and after you cross Avenue Foch at the end of the French Concession, the street will become Yates Road."

The officer smiled again. "Thank you, very much."

Vickie hesitated for a moment, then nodded and walked away. She was enormously pleased with herself. In this, her first encounter with an American, she had had no trouble understanding his English.

No one answered the doorbell at Zoya's apartment and Vickie turned back, walking slowly toward home. As she neared Route Père Robert, she saw the American officer standing on the corner and looking up and down the street.

She stopped. "What's the matter?"

The officer spread his arms in a helpless gesture. "I walked the three blocks as you said, but the street I came to was not Route des Soeurs, but this one, Route Père Robert. I don't get it."

"How silly of me. I forgot to tell you that on this side of Avenue Joffre the street is called Route Père Robert, but to the right it becomes Route des Soeurs." Vickie smiled and shrugged. "Don't ask me why."

"I see," he said with a grin. "Instead of sisters, I stumbled on the father, eh?"

Puzzled, Vickie frowned, and he laughed. "You missed my joke. I know a little French. On the right are the sisters, and on the left is the father. *Soeurs* and *père*."

Vickie laughed. "I guess it is rather confusing, isn't it? And then farther on, the Sisters become Yates Road."

"You wouldn't by any chance be going in my direction?" he asked. "I'd sure appreciate your guiding me to Yates Road. Otherwise I may stumble on some other family members."

Vickie hesitated only a moment. "I'll be glad to," she said, and he tipped his cap once again. "Good. Let me introduce myself: Lt.Colonel

Brian Hamilton of the United States Army at your service." He bowed with exaggerated panache, his smile so infectious that Vickie smiled back and introduced herself.

"I'm supposed to meet two of my friends," he said, "on the corner of Yates and Bubbling Well Roads. We were planning to do some shopping for our families. Do you mind if we take a pedicab instead of walking? I'm a little late."

As they rode in the pedicab, Vickie wondered if any Russian friends of her family would see her and start to gossip. She didn't care. She settled back and listened to the American accent of Lt.Col. Brian Hamilton.

She spent the better part of two hours leading the three men from shop to shop, teaching them how to bargain. She told them that it was best to be the first in a shop, for the Chinese merchants believed that if they didn't make a sale to the first customer, they would have a bad day. She couldn't help but notice that while the other two officers bought gifts for their wives, Brian selected things for his mother.

When they were through, he offered to take her to dinner but she declined.

"Why not?" he asked. "We really appreciate your time and effort." When she hesitated, he added with a twinkle in his eye: "there's safety in numbers."

"I'm sorry, but I have to go home," she said.

"Well then, may I have your telephone number?"

Vickie gave him her phone number and fled.

The phone rang the next afternoon and she wasn't surprised to hear Brian Hamilton's voice say, "Hi! How about dinner at the Club in the Broadway Mansions? It's now our Air Force bachelor officers' quarters."

Vickie accepted, and he called for her at seven o'clock. He pulled up to their bamboo gate in a jeep and took the steps two at a time. He shook hands vigorously with Kiril and Lydia, smiled at Nina, and then haltingly said in Russian: "*Dobry vecher.*"

Surprised, Kiril asked: "*Govorite po Russki?*"

Brian shook his head. "No, I don't really speak Russian. I took it for a coule of years in college, but without practice—" he spread his arms in a helpless gesture…

"What branch of service are you in?" Kiril asked.

"Intelligence," was a short reply as Brian scanned the room with a quick glance. It was an open, frank appraisal, not particularly tactful as Henri's had been. She pushed the unwanted comparison out of her mind.

In spite of Kiril's stiff formality and Lydia's raised brow, it was impossible for Vickie to take offense at this friendly man with his warm and smiling gray eyes. Although he did not kiss her mother's hand, nor click his heels on greeting her, she was charmed by him and by his fresh, colloquial expressions.

He treated her to a delicious dinner of lamb, vegetables, and deep fried potatoes, which was followed by ice cream and coffee with real cream. They danced to a three-piece band playing foxtrots and American waltzes, but she found Brian struggling to follow the music and she couldn't erase the image of Henri leading her expertly on the dance floor. When the band played *Blue Tango,* Brian sighed. "When it comes to a tango, I have a wooden leg."

Stealthily Vickie looked down but Brian caught her glance. "I'm kidding."

Puzzled, Vickie asked: "Kid? A child? I'm sorry, I don't understand."

Brian grinned. "That's American. It means that I was making a joke, teasing you."

And so it went the whole evening. He asked about her background and listened attentively, interrupting once in a while with the kind of question that prompted her to go on. Vickie couldn't remember when she had laughed or talked about herself so much.

After a while, he said: "Your family has suffered a great deal. All those moves, tough to be continually uprooted. Too bad your people waited so long before doing something about the Tsar."

"Oh, but we tried once before. Way back in 1825. Unfortunately, the attempt failed. It was tragic because the revolutionaries wanted a democratic government, something like the one you have." Vickie paused, then added: "You were lucky to have succeeded so well with your revolution."

"Yes. I think we've set an example for the world. I've been to Europe several times with my parents. I enjoyed England, France and Germany, but I was always glad to get home. I've never taken my government and our way of life for granted." His mouth stretched into a shy smile. "Maybe that's why I chose to go into the army."

Vickie leaned forward. "What was your life like before that?"

Brian dismissed her question with a wave of his hand. "Not as spectacular or dramatic as yours. I'm an only child, born in San Francisco..."

"Oh, the city of the famous Golden Gate, isn't it?" Vickie interrupted.

"Right you are, and a few other famous things, as well. My father owned several hotels and expected me to join him in business. But I upset the apple cart not only by choosing to go to West Point, that's the army military school, but by deciding to make the army my career." Brian toyed with his spoon for a few moments, then added: "Dad was very upset."

What about your mother?" Vickie asked.

Brian's face lit up. "Oh, my mother is a petite blond package of hidden steel. She was on my side and argued with my father."

"And did she convince him?"

"Unfortunately not. He died recently...unreconciled."

Vickie was certain there was more to his story than he cared to divulge, but asked no more questions. She wanted to know about his personal life and whether he had ever been in love. He had already told her that he was thirty years old and not married. But then, why should she be surprised? She hadn't told him about Henri either.

*   *   *

During the autumn of '46, Vickie saw a lot of Brian. He usually waited in his jeep outside her office, then took her to dinner either at the Broadway Mansions Officers' Club or to one of the many Chinese and Russian restaurants. Sometimes she suggested they hear an opera at the Lyceum Theater and although Brian confessed that his music preference ran to a lighter genre, he went willingly. He even accompanied her once to an operetta but because it was in Russian, he missed the humor, but did not seem to mind, enjoying Vickie's translations. He brought a light touch to everything, and the more she learned to understand American, the more she laughed at his jokes and appreciated his ability to see the funny side of things.

Lydia kept bringing Henri's name up, mentioning that he hadn't left for France, was still in Shanghai, was still unmarried. Vickie kept silent, but when Lydia started comparing Brian's lack of polish to Henri's exquisite manners, Vickie bristled. "Don't waste your breath, Mama. It won't work."

*   *   *

Her parents' elated mood of the postwar months gradually dissipated. Vickie was well aware that her mother and stepfather were alarmed by the rumors circulating for quite some time now, and intensifying as the months went by, about the Chinese Communists activity throughout China. In spite of the giddy affluence now enjoyed by many foreigners and Russians in Shanghai, Manchuria was already under Mao Tse-Tung's control. How long would it be after the Allies left China before the Communists posed a real threat to Shanghai? Vickie shuddered to think of what would become of them if that happened. It was clear to her that she and her family had to leave China.

During the Japanese occupation their reduced circumstances had been blamed on war conditions and the most frequent phrase spoken had been: "This is all temporary. When the war is over…" as if that were going to restore Kiril's health and with it, his busy practice.

Their life had been easier to tolerate then, because others had shared their fate, but now, with many Russians back at work in foreign companies and getting good salaries, the Muravins' status became an embarrassment. So, the time Vickie spent with Brian was a charmed existence in which the rooming house on Rue Cardinal Mercier was pushed to the background and she was transported into another world where money was no problem, where good food and good humor were always in great supply.

One day, Brian mentioned that he'd like to taste a Russian home-cooked meal. Pleased, Vickie asked her mother to prepare borscht and beef stroganoff for him.

"I know it's hard for you to cook in our communal kitchen, Mama, but just this once, I think we should have Brian over for dinner."

Her mother obliged without comment, and when the evening came, Brian ate with great enjoyment, complimenting Lydia on her culinary talents. Vickie noticed that her stepfather sat stiffly, watching Brian eat his borscht from the broad side of the soup spoon. Anxious to distract her stepfather, Vickie recounted their first date when Brian told her that he had a wooden leg. Brian laughed.

"I have thin legs, and they don't obey me when I dance," he said, all seriousness on his face. "I don't even dare to appear in swimming trunks on our California beaches. I'm afraid they'd arrest me for vagrancy, no visible means of support."

Vickie laughed, but Kiril and Lydia missed the humor. When she explained in Russian, Lydia laughed, but Kiril gave Brian only a polite smile.

"I guess it loses in the translation, huh? That's what we call a 'dud'," Brian said.

After dinner, she walked out with him to his jeep.

"That was a wonderful meal, Vickie," he said, pulling her to him and kissing her lightly on the mouth. Vickie found herself responding with warmth. Brian released her, noticing a Chinese beggar boy who stopped to watch. "I wasn't aware that we had an audience," he said, his voice breathless. "On second thought, shall we give him another lesson?" and without waiting for her answer, he pulled her closer and kissed her again.

His face was flushed, and she tasted a faint flavor of borscht and sour cream in his kiss. Not very romantic to be sure, but he was so easy to be with and there was something endearing and warm about him.

When she joined her family inside, Kiril frowned. "Your young man drinks his soup from the broad side of the spoon. Certainly different from our table manners. And I was shocked when he made fun of his physical shortcomings in front of the ladies. So undignified."

Vickie put her arms around her stepfather and hugged him. "No one can live up to your impeccable manners, Papochka. But he's fun to be with and I enjoy his company."

"You do?" Nina asked. "I can't imagine what you can have in common with him." She paused, then snickered and added: "I suppose it doesn't matter since he's a rich American of course."

"You'd be surprised," Vickie snapped. "I really do enjoy his company." As soon as she said it, she flushed, ashamed of the defensive tone in her voice.

*   *   *

At the end of December, Brian asked Vickie to the New Year's Eve dinner dance at the Officers' Club. It was to be a formal affair. Vickie pulled out her only long gown, the peach one she had worn to the French Club five years before, and scrutinized it critically. It looked juvenile. With manicure scissors, she cut off all the tiny bows scattered over the skirt, pressed the dress and tried it on. It needed an accent. In a yardage store on Avenue Joffre, she bought a brown velvet cummerbund and a matching narrow ribbon to tie around her neck. The effect was demure yet elegant.

She couldn't remember when she had ever felt so lighthearted and cheerful. Going out with Henri had always been intense and ardent, never so buoyant or carefree as with Brian. He was not handsome like Henri, but there was a twinkle in Brian's eyes, and an appealing charm in his outgoing personality that enchanted her. Was he serious about her or was she a fling for him like Zoya's friend and her American officer? Surely not. That was an affair, this was different. Brian was *courting* her.

At the club, the band played *Don't Fence Me In, Sentimental Journey, As Time Goes By,* and other popular tunes, but when it struck up *I've got you under my skin,* Brian stopped dancing, took Vickie by the wrist and led her out to the elevator.

Vickie stiffened. "Where are you taking me?" she asked.

Brian winked. "To my apartment on the upper floor. My roommate is out of town and we need privacy."

Vickie tensed, her heart pounding in her chest. "Brian, I can't go to your apartment. Not all Russian girls do that sort of thing."

Brian took her hand and squeezed it. "Don't worry about the Russians. You're on American territory now. No one has seen us and what I have to say is for us alone."

As soon as he closed the door behind him, he took her into his arms, nuzzled her neck, and kissed her face. "Vickie, you're very special. I've fallen in love with you."

With an enormous effort of will, Vickie pushed his arms away and stepped back.

"Brian, I can't stay here tonight. I..." her voice shook with disappointment and hurt. "I'm not the kind..."

Brian pulled her back to him, and lifted her chin. "I know what you're thinking. Why don't you let me finish what I want to say before you jump to conclusions? Look at those big frightened eyes!"

He buried his face in her hair. "Vickie, honey, I want to marry you."

Vickie's head whirled. It was what she had hoped to hear, but now that he had said it, a torrent of doubts assaulted her. She would be marrying a man she only liked and did not love. But what was the alternative? Staying in China with the Communist threat? What would the Communists do to her stepfather, a Russian prince, or her impetuous, beautiful sister? Here was a chance to help her parents and sister leave. As for falling in love with Brian, how could she, when she loved another man? But she felt comfortable with Brian, liked him enormously, and marriage to him would be pleasant, not something she would have to endure. Perhaps with time she would even learn to love him.

She leaned against him. "Oh, Brian, I love you too."

How easy it was to lie.

Brian stepped back. "Now you see why I had to bring you here? I could hardly sit at the table with others and between comments on a good steak and tomorrow's weather, say, 'By the way, Vickie, I want to marry you'!"

They both laughed and then Brian took her face in his hands. "I want to do so much for you, honey," he said. "I want to make you laugh. I want to make you feel secure and happy. And you know, I think you'll love living in the States."

Brian's words sent a new kind of thrill through her, the thrill of the unknown, exciting world she would be entering, the lovely world to which he belonged. Perhaps love, after all, was not for her. She had refused to go with Henri to Russia and so lost him, but there were other ways to seek happiness. She would bring her parents to America, where they would be safe and happy. Her mother would be so pleased and Nina would have a promising future with all sorts of opportunities in her young life.

As for herself, Vickie made a mental vow to Brian to be the wife he deserved. She couldn't give him passionate love, but she could lavish care and affection on him. He would never know the real reasons she married him.

As they stood by the window looking down on the lights illuminating the street far below them, Brian told her that his parents wanted him to marry his childhood friend, Ellen Bradford. "But I didn't love her. She was just an old friend, so nothing came of it. Now then," he smiled mischievously. "I've let the skeleton out of the closet."

Vickie frowned. "Skeleton? What skeleton?"

"I get such a kick out of you," Brian said, scooping her into his arms.

Vickie raised her brows. "But I didn't kick you."

Brian laughed. "Wow! Poor kid, you've got a lot to learn. But I'm going to have such fun teaching you our American vernacular!"

When he explained the idioms, Vickie said: "I too have a...a skeleton in my boxroom."

"Boxroom?"

"I mean closet," Vickie corrected herself, and then told him about her engagement to Henri. When Brian asked why they broke up, Vickie hesitated. "We...didn't agree on some things that were very important to me, and he wasn't honest with me." She spread her hands. "I lost my trust in him."

"I understand. Well, you don't have to worry about me. The only thing I can't talk too much about is my work. Some of it is top secret." He lifted her chin again and brushed her lips with a light kiss. "Tomorrow I'll start paperwork for our marriage."

Vickie said nothing at home. She hoped that when all the paperwork was done, her parents would be less inclined to object to her marrying Brian.

A few days after New Year's, Brian rushed to Vickie's office at the Jobert Trading Company, waving a bunch of papers in his hand. Once there, he sat down on a wooden chair by her typewriter and said: "Honey, I've received orders to return to the States in six weeks. We must get married before I leave, so you can go with me. Otherwise, as my fiancée you'd have to wait two years for your visa."

Without waiting for her reaction, he took her arm and pulled her up.

"Let's get out of here."

The rest of the day was a blur in Vickie's mind as they made lists of what had to be done before the wedding. They joked about his impatience to tell her about their marriage in a roomful of office people.

"I couldn't have picked a less romantic place, could I?" Brian mused as an afterthought.

Vickie, always analytical, replied: "It wasn't exactly a proposal, Brian. Remember, you already did that on New Year's Eve, which was much more romantic."

"Have you told your parents yet?" Brian wanted to know. "Shall I go with you when you do?"

"No," Vickie said. "I'll do it myself. They'll be delighted." She hoped that her voice was convincing.

*   *   *

But the opposition she encountered at home was greater than she expected. Kiril pressed his lips together and rising from the armchair, paced the floor. "His breeding leaves much to be desired, Vickie. I question his background in spite of his father's wealth. Take his manners, for instance…"

"What's wrong with his manners, Papa?" Vickie interrupted defensively.

"Lots of things. Haven't you noticed how he sits in an armchair? He slouches, crosses his legs with the foot on the knee. Now where have you seen any gentleman doing that? Then too, his speech is flippant, he doesn't bow or kiss your mother's hand, and in general his familiarity irks me. I'm accustomed to a more deferential manner in young people."

"Oh, Papa, American manners are different from ours. In his country his behavior would be considered only friendly, I'm sure. After all, there's much more to a man than his manners. If I'm to marry an American, I should adjust to his customs instead of judging him by ours."

"Well, speaking of marriage, I think he should have sponsored you to come to America as his fiancée and let you see how you like it over there. A two-year wait would have given you plenty of time to think things over and make sure you want to marry this foreigner. Too bad he's rushing you. He hasn't even had the courtesy to ask me for your hand in marriage."

Aware that she had kept Brian from doing just that, for fear of Kiril's cool reception, Vickie said: "He's informal, that's all!"

Nina, who had been dusting the porch and listening, now stepped into the room. "Oh Papa, don't be so stuffy. Vickie is right, manners are different in a foreign country. She'll get used to them. Just think what it means to the rest of us. We may all go to America now."

Kiril frowned. "Shame on you, Nina. Where did you learn to be so calculating? A well-bred lady never says such things."

"You mean she only thinks them?"

Kiril gasped, but Lydia walked over and put her arm on his. "Darling, the world is changing rapidly, and we must try to adjust. Vickie seems to be happy again, so let's not spoil it for her with our doubts. After all, she is marrying an officer in the American Army."

Nina put down the dust cloth and looked at Vickie. Her eyes were sharp. "So, dear sister, you've hooked another one. I wish I knew the secret of how to catch a foreigner. Anyway, a family celebration is in order. Papa, stop pouting and let's invite Brian to *our* Officers' Club."

There should be a celebration indeed, but Vickie's heart ached. The Officers' Club would bring unwanted memories. That's where she and Henri danced the hours away cheek-to-cheek. That's where she would feel his presence, and it would torment her.

What have I done? I don't love Brian, Vickie thought in panic.

But she had made her choice. Her parents and her sister's security depended on her now. By marrying Brian her family problems would be solved. If Henri would haunt her dreams in the future, she would be the only one to know it and no one would be hurt, because that dream could never be realized.

CHAPTER THIRTEEN

The next afternoon Brian picked Vickie up at work and took her to dinner at the Broadway Mansions Officers Club.

"Honey," he said passing a plate of vegetables to her, "I've had another snag in our plans."

When Vickie gasped with fear, he raised his hand. "Don't worry, just another bureaucratic run-around. I was told that army regulations require a three-months period to investigate a non-American fiancée before marriage can take place. But they also say that in special cases, it's up to the commanding general to decide whether to grant permission to marry.

"The Commanding General of the U.S. Armed Forces in the Far East is General Albert Wedemeyer. I went to see him this morning." Brian paused, took a spoonful of clam chowder, then went on. "I must admit, I was taken aback when the general refused to grant permission, sight unseen. He wants to interview you first."

Vickie gasped. "Are you serious? We're talking about marriage, not a job!"

Brian patted her hand. "Have no fear, hon, you'll charm him."

★   ★   ★

Vickie didn't tell her parents of this latest development. She could guess what their reaction would be, not to mention the barbs from her sister. It was all she could do to cope with the humiliating prospect of being put on display before an American officer, never mind that he was a commanding general, who would decide her future. What if he took a dislike to her? Her happiness was at stake because of a stranger's opinion.

The next morning she dressed carefully for the interview, put on her fur-trimmed boots, the remnants of better days, her three-quarter length muskrat coat, a matching hat, and, armed with anger, went to the commanding general's office.

A young lieutenant ushered her into a large carpeted office and announced: "*Princess* Victoria Muravin," and then closed the door behind her. Somehow, she had conjured up an image of a commanding general as short, fat, and baldheaded. Instead, she was staring at a lean, tall man in uniform who rose from behind a huge mahogany desk and stood towering before her.

He has a commanding presence, flashed through her mind as she approached him hesitantly. His short dark hair was parted off center and combed back, accentuating dark, slightly elongated eyes that studied her without a trace of a smile. He was handsome, militarily erect, and stern. He couldn't have been more than in his mid-forties and the three shining silver stars neatly arranged on his shoulders did not in the least make him look older. His brows climbed up as he asked: "**Princess Muravin?**"

Vickie did not like the emphasis on her title. She jutted her chin forward and surprised herself when her voice resounded in the quiet office. "Yes, General, my name is Princess Victoria Muravin."

With hands clasped behind his back, General Wedemeyer started to walk up and down in front of his desk, glancing at Vickie sideways. Stopping for a brief moment, he pointed to a leather armchair. "Please sit down, Miss Muravin. I have to warn you that in America we do not have titled aristocracy and if you marry Colonel Hamilton and become an American citizen, you will lose yours. Do you know that?"

"I am well aware of that, General. I would lose my title if I married any man without a title, be he American, Russian or any other nationality."

"So, your father is a prince. How far back does his family name go?"

"Prince Muravin is my stepfather, General. I am not a princess by birth but through adoption only."

General Wedemeyer stopped pacing the carpet and studied her. "I admire your candor, unsolicited, I might add." He pulled up a chair and sat across from her. "Now tell me a little about yourself and your family."

She told him about her life both in Harbin and Shanghai, and after she had finished, she watched as General Wedemeyer rose, clasped his hands behind his back again, planted his feet slightly apart in an intimidating stance, and looked down at Vickie.

"Miss Muravin," he said, "I feel obliged to tell you that not everything in America is as glamorous as you see in the movies. Not every home has push-button conveniences, and you may find some areas of the United States not as modern as you might think. Are you prepared for that?"

Vickie rose abruptly from her chair. This was too much. What did Sara call those other women? Gold diggers? Was that what this general was implying now?

"General," her voice rang loud as she looked him straight in the eye, "My family suffered during the Japanese occupation. We had to do without many basic necessities, but we kept our dignity. We never forgot who we are." Vickie couldn't control her shaking voice and coughed to cover up. "When two people love each other," she said, "does it matter where they live?"

She waited for an answer, and watched in amazement as his eyes twinkled, softening his face, followed by a smile that transformed this formidable person into a warm human being. "I have nothing to say to that, Miss Muravin," he said. "You may get married as soon as you wish."

Vickie wasn't sure how she managed to walk out of the general's office with dignity. It seemed that her feet floated on air. As soon as she was out of his sight, she ran to Brian's office, past his staff's desks, ignoring amused smiles. Dashing breathlessly into his small cubicle of an office, she told her startled fiancé her good news. He kissed her cheek, and handed her a folder.

"Wonderful, darling, but I'm not at all surprised, in fact I expected it. Now, the next step is to go through these tests, and then we're in business."

Vickie stared at the sheaf of official looking applications and slips. "What are these for?" she asked opening the folder.

"The necessary medical tests. American law requires that before we're married, we must take a blood test to make sure we're free of syphilis. But here," Brian pointed at the folder Vickie was holding, "there are a couple of other tests for you to go through."

Vickie was shocked at the way Brian spoke of the dreaded disease. One did not mention such matters so casually; surely not even between fiancés.

"What must I do then?" she asked when she found her voice.

"I'll take you to our dispensary where they'll take a chest plate to make sure you don't have TB, and then you'll go for a GYN exam."

"GYN?"

Brian smiled. "Sorry, I forgot. It's short for gynecologist."

Vickie's face grew warm. Was this Brian's idea to determine if she was still a virgin? How degrading. Was he that Victorian?

"Why the gynecologist?" she managed to ask.

Brian shrugged. "It has nothing to do with you personally, hon, believe me. Every foreign bride has to submit to such an exam to make sure she does not have any other venereal disease."

My God. Was there nothing sacred left between them? Is he always going to call a spade a spade? Would his approach to lovemaking be equally pedestrian, stripped of all mystery? She imagined him giving her casual instructions in their marriage bed. She couldn't resist a smile.

"That's my girl. See the funny side of it. I always try to. It'll soon be all over and we can set the date. There isn't much time left, you know."

The rest of the day was spent in taking the blood test, x-rays, and finally, the gynecological exam.

Vickie had never had such an exam and was mortified when, after being placed on an examining table with her legs spread apart and feet hooked into what looked like stirrups, she saw that the examining physician was a man. Her mother had always gone to a woman doctor for such matters, but she, Vickie, had to submit to the excruciatingly embarrassing experience of being examined by a male gynecologist. Thank God that the nurse was a woman. But then the nurse stepped forward and said: "Major Anderson, this is Miss Victoria Muravin." Vickie closed her eyes to avoid meeting the doctor's glance and was grateful that he did not ask her any questions.

After it was over, Vickie dressed quickly and put distance between the dispensary and herself as fast as she could.

It took a couple of days for all the results to come in, and Brian called to tell her that everything was OK and they could set their wedding date. Vickie announced then, that she wanted his army chaplain to perform a private ceremony.

"How come?" he asked, "Don't you want a big wedding in your Cathedral on Route Paul Henry? I visited it a while ago. It's beautiful."

"There isn't enough time left to plan it," she said. In part, that was true, but she was too proud to tell him that her parents couldn't afford the expense of a traditional wedding.

At home, Kiril shook his head. "You should be married in our Orthodox Cathedral, not by an American Chaplain," he said, disapproval clear in his voice.

"But dear," Lydia said, "a big wedding in a Cathedral and a reception afterward would—"

"Papa, it was *my* decision," Vickie interrupted quickly. "There isn't enough time to plan a church wedding."

She turned and looked at her mother. When their eyes met, Lydia nodded imperceptibly and lowered her gaze.

Nothing more was said.

That evening, after dinner at the Broadway Mansions, Brian brought her home, kissed her at the bamboo fence gate, and pulled away in his jeep. Vickie was about to go inside, when a shadow moved out from the dark and blocked her way. She gasped.

"Don't be frightened, darling," Henri's voice whispered in her ear, "it's me. I want to talk to you."

Vickie struggled to push him away, but Henri grabbed her arm and pulled her out into the alley. As they stood under the meager light of a single bulb hanging on the back door of the next boarding house, she asked: "Why are you lurking in the shadows like a criminal? Is that Igor's influence?"

"Igor has nothing to do with why I'm here."

"He has everything to do with us."

"I love you. You're Russian, and a Russian woman will sacrifice everything for love."

"I can forgive a lot, but one thing I will not do, and that's go with you to Russia. You're driven by a false illusion!"

She freed herself and stepped back. He was pale, his eyes bloodshot. Her hand went up of its own accord to touch his face, but she checked herself in time. "I feel sorry for you, Henri," she said. "You don't see where your loyalties lie. France is your country. You're betraying her. Where's your integrity?"

"*My* integrity? And what about you? You are marrying one man while loving another?"

Vickie began to tremble. "I love Brian. Do you hear? I love him!"

"I'll never believe it. You love *me*. I can see it in your eyes." Henri grabbed her arms. "Not everyone is given a love like ours. It will haunt you. I beg you, come back to me!"

Despite the cold January night, Vickie flushed. With one violent move she wrenched herself free and ran. Henri's anguished voice pursued her: "Some day you'll regret your decision!"

Through the long hours of that night, Vickie tried to escape the storm of her thoughts. Henri's face had looked tortured; he had lost weight. He said he loved her, but there was a rival, Russia, and he loved *her* more.

She tried to think of Brian, to bring his warm, impish smile to her mind's eye, but his image eluded her.

The next day, her mother asked her how she felt about Brian, and Vickie, caught unprepared, thought: How *do* I feel about him? And as she searched her mind, this time Brian's face came to her clearly.

"I'm carefree with him, Mama," she said. "Carefree and...secure."

Lydia nodded several times as if she knew exactly how Vickie felt. "Good. Hold on to that feeling."

"Is that wrong, Mama?"

"Is what wrong?"

"To feel secure, comfortable with the man you marry?"

"You mean instead of being passionately in love? No, it isn't wrong. Hang on to a man like Brian. Let me tell you something that I've never told anyone. When I met Kiril, I was looking for security, and I married him without love. And now, I'm the luckiest of women, for I fell deeply in love with him."

Impulsively, Vickie hugged her mother. "I love you, Mamochka."

Lydia sighed. "I'm still sorry that something happened between you and Henri. You threw away a rare combination few of us are privileged to have: wealth, citizenship, *and* love. But at least you are marrying an American and a decent one. For all our sakes, I thank God."

"There was something about Henri I could not accept. Please trust me, Mamochka."

Henri was a misguided man, but Brian had no such problem. His love for his country was uncomplicated, unassailed by other loyalties, and his desire to make her happy was disarming and endearing. When she was with him, there was ease and warmth and laughter.

Dear, kind Brian. Surely what she felt for him was just as important as love.

*   *   *

They were married with her family present. Brian's roommate was his best man, and Nina, her maid of honor. General Wedemeyer, who was out of town on business, sent his chauffeured limousine to take Vickie to the ceremony. He invited the newlyweds to spend their honeymoon weekend in the mansion requisitioned for him by the army, and left instructions to prepare for them the luxurious suite that was reserved for General George Marshall whenever he visited Shanghai.

When they arrived at the mansion after the wedding, Vickie had never seen such affluence, not even in the Jobert mansion. The huge bathroom in their suite was in pink marble. The wash basin, shaped like a shell, was inlaid with mother-of-pearl. Vickie stood there, running her fingers over the smooth surface, tracing its exquisite contour.

Brian came in and watched. "Decadent, isn't it? But the mother-of-pearl basin is here to be used, not caressed," he teased, reaching over her arm and turning on the water. "I'll do the caressing, and not the basin, either."

In bed that night, Vickie tried to conceal her nervousness as Brian's hands glided over her skin. His tenderness was sweet, but his caresses were awkward and Vickie was left unmoved. She submitted to his lovemaking without arousal and when she closed her eyes, it was Henri's face that floated above her.

She had loved him with the special beauty and consuming passion of first love. In her innocence then, she had believed that nothing could separate them, not war, not betrayal, not death.

With Brian there was no turbulence, no fiery expectations. Some time later, when his energy was spent, Vickie turned toward the wall to hide tears of disappointment.

He raised himself on the elbow and kissed her lightly on the mouth. "How does it feel to be Mrs. Brian Hamilton, honey?" he whispered.

She threaded her fingers through his hair and said: "Happy. Peaceful. Proud to be your wife, and—" she closed her eyes and lied, "content."

*　　　　　*　　　　　*

Three weeks later, they stood on board ship, ready to sail for San Francisco. But before she left, Vickie had gone to say goodbye to the Rosens and told Sara the hour the ship was to sail, but Sara shook her head. "I want to imagine that this is just another visit, and when you leave, I'll pretend that you'll soon be back to see me again." She made no effort to hold back tears that filled her eyes. "God keep you and give you happiness," she whispered hugging Vickie and nudging her toward the door. Afraid to break down, Vickie ran out of the apartment without looking back.

Now, she stood alone in a sea of strangers. Hundreds of returning GI's, soldiers, sailors milled around, talked about their homecoming. Happy faces, smiling faces, but all of them strangers. As the ship started to move away from the shore, the space between the pier and the starboard widened, and suddenly, Vickie was a terrified four-year old again standing in the dark corridor, staring through a window over the roofs of Harbin.

She couldn't remember what she had done wrong that night, but her mother had ordered her out of the room into a shadowy hallway of the rooming house, where Vickie stood by the open window shivering in terror of the darkness, and wondering if the fairy tale's cruel Baba-Yaga would fly down on the broom and steal her. With eyes wide open, she had stared into the dark unknown, waiting, listening for footsteps.

And now, so many years later, she was headed toward a vast new country across the ocean and she shivered with the fear of the unknown. She leaned over the railing and stretched her arms toward the small group of people waving at her, the three people she loved so much. How she wished she could scoop them into her arms and bring them aboard to sail with her.

A warm hand pressed gently on her shoulder. "Hon, I know this is a sad moment, but I'll do all I can to make things easier for you."

She wrapped her arms around his neck, buried her face in his shoulder and tried not to cry.

A few moments later, she raised her head and looked to the other side of the ship where the Whampoo River flowed into the Yellow Sea. Somewhere beyond the sea and the Pacific Ocean, there was America. With an effort, Vickie replaced her fear with hope that the beautiful, wondrous, bountiful America, was waiting to accept her and those she loved, with open arms.

PART II

UNITED STATES

1947-1950

CHAPTER FOURTEEN

San Francisco

On the morning of the eighteenth day at sea, Vickie peered into the milky curtain of fog that hung over the ocean. Their ship was to dock in San Francisco, and land should appear soon. But what if she missed the first sight of America?

The Pacific Ocean crossing had been a nightmare. Pacific indeed! High waves rolled the ship incessantly and she had spent the better part of most days flat on her bunk, weak from seasickness, embarrassed before her new husband. But Brian's tact and consideration eased her discomfort somewhat.

The small, dark cabin, the rhythmic squeaking of the ship as it rolled from side to side, her total concentration on lying still and controlling her nausea were all behind her now. She leaned forward straining, straining to be the first to see the shore. The land she had dreamed and fantasized about, the land she was about to claim as hers. As she stared into the ever moving, curling fog, she discerned a darker spot on her left; a shapeless blur at first, that thickened, took substance and emerged as a cone-shaped rock rising out of the restless water and foamy, white breakers.

"There it is! There is San Francisco!" she cried, tugging at Brian's sleeve, afraid to take her eyes off the wonderful sight and lose it again in the fog.

Brian grinned. "Not yet, hon. These are the Farallon Islands. We're getting close to the Golden Gate, but it'll be a while. Why don't we go down and have something to eat before we dock?"

But Vickie wouldn't budge. They were close to the city, and she wasn't about to leave the deck and miss the first sight of the famous bridge.

She stood motionless, waiting, and then the towers of the bridge with their suspended cables rose out of the low-lying fog and touched the blue of the sky. A mirage? Vickie stared, blinded by the sun as the fog melted away revealing the bridge in all its majesty. Soon, she could see the cars, small as ants, moving across it. But as they drew closer and closer to the bridge, Vickie was puzzled.

"Where's the Golden Gate?" she asked. "This bridge is red."

"You mean to tell me you thought the bridge was actually golden?" and when Vickie did not answer, he laughed. "The Golden Gate is the name of the strait that connects the ocean with San Francisco Bay, and the bridge is named after it. It has nothing to do with color."

Vickie tried to hide her embarrassment as she followed Brian to the starboard side of the ship. He pointed to a row of houses that hugged the steep side of a hill above a beach. "That's Seacliff." He paused, then added: "My parents' home is up there."

Vickie studied the two and three-storied mansions, each different from the next in size and architecture. As the ship floated under the bridge, she was caught up in the exuberance of the hundreds of soldiers on deck, who let forth with a powerful: "Hip, hip, hurray!"

Once the ship cleared the bridge, the emerging skyline of the city took her breath away. "So many buildings so close together!" she marvelled, drinking in the brilliance of the sparkling, pastel colors of the structures and the lush green of the park on her right. She saw cream-colored houses there with red-tiled roofs scattered among tall eucalyptus trees.

"That's the Presidio," Brian said, "and we'll probably live in one of those army houses." He turned and studied her face. "Quite a lot to learn, isn't it, hon?"

Vickie nodded. "As my mother would say, 'my eyes are running apart' at all this."

Ahead of her, the restless waters of the bay were sprinkled with small boats, their sails tacking in the wind. As the ship drew near the shore, she could see the dock crowded with people eager to welcome the heroes home.

Vickie felt Brian's arm slip around her shoulders. "I think I see my mother."

"Where, where?"

Vickie's hands went very cold and she tried to control an enormous surge of anxiety.

"Over there, to your right. That short, blond woman in a blue suit. And there's James, the chauffeur. See a tall uniformed man next to her?"

Vickie scanned the crowd and spotted the blue-suited figure of a petite woman waving a white handkerchief.

The disembarking procedure seemed interminable, and Vickie marvelled at her mother-in-law's patience: Mrs. Hamilton stood in the same spot without moving.

Then it was their turn to disembark. As she came to the bottom of the gangplank, Vickie's heart pounded in her chest. She lifted her right foot and slowly placed it on the ground. American soil. For a brief moment, she closed her eyes.

America. *My* country. Henri's impassioned words came to mind and she repeated them: Surely this is the country of *my* heart.

What a scramble to thread their way among the deliriously happy crowd greeting their loved ones with laughter, tears, hugs and kisses. Finally, they stood before Brian's mother. She hugged him, offered her cheek for a kiss, held his face between her gloved hands for a few seconds, and then, throwing her arms wide open, turned to Vickie. "Darling! Welcome to the United States and to the Hamilton family!"

"Thank you, Mrs. Hamilton," Vickie said, enormously relieved by the warm greeting.

"Not Mrs. Hamilton. You must call me Mother, or Mims."

Although Vickie was five foot five, she had to bend over to receive her mother-in-law's peck on both cheeks. Then the older woman pushed her slightly away and looked her over from head to foot. "My, but you are tall. And so thin!"

Vickie couldn't tell whether it was meant as a compliment. At a loss how to answer, she smiled and studied her new mother-in-law. Her pale blue suit fit her to perfection, and on top of her smoothly coiffed hair, she wore a small matching hat with a veil. Light gray eyes looked back at Vickie with frank appraisal. Under such scrutiny, Vickie felt inadequate in her pink wool travel suit tailored at a Chinese tailor shop on Avenue Joffre.

As they approached a black Cadillac sedan, Jane Hamilton leaned over to Vickie and whispered: "Make a fuss over the car, and tell James how well he keeps it." Vickie was startled, but Mrs. Hamilton went on: "Help is hard to keep these days, don't you know."

After they climbed into the car, Jane Hamilton looked expectantly at Vickie, and Vickie, feeling very foolish, said in a loud voice: "My, what a beautiful car this is, and so well kept!"

James turned his head just a little to the right and said with clear amusement in his voice: "Why, thank you, Ma'am."

They drove through downtown over the steepest hills Vickie had ever seen in a city, and all the while she stared in amazement at the old-fashioned architecture. Not at all like the modern apartment houses in Shanghai. She was surprised there were so few pedestrians on the sidewalks; the streets seemed deserted.

"Where are all the people?" she asked.

Jane turned to look at her, one eyebrow raised. "What do you mean, darling? Most people ride cars or buses."

Brian cleared his throat. "Vickie is used to seeing throngs of pedestrians in Shanghai, Mother, mostly Chinese scurrying along broad sidewalks. Few of them have cars."

"You mean they don't need any?"

Brian sighed. "Very few people in China can afford cars, Mother."

They pulled up in front of a three-story white house that seemed carved out of a steep cliff. An intricate filigreed iron screen protected the front door, and as they entered, Vickie found herself standing on a black-and-white checkered marble floor. The air was cool filled with the smell of fresh wax and a faint fragrance of roses. At the base of a curved, polished mahogany stairway, stood a middle-aged maid in a black dress and white apron.

"Darling," Jane Hamilton said, "this is Julia, who's been with us for many years. She takes good care of me."

"How do you do," Vickie said and was rewarded with a prim nod. A door opened somewhere in the back and a portly woman came toward them, wiping her hands on a large apron.

"And this," Brian's mother went on, "is Mrs. Lester. I have to exercise all my will power to keep from over-indulging in her divine cooking. But my dears, you must be starved. Let's have something. You haven't eaten, have you?"

"No, we haven't had any lunch," Vickie answered, silently congratulating herself for remembering to say lunch instead of tiffin.

To her unaccustomed eye, the oval dining room table looked cold and cheerless without a tablecloth. The ecru linen place mats and napkins, the silver bread-and-butter plates and tall crystal goblets, covered only a fraction of the dark and highly polished mahogany. In the center of each place mat was a dinner plate with a wide border of cobalt blue. As they sat down, Julia placed a smaller plate of something on the bigger one, then passed a silver filigreed bread basket filled with hot scones.

Vickie studied her plate. On a bed of raw greens there were alternating slices of what appeared to be an olive green pear and small sections of pomelo. Vickie never liked the bitter pomelos she had had in Shanghai. She waited until her mother-in-law picked up her fork, and then, for lack of the fruit knife that would have been included in a place setting at home, she took a dinner knife and sliced a section of the strange green pear. To her surprise, the blade went right through the soft flesh of the pear. She quickly replaced the knife on the table, leaning the blade on the edge of her plate. She picked up the fork with her left hand and carried the pear to her mouth. It had no appreciable flavor and was mushy on her palate. She managed to swallow it, but to tackle the pomelo slice, with mayonnaise on top, no less, was quite another matter. She scraped it off with the knife and as she picked up the pomelo section, she saw Brian's mother watching her.

"Darling," Jane said, her left eyebrow slightly up, "I know that in Europe you eat with the fork in the left hand, but you're in United States now, and also, I hope you don't mind my telling you, here we place the knife not against the plate, but *on* it and then take the fork in our right hand to eat. Like this, see?" She demonstrated the awkward procedure.

Why in the world had the Americans invented such complicated table manners? Vickie thought, trying to suppress a smile. I feel like I am from another planet.

After she struggled with the green pear and the pomelo, which Jane called avocado and grapefruit, Julia brought in large cups of cream of mushroom soup. This, Vickie found delicious. She drank it, half listening to the talk bouncing between mother and son. Mostly her mother-in-law bubbled.

"You remember the Blairs? She looks divine, and they're dying to see you."

"…yes, your opera friends."

"…I'm so glad this war is over."

"…We're investing in IBM stock."

"…I'm glad you didn't bring a Chinese girl home."

Vickie raised her head and met her mother-in-law's smiling glance. Vickie smiled back and ladling her soup, brought the silver spoon to her mouth with the narrowed end first. Brian's mother took her soup from the wide side of the spoon, and Vickie remembered Brian eating borscht in their rooming house the same way. How many times had her governess, Lisa, told her in Harbin never to do that. "It is not only bad manners, but easy to spill your soup on the tablecloth," she used to say.

Now, as she glanced at her mother-in-law, Jane smiled again, but this time the gray eyes didn't. "That's the way we use the soup spoon here, darling," she said.

Without thinking, Vickie blurted out: "My governess used to tell me it was bad manners to do it that way."

The moment the words were out, Vickie was mortified, expecting a sharp response, but instead, Jane said: "You had a governess?"

"Yes, Mother," Brian answered for Vickie, "all through Vickie's childhood and early youth."

Jane stiffened. "I don't know the Russian manners, but you're in America now, and here we do it this way."

Vickie looked to Brian for support. But Brian only patted his mother's hand. "You see, Mother, what fun I'm going to have introducing my wife to all our customs?"

Was Brian being obtuse, ignoring his mother's criticism? Vickie thought of her stepfather who had criticized Brian's manners, but who would never, never have said it to his face.

"I'll have Julia bring us dessert," Jane said, and moments later Julia appeared in the dining room as if by magic. Vickie did not see or hear a bell, and wondered if the woman had been standing just outside the door, listening to all the humiliating remarks directed Vickie's way.

"Tell Mrs. Lester that the soup was divine, Julia," Jane said, as Julia, her face dour, removed the plates and disappeared into the kitchen.

Why is Julia such a sourpuss? Vickie thought with amusement. Could it be that Brian's mother sprinkles her speech with 'darling' and 'divine' routinely and the servants see through her gushing compliments?

The delicious lemon cake was eaten without mishap, but the mystery of Julia's instant appearance worried Vickie. Later, when they were alone at last in the guest room, she asked Brian: "Does Julia stand by the door and listen to your mother's summons throughout the whole meal?"

"Why no, hon, whatever made you think that?"

"Because I didn't see a bell and yet every time your mother said she would call Julia, the maid would appear from behind the door."

Brian laughed. "Oh, that. There's a bell under the carpet within reach of mother's foot."

Relieved, Vickie admired the room. The two beds were covered with quilted bedspreads in a handsome pink and green print with matching easy chair and draperies. The partially lowered venetian blinds gave the room a cool, restful glow. With a tired sigh, Vickie sat down on the edge of the bed.

Brian picked up his briefcase. "Hon, I've got to go to the immigration office to take care of the paperwork. Why don't you rest while I'm gone? If you need anything, just ask Mother."

"O.K.," Vickie said and went to the bathroom. As she washed her hands, she realized that she was thirsty. In the bedroom, she had not seen a carafe of drinking water. Was keeping the boiled water out of the bedroom another American custom? What if her mother-in-law made another subtle remark that would sting like a wasp? Brian hadn't left yet, she could hear him talking to someone on the phone.

She dried her hands, walked out of the bathroom and stood by the door, waiting for Brian to end his call. He was standing with his back to her and evidently hadn't heard her come in.

"I've missed you, Keith," he was saying. "More than I thought…Yeah, it's been a long time…huh…Married in Shanghai…She's a great gal…She'll be an asset to me in the army…Well, you know, a family man, and all that…What? Right now? Let's see…I guess I could after I get done with the immigration officials. But just for a minute."

As he replaced the receiver, Vickie stepped into the room. "Is Keith an old friend of yours?"

Brian whirled to face her. "Don't ever eavesdrop on me again."

Vickie was taken aback. "Why are you so angry? I wasn't eavesdropping at all. I came back into the room because I'm thirsty."

Brian frowned. "Thirsty? Then why come here?"

"Because I couldn't find a carafe of boiled water anywhere. I came back to ask you about it."

Brian grabbed her hand and led her to the bathroom. He picked up a small china glass, filled it with water from the faucet and handed it to her.

She backed away. "But it's not boiled."

"For heaven's sake, Vickie, take it! You're not in China anymore. You can drink tap water here from any faucet."

What the mind understood, the instinct, programmed through a lifetime of caution, refused to accept easily. She took the glass and held it for a few seconds without drinking.

"Oh now, really!" Brian said with impatience, and walked out of the bathroom.

"I'll try not to be gone too long," he called from the bedroom and was gone.

After drinking the water, Vickie lay down on the bed and put her arms behind her head. For the first time she had seen Brian flushed with anger. Why was he so touchy about his phone call? He hadn't said anything secretive. Could it be that in his intelligence work he had been trained to be wary of anyone listening behind his back? She shrugged at the thought and a few minutes later fell asleep.

*   *   *

A low, repeated sound awakened Vickie. She checked the bedside clock. It was 5 p.m. She had slept for over two hours. She stretched and listened. The foghorn. Brian had told her about the frequent fog in the bay. How did people sleep through such plaintive hooting?

She heard no other sounds, and she wondered if her mother-in-law was taking a nap. Then the foghorn again. This time it reverberated mournfully through her head. She hugged herself. Aside from Brian and his mother she didn't know a single soul in this vast land of America. And Brian was the only one who was her friend. Her dear ones: mother, stepfather, sister, Sara, her friends and everything familiar were seven thousand miles away. What would Papa have said if he had heard the verbal exchange between her and her mother-in-law at the luncheon table, or rather, not so much an exchange as a one way conversation? Proud Papa. He would have found something tactful to say and at the same time make Brian's mother realize that she was unkind. Her qualifier 'darling' was meaningless.

On the round table by the chair, next to a picture of Brian in his cadet uniform, stood a crystal vase full of roses. Vickie smelled them. Their fragrance was more delicate than the roses in China. Henri had often brought her roses and carnations. He loved flowers as much as she did. When magnolias were in bloom, he had taken pictures of her burying her face in the huge blossoms in Jessfield Park, and had kept the framed snapshot on his desk.

Vickie inhaled deeply to calm a sudden flutter in her stomach. She wondered if Brian loved flowers. She must ask him.

The air in this house had a freshness that she had noticed at once. It smelled of polished woods, of new paint, of the clean starch of laundered linens. It had a gentility, a kind of calmness and order and harmony, from the quality of its scents to the coolness of shining silver that shut out the discordant world outside.

And far away, at the edge of the world, a rooming house was burdened by tired odors that dwelt in its decaying rooms.

The large room overwhelmed her. Her mother-in-law would never know how to treasure fully what she had. How could she, when she had not experienced anything less? Vickie felt a sense of heightened pleasure in being able to enjoy affluence again, after having been deprived of it for so long. Nothing terrible could ever happen to her in a house like this. Yet, the pleasure was tinged with guilt at the thought that her family was not so lucky.

An hour later, Brian opened the door and, after a moment's hesitation, scooped Vickie into his arms, whirling her around the room.

"Hon, everything is O.K. You're eligible for citizenship in two years. Then, as a blood relative, your sponsorship will allow your family to by-pass the long wait for their immigration quota. It's too bad that as an in-law, my sponsorship wouldn't allow them to skip the wait." He released her and winked. "But you have to stay married to me for those two years or else, as an unmarried immigrant you'll have to wait the full five years to be naturalized."

Vickie hugged him. "Whatever put such thoughts into your mind, honey? Just so *you* don't regret having married a foreigner." She threw him a sidelong glance. "I must have embarrassed you at lunch with my table manners."

Brian dismissed her words with a wave of his hand. "Oh, that. I knew I'd have fun teaching you. With that charming accent of yours, everyone will know you're new here."

Not a word about his anger over the phone call. Just as well. Better to forget it. But then, not a word about his mother's remarks. Perhaps he was so used to them that they ceased to affect him. She would be strong. She wouldn't complain to him about his mother's barbs.

She pointed at the roses. "Aren't they beautiful, Brian?"

"Yeah, they're O.K." he said absentmindedly. "I was gone longer than I thought because I couldn't resist dropping in at the Presidio and checking things out." He sat down in the easy chair and crossed his legs. "We're going to have a nice duplex with three bedrooms upstairs and a smaller one off the kitchen. I even met one of the neighbors. The Brennans. She's real friendly, and she's invited you to a welcome coffee she's giving in a few weeks. She does that every year when new people are assigned to the Presidio. You'll meet a lot of officers' wives fast and make friends."

Vickie was delighted. They would have a place of their own right away, and she would meet some contemporaries, women who were also far away from home. They would understand her loneliness. She would be able to learn the ways of America from them without enduring her mother-in-law's scrutiny. And the two years before she was united with her family would pass quickly....

CHAPTER FIFTEEN

A few days later, Brian and Vickie moved into a two-story duplex in the Presidio. The living room, dining room, and two of the three bedrooms upstairs overlooked San Francisco Bay and the island of Alcatraz with its federal prison. In the evening, when the setting sun played with the glass panes of the highrises, the glittering reflections splashed a rainbow of color on the city.

The house was spacious, and although it was not as elegant as her mother-in-law's, it was *theirs*. Vickie turned round and round in the living room, studying its dimensions with appreciative eyes. Mama, Papa, Nina, were squeezed into such a small area, but she and Brian had nine rooms counting the kitchen and two bathrooms. Imagine, all that for just the two of them. Once the furniture that Brian had accumulated during his bachelor days was out of storage and spread sparsely throughout the house, it became apparent that more pieces were needed.

"I'll ask Mother to take you shopping," Brian said. "She'll take you to the best stores for furniture. You need new clothes too, and she'll introduce you to the brand names."

Intimidated though she was by her mother-in-law, Vickie agreed, aware that she needed tutoring in almost everything in her new country.

"Why do I have to go to the best stores in town?" she asked. "Won't the prices be higher there?"

"Maybe, but then you're sure of getting good quality," Brian said. "You don't have to count every penny, hon. My income from father's estate is generous, and that, added to my army salary," he smiled and winked at her, "believe me, you can afford to shop at the better stores."

He paused, then cleared his throat and explained: "It wouldn't help my career if we flaunted our money, so that's why we're living on the post the way most of my colleagues do. Our income is our business. Now go have fun shopping. I have complete confidence in mother's good taste. She'll be lots of help to you. Until we open charge accounts, I'll ask mother to charge on hers, and I'll pay her back later."

Vickie decided that after one trip downtown, she'd learn enough about the stores to get to them by bus. She'd go back alone, then, and buy something to send home. Mama loved silk blouses, Papa needed a new robe, and Nina…well, Nina would love anything from America. It would be good to buy something special for the family, and from what Brian had said about their finances, surely he wouldn't mind. What a gratifying feeling, to be able to give something to her parents and sister that they could not afford.

The shopping was a success, one could say, if you ignored Jane Hamilton's left eyebrow that climbed slightly when it was discovered that Vickie didn't like black dresses, so 'in' at the moment, and climbed even higher at the discovery that her daughter-in-law had a mind of her own, when she politely declined a gift of a black straw hat.

"I'm not used to wearing anything black," Vickie said, and added quickly, "not yet," to soften the refusal.

On the whole, however, Jane was thoughtful, not too condescending and completely in her element introducing her to various American sizes and quality goods. Vickie was overwhelmed by such stores as I.Magnin and the White House where fine dresses could be purchased right from the rack.

"Go ahead, try it," Jane urged, watching her finger the cloth of a blue print dress. "See if it fits."

Vickie's head was spinning. In Shanghai, if one had the money, several elegant boutiques in the arcade of Rue Cardinal Mercier made clothes to order. Those who couldn't afford them, found a Chinese tailor somewhere in the back alley where, after he took your measurements and haggled over the price, he made you a dress copying a magazine picture. But here, in America, you could actually try a dress on before buying it.

From I.Magnin's, they went looking for furniture at Sloane's.

Vickie picked out a carved oriental chest and tried not to compare the price to what she would have paid on Yates Road in Shanghai.

That night, Vickie lay awake, happily reliving the pleasures of the day. What a thrill to be able to spend money without worrying if it would last until the end of the month.

A few days later, when all the purchases had been delivered, Vickie felt like a child with new toys. She tried on her new clothes, went from room to room, running her hand over the polished woods and quilted fabrics, and wondering where each piece would fit best. When Brian came home that evening, they worked past midnight, arranging the furniture and hanging the curtains.

With the exception of that one phone call, Vickie had yet to see Brian lose his temper or show any appreciable annoyance at anything. He was so thoughtful, so considerate, so eager to make her comfortable in her new country.

He complimented her on her cooking after she struggled with unfamiliar measurements and staples to prepare Russian yeast pancakes. Although they came out rather leaden, he ate them valiantly.

He even trusted her enough to tell her to shop as she pleased. And so one morning, as Brian was leaving for work, she asked for money without any qualms. He pulled out his wallet. "What do you want it for?"

"I'd like to buy a few things for my parents and for Nina."

Brian's eyes narrowed for a second. "Like what?"

"I—I don't know exactly...I have to look first."

"Why don't you ask Mother? She'd help you decide."

Flustered, Vickie stammered. "I—I thought II'd take a bus downtown. I mean, I have to learn to get around by myself without always bothering your mother."

Brian chuckled. "It wouldn't bother her in the least. She loves to shop. Anyway, here's some money. Have fun!"

Suddenly, the fun she had shopping the first time, vanished. She found herself adding up the prices, careful to spend only what he had given her. She selected a white blouse for her mother, and a blue wool robe for her stepfather, but it took her a long time to find something that would please her sister. Finally, she chose a cotton print skirt with a matching scarf.

A few mornings later, Vickie dressed with care for her first coffee in an American home. She had never heard of a morning party. At home, ladies got together for afternoon tea, but Mrs.Brennan had specifically invited her for ten o'clock.

"What should I wear, Brian?" she asked with apprehension.

"Call Mother, she'll advise you better than I can."

Vickie called.

"Why, your blue and white silk with the matching bolero jacket, of course," Jane said. "And don't forget the gloves."

So Vickie put on her new dress, ankle-strap, high-heeled blue shoes, pulled on a pair of white gloves, and headed out. The Brennans lived just three doors down the block on Simonds Loop.

The hostess was a plump woman in her thirties, exuberant and loud. Ten women were seated in the living room, and although Sue Brennan introduced everyone, Vickie could not remember all the names. They sounded so foreign to her ear. Most of the women wore skirts and blouses with sweaters casually thrown over their shoulders, and sensible pumps with medium heels. Clearly, Jane Hamilton moved in different circles and had never attended a coffee in an army home.

Vickie sat down on the edge of a straight chair and looked around her. The exact size of her own living room, it nonetheless seemed different with oval braided rugs on the floor, white crocheted doilies on maple furniture, chairs with cushions and pleated skirts. She listened to the conversation.

"...We were stationed at West Point too. Jack is Class of '33."

"...My Frank is Class of '40."

"...I miss the East Coast. This is like a foreign country to me here."

"...We have so many pidgeons in our back yard. How do you get rid of the things? Their cooing is so sad, it makes me homesick." The woman who said this turned to the hostess and nodding in Vickie's direction, said: "Does she understand what I'm saying?"

Vickie spoke up: "Yes, I do," then added, "I spoke English long before I married Brian." She was immediately annoyed with herself for adding that qualifier. She didn't have to explain.

The woman studied her for a moment, then said: "I wonder if my Charles knew your husband at West Point. What Class is he?"

Vickie couldn't remember, and why was it so important to know what Class each husband belonged to? She made a mental note to ask Brian, but right now Sue, tactful Sue, saved her.

"Who would like some more coffee, girls?" she said going for the coffee pot.

Vickie turned away from the woman and studied the round mirror hanging on the opposite wall. A brass eagle was carved on top, and the miror's convex shape distorted her image so much, she tried hard not to laugh. Why did such a mirror exist at all? But it was the ancestral portraits of a man and a woman on each side of the mirror that drew her attention, especially the portrait of a woman in a white bonnet, who resembled Mrs. Brennan. During a break in the conversation, Vickie turned to her hostess.

"Are those *your* ancestors, Mrs. Brennan?" she asked.

Sue Brennan blinked rapidly. "Why, no, Mrs. Hamilton, that's Martha and George Washington."

Vickie heard a few giggles behind her and when she turned, one of the women said: "That's our first president, Mrs. Hamilton."

Vickie felt her face grow warm. "I know that George Washington was your first president, but I don't remember seeing his picture before." She cleared her throat and smiled sweetly. "I'd have no trouble recognizing Michael Romanov, the first Russian Tsar."

When later that evening Vickie related her blunder to Brian, he exploded with laughter. "That's one for the books! It's O.K. hon, but if I'm ever assigned to the South and you see a portrait of a general on a white horse over someone's mantel, don't ever ask who *he* is!" He explained just who the General was.

Vickie sighed. "I better not ask questions of anyone but you."

As weeks and months slipped by, she wrote ecstatic letters to her family. She described the busy waters of the San Francisco Bay, the sparkling diamonds of the Berkeley night lights, even the subtle fragrance of the eucalyptus trees populating the Presidio. She detailed her mother-in-law's elegant home, told them about Jane's guidance in everything that was new to her, and went to great length assuring them how happy she was with Brian.

Although their lovemaking had not improved and usually lasted only a brief few minutes, Vickie preached to herself that sex was less important than all the blessings bestowed upon her now. In her letters to Sara, though, the truth trickled through.

> ...I miss you, dear Sara, Vickie wrote, more than you can imagine. There are so many things I'd like to discuss and share with you that of necessity must lie fallow in my soul. My mother-in-law is trying hard to teach me American customs, from table manners to shopping to learning the idioms. I suppose she too has to go through a period of adjustment in getting to know

her foreign daughter-in-law. There are times when I would like to sit down with you and ask you how to cope with this or that on this huge continent inhabited by people so new to me, and there are times when I catch myself talking to you and then, startled, I turn around and the room is empty..."

Clearly, Sara understood Vickie's loneliness which was evident in her own letters, although she never said as much. Instead, she commented on how fortunate Vickie's life was turning out to be with financial and political security in America, surrounded as she was by a good husband, a helpful mother-in-law, and new friends. She wrote guardedly about her own life in Shanghai:

Jacob's practice is as busy as ever and I hardly see him until late in the evening. I don't see much of Joseph for that matter, for he's either studying late, or over at Nina's. I don't mind it though, as long as he's O.K., so am I. I keep busy straightening Jacob's files and scheduling his appointments. In a way I'm glad Joseph didn't want to be a doctor. He'll get his engineering degree and will have a good position with regular hours.
Dear girl, I miss you, and our little chats. But who knows, in this changing world, we may yet meet again. In the meantime, our letters will do. I catch myself waiting eagerly for the mail and when your letter comes, it's a holiday for me. I read it over a cup of tea and talk to you, and pretend we've had our visit. Joseph tells me all is well with your family, but then I'm sure your mother keeps you well informed...

Vickie could picture Sara sitting straight up at the dining room table, one veined hand holding the teacup, her soft eyes scanning the letter. From what Sara said about the Muravins, Vickie deduced that the social contacts between the two families had not improved and she was sorry. But then it was unrealistic to expect her stepfather to change. Sara never mentioned the Joberts and although Vickie appreciated her friend's tact, she nonetheless searched her letters for any scrap of news about the inhabitant of the top apartment of the mansion on Rue Delastre…She avoided saying his name even in her mind, wrapping his image in darkness, as if by doing so, everything personal between them would be buried in her subconscious forever.

When February came, Brian took a few days off and they went to Lake Tahoe. It had been many years since Vickie had seen so much winter. The crisp, frosty air, the sound of crunching boots on the ground, the white-capped mountains, the snow-laden evergreen forest, all reminded her of the Manchurian winters. It brought back memories of her childhood, when she waited for the wild game her stepfather would bring home from his hunting trips, and the delicious meals that came afterward. The memory stirred a sudden hunger for her favorite pheasant in sour cream.

She turned to Brian who was exhaling warm air into his cupped palms and pressing them against his reddened nose.

"You know, dear, this snow-covered forest reminded me of Manchurian winters and the hunting season when my stepfather used to go hunting. I loved the wild game he always brought home. Next week I'll buy a pheasant in the grocery store and prepare it the way our cook used to do in Harbin. It's delicious."

"You can't buy pheasant in the markets," Brian mumbled from behind his gloved hands. "You have to shoot one yourself on a hunting trip."

Vickie was stunned. "America, such a rich country, and you can't buy a pheasant? In Harbin, during hunting season, pheasants were sold cheaper than chickens."

"Sorry about that."

Vickie sighed. "We not only had pheasant and duck and snipe, but deer as well."

"Wow! What else did your stepfather hunt?"

"Sometimes he went to Korea and hunted wild hoars there."

Brian roared with laughter. "Didn't your mother object?"

Vickie stared at him. "Why should she?"

"Hon," he said, still chuckling, "we hunt *boars* in this country." When he explained what 'whores' meant, Vickie laughed. "Well, they never taught us that word at the convent. I have lots to learn yet."

But learning did not come easy. She avoided asking Jane for advice too often, not because Brian's mother would not help her, indeed she would, but her whole attitude, her tone of voice, the perennial arched left brow, all grated on Vickie. She made friends with Sue Brennan who never made her feel ignorant or inferior; on the contrary, Sue asked her a lot of questions about her life in China, and Vickie was happy to reminisce about the years in Harbin, omitting her life in the rooming house in Shanghai. Sue would have been shocked, or worse, pitied her.

"And what about you?" Vickie asked. "Tell me about yourself."

"Absolutely dull by comparison," Sue said. "I'm an only child. My father is an accountant and my mother is a schoolteacher. I met my husband at a senior prom and after he graduated from West Point we were married. We've been travelling ever since, but have yet to be assigned outside the country. I'd love to go abroad."

She endeared herself to Vickie, who appreciated in her new friend a genuine interest in other places and people.

*   *   *

During that year of '48, Vickie got her driver's license. Brian assured her that if she could negotiate San Francisco's steep hills, shifting gears at the top of the street without slipping back, she could drive anywhere. She also learned to operate the washing machine, the vacuum cleaner— what heaven not to have to sweep the rug with a broom—and such marvelous kitchen helpers as a mixmaster and an electric toaster…

Her kitchen was small, and she particularly appreciated the free-standing cabinet on wheels which she filled with extra china and glassware, until Sue caught her washing dishes by hand and asked her why she wasn't using the dishwasher.

Hands in soapy water, Vickie looked at her. "What dishwasher?" she asked.

Sue leaned over the free standing cabinet, pulled out the hoses from the back, and showed Vickie how to connect them. Vickie sat down at the kitchen table and laughed.

"And I thought this was an extra storage cabinet," she said. "With all the household conveniences, I feel like a lost ship."

Sue chuckled. "Don't you mean 'a lost sheep'?"

Vickie stared at her for a moment and then burst out laughing again. "There I go again! In Russian, we have no distinction between the short and the long 'e'. Let me tell you what happened when we first moved here. Before our dryer was delivered, I hung the wash on the clothesline outside and it started to rain. Brian was planting some flowers in the backyard and I opened the window and shouted: 'Brian, hurry! Take the shits off the line!' You should have seen Brian sprint to the window waving his arms: 'O.K., O.K. hon, I will!' I had no idea why he got so worked up."

Sue laughed hard. "I bet the neighbors loved it!"

There were other, more pleasant discoveries. Vickie found she could go into any store, check the price and know that it was what she had to pay without bartering and matching wits with the shopkeeper. And the meat in grocery shops was refrigerated. Green, buzzing flies were nowhere to be seen.

At home, she worked hard at becoming a good army wife. Under Sue's tutelage, she cooked American dishes, entertained Brian's colleagues and their wives, and listened dutifully to their chitchat. At one of such parties, she moved closer to Brian who was visiting with the men at the other side of the room. Although his humor often kept his guests laughing, right now he was serious.

"…I was in the CBI Theater during the war," he said, then noticing Vickie by his side, put his arm around her shoulder and smiled. "This is the prize I got in China," he said. "You might say, one of us Shanghaied the other. So I have a soft spot for that country. But in India people looked depressed and miserable. Monsoons, flooding hurricanes." He paused for a moment, then smiled. "Leave it to our GI's though. They'll find humor in anything. While I was in India, the GI movie theater was blown down in a storm and the next day a new sign appeared on the billboard: Coming attraction: Gone With The Wind."

The men laughed, and one of them said: "I just got back from Calcutta and that's what it's like. But India's culture is amazing. I sort of liked it."

"Do you think they're still in shock over Mahatma Gandhi's assassination?" Vickie said.

One of the men shrugged. "Who knows? Their political situation is so complex."

"I didn't mean politics," Vickie hastened to explain. "I meant the religious side of the man. He was so revered as their spiritual leader."

"You're right, hon," Brian said, "but as far as the political situation goes, not only India, but the whole world is in turmoil. The Soviets are stirring up mischief with the Berlin Blockade and now, as Bernard Baruch said, we have a cold war on our hands. Thank God, *our* democracy remains solid."

Democracy? The word teased a memory to surface, but it eluded Vickie, and when one of the wives, a short, rounded girl, came over to her side, Vickie forgot what it was that bothered her.

"When we visited my family in New York this year," the girl said, "we saw the ballet Orpheus with Maria Tallchief in the title role. It was choreographed by George Ballanchine." She smiled at Vickie sweetly. "Isn't it too bad that the government in your country censored your own great composers this year and called their work bourgeois decadence?"

"The Soviet Union has never been my wife's country," Brian said. "She was born stateless, and is now about to become an American citizen."

The girl shrugged. "Anyway, there were three of them, the composers, I mean, but I can never remember those Russian names, they're impossible to pronounce."

Vickie was amused. "You mean Khachaturian, Prokofiev and Shostakovich?" she offered. "It's true that Russian names are sometimes long, but every letter is pronounced exactly as it is written. English words may be shorter, but in some cases the same combination of letters can sound entirely different."

The girl raised her brows. "I don't know what you mean."

"I'm talking about words like 'enough' and 'through'," Vickie said, and saw that Brian's eyes were dancing.

"I still say that Russian words are impossible to pronounce," the girl persisted. "I just hope we'll never go to war with Russia."

"After reading Norman Mailer's *The Naked And the Dead*, I think no one would want to go to war," Vickie said.

"Tell that to the Russians."

Vickie spaced her words carefully. "The Russians lost twenty million people in the last war. I don't think they have to be reminded what war is like."

Why do they always say Russians and not the Soviets? Vickie thought in dismay, but before she could say anything, she caught Brian's warning glance. To fill an uncomfortable lull in the conversation, she said the first thing that came to mind: "I read recently that a new drug for seasickness, called Dramamine, was discovered this year. Too bad it wasn't available when Brian and I were honeymooning aboard ship."

Everyone laughed and the tension was broken.

After the guests had left, Brian came into the kitchen to help clean up. Although Vickie had heard that American husbands often helped their wives with the housework, she had been nonetheless surprised and pleased the first time he had done it. She suspected that he had never had to help with the dishes at his parents' home.

"Ilon, you know that we can afford to hire help," he said, "but for a small dinner of eight, army wives as a rule do it themselves, so..." he shrugged, and Vickie understood it was another custom to observe.

This evening, he was silent for a few minutes, then said: "You have to brace yourself for comments. Nobody understands that there's a difference between the Russian people and the Soviet government. Don't take it personally. Anyway, you ought to start thinking more as an American than a Russian. We're all immigrants here, and that's what's so wonderful about our country, it assimilates everyone, all equal under God."

Confused about her reaction to the evening's conversation, Vickie remained silent. She was trying hard to become an American, to forget her Russian background, so why did she feel compelled to defend her heritage?

Suddenly she remembered what it was that eluded her earlier in the evening.

"Brian," she said, "When Israel became an independent state last May, wasn't our country—" *how good it felt to say our country,* "the first to recognize it officially?"

"Yes, it was."

"Yet there are clubs in America, Sue told me, that won't admit Jews as members."

"That's right."

Vickie stared at Brian. "You mean to tell me that a democratic country like this, a country which champions equal rights, would exclude Jews from membership in clubs?"

Brian nodded.

Vickie put down her towel. "Why, that's a greater prejudice than class distinction in other countries."

"They are private, not government clubs, and that's the kind of democracy we have—" he gave her a crooked smile, "freedom to indulge our individual prejudices. Now, be a good girl and pass me the towel."

She stole a sidelong glance at him. He always brushed things off, never discussed any subject in depth. Once again, it hit her: they really had little in common. For one thing, he never shared anything that went on in his office, and now she asked him about it.

"I have top secret clearance and I can't talk about my work with anyone outside my office. Besides, the details of my job would bore you."

"You don't trust your own wife?" she asked piqued by the implication that she wouldn't understand.

Brian sighed impatiently. "Hon, it's not a matter of not trusting you. I'm under oath, that's all."

Vickie said nothing more, but there were things that bothered her nevertheless. Sometimes when he came home late, his eyes shone particularly bright, his face was flushed, and on those nights he was reluctant to make love.

She sighed and picked up a fresh towel. After the dishes were done, he took her hands in his. "I know you're bored, so why don't you ask Mother or Sue Brennan to go to the opera with you? Get good seats. I know you like classical music. As for me, I'll beg off." He grinned self-consciously. "Give me Glen Miller or Benny Goodman anytime. I'm a peasant at heart."

Somewhere, from the hidden recesses of her mind a picture emerged of herself and Henri walking home from the Lyceum Theater after hearing Tchaikovsky's *The Queen of Spades*. They had shared their impressions, hummed the tunes, discussed their favorite arias, argued in favor of one or the other. How long would it be before she wiped such memories from her mind?

The noisy clock on the kitchen wall ticked the seconds off, but the picture lingered. There was no such communication between her and Brian. They lived parallel lives with no common interests to share. But she had gone into this marriage with open eyes and the benefits were many. Dwell on those!...

Her hands shook as she put the last dish away. Think of today, of now. What was left yet to do tonight? The tablecloth needed to be checked for spots before folding it away; napkins to be thrown into the washing machine; the chairs in the living room had to be straightened. Homey, secure things. Unthreatening.

That night, Brian made love to her hurriedly, then brushed a kiss on her forehead. "Good night. It was great."

Vickie lay still, waiting. Moments later, however, he was asleep. No gentle lying in each other's arms, no tranquil sharing of the spirit.

He took it for granted that she had been satisfied. Was it because she responded with tenderness to his lovemaking that he assumed it was good for her too? He never asked, and if he had, she could have truthfully answered that she was not left frustrated. But she would not have added that it was so because she hadn't been aroused in the first place.

Lips pressed together, Vickie tried to rein in her galloping thoughts. Henri's handsome face...the eyes darkened with passion...His lovemaking...She moaned. How disloyal to open the door to those memories. A good man, a generous man slept beside her, a man who must be everything to her now. True closeness would come in time, grow with the years. It must. For now, there was much to be grateful for.

She turned toward Brian, and gently stroked his sleeping face. He did not stir. She rolled over on her back and crossed her arms behind her head, careful not to awaken him. Staring into the darkness, Vickie listened to the whispers of her soul, the hollow sounds of her heart.

There was another reason for her frustration. They had been married a year and a half, and she still wasn't pregnant. She wanted a child, wanted desperately to give birth to an American citizen, a son or daughter who would be born with a country. A child who would never experience what she herself had gone through. But the baby didn't come. What was wrong with her? Was she barren?

Finally, without telling Brian, she made an appointment and saw the army obstetrician. After a thorough exam, he could find nothing wrong.

"Sometimes," the doctor said, "it is difficult to get pregnant when you're under any kind of stress. You haven't been in this country long. Give yourself time, relax, and things will take care of themselves."

Relieved to learn that she was capable of having children, she now wanted to make sure there was nothing wrong with Brian. That night after dinner, she suggested that he be examined.

"I get yearly physicals. I'm perfectly healthy," he snapped, annoyance clear on his face.

Vickie touched his cheek with the palm of her hand. "I didn't mean to hurt your feelings, darling. It's…just that I want so much to have a baby."

"There's plenty of time. Don't rush things."

Vickie sighed. That's what the doctor said, *give yourself time.* How strange that Brian had flared up at the mere suggestion that he might be less than virile, not capable of fathering a child. What egos men had. She'd have to wait and hope.

But in the meantime, she didn't want her mother-in-law to think that her son had married a barren woman, so she told Jane about having seen the doctor and what he had said. To her surprise, Jane's reaction was the same.

"Don't rush into it, darling," she said. "It takes a lot of effort to make a marriage work. You and Brian didn't really know each other well before you were married. Wait awhile before saddling yourself with a child."

Vickie was astounded. Was Jane implying that their marriage wasn't solid? Or was Vickie to infer from her mother-in-law's tossed off remark that she didn't care about having a half-Russian grandchild? Was she forever destined to suffer for her Russian legacy?

Vickie began to study the Constitution in preparation for her naturalization, the day that would realize her long awaited dream. Then, as an American, she would immediately sponsor her family.

But the news from China was alarming. Communists were gaining in strength and it became evident that it was only a matter of time before there would be a complete takeover. It had become a private race between them and Vickie's naturalization. What would happen to all the White Russians trapped in China?

Letters from her parents were no less disturbing. Lydia reported daily events in Shanghai, occasionally asking if there were any rules that could be bent to expedite their visas. In the Fall of 1948, her mother's letters became more frequent, breathing urgency and indignation:

> ...Do you remember the Chinese shopkeeper we've dealt with all these years, so obliging in the past? Well, he has suddenly become undisciplined, his attitude insolent. We still need his trade, so I'm afraid to complain and upset Kiril. Rickshaw coolies are impudent and even beggars have become brazen. I was carrying bread the other day and a boy in rags ran up, grabbed the parcel right out of my arms and took off in full view of the policeman who stood on the corner pretending not to notice. Can you believe it? What are we coming to? Such lawlessness. The police enter our homes unannounced, sprawl unceremoniously in our chairs under the pretext of checking the number of Europeans living in each house, and we're forced to bribe them with our UNRRA rations to get them out. Our only hope is the new organization that came out of UNRRA, called IRO, International Relief Organization, or as we affectionately call it, Auntie Ira. It is preparing to take out all White Russians who wish to leave China before the communists take over. Unless foreign visas come soon, it looks like we shall all be transported to the small island of Tubabao in the Philippines, to await our visas. Rumor has it that General MacArthur put pressure on the Philippine President Quirino to shelter us. We have become true migrants. When will it all end?

As she folded the letter thoughtfully, Vickie noticed a P.S. on the other side of the paper.

Jacques Jobert has already liquidated his business and taken Claudette to France. Katya worries me. The bronchitis she had last winter turned into pleurisy, and although her cough seems to be better, she has lost a lot of weight and grows weaker by the day. I don't know why she refused to leave with her husband, but Henri stayed behind to care for her.

The name leaped at Vickie with unexpected force. Henri was still in Shanghai...He hasn't left for Russia yet. Has he changed his mind?

CHAPTER SIXTEEN

Vickie sat by the guest room window gazing at San Francisco Bay. Ordinarily, the view was best from that room, but dense fog blocked Alcatraz Island and the Golden Gate Bridge. The foghorn hooted with mournful regularity. Forlorn, it nagged. It wept. How could anyone learn to like it? She could not shut out its plaintive voice. In the middle of the afternoon the house was quiet. So quiet, she heard the slight rustle of paper as an envelope slid off her knees and dropped to the floor. Brian had brought the mail from the office during lunch hour and on first glance, Vickie saw only bills and magazines, so she put off sorting the thick stack until after her chores were done and the house was in order.

She looked down at the fallen envelope and saw her mother's handwriting. Her heart quickened with apprehension: First letter from the Philippines. She tore it open and started to read:

10 February 1949

My dear Vickie,

Here we are, in this awful place with the jungle for our bedroom. It turned out much worse than we expected. We were scheduled to leave Shanghai in groups of four to five hundred people. Both Rosens and ourselves were on the first ship, the *Hua-Lien*, with four hundred ninety refugees aboard. We were so happy to have escaped the communist takeover, that we ignored the IRO warnings about primitive conditions on Tubabao Island: no electricity, no water supply, no sanitation. We thought that if President Quirino offered shelter to six thousand refugees, surely something would be done for us. How naive we were!

When we approached the coral island, it appeared as an emerald gem rising out of the sea. Huge fronds, lianas, tall coconut palms. It appeared like a tropical paradise.

It took two days to unload the equipment and disembark all of us. At least we were lucky that Russian engineers had been flown in earlier to clear some ground for us. All we found were a few quonset huts and large, dilapidated tents abandoned by American troops during the war. Near the clearing, a small creek meandered through a ravine at the edge of which was a long, communal outhouse. On the other side of the ravine, we saw native huts built on stilts near the beach. A large sign in front said in English: 'Forbidden Zone.' We found out later that we were placed near a leper colony. Can you believe it?

We were given cots, mosquito nets, candles and matches, and assigned to a tent for forty people, each family partitioned from the other by flannel blankets thrown over a length of rope. Rosens were in a nearby tent with seventy people. That first night all we had to eat were canned rations given to us by the IRO officials. They told us that when the jungle was cleared enough to give us more room, we would be issued smaller tents which we would have to put up ourselves. Soon after our arrival, more trees were cut down, and we were able to get a private tent, as did the Rosens. Theirs is right next to ours, and it turned out to be a stroke of good luck because Joseph, bless his heart, helped us to put up the tent. And, when we were told that we had to dig a ditch outside our tent for water runoff,

Joseph relieved Kiril from that humiliating job. Can you imagine, Papa, a prince of blood, having to dig a ditch?

We brought most of Papa's medical supplies and instruments,
so he will be in great demand here. But you know his heart condition. I worry that he may not get as much rest as he should.

By the way, before we left Shanghai, I went to say goodbye to
Katya Jobert. I hadn't seen her for a couple of months and was
shocked by her appearance. She was lying on a chaise longue,
pale and coughing. Henri sat beside her. He rose when I came
in, but his greeting was icy. What have I done to deserve that? I
wanted to know why she hadn't left Shanghai with her husband and daughter, but she refused to talk about it. And that
was that! I can't understand why she is staying behind and
jeopardizing her son's safety in the process."

Vickie's heart lurched painfully. She closed her eyes and inhaled
deeply. *Dear God, will I ever say his name without an ache, without
remembering?* Her hands trembled as she read on:

But back to our life here, In the communal kitchen all women
are assigned chores. I have to peel potatoes and do some cooking, but I don't mind that. Nina pouts but it's good for her to
do a bit of kitchen duty. I am so glad that you'll be getting your
citizenship soon and we won't have to stay here much longer. I
feel so sorry for those who have no sponsors and have to wait
for the immigration visas to the countries willing to take them.
Papa and Nina send their love. As you know, neither of them
are letter writers, so I'm the one who will keep you informed
about us. Stay well, dear girl, and kiss that dear husband of
yours for us.

Your loving mother."

Vickie reread the letter and folded it slowly. Her mother was trying not to complain too much about the shocking situation, but the truth was apparent between the lines. With a hollow feeling in her stomach and trembling hands, Vickie put the letter away. Here, in San Francisco, she lived in a comfortable home with all the modern conveniences while her family was forced to exist in appalling conditions.

Terrible to be helpless. There was nothing she could do until she became naturalized and that wouldn't be for a few months yet. Thank God that their time on Tubabao would be counted in months instead of years.

Katya Jobert was probably dying and Henri stayed by her side as a dutiful son. What was he going to do after she died? Remain in Shanghai? Vickie sighed. Better concentrate on the remaining chores to keep away from disturbing thoughts.

She went to the master bedroom and saw Brian's scattered clothes. Once out of his uniform, he always wore a suit and looked well groomed when they went out, careful that his socks were the same color as his shoes even to the right shade. But at home, he didn't care if his Sulka ties and Hickey Freeman suits were left all over the room and his closet so disorganized that if Vickie didn't straighten it out regularly, she was sure he would never find anything. When she once asked him to put his things away, he shrugged. "I'm always in such a hurry, hon. Who looks into our closets, anyway?"

"*I* look into the closet, and it bothers me."

"Loosen up. You don't have to prove yourself to anyone."

Not to anyone, she thought, only to myself. But, rather than become a nagging wife, she continued to pick up after him. Actually, she enjoyed hanging his ties according to color, lining up his shirts and suits in a row. It was important to have her home in immaculate order, dusted and shiny. She had this compulsion to keep the house spotless and neat. No one was ever going to say that a Russian woman was not tidy.

Once, when she was on her hands and knees buffing a small area of wood floor in the entry, Sue came to visit. Vickie asked her to sit down. "I'm almost finished. I'll be right with you."

Sue watched her, then said: "Why are you doing this? Don't be a slave to your home. Far better to spend time on your own self than on your floor. Be good to yourself. By the way, you said you wanted to know a little about makeup. Come with me!" Her round, jolly face was skillfully covered with a thin layer of makeup giving a fresh glow to her face.

At her house, Sue showed Vickie a whole array of makeup bottles and jars and offered to take her shopping for cosmetics.

Vickie went to Elizabeth Arden's for a demonstration and was amazed how much better she looked with tinted foundation, rouge, and a touch of mascara. She hid her makeup in a drawer, keeping only a few bottles of perfume and cologne on her dressing table. After that she applied makeup every morning before coming down to breakfast with Brian. She remembered her mother saying that a smart wife must never let her husband see her unwashed face and uncombed hair in the morning.

And now, deep in thought, Vickie sighed. Time to go downstairs, and start dinner.

* * *

In the next three months, Vickie tried not to dwell on what was happening on Tubabao. Letters from her mother became scarce and terse. There was no word from Sara, and Vickie missed hearing from her. She sent frequent packages to her parents, mostly flour, sugar, tea, and some canned goods.

To make the time go faster, she continued to entertain a lot, shopped downtown, went to the movies either with Brian or with other wives. But all that was not enough. Something was missing. So, with Brian's encouragement, she auditioned at the San Francisco Conservatory of Music on Sacramento Street, and was assigned a teacher on the collegeate level. Brian bought her a Baldwin Acrosonic spinet, explaining that a baby grand piano would be impractical as long as he was in the army. "Every time we move, it would create a problem, hon. We'll never know what our housing situation will be at the next place," he said. Vickie didn't mind. She was thrilled to have a piano after all the lean years in Shanghai, and started practising three to four hours a day. Keeping an immaculate house and playing the piano required quite a balancing act on her part, but she managed.

Brian was proud of her and told his mother that his wife was going to be a concert pianist. Vickie smiled to herself, sure that her mother-in-law was going to be delighted to compensate for Vickie's lack of college degree by telling everyone that her daughter-in-law was a student at the conservatory.

Then, in early June came another letter from Lydia, much more detailed than the previous ones:

2 June 1949

My dear Vickie,

First of all, thank you, dear, for the latest package of much-needed staples that you have sent us. Sugar and coffee are especially welcome. We are forbidden to shop in the neighboring Philippine barrios, and have to make do with what we can get at the shacks that sprang up across the road from our tents. The natives peddle produce and housewares at exorbitant prices, and we have no alternative but to deal with them.

We are going into our fifth month in this God-forsaken place, and my nerves are getting more frayed by the minute. We are warned about the poisonous snakes and about the jelly fish on the beaches; We are forbidden to kill either tarantulas or huge lizards, for we are told that they are necessary predators.

I feel that we live in a prison without bars. The international staff of IRO is housed in separate wooden barracks and quonset huts. They censor our in-coming mail, and demand that all out-going letters be submitted unsealed. It's insulting to be treated like common criminals. All because we're refugees and at their mercy. Let them read this letter and learn how all of us feel! All around us tempers are short, and arguments flare up at the slightest provocation. During the drenching rains, water soaks through our tents and mud fills the ditches. Papa is so busy caring for the sick who suffer with intestinal problems from unrefrigerated food, that it always falls to Joseph to clean out the ditches.

Jacob has made up his mind to immigrate to Australia. He thinks it's still a pioneer country and the easiest to enter. Besides, he speaks English well and feels that he would have an easier time getting his medical license in English than in another language. Nina spends a lot of time with Joseph and I am afraid their friendship has gone beyond simple infatuation. Papa is not happy about it, and said so to Nina, but she refuses to listen. How can we interfere, when the whole Rosen family has been so helpful to us?

We have a new interesting person here. A group of American officials paid us a visit and promised to do what they could to help. One of them is a young engineer of Russian parentage, Rostislav Antonov, who decided to stay on the island with the IRO. He has met Nina and gotten her a secretarial job at the IRO offices. You can imagine how very happy she is to be free from kitchen duty.

This Ross Antonov has a Slavic face with blue eyes and light brown hair. He is tall and spare of build. He told Nina that he is an only child and that his parents had died in a car crash when he was in college. He is now thirty-two, but he has not forgotten his Russian, and speaks it well. It is very helpful to those of us who do not speak enough English to communicate our complaints. I hope that Ross Antonov will take an interest in Nina. American-born ethnic Russian with an engineering degree! I can dream, can't I?

Well, my dear girl, judging from your letters, you are both well
and happy. I hope that we shall be reunited very soon.
As always, Papa and Nina send their love.
Your loving Mother."

Vickie sighed as she read the letter. Poor Mama. Her pride is chafing
and the long wait for their visas must be taking its toll. Thank God my
naturalization exam is soon. Once I have my citizenship, things would
move fast.

Perhaps it was good that the Rosens would be leaving for Australia.
Joseph's growing affection for Nina was unfortunate. Vickie couldn't
believe that her sister was serious about him. This new American, Ross
Antonov, appeared just in time and with luck he would fall for Nina.

Vickie put the letter in her desk, walked out of the guest room and
headed downstairs. But as she passed their bedroom she saw Brian's
shoes and socks by the armchair. She went in, picked them up and put
them in the closet.

As she straightened up, she knocked his Harris tweed sport coat off
the hanger and saw a stain on the sleeve. It would have to go to the
cleaner's. She went through his pockets and in one of them found a
business card. Keith Engstrom, commercial artist, it said. She felt a pang
of guilt. That was the man Brian went to see on the day of their arrival.
Keith must be a close friend of his, and she had neglected all this time to
ask him for dinner. She must do it soon.

She placed the card on the dresser and made sure that everything else
in the room was tidied up. She took comfort in seeing order in the
house and now, after running a comb through her hair and powdering
her nose, she went downstairs.

The front door slammed and Brian called from the hallway: "Hon,
I'm home! Mother phoned at the office and said she couldn't get you,
but she expects us for dinner tonight. Just us and her old friend, Louise
Chambers."

As Vickie came out of the kitchen to greet him, he brushed a quick kiss on Vickie's forehead and handed her a letter with a happy smile. "Here's another letter from Tubabao. This time from your friend, Sara."

Vicky tore open the envelope and sat down in the living room.

Brian started up the stairs, then paused: "I hate to rush you, but you better get dressed. You know how Mother hates it when anyone's late."

Vickie nodded, then started to read:

10 July 1949

Dear Vickie,

I hear great reports from your mother about your life in America. I am so happy for you. My only regret is that it may be a long time before I see you again, if ever. Jacob has decided that we shall go to Australia. Many of our friends made the same plans, so I know we won't feel lonely when we eventually get there.

As time passes, everyone is feeling somewhat stressed, but the young are enterprising and it is amazing what they have done here. Among us are fine musicians who brought their instruments to the island and have now organized an orchestra. On a makeshift platform they stage performances for us with excerpts from symphonies and musicals. Amateur singers entertain us with folk songs and encourage us to participate. The musicians put up a large tent in an open area and nicknamed it Theater Square. Leave it to our Russian humor!

Our tents are lined along several dirt roads and named grandly *the Avenue Joffre, the Nevsky Prospekt, the Tverskaya*. We try to keep our hopes high, and make the best of our situation. We have to remind ourselves often that this is all temporary, and we should count our blessings for having escaped the communists in China.

Joseph is very fond of Nina and the two young people spend a
lot of time together. I worry about it and hope that when we all
leave Tubabao, they will accept their separation as inevitable.
Try not to worry about your parents. They seem to endure the
hardships fairly well and we try to help whenever we can.
God keep you well and happy and I know you shall be reunited
with your family soon.
Your loyal friend, Sara.

Vickie closed her eyes and pressed the letter to her chest. Dear, dear
Sara. How typical of her to see the positive side of things. And how different was the letter from Lydia. Vickie kissed the pages and went
upstairs to dress.

*   *   *

Over the past two years Vickie learned to dislike her mother-in-law's
elegant house. Jane's patronizing attitude had not changed since the
first day of their arrival. She assumed the role of a teacher and acted it
out to the hilt whether Vickie asked her advice or not. "…Really, Vickie,
I know you're slender, but you should still wear a girdle. In the back, you
know, it shows the wobble…Be sure and call your dinner hostess to
thank her the next day. Or write a thank you note, it's expected…" and
all this slipped in smoothly between martinis and discussions of a current opera or charity ball she attended. It all seemed to go over Brian's
head, and when Vickie finally swallowed her pride and mentioned it to
him, he seemed annoyed.

"Mother means well," he said, "She's only trying to be helpful."

But Vickie felt the sting. She found it difficult to make the calls. She
never learned how to rave over a dull dinner party. Some of these social
graces were nothing but a bunch of white lies. Yet Jane did it. Other
wives did it. And she wanted to belong, to be accepted. So she wrote the
notes.

Louise Chambers, that old gossip with a perennial self-serving smile on her wrinkled face, was already there when they arrived at Jane's home. Her glance slid down Vickie's simple blue dress. "Hello, dear," she said in her hoarse tobacco voice, her taut skin under her beak nose stretching over a smile. "What a dear little dress. Are you young people wearing them shorter this year?"

And that, Vickie thought, translates into an inexpensive dress. Aloud she said: "Oh, haven't you noticed, Louise? The saleslady at I.Magnin told me everyone is wearing shorter skirts this year. I'm glad you like my *little dress.*"

Jane winced.

Two years of apprenticeship under Jane, and I've learned more than she bargained for, Vickie thought nastily. Louise grunted and turned her attention on Brian.

"You want your usual rum and coke, Vickie?" Jane asked.

"No thank you, Mims. Brian suggested that I try Bourbon and coke instead. Many of our army friends don't stock rum and I don't want to embarrass our hosts. Actually, I'm getting to like bourbon."

Jane raised her left brow. "Well then, perhaps you'll want to try the more conventional bourbon and soda."

"I already did and I don't care for it." Softer to say 'don't care' than 'don't like'. Keep it smooth, don't rock the boat.

The conversation hummed around her. Vickie tuned it out and concentrated on the cool drink in her hands.

"Vickie! You're miles away. Louise asked you a question."

Jane's bristling voice started Vickie. "I'm sorry," she said, "I guess I was daydreaming. What did you say, Louise?"

"I asked about your family. Any idea when they'd be coming to the States?"

"Soon after I get my citizenship," Vickie said.

"I look forward to meeting your parents, my dear," Louise said without much enthusiasm.

"Prince Muravin is a charming gentleman, and his wife a lovely lady," Brian said.

"Speaking of princes," Louise said, "I ran into Ellen and Keith Larsen yesterday. They asked about you, Brian."

"I don't think I know them," Brian said.

"Of course you do. They're your mother's friends."

"I'm sorry, I don't remember them. What has that to do with Prince Muravin's arrival?"

"Oh, I meant to add that they were entertaining Count and Countess de Massenet from Paris last week and I met them. Such a cultivated, charming couple."

"So are the Muravins," Brian said. "You'll be impressed."

Loyal Brian. Thank you!

And so it went the whole evening. At home, Vickie went to bed without discussing the evening with Brian. No use sounding like a complaining wife, especially about his mother's close friend. Actually, she found the whole dialogue with Louise rather amusing. Louise's pretentiousness at something she was not, was so transparent, it was funny.

CHAPTER SEVENTEEN

The months since she became naturalized flew by quickly. How happy she had been to stand with other new citizens and pledge allegiance to her flag. Her flag! In looking over the crowd, she had wondered how many of them had been born stateless like herself and were experiencing the same incomparable thrill of acquiring citizenship for the first time in their lives. Hard as she tried, she could not restrain the tears from flowing down her cheeks.

It wouldn't be long now before her family would be joining her in the States. Daydreaming about their forthcoming arrival, she didn't open her mother's latest letter until she had finished her tea. This was one of the routines she carried over from her mother's custom to have an afternoon tea with a piece of cake or a cookie. She looked down at the letter now and opened it with happy anticipation:

16 September 1949

My dear Vickie,

I have some wonderful news to share with you. Ross Antonov has proposed to Nina and they will be married here, so we can all come to America together. Ross is not of noble birth, but his father, Stepan Antonov, was a rich merchant of the First Guild in Russia. Ross is well educated. He charmed us with his respectful manner, and his broad knowledge of Russian history. Papa realizes that there are no aristocratic titles in America, and has accepted Ross as his future son-in-law.

Our papers have been processed and you can't imagine how thrilled we are to be leaving this place. I'm packed and ready to go at a moment's notice. It will be so good to see you and Brian. Thank you my dear for renting an apartment for us. I'm sure that after Kiril starts his practice, we'll be able to buy our own little house. I don't remember when I've been so happy.

For the next two pages Vickie's mother extolled Ross Antonov's virtues and gave details of the forthcoming wedding at the camp. Vickie lowered the letter for a moment. What happiness! She closed her eyes, trying to imagine her beautiful sister in a wedding dress, and she was sure that in spite of their circumstances, her mother would have managed to make something lovely for Nina. With a happy sigh, she read on:

So much good fortune has come our way, that I hate to spoil this happy letter by telling you sad news. We had our first major typhoon this month. For several days before it, the rains were relentless. The squalls alternated with the hot sun that made everything steam. There was no escape anywhere. Then, one day, a warning was issued that an approaching typhoon could hit Tubabao, but we've been used to false alarms and weren't worried. In late afternoon, however, the wind came in strong gusts. We secured the ropes that held our tent and waited inside. Soon the wind picked up and it had a voice, I swear. It bellowed, it howled, it wailed.
Our tent held up and we were safe, but some others were not so lucky.
There was violence in the atmosphere. Violence in the roar of the typhoon, in the creaking sound of collapsing tents, in the

whine of sheared off metal roofs. I can still hear the screaming, the sobbing, the children crying.

When the storm hit, Sara ran into the jungle to find Joseph who had gone for a walk earlier. A while later he came running to the tent, but Sara was not with him.

Vickie, my dear, I am so sorry to tell you that the next morning she was found dead.

Vickie gasped, dropped the letter and covered her face with her hands. Sara dead? No. It couldn't be. How? Frantic, she picked up the fallen sheets. The words jumped before her eyes:

She was killed by a section of a metal roof that had sheared off one of the quonset huts. She died instantly, they tell us, so at least she didn't suffer. I know how much she meant to you, Vickie, and I am so sorry that this terrible accident happened to our friend. Jacob and Joseph have withdrawn into themselves in their grief and we respect their privacy. They will be leaving for Australia soon, away from the tragic reminder of their loss.

Until we see you soon, all our combined love to you both,

Your loving mother"

Shaking, Vickie folded the letter but her fingertips were so cold she had difficulty slipping the pages back into the envelope. Her Sara.... Gone.... What a terrible way to die. Tears stung, then fell down her cheeks and she wept for her friend. Sara's face floated before her, the gentle smile, the kind eyes, the soothing voice. Why did her mother leave such tragic news to the end of the letter? How could she be so callous? She rose and walked to the drop-leaf desk at the other end of the room, her legs weak, a chill in her heart. She dropped the letter on top of a pile of papers and then sank into a nearby armchair.

Her mother was so wrapped up in Nina's marriage she had forgotten to include the Rosen's new address. Nina was marrying a Russian-American. She, her sister, should be sharing in her joy, looking forward to meeting her brother-in-law. She should be glad they were all out of China, especially since it had been taken over by the Communists last October. Instead, all she could think of was Sara. She had such a yearning to hear her voice once more, to see her face, to touch her. And what about poor Joseph and Uncle Jacob? What a shock for them! Where were they?

The room was getting darker and Brian was not yet home. She wanted to be held by him, comforted by him, but he wouldn't understand her grief. How could he? She had never told him how much Sara meant to her. No, her light-hearted Brian would not understand the loneliness that filled her.

All she wanted to do was to sit and cry and remember.

She paused at the door and looked back. Sorrow lingered in the room, hidden in the desk. She went over, and brought her fist down on the polished wood. "Damn! Damn!"

Tears blurred her vision as she went downstairs. She heard the key turn in the front door lock. She ran out of the kitchen. Brian. His happy face, his smiling eyes. Vickie threw her arms around his neck, pressed her head into his shoulder. "Oh, Brian! My friend…Sara…she's dead!"

His arms went around her, squeezed hard. "What happened?"

"There was a typhoon and Sara was killed by a flying piece of metal roof."

"Oh, hon, how dreadful. I'm so sorry. Wasn't she your mother's friend?"

"Yes, but she was also my friend. I loved her!"

"You must feel terrible. It's hard enough to lose a friend, but to have it happen in such a tragic away." He shook his head and released her. "We must find you a friend here soon. How about Sue? Give her a call."

He didn't understand how much Sara meant to her and it was no use explaining. She reached up, wrapped her arms around him and leaned her forehead against his cheek. "Oh Brian, now you're my closest friend."

"Of course I am, but you need a woman friend, too. Give Sue a chance." He kissed her on the cheek, then pushed her away and laughed self-consciously. "I need a shave."

After touching his chin, Vickie said: "No, you don't. I have some good news too. Nina is getting married to an American of Russian descent."

"An American? What was he doing in Tubabao?"

When Vickie told him, he said: "That's great! I'll call Mother and tell her the good news."

Vickie didn't hear the conversation, but in a few minutes, Brian called: "Hon, Mother wants a word with you."

Reluctantly, Vickie picked up the receiver.

"I'm sorry to hear about your friend, dear," Jane said in the same detached tone of voice she would have used if someone's pet dog had been lost. "But what great news about your sister!"

"Yes, thank you. They'll be coming here together with my parents. I expect a telegram any day telling us they're on their way."

"How nice, darling," Jane said. "Is she marrying one of the refugees in the camp?" she asked.

Vickie was waiting for just that. "No. His parents came to the States before the Revolution, so Ross is a native American. He's an engineer who worked at the camp with the IRO."

"I'm happy for your sister, darling," Jane said without enthusiasm. "I'll entertain them of course when they arrive, and I certainly look forward to meeting your parents."

*   *   *

That night, Vickie wept into her pillow. Brian took her into his arms. "Hon, please don't cry. I'm sure your friend Sara wouldn't want you to. Think of the good times you had together. Tell you what, why don't we go to the movies tomorrow night? I heard that *The Third Man* with Orson Welles is great. It'll take your mind off things."

Vickie shook her head. How could a movie take her mind off Sara? Her friend was killed and she was supposed to enjoy a movie?

Brian sighed. "O.K. What if I take a few days off and we fly to New York to see a couple of plays or a musical? They say *South Pacific* at the Majestic Theater is a real smash. I'll have fun showing you around New York."

"I'm sorry, Brian, I just can't. Besides, I can't leave right now, you know that. Any day my parents may send a telegram that they're on their way."

Brian threw his arms up. "For heaven's sake, Vickie, what else can I do? You Russians are so emotional!"

Vickie swallowed. "I'll be fine. I'll read, that will take my mind off things."

"Good. What are you reading now?"

"I just finished George Orwell's *1984*."

"Did you like it?"

"It's frightening. He talks about a totalitarian society where the authorities control the minds of the people."

"That's just one man's idea."

"Except that it could well happen if we're not careful."

Brian leaned over and kissed the tip of her nose. "Don't clutter your mind with doomsday thoughts. Have I told you what a cute nose you have?"

Henri would have discussed the book's premise, she thought, would have developed the idea, argued the point in depth. She swallowed and said nothing.

Brian whistled a tune, threw his tie across the room trying to hit the chair and missed. Vickie bit back a remark, picked the tie up and put it on the chair.

"Do you think my hairline is receding, hon?" he said, peering at himself in the mirror.

Vickie examined his hairline. "Not at all."

He turned to her and smiled. "Just think what fun you'll have showing America to your parents and your sister. You'll have your whole family in the same city. And I'm looking forward to meeting my new brother-in-law."

She sighed, smoothed his hair, then wrapped her arms around him. "Brian, I need time to grieve for Sara. Please be patient." She hesitated, then added, "I love you."

He grinned. "You're the greatest. I'm lucky."

*   *   *

They didn't come by ship after all. Ross had arranged for them to fly out of Manila.

The last few days before their arrival, Vickie spent hours fixing up the two furnished apartments she had rented for her family in the Richmond district. A block apart, they were near her home in the Presidio. The day before the family was due to arrive, Vickie purchased carnations, her mother's favorite flower, and arranged them in crystal vases she brought from home. How grateful she was that she had a husband who watched her activities with amused tolerance and did not suggest his mother's help.

The next day, she insisted on being at the airport an hour before the plane was scheduled to land. "What if the plane comes in early and we aren't there?" she said to Brian when he tried to talk her out of leaving the house so far ahead. The plane arrived in the middle of the afternoon and as soon as she saw them, Vickie hugged both her parents with arms spread wide, kissing one face then the other with trembling lips. How hard it was not to stare at them, not to show how shocked she was by Kiril's drawn face, by the web of wrinkles on her mother's tanned cheeks and the rough skin on the palms of her hands.

Lydia pulled away first. "I want you to meet my new son-in-law," she said, beaming. Vickie had never seen her mother's face this radiant before. She hugged and kissed her sister, then turned to meet Ross Antonov. A tall, muscular man looked at her with a face so open and friendly, one couldn't help but like him immediately. An American and a Russian. How lucky for Nina.

"Ninochka, I'm so happy for you," Vickie said, still looking at Ross and catching herself smiling at him.

"Pretty lucky break for me, sister," Nina said, slipping her arm through Ross's.

"I'm the lucky one," Ross said, taking Vickie's hand. "A ready-made family for me as well as a beautiful wife."

How strong his hand felt. He'll be good for Nina. He turned to Brian and put out his hand. "A fellow American! Pleased to meet you, brother-in-law."

Brian laughed. "Welcome into the family, Ross. I guess we'll feel out-numbered for a while, what with all these Russians around us, but we love them, don't we?"

Kiril cupped Vickie's chin. "You look wonderful, my dear. Married life agrees with you. I'm so glad."

"Thank you, Papa," Vickie said, and thought: That dreadful climate didn't do him any good. I'll show mother what food to buy and how to measure ingredients the American way. He'll gain weight, dear Papa. She kissed him. "You can't begin to imagine how happy I am to have you here!"

"My mother expects us all for dinner tomorrow night," Brian said. "We'll drive you to your apartments now, let you catch up on your sleep, then pick you up tomorrow evening at six-thirty."

They dropped Ross and Nina off, then drove one block farther and stopped in front of a two-story apartment house perched atop a one-car garage. After unloading their luggage, Brian handed Kiril the keys to the front door. Vickie's eyes filled as she watched her stepfather's hand shake so hard he could not insert the key into the keyhole.

"Here, Papa, let me help. These American locks are different from the ones we had in Shanghai." She took the key and opened the door.

They climbed the stairs into the spacious two-room flat with a large kitchen. Vickie had stocked it with food and dishes and pots and pans; had placed a few scatter pillows on the living room sofa to make it look homey; had hung an icon with a vigil light in the right corner of the bedroom, according to the Russian Orthodox tradition. She tried to forget that Brian had winced at the price of the icon when she bought it. He had mumbled something about unnecessary purchase as her parents surely would bring one with them. It was the only time Brian made a criticism about her purchases for the family and she let it pass.

As Lydia entered the bedroom, she noticed the icon, crossed herself, and made no effort to wipe the tears that trickled down her cheeks. "Thank you, Vickie," she said in a choked voice. "We're so tired. We'll see you tomorrow then."

Much as she wanted to question her parents about the Rosens, and Sara in particular, Vickie knew this was not the time to do it.

Outside, Brian squeezed Vickie's elbow. "We must leave them alone for a while. They need time to get their bearings."

*   *   *

Dinner the next evening was something Vickie would remember for a long time. How different it turned out to be from her own first dinner at her mother-in-law's home! "Why, Prince Muravin, I'm honored to have you in my home!" cooed Jane as Kiril, dressed in his striped gray flannel suit Vickie remembered from Shanghai, clicked his heels and bent over to kiss her hand.

Vickie watched with amusement as her mother-in-law flushed with pleasure. She could almost read her mind: A man with an aristocratic title and now a relative at that! Vickie was sure her mother-in-law would phone Louise Chambers the next morning to relate every word of tonight's conversation, embellishing it with relish.

"Sit by me, Prince," Jane said, indicating the seat to her right. Vickie glanced at Lydia. Her mother was glowing from the attentions poured on her husband. She wasn't at all jealous. Poor mama. She was so pleased that he was being honored again that she wasn't even aware that she was overdressed. Although her outmoded black velvet dress made during the war by a Chinese tailor, looked unfashionable next to Jane's elegant two-piece navy Mainbocher, Lydia had a presence, and carried herself with natural dignity.

"You must forgive my imperfect English. I need much practice," Kiril said, spreading his arms in a disarming gesture. "My French is much better. Do you speak French?"

Jane emitted a tiny laugh. "Oh, my dear prince, my French of school years is quite rusty I'm afraid. Far below your charming English."

Tomorrow she would report to Louise that her in-law had a divinely halting English, Vickie thought. She watched her father use European table manners, just as she had two years ago. But when she glanced at Jane, her mother-in-law seemed not to notice.

"You must still be exhausted, Princess, after your long flight," she said to Lydia. "I'm utterly selfish to have asked you here tonight, but I'm sure you understand how eager I was to meet you all and welcome you into the family."

Lydia smiled politely. "Of course. We also looked forward to meeting you. Vickie has written so much about you, we feel like old friends already."

Appropriate answer. Good for you, Mama.

"It must be such a relief for you to be out of that camp and in a civilized world again. Was it dreadful?" Jane said between bites of meat. She might as well have been commenting on the weather.

Lydia stiffened. "We managed."

Vickie glanced at her mother's hands and wondered how many potatoes she had peeled in the camp's steaming kitchens. But of course her mother would never admit it to Jane.

"I can't wait to see downtown San Francisco," bubbled Nina. "Will you take me, Vickie? Soon?" She paused, looking at Vickie's silk dress and her manicured fingernails. "I've got to keep up with my sister, don't I?"

Vickie ignored the last remark. "Of course, Nina, as soon as you're settled, and Ross lets me take you away from him."

She glanced at Ross and was surprised to see him studying her with his warm blue eyes as if he were trying to solve a riddle. She moved uncomfortably in her chair.

The maid glided around the table, her starched apron making a tiny rustle behind Vickie's chair. Glasses tinkled, someone coughed.

"Ross has to start his job right away," Nina said. "He's going to work on some project or other, so I'll be free to do as I want." Then turning to the maid who held a bottle of wine wrapped in a linen napkin, she lifted her empty wine glass. "Yes, please."

"Not yet a project, dear," Ross corrected. "Just an idea I want to develop."

Brian raised his head. "What kind of an idea?"

Vickie could see he liked his new brother-in-law. Could it be because he had never had a brother, she wondered, or was it because Ross was American born and would balance the Russian contingent of the family?

Ross shrugged. "I'm not sure it's feasible yet."

"An idea about what?" Vickie asked.

"About a device that would be used in hospitals."

She leaned forward. "In hospitals? Tell us about it."

Ross gave her with a searching look. "You're really interested, aren't you?" He appeared flattered.

"It's an alarm system," he explained, "that would alert the hospital staff when a patient is having a heart attack. I'm not sure yet how I'll make it work, but the possibilities are there."

"What made you think of this?"

"My mother's friend died in the hospital of a heart attack during the night and she wasn't discovered until morning. I keep wondering if she could have been saved if the staff had been alerted when it happened. I spent the war years in the army, working in maintenance of medical hardware at a military installation in Indiana. That experience sparked my interest in developing new applications for some of the sophisticated equipment, especially in the medical field."

Nina toyed with her crystal goblet, twirling it against the candlelight. She set the glass down. "How come you never told me about this, Ross?" Her voice sounded petulant.

"It just never came up, darling, and I didn't want to bore you."

"What a marvelous idea," Vickie said. "It could prevent so many unnecessary deaths."

"Yes, I'm sure it would."

Brian squeezed Vickie's hand. "That's my wife, interested in everything."

Vickie smiled. "I have so much to learn."

The conversation flowed. Pleasantly, courteously, everyone on their best behavior.

It couldn't last. They were all so different; Jane, Brian, Ross, all American products, and she, Nina, and their parents, from another world. How could these others ever understand? Maybe Ross could with his Russian background. Whatever made her think that marriage could bridge the gap? She admired Brian, maybe she even loved him. He seemed on *her* side, but she couldn't talk to him from the heart. There was something there…a wall she couldn't penetrate.

CHAPTER EIGHTEEN

The next day Lydia called Vickie. "You can't imagine how happy we are to be in America, dear. We'd like to go to church this Sunday and ask the priest to serve a thanksgiving *moleben* after the liturgy. Where do you go?"

"I go to the cathedral on Green St., Mama. I'll be glad to pick you up at eleven."

"Good, I'll be ready."

"Mama, wait! I want to ask you something."

"Yes?"

"It's about the Rosens. What was Joseph doing in the jungle during the typhoon?"

Lydia didn't answer.

"Did you hear me, Mama?"

"I heard you. I don't know why you want to open up old wounds. I already told you that Joseph went for a walk before the storm, and when the typhoon hit, Sara ran out to find for him."

"I still don't understand why Sara ran after him. She must have known that Joseph would have run back."

"Oh, for goodness sake, Vickie," Lydia's voice sounded exasperated. "If you have to know, that afternoon Joseph proposed to Nina and she turned him down. He was upset when he went into the jungle and that's why Sara went after him."

Vickie gasped and was silent for a few seconds. So that's what was behind it all. "I see," she said at last. "How dreadful for Joseph! Give me their address, Mama, I want to write him and Uncle Jacob."

"I don't have it. All I know is that their ship was to take them to Sydney."

Vickie was astounded. "Haven't you heard from them since?"

Again a brief pause, then: "No, we haven't." Lydia's voice was cautious.

"Mama, you're not telling me everything. What happened?"

"There's nothing to tell." Lydia's voice took on an edge. "We had a...a misunderstanding and they left in a huff. That's all."

Vickie's hand tightened on the receiver. Some inner voice warned her against pushing for further details.

"I'll see you Sunday, Mama," she said.

"I'll be ready," her mother said and hung up.

*   *   *

Two days later, Lydia called again. "I've met our neighbor, a friendly Russian lady who has lived here for many years. She says that there are two Orthodox church jurisdictions in America and we should join the Russian Orthodox Church in Exile. She says that although your church has been in America longer, your priests communicate with the Soviet priests. I wouldn't even shake hands with one of them." Lydia's voice rose. "You're going to a Bolshevik Church, Vickie. How could you?"

Vickie held her temper. "That's not true, Mama. You're talking about the Reds and the Whites again. There's no room for politics in a church. We pray to the same God, remember?"

"But your priests recognize the Soviet Church!"

"My church takes no orders from the Soviet Patriarch because it's autonomous and was established in America long before the Revolution. The Church in Exile accepts America's hospitality on a temporary basis, waiting for the day when she can return to her motherland. We all intermingle and go to one another's church, regardless of its jurisdiction. So where's your spirit of true brotherhood?"

Lydia sniffed. "I couldn't imagine Papa taking communion and receiving a blessing from a Soviet priest."

"But we don't have Soviet priests in our church, Mama. I just told you," Vickie said testily.

She had forgotten how strong Kiril's influence was on her mother. It was no use. Why quarrel? The main thing was to keep her parents happy in their new country. God only knew, there were many adjustments to make, and if that church brought them solace and a feeling of belonging, then it was the right one for them.

*　　　　　*　　　　　*

Christmas season came without snow, without cold weather. People shed their coats to bask in the sun's gentle warmth. Vickie couldn't get over it. In Harbin temperatures hovered around twenty below zero with snow piled several feet high along the sidewalks. In Shanghai, the damp wind blew from the Whampoo River and chilled pedestrians to the bone. But here, in San Francisco, pink clouds hung in the sky, wispy, precarious, then melted into the blue. Downtown's Union Square was bubbling over with holiday spirit. Salvation Army workers rang their bells on street corners, and both live and mechanical Santa Clauses vied for the children's attention. A decorated Christmas tree several stories high, graced the venerable City of Paris Department Store, and shoppers crowded around to enjoy the elaborate window displays at Gumps'.

Vickie could hardly contain her excitement. "Imagine, Brian," she said, "This is the first Christmas in years when my family won't be plagued by insecurity and fear of the future. Everyone can be together for dinner."

"Great. I'm sure Mother will be delighted to have us all."

"There's plenty of room in our house," Vickie said quickly. "We've had as many as twelve. We can easily have the whole family."

"I only wanted to save you the trouble of cooking. After all, Mother doesn't have to lift a finger in the kitchen."

But Vickie was firm. "I don't mind preparing a meal for all of us."

Suddenly, she remembered something. "Brian, I feel bad about not asking your friend Keith, over. Why don't you ask him to join us for Christmas dinner?"

Brian reached for his uniform coat. "He has his own family."

"Oh. I don't know why I assumed he was a bachelor."

"He is, but his parents live in Marin County."

"Well then, we'll have him over another time. He must feel hurt that we haven't asked him by now."

"Don't worry about him." Brian's voice was brusque. "He's a loner. I doubt that he'll come if I ask him."

With that, Brian grabbed his army hat and was gone.

Vickie stood still for a few moments, then shrugged and dismissed the whole idea.

It was fun introducing her family to a turkey dinner with stuffing and cranberry sauce, sweet potatoes with marshmallows, mincemeat and pecan pies. Everyone enjoyed the food, and even Jane refrained from arching her left brow. Only Nina wrinkled her nose after tasting the mincemeat pie and left it on her plate uneaten.

At the end of the meal, Vickie started collecting the dirty dishes. Nina and Lydia rose to help, and a moment later, Jane rose too. Hesitantly, she picked up two plates, then watched the other women. Up went her brows.

"Oh!" she said with genuine surprise. "You stack them!"

Vickie had a hard time suppressing a smile as Jane followed suit.

When the dishes were cleared, Ross raised his glass of wine, his glance lingering on Vickie. "I want to propose a toast to our hostess, and thank her for a marvelous dinner." He bowed in her direction. "Congratulations on having learned our American cooking so fast.

Everything was delicious, including the mincemeat pie." He winked at Nina, who pursed her lips, then turned to face the others. "And now, I have a wonderful surprise for you all. Ladies, Prince Kiril, in a few months, Nina and I are going to make you grandparents, and Vickie, an aunt."

The oh's and ah's reverberated in Vickie's ears, as envy, deep and immediate, stabbed her. The chair scraped on her carefully waxed floor when her mother got up to hug and kiss Nina. Her sister smiled sweetly, but there was no glow on her face. I would have been beaming, Vickie thought. I would have shouted it, told everyone as soon as I knew. How could Nina have kept this secret even for a day?

Brian kissed Nina, and now it was her turn. "Wonderful news, *sestry-onka*. I'll be an indulgent aunt, you'll see." The words sounded trite, but she meant them. Until she had a baby of her own, she would at least have a niece or a nephew to love. A baby in the family. Such happiness for her parents!

∗   ∗   ∗

They were so pleased with everything in America. The abundance of food, the modern appliances, the privacy of their apartment. "Especially the privacy," her mother told Vickie. "What a joy not to have to lower your voice for fear the people in the next tent will hear you. To have a bedroom, a living room, and a kitchen! Before Tubabao, I took these things for granted, for even in the rooming house we had a modicum of privacy, but after Tubabao, every detail thrills me." Lydia smiled sheepishly, "I'm still a little frightened of the fast speed Waring blender, but I can't help but have tears in my eyes when I look at the large gas stove in our kitchen now. It's all mine!"

Vickie listened to her mother with an indulgent smile.

"I have so much to be thankful for, Vickie," Lydia went on. "You and Nina have married well and soon I'll be a grandmother. What happiness!"

Vickie hugged her mother and wished that she too could have made Lydia a grandmother.

Soon after the holidays, Kiril applied for his license to practice medicine. Vickie went over to her parents' apartment and waited for the results with apprehension.

She knew that her stepfather's poor English would be a real stumbling block. Besides, there were new diagnostic methods now, different terms for ailments, new drugs to prescribe. How could he learn all that in a foreign language and pass a State Board Exam?

After years and years of successful medical practice, his professional expertise was no longer sufficient. Vickie smiled bitterly. Prince Kiril Muravin, a respected and admired physician, would be out of work.

When her parents came home, Lydia confirmed Vickie's suspicions, but concealed her disappointment well. "Why should Papa go through all this at his age?" she said. "He's sixty one years old and doesn't have to practice medicine at all. He'll enjoy semi-retirement, and can use his beautiful Russian to teach it. That's what he will do," she emphasized the sudden thought. "We'll advertise in *The San Francisco Chronicle* and he'll give Russian lessons. Meanwhile, we'll get along on what's left of our savings."

Before long, to Vickie's relief, Kiril had a full schedule. Most of his pupils were children of Russian immigrants, who were anxious to have their offspring preserve their mother tongue. Her mother, in the meantime, glad for her past experience in bookkeeping, became a teller at the Bank of America branch in the Richmond district where they lived.

Nina and Ross bought a small cozy house on Sixth Avenue near Lake street, not far from the senior Muravins. Ross was earning a good salary at the engineering firm downtown, and Nina spent a lot of time shopping with Vickie and decorating the nursery.

*   *   *

As the months passed, Vickie became more and more aware that to the average American, Soviets and Russians had become synonymous. How easy it was for Brian to say that she should react more as an American than a Russian. But every major event that had to do with the Soviets affected her personally. One sensational case after another filled the newspapers. Alger Hiss was found guilty of perjury for concealing his membership in the Communist Party; Klaus Fuchs and Harry Gold were imprisoned for giving atomic secrets to the Soviets. The House Unamerican Affairs Committee was ferreting out American Communists in the country, claiming internal subversion in the government. And when the Korean War began in June, a terrible paranoia swept the United States and triggered a wide attack on American communists. It was not popular to be a Russian.

Shortly after the Korean conflict started, Vickie and Brian sat in the living room one evening sipping a drink before dinner. "When people hear my accent and ask me where I'm from," Vickie said, "I tell them I was born in the Far East. I say very little while I'm out shopping. When anyone guesses that I'm Russian, I feel compelled to say that I'm not a communist but a White Russian, and then explain what that means."

"Nonsense," Brian said. "You're an American now. You have nothing to do with the communists. You were never a Soviet citizen and you weren't even born in Russia."

"I feel so much on the defensive." Vickie sighed. "Brian, is there a chance they'll send you to Korea?" she asked, dreading the answer.

"I don't think so. I went to the Far East during the last war, and my guess is that if I'm sent overseas, it will be Europe this time."

Europe. Oh, how she wished that would happen. Surely in Europe she would not feel so defensive about her background. The Europeans lived close to one another, they were used to foreign accents, they tolerated a different culture and they would understand better what being a White Russian meant.

*　　　　　*　　　　　*

Brian received his orders in August. What a thrill it was when he came home and told her that he was assigned to the G-2 Section of the U.S.Army Headquarters in Heidelberg, Germany.

"We're to leave in three months," he said twirling her around the living room. "Just think, we'll travel! We'll go to Paris, London, Rome!"

Vickie threw her head back and laughed in sheer joy. "And Venice, Florence, and Vienna, Madrid, and…"

"Wow! Hold it! I do have to work somewhere in between," Brian interrupted kissing her on the forehead. "We'll have plenty of time to plan everything." He pulled back and searched her face. "Will you miss your family a lot?"

Vickie swallowed hard. In her excitement over the prospect of going to Europe she hadn't had time to think of her family. "Of course I'll miss them," she said, and thought: Why did he have to spoil it right now? It won't be as bad as when I left them in Shanghai. They're all in the States now, and safe.

A few days later, Ross called to say that Nina gave birth to a baby boy. Nina named him after Kiril but Ross said Kenny would be easier on American ears "and, after all," he added, "Kenny was born an American. He's a plump little fellow."

Vickie rushed over to see her new nephew. A good baby who cried regularly every four hours for his feedings, Nina told her, and slept the rest of the time.

"Do you have enough milk for him? Vickie asked, aware that her sister had small breasts.

"No. I bound my breasts and won't nurse him. Nursing pulls the breasts down," she confided. "I don't want to ruin my figure and besides, I don't want to tie myself down to rushing home to nurse him. This way I can take him with me when I go out and give him the bottle. Easy."

Vickie kept silent. What a joy it would be to hold your own baby and feel his tiny mouth suckle at your breast. Didn't Nina have that maternal urge? God worked in strange ways. Her sister did not pine for a child, yet had one right away, while Vickie had gone for three years without getting pregnant. She thought of going to the doctor again. But what could he tell her that would be different? Maybe in Germany, in a romantic European setting, they would make love more often and she would get pregnant.

Soon after Kenny's birth, Ross had fallen into the habit of stopping by their Presidio quarters once in a while. "Nina is home with the baby," he'd say and then sit and talk to Vickie and Brian.

One afternoon, shortly before they left for Germany, Vickie asked: "How is your project coming along?"

Ross sighed. "I've been so busy at the office, I haven't had any time to work on it." He looked across the room, his gaze unfocused. "Used to be I could think about it at home after work, but now, what with Nina and the baby needing my attention…"

Something in his voice made Vickie look up sharply.

"Isn't she well?"

"She's not sick, but…" Ross said, glancing at Brian, then looking back at Vickie. "Your sister has her moods."

Vickie sat up straight. Was there something else? What was he hinting at? For a few moments she was silent, then returned to her question. "We were talking about your project," she said.

Ross studied her speculatively. "You really want to know. You're not just being polite."

His open, friendly face shone with intense pleasure.

"I don't ask idle questions," Vickie said quietly.

"The alarm device I thought of designing is going to be cumbersome. Too heavy. There should be a better way."

"Is anyone else working with you on this? A cardiologist perhaps?" Brian asked.

"Not yet. I want to have something a little more developed first. I did discuss the idea with my family physician. He was quite enthusiastic about it but thought I was way ahead of my time."

Brian rose and went into the kitchen to freshen their drinks.

"You should bring Nina and the baby to see us in Germany," Vickie said.

Ross gazed at her pensively. "I'll miss you when you leave. You know how to listen."

A message fluttered in the air, then darted away. What was he trying to say?

Brian came back into the room. "When Kenny is a little older, I hope you'll take time off and visit us in Heidelberg. Use our house there as a base of operations and see some of Europe."

That would be lovely. She'd see Kenny at his cutest age. How thoughtful of Brian.

Now he glanced at his watch. "Ross, will you excuse me if I run out on you? I've got some urgent work to finish up at the office." He kissed Vickie on the forehead, waved to Ross and headed for the front door.

Vickie watched him leave with narrowed eyes. How odd. She frowned to shake off a vague uneasiness and turned to Ross.

"Would you like a liqueur?" she asked.

"No, thank you." He seemed preoccupied.

"Your mind is somewhere else, right?" Vickie asked.

He gave her a rueful smile. "Yes. I was thinking of your assignment in Germany and how much you'll love seeing Europe. I know you'll enjoy all the treasures it has to offer."

"Have you been there?"

"I have. When I was in college, I spent a summer seeing Europe on a shoestring. It was a great education, and I've never forgotten it."

"Where did you go? What did you like the most?"

"I toured the usual places, of course, Rome, Paris, Vienna. But what I enjoyed most was Leonardo da Vinci's home in the Loire Valley in France."

Vickie raised her brows. "Da Vinci in France?"

"Yes, he lived there. The house was filled with his mechanical inventions. What a genius he was. Did you know," Ross leaned forward, his voice animated, "that he had devised a kind of air-conditioning for his home?"

"No, I didn't."

"Well, it was quite a contraption, but considering the age he lived in…revolutionary. He built a huge wheel that rotated slowly in a pan of water, and cooled the air in the house by evaporation."

"Fascinating!"

Ross smiled sheepishly. "Since I fancy myself a kind of an inventor, I was very impressed."

"When you visit us, we must all go there together."

Ross sat back in his chair. "I don't know if Nina would be interested in anything like that. I think she'd enjoy the glamor of the big cities more."

His eyes clouded with hidden thought and he slumped in his seat, lowering his head and sighing. After a few moments, he ran his hand through his thick hair, sat straight in his chair as if he had come to a decision and looked at Vickie. "I have something to ask you."

Vickie waited.

"It's…" he paused and coughed, gaining time.

"About Nina?" Vickie prompted.

"Yes. You're very perceptive. Thank you for making it easier for me." He rubbed his hands. "I don't know what's happening to her. She was so full of fun when I married her, but once she became pregnant I noticed a sharp change."

"In what way?"

"She's irritable, critical…but that's not what really worries me." Ross glanced at Vickie and lowered his eyes again. "We all enjoy our drinks and there's nothing wrong with that, but Nina never stops with one glass of wine. And she wants them every night. I'm worried."

"Why don't I talk to her?"

"Would you? I know families often hesitate to interfere, but I thought…"

The sentence trailed and Ross looked at her with such pleading in his eyes that Vickie said: "I'll see her tomorrow, Ross. I'm sure it's a passing phase." She patted his hand and he caught it in his.

"Vickie, what a loving sister you are." Impulsively, he kissed her hand, then smiled. "You see, you bring out the old-fashioned chivalry in me."

Vickie kissed him on the cheek. "And I'm grateful for the brother I've acquired."

The next day she went to see her sister.

Nina was changing Kenny's diaper on a bassinet in the kitchen and greeted Vickie without a smile. The baby cooed and kicked his legs happily and Vickie couldn't resist tickling his tiny feet. "He's going to be a big boy, this nephew of mine," she said, picking him up and cradling him in her arms. How wonderful it felt to hold this live bundle, this warm, cuddly baby.

Suddenly, she was too consumed by envy of her sister's motherhood to smile at her, too busy resenting her own inability to get pregnant to say anything else.

Nina watched her for a few moments, then took him out of Vickie's arms. "It's nap time, I don't want him to start crying," she said, nuzzling him in the neck. The child gurgled happily as she carried him to the bedroom.

While she waited, Vickie looked around the kitchen. Morning dishes were still in the sink, the room smelled of rancid fat and something sour that she could not identify. On the kitchen table, next to a baby bottle was a half-empty glass of wine.

"Well, big sister, are you satisfied with the inspection, or are you going to give me a lecture on housekeeping?" Nina's voice oozed sarcasm.

Vickie started. "What's happened, Nina?" Vickie pointed to the glass of wine. "Since when have you started drinking before lunch?"

"And what's wrong with a glass of wine before lunch? I'm bored stiff sitting in the house all day, and taking Kenny out with me is more trouble than it's worth."

"What about hiring a babysitter for a few hours?"

"Don't ask me why, but I'm afraid to leave my baby with a stranger. I'm afraid something would happen to him and then I'd never forgive myself. So, I'm stuck here. I didn't expect to be saddled with motherhood this soon. Even Mama gets out into this new world more than I."

"My God, Nina, how can you say that? It's not fair to Ross. You have a beautiful, healthy child. I'd give anything to trade places with you."

Nina gave her a crooked smile. "Including my husband?"

Vickie gasped, but Nina silenced her with a wave of her hand. "Don't pretend innocence, dear sister. Don't think I haven't noticed how cozy you two are together. 'How is your invention coming along,'" she mimicked Vickie.

Vickie's voice shook: "Don't insult me. How can you even think such a thing? If you showed more interest in your husband's work, he wouldn't find it necessary to tell me about it."

"Don't meddle in my life. You're so sanctimonious, you make me sick!"

"Nina! I can't believe my ears. What would Mama and Papa say if they heard you now?"

"Ha! Mama would find some excuse in my defense. She's always been on my side, you know. As for Papa, he'd find something to be critical about. I'm his natural daughter, but you're the one who's his favorite. Don't deny it. It's always been, 'good Vickie, smart Vickie!' But you know something? You with your righteous attitude don't fool me. Why don't you be honest about one thing? We both married for two reasons, security and an American passport."

Noticing Vickie's face flush, she chuckled. "What's the matter, the truth hurts? At least you had fun while I got pregnant right away." Her eyes drifted toward the bedroom and her face softened. "I must say though, Kenny is adorable. It's just that he came too soon."

"Count your blessings, Nina."

"And do you? You don't love Brian any more than I love Ross. Only I admit it, and you're still trying to convince yourself that you love Brian and not Henri."

Vickie caught her breath. "How can you say that? I *really* love Brian!" she shouted, and was instantly appalled by her reaction.

Nina's mouth twisted in a crooked smile. "I see I've touched a nerve. But that's the truth, isn't it?"

Vickie lost control. "What about you and Joseph?" she cried. "You led him on, didn't you? You knew he was in love with you, but for you it was just a fling, wasn't it? You broke his heart. Do you ever think about that day?"

Nina turned deathly pale. "I don't want to talk about it." She opened the refrigerator, took out a bottle of white wine, refilled her own glass with shaking hands, and poured one for Vickie. After a few moments, she steadied herself, then said with a sad smile: "Here, let's drink to our good fortune, big sister, and forget what we've said to each other, O.K.?"

Swallowing hard, Vickie said: "I don't drink this early in the day. I better go."

"I've never known you to carry a grudge, Vickie. You've changed."

"Remember Mama's favorite saying—words are not like birds, once out of the cage, you can't catch them."

They both fell silent remembering. Vickie put the palm of her hand on her sister's cheek. "We both said things we shouldn't have, and I'm sorry. But do think about what I've said about Ross. Men like him are hard to come by. You'd be a fool to lose him."

*   *   *

Vickie didn't tell Brian about her visit to Nina. It would have been betrayal of loyalty to her sister. But she worried. Was Ross aware that Nina was drinking during the day? She phoned him at work and told him that she had heard about mood changes that happen after childbirth. It was called postpartum depression. But, if things didn't improve, he should take her to a doctor.

The sisters did not speak alone again, until Brian and Vickie went to say goodbye before leaving for Europe. While the men were in the living room, Vickie followed Nina into the kitchen. "Take care of yourself, Ninochka," she said hugging her sister.

"I'm sorry about what I said to you last time," Nina said with tears in her eyes. "I'll miss you, Sis. Write, will you?"

Vickie nodded. "Of course I will. You must visit us while we are in Europe."

In parting, Ross took Vickie's hand and patted it. "Nina and I will miss you very much. You're not only a sister, but a good friend as well."

Vickie hugged him. "Take care of Nina, will you?" she whispered, brushing his cheek with a kiss. Then, pulling back, she smiled. "And I won't worry about leaving my parents behind. I know you'll look after them," she said.

But that wasn't quite the truth. The next day she said to her mother: "I worry about you, Mama. You know so few people yet."

"How can you say that, Vickie? Most of the Russians we've met live around here, in the Richmond district, and Papa and I are active in our church." Lydia paused, then added: "Too bad you don't belong to our church."

Vickie leveled her gaze at her mother. "I'm an American now, Mama, and I belong to the Orthodox Church in America."

"Just because your husband is an American, doesn't mean you should ignore your Russian heritage. You should be proud of it," and before Vickie could answer, Lydia abruptly changed the subject. "In Germany you'll be able to do translating again. I don't suppose you did any of it here in San Francisco, did you?"

No, she hadn't. How could she? There were demands on her as an army wife and a hostess and she tried hard to do justice to both. It wasn't until her mother had mentioned it, that she began to miss her work. Her work at the Jobert offices. Memories flooded in. But she must not think of *him*. She busied herself with packing. Their belongings had to be separated into three groups. The furniture would be stored for the duration of their assignment in Germany, because houses in Heidelberg were furnished with quartermaster issue furniture and china. But kitchen utensils, linens, clothing, favorite bric-a-brac and her piano would be shipped overseas. She enjoyed her studies at the San Francisco Conservatory of Music and wasn't about to stop playing in Europe. Their cabin baggage however, had to be kept hidden from the packers.

"The movers will pack anything in sight," Sue Brennan warned. "My neighbor forgot to empty a garbage can, and two months later found the can full of slimy lettuce."

*　　　　　　*　　　　　　*

Before they left, Vickie hugged the first passport she had ever owned in her whole life. How inferior she had always felt because she was a refugee without a country, and how proud she was now, a lawful citizen of the United States of America! Reverently, she examined it again. Its green cover was designed with rows upon rows of the American seal, a larger gold seal was superimposed in the center, and the gold lettering said *Passport, United States of America.* Her hands trembled as she opened it and read: "I, the undersigned, Secretary of State of the United States of America hereby request…to give all lawful aid and protection to___" there followed her name written in ink and below it, the magic words: "a citizen of the United States." She didn't mind at all that her face on the photograph was partially distorted by the kiss of the embossed seal.

On November 1st, 1950, Vickie and Brian left by train for New York, where they sailed for Bremerhaven, Germany.

PART III

GERMANY

1950-1954

CHAPTER NINETEEN

Heidelberg

As the ship inched its way toward the dock in Bremerhaven, Vickie stood at the railing trying to take everything in. This time, with the help of Dramamine, the crossing had been pleasant, and after seven days at sea, land was a welcome sight. Germany. She was excited about this country with a language she did not understand, new challenges, a culture to explore.

The noise hammered at her ears: the clanking of chains as the gangplank was lowered, the scraping of wooden crates on the ground, the guttural sounds of German as workmen shouted to one another. Further back, a band struck up a welcoming German tune.

Brian chuckled. "They're playing '*Ich hab mein Hertz in Heidelberg verloren*', which means 'I've lost my heart in Heidelberg'. Just for us, huh?"

Vickie was amused by the musicians' lederhosen and green hats, a saucy feather clipped to the side with a silver emblem. In spite of the brisk November wind, the men showed no signs of discomfort. A hearty lot, Vickie thought, her attention drawn again to their velour hats. Papa would look smashing in one of those. She'd have to find out where to buy one.

In the crowd, she spotted U.S. Army personnel waiting to assist the disembarking passengers. Men in familiar uniforms…And here, on German soil, for the first time Vickie felt truly American.

*   *   *

They were given a requisitioned German house. It perched high on a hill overlooking the Neckar River that meandered through a narrow valley between tree-lined hills dotted with substantial red-roofed homes.

Their house was arranged on five levels, far too large for us, Vickie thought. She was intrigued, however, by the floor plan. The street entrance led into an inside stairwell which climbed to the front door. That level housed the coal furnace room and the maid's two-room lodging. On the next level, there were living room, dining room, kitchen and a chute in the hall. Vickie looked inside it and turned to Brian. "Is that what you call a silent butler?"

Brian roared with laughter. "No, hon. This is not a silent butler, but a dumb waiter!"

Vickie smiled sheepishly as they climbed another flight of stairs. This floor held three bedrooms and one bathroom, and higher still, two more rooms in the mansard area.

What in the world will we do with all these rooms? Vickie wondered, and decided to make one of the bedrooms into a study for Brian. The top floor would be left for storage. The house was furnished with Quartermaster walnut furniture, stocked with Rosenthal China and Bavarian crystal.

Vickie worried about the owners of the house. "I hope they found a good place to live," she said to Brian.

"Don't worry about them, hon. The U.S. Army pays them a handsome rent price for the use of their home, and we in turn, have our quarters allowance withheld from my salary. So you see, nothing is given or taken for free."

The army assigned them the required German caretaker, a widow who turned out to be an excellent cook.

Brian's office was on the other side of town, housed in the old sprawling German compound, now called Headquarters EUCOM. For Vickie, the only inconvenience about living on the Neckar, was that she had no car when Brian drove the carpool. Still, on those days, she relaxed on the small concrete balcony off the dining room, and watched the busy river traffic below. At night, she and Brian enjoyed the multi-colored water display that fanned out of the river in front of the Harlaas Café directly across from their house.

She picked up German quickly, whole phrases at once, ignoring correct grammar and speaking in colloquialisms she learned from her cook. Using *putz-frau Deutsch*—charwoman's German—she delighted local grocers with her fluency when she shopped for fresh produce. The open marketplace behind the elegant Hotel Europa on the Anlage street, made such shopping a treat...

She couldn't get enough of Heidelberg. After all, she was Old World herself. Nestled between the river and the hills, the old town was dominated by the spectacular ruins of the Schloss. The castle, burned by the French in 1693, had become more picturesque as a ruin than perhaps it was in its heyday. She roamed the narrow, cobblestoned streets of town, paused at the quaint city squares with their ancient wells and cooing pigeons, admired the Baroque churches, stood at the Universitäts Platz, gazing in awe at Germany's oldest university founded in 1386. Papa would love to see this, she thought, aware that the university boasted one of the most famous medical schools in Europe. Such street names as Akademiestrasse and Seminarstrasse were a constant reminder that it was primarily a university town.

Brian was happy with his work. "I hope you make friends here soon," he told her after they arrived. "I'll have to be on TDY often," but when he saw Vickie's questioning look, he slapped his forehead, "I'm sorry honey, I keep forgetting that you don't know our military terms. TDY stands for temporary duty. Anyway, I'll be both in Berlin and in the Army Language School in Oberammergau. Come to think of it, it's a short drive from Garmisch, and sometimes you can come with me. You'll love Bavaria. But while you're here, I understand there's an active social life and an officers' club across the river called the *MACOGEN*."

"What a strange name," Vickie commented, and Brian laughed. "It's a field grade officers club. Short for major, colonel, general, MA-CO-GEN, see?"

She discovered that they had only to cross the old bridge and double back a short way to reach the Macogen and enjoy the intimate atmosphere of the small club.

Still, with no child to occupy her time, and a servant to do her housekeeping, the hours dragged. Living in a foreign country, hearing a foreign tongue, the desire to speak the languages she knew, strengthened.

"Couldn't the army use my skills?" she asked Brian.

His reaction was immediate and firm. "I'd rather you didn't work, Vickie. Get involved in women's clubs and local charities. There's plenty to do, not to mention our travels. Besides, how many interpreters can they use in Heidelberg? This is not Bonn, or Frankfurt."

"But Brian, I need to do something stimulating, useful."

"I don't *want* you to work. It wouldn't look good. The army is a small family and rumors will start that we can't make it on my salary. It may not set well with my superiors. I'm sorry, but I have to think of my future."

Vickie dropped the subject for the time being. She couldn't believe that Brian's commanding officer would object. What business was it of his? She had the qualifications. Where could they find a trilingual translator and interpreter who was an American citizen and available on short notice?

The month of May splashed cherry blossoms all over the hills, flowers bloomed in the city squares, and the air was redolent with the freshness of spring, the kind of days one wanted to do something wonderful, memorable, instead of counting the hours in boredom. She played the piano to keep up her technique but that was not enough. Life was passing by and she did nothing about it. Below their house on the Neckar, accordion music from the daily excursion boats floated on the air waves. She yearned to take one of those rides but Brian kept putting her off.

"I'm too busy right now. When the summer comes, I promise we'll do it together."

The Gastätte, the small restaurants, the paths through the wooded hills, the abandoned castles along the river, all beckoned, but her husband showed no interest in exploring them. Vickie fretted. Surely there was more to life than his work and her duties as an army wife.

Then, toward the end of May, Brian brought home an invitation to a diplomatic reception to be held at the Macogen Club the following week.

"There'll be members of the Allied Military Mission from Frankfurt at this reception. Your languages will really come in handy. I'll be so proud of you."

He patted her on the cheek. "Brush up on your French, and I don't need to tell you about the Russian."

At the thought of speaking French, Vickie's mind flew away. Henri. She reread her cherished French edition of Flaubert's *Madame Bovary*, becoming engrossed all over again in Emma's love affair.

She chased away those other thoughts at once. Paris was a long way from Heidelberg, Henri was not in the military, and he wasn't even in France. He was in Russia, probably in Leningrad or Moscow. Foolish to feel his presence at the mere mention of the French language.

She couldn't decide what to wear to the reception. She missed Sue Brennan. The bad part about the military was that as soon as you got to know someone in whom you could confide, orders came and you had to start all over again. She had already met a few wives, and one in particular, Betty Campbell, appealed to her. She was a chatty, tall brunette from Southern California whose husband was a major in the engineer corps. But they lived several miles away in an apartment complex called Mark Twain, near army headquarters, and it wasn't the same as having Sue Brennan practically next door where she could run over and ask her questions.

Nevertheless, she did call and ask Betty what she should wear to the reception.

"This will be a big affair," Betty told her. "I'm wearing my dressiest cocktail outfit. Your black and white organdy dress sounds chic. I'd wear that."

Vickie hung up, relieved.

On the night of the reception, Vickie dressed carefully. The full length mirror in their bedroom reflected her stunning figure tightly draped to the hips in black organdy. A full white skirt flared out in a swirl to just below her knees in the front and dropped down to her ankles in the back. Jane's wedding gift, a sapphire-and-diamond brooch sparkled at her mandarin collar, and aside from her wedding band and the diamond engagement ring, she wore no other jewelry.

Brian looked impressive in his blue uniform with silver leaf shoulder boards and military insignia on the lapels. It was the first time she had seen him in the dress uniform and impulsively, she threw her arms around his neck and kissed him.

"Darling, you look dashing. I'm so proud of you!"

"You don't look too bad yourself, Mrs.Hamilton," Brian said and turned to leave the room.

Vickie smiled seductively, and raised her arms to her hair. "Well, then, maybe my outfit and your glamorous uniform will help us make a baby later?"

"Sure. Would be nice to have a family." The words were thrown casually over his shoulder, as he left the room. Vickie dropped her arms to her sides and followed him.

On the way to the club, Brian said: "Vickie, just in case you get carried away talking to the Russians, please don't forget our French guests."

"I won't forget."

Vickie could hardly contain her excitement. She was going to interpret again, use her languages with fluency, be useful at a diplomatic reception.

The Macogen club was already full when they arrived. No wonder it was reserved for only the field grade officers: the place was too small to accommodate all ranks. Vickie was dazzled by the colorful mixture of dress blues and foreign uniforms.

Brian, his hand under her elbow, guided her toward a group of Soviet officers standing in one corner of the reception room. With a friendly nod to one of the Russians, Brian said: "I'm Colonel Hamilton. We're so pleased that you are with us today. My wife, here, will translate for me."

Vickie repeated his words in Russian and was amused to see the surprise and the smiles spreading on the Soviet faces.

"Why, our countrywoman!" a portly officer said with a firm handshake. "Allow me to introduce myself: Colonel Ivan Rostenko." He turned to a short officer with a crewcut standing beside him. "This is our Mission doctor, Colonel Roshkov."

Vickie inclined her head politely, and was going to repeat it in English, but Brian had already moved away.

"Well, well," Col. Rostenko's voice boomed, "What part of the motherland are you from?"

Vickie smiled. "I'm not from Russia. I was born in China, after my parents fl..." she cleared her throat to check herself, for she almost said 'fled', "after my parents left Russia."

"Amazing," the man said, his voice suddenly cautious. "You don't have a trace of an accent."

"That's because I was born in Harbin."

"Harbin? Where's that?"

"In Manchuria. The Russians built Harbin at the turn of the century when they were shortening the railway to Vladivostok. So you see, my parents and I lived in a Russian community."

Col.Rostenko raised his brows. "Never heard of it."

"You'll be interested to know that in the thirties, there were over a hundred and fifty thousand Russians in Harbin," Vickie said, and with that, Rostenko slapped himself on the forehead.

"Of course. The non-returnees."

Vickie smiled politely. "Actually, in the west, they are called Russian émigrés."

"Ah, yes, the double-eagle, the white, blue, and red. All that ancient history. After the war was over, many of them returned to the motherland."

Vickie looked at him hard. "Yes, they did," she said. "They thought they'd be given work in their professions, but instead, many were sent to remote places as laborers."

"We lost twenty million people in the patriotic war, but not a single so-called émigré fought to save our motherland from the fascists. So it's only fair to put them to work where they are needed the most, don't you think?"

Vickie felt a surge of such hot anger, she knew that if she continued the discussion, she would say things she would regret later. This was a diplomatic reception, and diplomacy required tact and courtesy, from the host nation.

She turned to the Russian doctor, who stood listening.

"Colonel Roshkov," she said, "My stepfather is a doctor too. What's your specialty?"

The man's face brightened. "I'm a surgeon," he said.

When Vickie didn't immediately respond, he added: "*zhivot polosuyu*," and swept the edge of his hand across his abdomen.

He used a crude, peasant term for 'cutting the abdomen' and Vickie had trouble keeping a straight face.

"Have you been in Germany long?" she asked, regaining her composure.

"Long enough. I'm due to go home. My mother is ill."

"I'm sorry. Is it serious?"

"Yes. She's had pneumonia and pleurisy. Her recovery has been slow."

"When I was a child and had a cough, my mother put suction cups on my chest. Do you still use them?"

"Oh yes, indeed. I remember a funny incident in my town. A hospital patient with cups on his back jumped out of bed and ran down the corridor yelling for his nurse who had left him alone for too long. It was quite a sight, I tell you!"

Col. Roshkov laughed, carried away by the memory.

A simple soul, this one, Vickie thought, then, noticing Rostenko's frown, changed the subject.

"Is Madame Rostenko here?" she asked.

"No. Our wives are in Frankfurt minding the children," Colonel Rostenko answered and Vickie thought: With German servants readily available, their wives didn't have to stay home. Either they were afraid to let them see stylish western women, or else had orders to keep them at home.

Brian put his hand on her arm. "Hon, I hate to take you away from these gentlemen, but there are French guests at the other end of the room who would like to chat with you, I'm sure."

Glad to leave these stiff Russians who appeared to be afraid of the foreigners, or more probably, of one another, Vickie nodded, and giving Colonel Rostenko a polite excuse, allowed herself to be led away.

They went up to a group of French officers and their wives who stood drinking champagne and chatting quietly among themselves. What a pleasure to see these women, elegant and relaxed and smiling.

The men bowed over her hand, murmured *'enchanté,'* introduced themselves, then moved aside to allow a man in civilian clothes to step forward. One of the officers smiled.

"Permettez-moi, Madame, de vous présenter le vice consul de notre consulat à Francfort, Monsieur Henri Jobert."

Cold air filled the room; the warmth seeped out of her skin. For a brief moment blue-green eyes touched hers and then he was bowing over her hand. She willed it not to tremble.

"Madame and I have met before. In Shanghai."

His voice. Vickie breathed slowly trying to control her racing heart. Oh God, help me!

The French officer bowed. "Well then, I shall leave you two to reminisce."

"Brian, this is…" but Brian had already left her side, and was lost in the crowd. One of the French women looked at her curiously, whispered something to another woman and moved away.

Facing each other, they stood alone among strangers. How one person can fill a room! The sheer force of his personality made her weak. He hadn't changed. Perhaps slightly more defined lines around his nose, otherwise the same handsome face, the same intense look in his eyes. She was afraid to look at him more carefully, afraid that her eyes would betray her and he would find love in them, that special love she had been so sure she had conquered.

"I never dreamed I'd see you again," he said softly.

Under an avalanche of conflicting emotions, she found her voice.

"And I'm even more surprised," she said, and added in Russian: "I thought you'd be in Russia by now."

"They wouldn't let me immigrate," he answered.

"Why?"

"It's a long story."

"And Igor Sevich?"

"He's in Moscow."

"So you correspond with him."

"We keep in touch." Then: "Vickie, you look wonderful."

"Thank you. I'm happily married. Are you?"

"No. And I doubt I ever will be."

An awkward pause. She should veer away from dangerous words, think of something innocuous to say. But ordinary social dialogue abandoned her. She remembered his last plea to her, his warning that their love would haunt her. She remembered the pain in his eyes when they parted. She remembered too many things.

"How is your mother?" she managed to say. "Where is she?"

"Mother died in Shanghai."

"I'm so sorry. Did she have complications after her bronchitis?"

Henri hesitated. His eyes darkened. For a few seconds he seemed to struggle for control, then his lips pressed into a thin line. "Complications yes, but not from bronchitis."

"Another illness?"

"You might call it that."

His voice was so full of bitterness, Vickie dared not pursue the subject.

"And your father, Claudette, where are they?"

"Father lives in Fontainebleau in his country home, and Claudette is in Paris, working in the fashion house of Dior. She turned out to be a talented designer. She'd love to correspond with Nina. They were such good friends in Shanghai. Where is your sister?"

"Nina is in San Francisco. She's married and they have a little boy. I'll give you her address."

"And your parents? How are they?"

"They are all in San Francisco now."

She heard her own voice, yet it seemed detached from herself, the banal exchange going round and round the real issues that remained untouched. They talked on, captives to the situation. She answered his questions all the while thinking that soon the reception would be over and she would go with Brian to their home on the Neckar, and Henri would leave for Frankfurt…Only an hour away…yet everything was futile and wrong. Wrong!

Then a stabbing thought. *He didn't go to Russia after all. He lived in Europe, a French citizen, still serving France. If she had waited…*She remembered his threat that she would regret the wasted years.

Henri took her hand in his. "Vickie, people are beginning to look at us. Your husband is here. We have to meet again, talk."

She shook her head, unable to speak. His pleading eyes were so close. I love you, they said. She read them clearly, there was no mistake.

"Please," he said, still holding her hand. "I'm staying at the Hotel Europa for a couple of days. I'll wait for you tomorrow in the afternoon."

"No! It's impossible. The hotel is requisitioned by the U.S. Army, you know that. Someone will recognize me. I can't. In broad daylight—"

"If you don't come, I'll come to your house."

"No! You mustn't! There's a cook in the house. We—we can't…we mustn't…"

"You'll find a way." He said with assurance. "You must. I've found you now, how can you even think that we won't see each other again?"

She should be telling him that it was all over between them, saying again that she was a happily married woman, that she loved Brian. But her voice failed her while her heart cried out: *Yes. Yes. I want to see you. I still love you!*

Finally, she whispered: "We mustn't."

"Nonsense. I'm going to call you tomorrow morning and tell you where we'll meet."

Brian came up. Smiling, relaxed Brian. "I see you're taking your job seriously, hon."

"Brian, this is Henri Jobert from the French Consulate. We—we knew each other in Shanghai. His mother was my mother's friend in Russia. That's why we're speaking Russian instead of French."

They shook hands. "I'm pleased to meet you. What a small world this is." A courteous, reserved voice. Not at all like the usual, expansive Brian. Had he guessed? He turned to her: "My dear, there are other people who want to meet you." He bowed to Henri and led her away.

She hoped that he could not feel how her arm trembled.

CHAPTER TWENTY

All morning Vickie argued with her conscience. She should leave the house, not wait for his call. Yet she was afraid to step out into their back-yard for fear of missing it. Unnerved, she took a hot bath to relax. She came out of the bathroom determined not to see Henri, until the cook called from the kitchen: "*Frau Hamilton, ein Mann hat enrufen und hier ist die Nummer.*"

Vickie took the slip of paper with the telephone number and stared at it. Some stronger power had wiped out all caution and she had no will left to quarrel with herself. And she needed that caution, for Brian had indeed guessed.

On the way home from the Macogen Club, he had said: "This Henri Jobert. He's the one you told me about in Shanghai, isn't he?" and when Vickie nodded, he said: "Must have been awkward for him." He looked at her sideways and squeezed her hand. "But you're mine now."

Vickie had prayed that he wouldn't make love to her last night, but he did, and she, desperate to convince herself that Brian was the one whom she now loved, responded with abandon striving for fulfillment. It hadn't worked. His caresses were fleeting and rehearsed, as if he had memo-rized the obligatory pattern and stuck to it each time they made love.

After he rolled off her, he was asleep in moments, but Vickie lay there staring into darkness, her body throbbing with frustrated desire. Her mind screamed for Henri's naked, muscular body to cling to her and appease her thwarted passion.

Now, in the morning light, the black phone glistened in front of her like a predator ready to strike. No. She was not going to see him, she thought, even as her finger dialed the number.

He would wait for her, he told her, at the *Zum Roten Ochsen* on the Hauptstrasse. It was at the top of the street, far from the usual shopping area where they might run into familiar faces.

"No!" she cried.

"Please," he pleaded. "I've got to see you. Just this once. Please."

She hesitated, then, "Just this once. But not at that student tavern. It's too famous to be safe. Everyone takes their out of town visitors there."

"Very well then, the other one, *Zum Zeppl*, is less popular. I'll meet you there."

She went. She wanted to talk to him about Katya, about his work, about his life. That was all she wanted to do.

He was sitting at a table against the far wall where it was dark enough not to be noticed easily. She sat down opposite him with her back to the entrance. The place smelled of beer, sauerkraut, and smoke.

"Would you like a glass of wine or their draft beer with your sandwich?" he asked.

"Just wine, please."

When a buxom, middle-aged waitress came to their table, he ordered a roast beef sandwich with beer for himself and a glass of wine for Vickie.

"How long have you been in Frankfurt?" Vickie asked. "I didn't know you spoke German."

"I started studying when I came to Frankfurt, about six months ago. How long have you been in Heidelberg?"

"About the same time."

"To think that we've been so close to each other and didn't know it. If not for the kindness of fate, we might not have met at all."

"You call it kindness, and I think of it as mockery."

He reached over and covered her hand with his. "For me, it's immeasurable kindness."

Vickie turned away, her eyes drifting over a cluster of heavy signs crowding the walls. *'Anlage'* one said, *'Rohrbacherstrasse'* said another. Why had they decorated their walls with street signs?

Henri caught her glance. "I was told that all of these were stolen by students. To my knowledge, no one had ever been caught and the signs never returned. Now, it has become a tourist oddity."

"I haven't been here before."

"From what I understand, *Zum Roten Ochsen* is the number one tourist attraction. I'm sure you've seen photographs of famous people on their walls. Even Mark Twain's."

But Vickie wasn't listening. Other people came in, sat close to them. Some spoke German, others a language that sounded Scandinavian. She looked at them, imagining criticism in their scrutiny, as though they recognized what she was doing and had become her accusers. Panic seized her. Any minute, any second, Brian could walk in with a visiting officer from Frankfurt or Berlin and—the thought was too terrible to finish. She picked up her purse.

"Henri, I want to leave. This minute!"

He paid for the uneaten food without a word and ushered her out. Outside, she looked up and down the street, frantic to break free, but he held her firmly under the arm.

"There's no one in sight, Vickie. Relax. My car is around the corner in an alley. I'm not going to let you leave. Not yet. We've hardly had a chance to talk. I checked out of the Hotel Europa this morning and rented a flat on a quiet Dantestrasse. No one will ever find us there."

Once in his Citroen, she felt reasonably safe. Then a thought struck her. "Why did you rent a flat when you're going back to Frankfurt in a few days?"

"I'll keep the flat for as long as you are in Heidelberg and I am in Frankfurt." He jutted his chin forward. She had forgotten that defiant habit of his and the familiar gesture broke her resistance. She sat back in her seat, leaned her elbow on the door arm and shielded her face with her hand. Dreadful to hide like this, to fear being recognized by someone.

The apartment was on a residential street, right off the busy thoroughfare of Rohrbacherstrasse, where Brian and other senior officers drove every day to their offices. And here she was, not a block away from that traffic, doing something that could create a scandal and ruin her marriage. Risky? Foolish? Daring her fate? All of those, but she was beyond reasoning, beyond retreating.

Henri slowed down, turned into a breezeway and drove over bumpy cobblestones into an inner courtyard. There he parked and led her to the second floor apartment. It was a small place, a living room, bedroom, and a tiny kitchen. A bachelor's retreat, a hideaway cozily furnished with Danish furniture and pictures of Heidelberg and the Bavarian Alps on the walls. Even flowers…

"How did you find it so fast?" Vickie asked.

"The owner's son is a concièrge at the Hotel Europa. It was that simple." He pulled out a scarf he'd bought her, draped it around her neck and pinned it with a gold leaf. "I saw these this morning and thought you'd like them."

"How thoughtful. Thank you."

She ran her hand over the delicate silk, fingered the gold veins on the pin. She had forgotten how Henri used to surprise her with little gifts in Shanghai. "What's the occasion?" she would ask, and he would kiss her and say: "The occasion is you!"

They sat down on a sofa and looked at each other. The tension between them was charged, magnetic. She must talk, say something, anything, but keep talking.

"You have me at a disadvantage, Henri. You know about my life, my family, that I'm now an American, but I know nothing about what happened to you after I left, or what you're doing now."

"You know that I am vice consul at the French Consulate in Frankfurt."

"That's not what I meant. I want to know what happened to your relationship with Igor Sevich."

"I told you that already. We correspond occasionally."

Vickie studied him for a moment, then tried another approach. "I see. Tell me, do you miss Shanghai?"

"Only the happiness I knew with you there. Those precious memories...I'll never lose them. They are mine."

He looked at her with such longing, she quickly changed the subject. "What about China in general?"

Henri rose abruptly, started to pace the room, then stopped in front of her. "I hate it! I don't ever want to see a Chinese face again!"

His outburst was so unexpected that Vickie was taken aback. "But you had such a good life there. Friends, faithful servants. I remember your good amah. Why such a sudden change of heart?"

Suddenly, Henri blurted out: "Because mother was killed!"

"How? What happened?"

Shaking, Henri lowered himself on the sofa, then clenched his fists. "How fickle the human animal. She was killed by the people she trusted most. Betrayed by our faithful amah."

"My God, why?"

"I'm not sure you knew that my mother was a confirmed socialist. She never talked about it because all of her friends were loyal monarchists, like your parents for instance, and she didn't want to lose her friends. But Mama believed in the new Russia, and I inherited that belief. That's why we both stayed in Shanghai and didn't go to France with my father and Claudette." Henri's mouth twisted in a sardonic smile. "You could say that we were an evenly divided family. Mama and I on one side, Papa and Claudette on the other. Anyway, Papa arranged through a Swiss bank to provide a steady income for mother, and left her in my care. She was weak from prolonged bronchitis but our amah and I took good care of her and she recovered. I was reasonably sure that we could immigrate to Russia together, and Igor Sevich was eager to help. Imagine my shock when one day he told me that Soviet authorities said that I could be of much more use to them if I remained in the west and kept in touch with Igor.

"The political situation was tense, and Mama was still waiting for her visa to Russia. She begged me to leave, afraid that I'd be trapped in China. I didn't like to leave her, but I had no reason to suspect any trouble, especially since I thought she'd soon be on her way."

Henri's voice broke and he paused for a moment before going on. "So I gave in to her pleas, but before I left, I went through our house one last time. In the unused rooms I saw nothing but emptiness, felt the dampness clinging to me with odors of dust and mold and—" he looked at her, "destroyed happiness. It was sad for me, Vickie, painful. But I did not linger." He clenched his fists and swallowed hard. "I had faith in our amah. I left, and the last memory I have of Mama is her relieved face as she kissed me goodbye."

Vickie waited for him to go on, but Henri seemed transfixed struggling with some inner memory. She took his hand. "What happened next, Henri?" she asked gently.

"I gave Igor Sevich my father's address in Fontainebleau and that's where I found the letter. The Chinese communists overran the city and our amah, our faithful amah whom we treated so well over the years, denounced my mother to the authorities as a rich capitalist. One night, a gang of young ruffians stormed the house, dragged mother out of bed and bludgeoned her to death."

Vickie's eyes filled and she opened her arms to Henri. "Oh my dear! How awful!"

Henri stared at her in surprise. "You know, you're the first person I've told this to. I couldn't even tell it to Papa or Claudette. I just said that

Mama died of her illness." His face twisted in grief. "I couldn't even cry. Can you imagine that? My mother whom I adored. We were close, you know that! Oh, God!"

He went into Vickie's arms, and she cried with him. She cried for Katya and for herself and for what could never be. After a while, he pulled out his handkerchief and wiped his eyes, then hers. "I'm sorry. I never expected this to happen." He grasped her shoulders. "I couldn't talk about my mother. But you...oh, you!"

He released her and sat still, staring at her.

"Did you know that Sara was killed in a typhoon in the Philippines?" Vickie asked.

Henri gasped. "How dreadful. I didn't know."

"I loved her deeply, and when the news came I wept and grieved. She was like a second mother to me. There...there was no one to whom I could have explained the depth of my grief."

Tears filling her eyes again, she reached over to stroke his cheek, and this tender touch detonated an explosion. With a sudden intake of breath, he pulled her to him, frantically seeking her mouth. In an instant they were entwined, tearing at each other's clothes. At that moment, doubt had no space, thought no dominion. There was only the need to experience again that original white-hot moment of passion she knew in Shanghai.

Later, cradled in the warm hollow of Henri's shoulder, she inhaled his familiar scent, and let his hand glide over the length of her body. How wonderful it would be to stay like this, without moving, without setting the clock in motion. How could she ever have thought she'd be able to put him out of her mind? She had distanced herself from the truth in cunning self-deception, but her heart had clamored. Always.

Henri traced the outline of her cheekbone and jaw with his finger. "I love the mole behind your ear." He kissed it, sending shivers through her. "And the pulse at the corner of your eye." He touched it lightly with his lips. "I know every particle of you, your thoughts, your heart without your having to say a word.

"You see, you're luckier than I am," he said after a pause. "You have your Russian family around you. I know that our lives can't be patterned to our liking, but to the very end I believed that you would change your mind and share my dream of living in Russia. Even now, four years later, I remember my agony on your wedding day. That was the worst day of my life. Do you have any idea how alone I feel?"

"How can that be, Henri? You're French, too. You must have some ties to your father's roots."

Henri shook his head. "For a while I thought I had adjusted to my new life, but now that I've met you again, I realize how empty it has been. This is my second chance. I won't let you go, Vickie."

He bent over and kissed her on her lips. She stirred.

"Darling," he said, "I know that we can't meet on weekends, but I can always get away during the week. I'm only an hour's drive from you." He took her in his arms again. "*Moya rodnaya,* my very own!"

This time his lovemaking was slow and sinuous. His fingers feathered her skin, his lips followed his hand with delicate, moist kisses. Vickie was lost. Every nerve, every muscle in her body pleaded for release. The world had stopped. The rush of hours suspended.

But afterward, suspicion would not go away. Vickie rose and picked up her scattered clothes. "Tell me something," she said starting to dress, "when the Soviets said you could be of more use to them abroad, what did they mean? What are you doing for them?"

Henri sighed. "Not much. Sometimes Igor's contact in Frankfurt asks for something, and I give it to him."

"So, you're working secretly with the Soviets, yet they won't allow you to immigrate. What happened to your dream?"

"I haven't given it up. In the meantime, I'm needed here."

"You may love Russia, but you are a French citizen and you're betraying your country."

"I look at it differently. I'm helping the country I love best."

"You're selling the country of your birth."

"I'm not selling anything. I don't get paid for what I do."

"Doesn't your conscience bother you?"

"Conscience? It would bother me far more if I didn't do everything I could to help Russia. I believe in socialism and so did my mother. If I gave up this work, I'd feel I had betrayed my mother's memory."

"And if someone else betrays you? What then?"

"Why so negative?"

"Not negative. Realistic. Look what happened to the British diplomats, Burgess and Maclean last month."

"But they were warned that their cover was blown and they're safe in Russia."

"You may not be so lucky. You may be caught, and besides, it was the communists who killed your mother. How can you help them?"

"The Chinese killed my mother. I won't get caught. I'll take my chances. I know where my loyalty lies. What about you? You've become an American citizen but you'll never be able to trade your Russian soul for an American passport."

He looked at her for a few moments, then smiled. "Put your mind at rest, and let me make love to you again."

He reached for her, but Vickie eluded him. "Please, Henri! No!" She picked up her purse. "Take me back to my car. I want to go home."

*   *   **

Vickie drove home slowly along the waterfront of the Neckar. It was a busy river. Barges with cargo floated downriver, gaily decorated white excursion boats idled near the City Hall, waiting for passengers. A few German women in sturdy walking shoes held their rosy-cheeked children in their arms, pointing at the passing boats. The warm sun shone on the City Hall's windows in blinding reflections.

Suddenly, Vickie gripped the steering wheel. She pulled over to the curb, turned off the ignition, and sat staring out the window.

It was hard to believe that a few miles away she lived as an army wife of another man to whom she owed so much.

What had she been saying to herself these past three years? That her dreams were understandable for a stateless girl, security with a husband, a country to belong to, children born as native citizens. She had the first two now and the third would come later. Brian was a caring husband, a hard worker, a good provider. And as an added bonus, he was independently wealthy. She would never again want for anything.

She shouldn't have gone to see Henri. Agitated, yearning for his arms and love, she had thrown caution away without a thought for the future.

She must break with Henri, erase the past and be faithful to Brian. That's what she should do, but knew she wouldn't.

*   *   *

They found ways to meet at odd hours of the day, a morning here, an afternoon there, telling the cook that she was going for a drive or to shop, always careful to bring home purchases or drive out into the country afterward to see what she was supposed to have seen. Her restlessness had disappeared, and to her surprise, she was able to give more of herself to Brian, trying to please him by entertaining more, and even doing some volunteer work at the German-American Women's Club.

Brian was pleased. "You see," he said to her early in July, "I told you you'd find something worthwhile to do. Glad you stopped thinking about a job."

"As long as you say that there's no demand for my services here in Heidelberg, I have to be content with what I'm doing."

"That idea about working as a translator was silly anyway."

Vickie bristled. "It isn't silly, Brian, and I would still prefer to do that over anything else."

His usually warm, smiling face turned red and angry. "Damn it, Vickie, I don't want you to work!"

Shocked by his outburst, Vickie gasped. "Brian! Don't raise your voice to me. I don't like it."

"You're exasperating. I don't know why you can't be like any other army wife. You have a good home, friends, and plenty of money to spend. There's so much to do and see right here, in Heidelberg. I don't understand you."

After he stalked out of the house, she sat for a while in the living room, wondering what she could say to him when he returned. But when he came home, he refused to discuss the subject.

A few days later, he told her: "I have to go to Oberammergau and I'm real sorry to miss the yearly pageant of fireworks and simulated burning of the Schloss. John, my assistant, was telling me about it. It's a spectacular event recreating the time when the French burnt the castle in the 17th century. I think you should see it. There'll be other occasions when you can come with me to Bavaria."

*   *   *

The pageant was indeed an unforgettable sight. The hot summer day had faded into a balmy July evening as Vickie and Henri climbed the steep narrow streets to the Philosophenweg across the river, a path where Germans took their Sunday walks high above the Neckar. They stood spellbound admiring the famous scene across the river: the Schloss high in the hills and the old bridge below.

"It's amazing how well they restored the bridge," Henri said. "Part of it was blown up in the last days of the war by Germans themselves. Now you can hardly see the line where the old masonry ends and the new begins."

On the banks of the river, crowds of Germans and Americans alike had spread their blankets, drinking beer and singing, waiting for the illumination. Vickie chose this spot deliberately, for she knew that most of the Americans would be down by the river or in the boats, and those who thought of the Philosophenweg, would not venture far beyond their parked cars.

She listened to the faint sounds of the accordion playing Gaudeamus Igitur. It reminded her of Sigmund Romberg's delightful Heidelberg operetta, *The Student Prince,* in which the old student song was used.

"We're safe here, lost in the crowds," Henri said with a smile. "We're lucky to have a place to sit down. See those people hanging out of their windows?" He pointed to the houses below them.

Vickie smiled. "Look how crowded those boats are on the river."

The excursion boats loaded with spectators positioned themselves for a better view. As they waited, the twilight haze that shrouded the red-tiled roofs, melted into the night. At nine o'clock sharp the whole city, an instant before studded with glittering lights suddenly was plunged into darkness. Henri turned Vickie's head toward him and kissed her deeply on the mouth. "Don't!" she whispered, pushing him away, "There are people around us."

He laughed. "So what? You think we're the only ones doing this?"

An explosion echoed through the valley drowning his words and an instant later, a cloud of red smoke billowed from the castle's windows. Soon, the whole fortress was silhouetted in crimson light against the dark mountain. For a while, the air hissed and the castle burned until its sharp outline began to blur and recede into the night.

So realistic was the eerie sight, that only when the old bridge below was illuminated in a similar manner and the fireworks mushroomed in the sky, did the illusion of the seventeenth century fire disappear.

"No wonder Goethe called this bridge the most beautiful in the world. He was inspired by this city," Henri said.

"I know," Vickie replied. "I've seen the house on Hauptstrasse where he lived when he visited Heidelberg."

The spectacle was so impressive that they drove to Dantestrasse without speaking. Vickie did not mind the late hour, did not ask to be taken home. With Brian gone, she had given the cook a few days off; there was no one to check on her whereabouts, and for the first time, she stayed with Henri overnight.

In those unhurried hours she enjoyed the comfort of the mind not burdened by the limits of a stolen moment: The pleasure of endearments, the contact of their bodies, the stirring in her veins, the closeness of his face above her.

In the morning, Henri said: "I have the whole day off today, Vickie. Why don't you be my guide for the Schloss?"

Vickie demurred. "I don't dare, Henri. It's the most likely place to run into people I know. Everyone takes their visitors there."

Henri studied her for a few moments. "My darling," he said softly, "we can't go on like this forever. You know that, don't you?"

Vickie waited.

"We stumble through life sharing crumbs of time. When are you going to tell Brian?"

"Tell him what?"

"About us, ask him for a divorce."

Something tightened her stomach, then reached up and squeezed her heart. "I can't, Henri."

"What do you mean, you can't?"

"Nothing has changed between us. I love you and always will, but I can't marry you."

"My God, what do you want from me? I'm living in Western Europe, I'm not in Russia, so why can't you ignore what I do with Igor? Are you going to let your happiness slip away a second time?"

"We're both prisoners of our convictions, aren't we?" Vickie said. "But that's not the point, Henri. Too many things have changed since Shanghai. I wouldn't hurt Brian. My family is in America now. Too many people would be hurt." She shook her head. "I can't."

He pulled her to him. "Isn't love supposed to conquer all?"

"Only in romantic novels. But in real life we don't have that luxury. We're not an island to ourselves, Henri. I love you, but I won't leave Brian. So let's take this moment while we can."

Henri showered her with kisses, held her close. "No! I'll never let you out of my sight again. I'll follow you wherever you go. You're mine, if not in the eyes of the law, then before God. He gave us our love, a true bonding. Nothing will ever change that. Surely you know it."

CHAPTER TWENTY-ONE

The next day Vickie was due for her routine physical exam. On the way to the 130th Station Hospital, she tried not to think of her parting dialogue with Henri. In spite of his admission, she knew she would continue to see him for as long as she and Brian remained in Germany.

After the doctor examined her, he looked at her with a broad smile and asked: "Are you feeling all right? No nausea?"

Surprised by his question, Vickie answered with a question of her own: "I'm fine, why do you ask? Is anything wrong?"

The doctor laughed. "Nothing is wrong. On the contrary, I'm delighted to find you in such good shape early in your pregnancy. Congratulations!"

Vickie gasped. "Are you sure?"

"As sure as I can be. The pregnancy test will confirm my findings. Haven't you wondered about missing your period?"

Yes, of course. She had been so involved with her clandestine meetings with Henri, she had given it little thought. She left the hospital as if propelled by wings.

I'm going to have a baby, she thought. A cute, plump baby all my own to cuddle and love. Brian is due home tomorrow. I can hardly wait to see his face when I tell him.

Driving home from the hospital, she watched the streets with a smile on her face. Women hurried along the sidewalks with bland, pensive faces, carrying knitted sacks loaded with heavy groceries and walking with a purpose. Stodgy people, those. She didn't understand them. But today it didn't matter. Today she loved everyone.

The next day, when Brian climbed the stairs to the living room, Vickie was waiting for him with a bottle of champagne and three glasses.

"What's the occasion?" he asked, a little annoyed at the third glass. "Who's coming?"

"I need two glasses for myself," Vickie said with a mischievous smile, and when Brian raised his brows, she pointed to her belly, "because there are two of us now."

He gasped, stood for a moment transfixed, then grabbed her by the waist and lifting her off the floor, twirled around.

"I can't believe it! After all this time! My wife is pregnant, I'm going to be a father!"

And in the days and weeks that followed, he walked about with a perpetual smile on his face.

Vickie's morning sickness was mild and soon disappeared. Emotionally, however, she was torn. After her initial elation, the thrill of long-hoped motherhood was tainted with doubts. Whose child was she carrying? She wanted to believe it was Brian's; it would be so much easier if it were Brian's.

She didn't tell Henri about her pregnancy. He would be sure that the baby was his. He mustn't know. She couldn't risk the possibility of his going to Brian and insisting on a divorce. He had called their love a bonding of body and soul. Much as she yearned for motherhood, she caught herself willing the days and weeks to slow down before the change in her figure forced her to break with Henri.

Even sleep brought no respite. Her dreams were disturbing, for although the scenes were different, the theme was always the same. Once she dreamt that she was pushing a cart up a slippery mountain, and like Sisyphus' stone, every time she was within reach of the top, the cart would slide down to the bottom. Another time she was swimming toward shore but instead, was pulled by an undertow farther out to sea.

There was something else: during one of Brian's trips on TDY, she had defied him. When she had mentioned to Henri her desire to work, he said he was sure her services would be welcomed and recommended she ask at the Public Affairs Section of the Army Headquarters. She was skeptical, remembering what Brian had told her. Nevertheless, she checked, and was surprised when the officer in charge seemed eager to give her work.

"We have no trouble with the German language, Mrs. Hamilton," he had said, "but we always need help with the French."

So, Henri had been right. Had Brian deliberately misled her? Well, so be it. She got a contract translating from French into English, and English into French, and did her work at home.

Upstairs, in the mansard room, she spread out the papers and her dictionaries on a table, and worked undisturbed several hours a day. She was not going to hide it from Brian, but then why volunteer the information? Her papers were left on the table in full view of anyone who entered the room. Translations were easy, mostly resumés of public affairs activities.

Although she enjoyed her work, she could not forget her heartache.

Every week when she went to meet Henri, she intended to tell him that their affair was over, but once in his arms, her mind was silenced. She mustn't go on like this. Brian was so happy about the baby, so solicitous of her, so kind. Ever since he learned that she was pregnant, he couldn't do enough for her.

She couldn't leave him. Not only because of her loyalty to him, but also because she was an American now. She remembered how often she had been overcome with an exultant emotion whenever she attended military parades at the Presidio and stood gazing at the flag. Her eyes blurred by tears, she listened to the band play the national anthem. It was *her* anthem, *her* flag, *her* country.

And Henri still hoped to live in Russia someday. She and her baby in Russia? She shuddered. Never.

So, it was a matter of loyalties: both to her new country and to the man who had given it to her.

One day, Brian discovered her work. Vickie saw the annoyance on his face as he tried to conceal it.

"If it fills your days while you wait for the baby, I won't object," he said. "But after the baby comes—" he shook his head and walked out of the room…

Vickie didn't want to start an argument. With the help of a nanny he had promised to hire for the baby, she should be able to spend a few hours a week on her work.

She yearned to go to Bavaria with him, where she hoped to renew that warm tenderness they had in the beginning of their marriage, and where she would try to cure herself of that other love that had such sharp edges of ecstasy and pain. But at the end of September, when she asked him again, Brian spread his arms apologetically and told her that he had to go to Berlin on yet another TDY.

                *   *   *

After he left, Vickie fled to Berchtesgaden. She left a note in Henri's apartment telling him that she was going away for a few days to think things over and for him not to look for her.

She made reservations at the sumptuous Berchtesgadenerhof, built by Hitler for his senior staff, and now requisitioned by the U.S. Army. Her suite of rooms overlooked the Watzmann Mountain that lorded it over Berchtesgaden from a distance. The luxurious appointments of her suite delighted her: A mahogany and glass cabinet filled with sparkling crystal goblets; soft armchairs upholstered in blue damask; a Meissen lamp on the marble-topped nightstand.

Enveloped in a cloud of warmth under the eiderdown comforter she slept later than she could ever remember, and discovered the unimaginable freedom of having no obligations to anyone. She realized she had never lived alone, had never had the opportunity to think singularly of her own needs. There had always been her parents, or Nina, or later, Brian and his career. Now, she had the leisure to balance the bank account of her life.

She left the hotel and walked down the main road to the village of Berchtesgaden. Although the day was overcast, and the smell of rain was in the air, she gave in to the temptation to stop at an outdoor café overlooking the valley below. Over a cup of hot chocolate, she admired the spectacular view. A row of houses, their balconies studded with flower pots, zigzagged up a steep hill on the other side of the valley, and somewhere high above them Hitler's hideaway, The Eagle's Nest, attracted a steady flow of tourists.

Vickie sipped her chocolate. Life pulsated and moved around her with a purpose. And what was *her* purpose? What was she doing alone in a Bavarian tourist town without her husband?

Avoidance. One of the emotional tortures she brought upon herself. Where was the strength to sever the cord that tied her to Henri? Her youth…Her Russian life in Shanghai…He had been such a vital part of both. Oh, dear God. How could she not see him again, not lie in his arms, not listen to his heart and his voice? Some people go through life without ever having to make such choices, but she was condemned to do so twice.

Two men drinking beer at the table next to her were loud, and suddenly their raucous voices grated on her nerves. She paid her bill and walked toward town, passing a small chapel in an old churchyard. But when she reached the village, the quaint tourist shops full of wood carvings and Hummels and velour Bavarian hats that had appealed to her so much when she had first arrived in Germany, now oppressed her. She turned around and hurried back to the hotel.

She walked out on the small balcony of her room. The towering mountains were so close, she imagined she could reach out and touch them. An illusion. Just like the illusion of being free of obligations, free of schedules, free of decisions. Especially of decisions.

Tomorrow she would take a tour of Hitler's *Eagle Nest* and then return to Heidelberg.

She slept fretfully, and in the morning, still tired, went on the tour. Standing on the concrete floor of the gutted bunker, she heard the guide's monologue, the tourists' questions, shreds of conversation floating in the dark and gloomy hideaway. Her body stiffened with a pervasive fear. Why had she come here into this place of lingering rage and madness?

Back in Berchtesgaden, she left the bus and walked briskly toward the hotel, welcoming warm rain on her face. Tiny rivulets of water gurgled in the gutters by the sidewalk. A Volkswagen rolled by, its tires hissing on the wet pavement.

A German woman caught up with her, the heels of her walking shoes clicking alongside. She raised her umbrella to share it. Vickie glanced at her gratefully. "*Danke schön!*"

"*Schreckliches Wetter,*" The woman said.

"*Ja wohl,*" Vickie answered.

They walked on, and at the red carpeted entrance to the Berchtesgadenerhof, Vickie thanked the woman and went in.

People walked, spoke of the chores at hand, laughed and loved. Vickie shook off the doubts of her mind. This was 1951 and the war was long over.

In her room, she took off her clothes, wrapped herself in a robe and lay down on the bed. The rain had stopped. A sparkling light from the window fell on her face, and she shut her eyes against its brightness. Somewhere in the hallway a door slammed and arrhythmic footsteps of two people passed by her door. Then the quiet, and something akin to a tentative peace. She yearned to still the rampage of her thoughts, to doze without disturbing dreams.

She slipped her hand inside her robe, moved her hand over her belly in circles. Please Lord, let the baby be Brian's. Everything would become good and simple: a close knit family, a child to cherish and love, with no place in her heart to mourn what could have been.

She must have slept, for when she opened her eyes, the sun was low over the mountains, its cool, opalescent light diffused in the murky skies. As she rose, she realized that she had not rid herself of the beehive of irksome thoughts she'd produced during the day. This then, was the scourge of loneliness, and suddenly, she wanted no part of it. Quickly, she put on a soft pink knitted dress, retouched her makeup with a matching pink lipstick, brushed her hair off her face, and glanced at her watch. Six o'clock. She should go down for dinner.

There was a knock on the door. She opened it and stood transfixed.

She had asked him not to follow her in the note she had left for him, but did she really mean it? Oh, nothing mattered, not her resolutions, her decisions, but to have him here, with her, alone in this idyllic town of Berchtesgaden. A wild, unreasonable joy surged through her. Her arms flew up around his neck and held him close.

"You came."

"I couldn't stay away," Henri whispered in her ear, holding her tightly in his arms. "I had to come. How could I pass up such an opportunity to have you all to myself for a few days?"

He smiled mischievously. "Your cook was most cooperative when I called. She told me where you were." He raised her chin, touched her mouth with his lips. "You smell of roses and lavender and your special scent I love so much. My darling."

Vickie pulled away in sudden alarm. "You can't stay here, Henri. This hotel is popular with a lot of families we know in Heidelberg. We can't be seen together. Oh, you shouldn't have come!"

"I've already thought of that and I'm taking you to Salzburg. I've rented a room at the Osterreichischerhof Hotel."

*   *   *

They had three days. Vickie insisted on taking a separate room under her own name. "I can't risk disappearing for three days," she explained. "In case of any emergency what excuse could I give for using an assumed name? Besides," she added, "I want to stay as close to the truth as I can. If Brian and I come to Salzburg, I don't want to pretend that I have never been here before."

Above the marble lobby the wide, red-carpeted stairs led to their second floor rooms overlooking the Salzach River and the old town of Salzburg. At night, the cathedral domes were floodlit in golden brilliance, and high on a cliff behind them, the fortress of Hohensalzburg glowed with a pale green luminescence, guarding the streets below from the twentieth century.

So beautiful.

In the mornings, they ate croissants, sweet butter and jam, orange juice and coffee, served with monogrammed paper napkins that said Good Morning in three languages.

"What luxury. You're spoiling me, Henri," she cried, "There isn't such elegance even at the Berchtesgadenerhof."

He smiled. "Nothing is too elegant for you, my love. That's why I chose this hotel. To me, it's the most beautiful in town."

He blew at her lowered lashes, watched her eyelids flutter like frightened butterflies. Leaning over, he kissed her hand, his voice choked with emotion. "I never want this moment to end. Let's stay in, the whole day."

She flushed and shook her head. "I want to see this charming town."

They drove across the river in his rented Opel and parked on the old market square below the geranium-dressed balcony of the Tomaselli Café, then walked to the narrow shopping street with its profusion of filigreed guild signs hanging suspended over the street: a twisted pretzel over a bakery, a bottle above the wine shop, a brass key over the locksmith's door.

The store windows were filled with brightly colored dirndles, woodenware painted with red hearts and flowers, long, curved smoking pipes, Tyrolean hats. But the street was packed with people, a sea of moving, staring faces. Vickie turned back. At the door to a sweater shop Henri stopped.

"How about one of those embroidered sweaters for you, darling?" he said.

Vickie paused. At the entrance, an old man in worn, shining lederhosen stood smoking a pipe. His blue eyes, deep-set in a weather-beaten, creased face, looked at her with sustained scrutiny.

Vickie turned and hurried on. "I'd rather have a glass of wine instead," she said.

They stopped at a restaurant in a shopping arcade, and drank a fruity Ausläse served to them in bulbous glasses with flared stems. In a nearby candy shop, they bought Mozart kugeln individually wrapped in gold foil with a picture of Mozart on top.

"Do you suppose this was Mozart's favorite candy?" Vickie asked, savoring the delicious marzipan-filled chocolate.

Henri smiled. "They didn't have chocolates in his day, silly. Whoever created these kugeln, though, was a genius."

Half a block away, they stopped at the house where Mozart was born and lived with his family. On the worn wooden floor of the walkup apartment they stood entranced before his piano, its keyboard protected by a glass cover. In the alcoved kitchen, Vickie looked at the blackened pots and pans stored on the wood stove used by Mozart's mother. The ceiling was low, the room dark.

"How tragic that Mozart died in the prime of life," Vickie said. But as they drove across the bridge to a flower garden, she added: "Yet the town is full of his music and I suppose always will be."

*   *   *

One more day, and then the final one. It must be final.

"What would you like to do this morning?" Henri asked, putting his arms around her as she stood gazing at the old town, its contours now softened by the falling rain. "This is our last day."

She freed herself. "We haven't gone up to the Fortress yet, or visited the Hellbrunn Castle. I've heard there are trick fountains in the park."

Henri laughed. "Yes, there are. I've seen them. Some of them are hidden in the center of stone benches. The castle was once owned by an Archbishop who was a prankster and delighted in soaking his unsuspecting guests. Can you imagine the havoc it must have caused as they sat on those benches in their seventeenth century finery? But darling, it would take our whole morning to visit the place, and we have so little time left. Let's have lunch at the Goldener Hirsch Hotel instead."

He took her back to the narrow street with the guild signs, and led her to the Hotel, its framed filigreed sign of a golden, leaping deer, hanging above the entrance.

They were ushered up narrow steps into a low ceiling dining room where they ordered lox sandwiches and dark Gösser beer.

After the waiter left, Henri looked around the room at the small tables covered with starched white cloths, then reached over and took Vickie's hand in his. "Remember when we used to sit in the outdoor café in Jessfield Park?"

She nodded and he went on, "We talked for hours about books and music." His eyes focused on a far memory. "Once we had a heated discussion about a book you read. I forget now what it was."

"I think it was Goncharov's *Oblomov,* and we discussed the term coined from that book."

"Yes, of course. I remember now. *Oblomovism.* I said that the indolent landowner like Oblomov was exactly the type who caused the revolution, and you argued that Goncharov created a fictional character who seldom existed in real life."

Vickie changed the subject. "We also talked about Tchaikovsky. Do you know that his First Piano Concerto is often played on classical music radio stations?"

"And hearing that Russian music doesn't make you homesick for Russia?"

"How can I be homesick for Russia when I've never lived there?"

"You know very well what I mean."

He turned her hand palm up and traced his finger over the creases.

"I wish I knew the art of palm reading," he said studying her hand. "My mother knew a peasant in Siberia who could do that."

"Why would you want to see into the future? It would frighten me to know when my life would end."

"I'm not afraid of death. If I knew how much time I have left on earth, it would give me an incentive to accomplish more in the years ahead."

"And if your life were to be interminably long, wouldn't that make you lazy?"

He laughed. "Not at all. I would only schedule my work at a less frenetic pace."

Vickie studied him. New lines had appeared at the corners of his mouth. Lines of stress? Surely not of age. His dark hair was still thick. He was only thirty-two.

"And you are working at a frenetic pace now?" she asked, pulling her hand away.

"I'm not sure. Perhaps I intentionally make it so to fill a void." He dropped his voice. "It can never be filled without you, Vickie."

He looked at her for a long while, his eyes intense, until she could stand his gaze no longer. This was the moment. It had to be. Where was her courage to say what she had intended to tell him all along?

"There's something I have to tell you, Henri."

She heard the words coming from a distance, as if another person was using her voice.

"And there's something I have to tell you, too. But go ahead, you tell me first."

"Henri, I want you to give up the apartment in Heidelberg. After we leave here, I can't see you again." She clasped her hands, then met his glance. "I can't. This is madness."

"My dearest, our lives are bound by destiny, and there's nothing you can do about it. I have a confession to make. I didn't follow you to Bavaria just to spend a few days alone with you."

When she started, he raised his hand. "I mean, that was only part of my reason. The other, the main reason, was to tell you that I have orders for a new assignment. I must leave Germany in a couple of days and I didn't want to be gone when you returned to Heidelberg."

So, destiny was helping her after all. She should feel delivered of a crushing burden, but something sharp and hot filled her chest, quickened her breath.

"Where are you going?" she whispered.

"To the French Embassy in Washington. So, you see, darling, fate would only have us meet again."

"Not like this. Never like this!"

"You're rejecting me? Just like that?"

Rejection. What a terrible word. A dreadful scene flashed before her eyes: Peter Sokolov throwing her, an innocent four-year old, out of his office and calling her a bastard…

"My love hasn't changed," she said softly.

The waiter brought their food, poured the beer.

"My dear," Henri said, "some day we'll see each other again. The day you return to America, I'll be there, waiting for you."

"America is big. We may not be anywhere near Washington."

"I'll find you."

"No, Henri. You mustn't. Ever."

"I won't accept that. You know it. Sooner or later, you'll be mine. But let's not talk about it now. Let's enjoy what hours we have left."

Vickie toyed with her fork. "I hope that after living in America for a while," she said, "you'll realize the folly of your Soviet connection."

"In that respect, I shall never change. The socialist system works well in Russia."

"Interesting, isn't it, that you continue to use the word socialism, rather than communism. Why not true democracy for Russia, the kind we have in America?"

"It would never work in Russia. For centuries the Russian was told what to do and how to behave. Given complete freedom, he wouldn't know what to do. He'd be lost."

Vickie spread her hands helplessly. "Oh, why are we arguing, forcing our differences upon each other! I'm glad you're going to America. You'll see for yourself that I'm right."

"I doubt it, and sooner or later you'll come to understand my faith in Russia."

They finished their meal talking about forgettable things. An air of unfailing politeness between them prevailed, and it widened her grief.

Driving back to the Osterreichischerhof Hotel, Vickie looked out the window. An old shopkeeper was sweeping the sidewalk with a broom, an exercise in futility, given the town's endless bustle. A thin woman in a gabardine raincoat, carried a shopping bag full of packages to the front door of a house. A recalcitrant gray cat, awakened from a nap on the steps, arched its back and, baring its teeth, refused to move out of the way.

Vickie turned, and as they crossed the bridge, she looked at the river, nothing human seemed to ruffle the placid waters…

That night, they ate lightly, drank champagne, held hands. In her room, as the ornate Dresden clock on the dresser ticked away, Vickie started to pack her suitcase. Something to do, anything, except sit idly and watch the minutes slipping away. Gently, Henri took the linens out of her hands, and pulled her toward him. She didn't resist. The last time. She must have cried the words in her heart. Her lips trembled.

The maid knocked on the door asking to ready the bed for the night; Henri sent her away. Outside the day darkened, then gradually, glittering stars filled the sky. The flood lights illuminated the domes across the river, and soon the city slept. In the muted light of the room, they clung to each other, and over and over their shadows blended and merged. Their passions soared to spend themselves, the sensations more intense in their awareness of tomorrow's parting. But neither the caresses nor the strength of his embraces could erase her sadness.

The sun shone in a blue sky the next morning. What right did the city have to look so stunningly bright and cheerful?

"I'll get the taxi to the train station myself, don't go down with me," she said to Henri. There was so much more she wanted to say, but didn't.

Quickly, blindly, while the porter was still in the room, she ran down the stairs and into the safety of the peopled street.

CHAPTER TWENTY-TWO

When Vickie got home, Brian was waiting for her in the living room. She walked in slowly, careful to conceal her shock at seeing him home early.

"I didn't expect you until tomorrow. Had I known, I would have come home earlier," she said dropping her purse on the couch and kissing him on the cheek.

"And I didn't expect to find you gone. Why didn't you wait until we could go together?"

"I asked you several times, and you always put me off, so I decided to go to Bavaria by myself before I got too heavy."

"Why didn't you at least tell me that you were planning to go? Why the secrecy?"

"No secrecy, Brian. I decided on the spur of the moment, that's all. Is that a crime?"

"There's no need to be sarcastic. You can't blame me for being surprised." Brian sat down at the table with a stack of mail. "Tell me," he said, "what did you do in Berchtesgaden?"

She told him about the quaint village and the Eagle's Nest and the beautiful hotel she stayed at.

"I hope you didn't go down the chute in the Salt Mines, did you? In your condition..."

"Salt mines? No one mentioned the salt mines to me."

"Then what did you do the rest of the time?"

Something alerted Vickie to the danger hidden in his question. Maybe it was his tone of voice that sounded too casual, or because he didn't look at her when he asked it, but pretended to busy himself with the papers. Suddenly, it hit her. He had asked what she did in Berchtesgaden. Of course! A giant wave of fear surged over her—he had found out where she was from their cook and called Berchtesgadenerhof…

She pulled out a chair and sat down, blessing her foresight in having taken a separate room under her own name in Salzburg. If Brian had checked, the desk clerk would have confirmed that her presence there.

He looked at her now. "I asked what did you do with the rest of your time in Berchtesgaden?"

She tried for a light touch. "There wasn't much to do in Berchtesgaden for a pregnant lady alone, so I spent three days in Salzburg."

"Did you rent a car?"

Vickie forced herself to breathe evenly. "This is becoming an inquisition, Brian, and I don't like it. But to answer your question: no, I didn't rent a car. A gentleman overheard me telling the desk clerk that I needed to get to Salzburg, and offered to drive me there. Once in town, I walked everywhere. I didn't go to Hellbrunn Castle, but we can do it together sometime. I understand it's great fun. Now, if you're through questioning me, may I please go upstairs and freshen up?"

Brian nodded, and Vickie fled to the bedroom. That was a close call. When he called the hotel, he must have learned that she had left with a man. He'd tried to trap her, he actually had tried to trap her. She pressed her hand against her chest to control her heart's galloping rhythm. Nausea rose to her throat and she barely made it to the bathroom.

When she emerged shaking, her skin clammy, Brian was there to support her around the waist. "Oh, hon, I'm sorry to have upset you," he said. "I'm a fool to have questioned you. Do you want some hot tea or bouillon?"

"No, thank you."

He hesitated, then kissed her on the forehead. "You better rest now." He turned to leave, then stopped. "Oh, I almost forgot. There's a letter for you from Ross."

"Ross?"

Brian nodded and brought the letter.

How strange. This was the first letter from her brother-in-law since they left the States. Why now? She tore the envelope open and began to read:

> Dear Vickie, Ross wrote, No doubt you're surprised to hear from me, and I'm sorry that Nina too is a poor correspondent, but I know that Lydia has kept you informed about our lives. I'm sure you're wondering why I'm writing now, so I'll come straight to the point. Nina has walked out on me. True, it's on a trial basis 'to find herself' as she put it, whatever that means. I'm wondering if she would have done this if Lydia hadn't made it so easy for her by offering to take care of Kenny while she's gone.
>
> Nina has changed since Kenny's birth. She is sullen, hardly talks, and I'm not sure she knows just what it is that she's searching for. Tell me, how do you feel about your Russian background? Personally I'm proud of it, but would you believe that Nina wanted me to change my name legally? When I refused, she asked that I at least change the 'v' at the end of my name to 'w' to make it sound less Russian. I wouldn't do it and we had a fight. After that, she decided to leave. She has divorced herself from everything Russian, doesn't go to church, and kept putting off christening Kenny until she ran out of excuses and gave in to Lydia's pressure. Nina has been corresponding with her old friend, Claudette Jobert in Paris and that's where she is now. I understand Claudette is not married and has a career in the fashion world. I worry what

kind of influence she'll have on Nina. What is this Claudette like, Vickie? If I knew what Nina's problem really is, we could work it out, I'm sure. But the truth is I don't know what made her change so, and she won't talk about it.

I don't believe in breaking up the marriage without trying to resolve our difficulties. How I wish you were here! I don't want to confide in Lydia because she is so protective of Nina, and I feel she would not be objective. You'd think that Russian-minded and religious as she is, she'd scold Nina for refusing to go to church or participate in any Russian Community functions, but instead, she is always able to find excuses for her daughter no matter how outlandish they are. I suppose I could talk to Kiril, but I don't want to cause him any stress and precipitate another heart attack.

I'm sorry to have to involve you in this. You're the only one I feel I can confide in. Could you write to Nina at Claudette's address which I'm enclosing, and ask her to visit you? I have such faith in your sense of values. Find out what's troubling her.

One more thing. Nina's drinking problem has not improved.

There followed a father's proud description of Kenny's proress and the closing words:

> "I feel very fortunate in having you as a sister-in-law. Somehow, and please forgive my sentimentality, I feel you are a kindred spirit and I only wish you were not so far away."

Vickie read the letter again: *Faith and respect for your sense of values*... What would Ross think of her if he knew that she was having an affair with Claudette's brother? Henri. Such an acute sense of loss. She looked out the window. Across the river, the Harlaas Café was lit up. People moved inside, talked and laughed. She could see the waiters bending deferentially over the customers, taking their orders. Far away, they looked like Lilliputians. Closer by, a barge floated downriver and a distant train blew a sharp whistle. Life was going on. Vickie rubbed her forehead and thought about the letter. Of course she knew what Nina's problem was: she didn't love Ross. Her shame at being a stateless Russian was the only reason she married him, but she wasn't trying to make a go of it. Vickie sighed. How could she tell this to him? Nina had accused her of the same thing, and if she ever found out about her and Henri...

Instead of writing, Vickie picked up the phone and called Claudette's apartment in Paris. She came to the phone on a second ring. "Allo?"

"*Bon soir, mon amie,*" Vickie said and to her surprise, Claudette recognized her voice.

"Vickie! What a pleasant surprise. How nice to hear from you." Her guarded tone belied her friendly words. "You're not in Paris, are you?" and when Vickie said that she was calling from Heidelberg, the tension in Claudette's voice eased.

They exchanged pleasantries, and Vickie told her that she was expecting a baby. Instead of congratulating her, Claudette said: "I've heard of a cream that you can rub onto your tummy to prevent stretch marks after the baby is born. If you like, I'll find out and send you a jar."

"Thank you," Vickie managed to say.

So much for the single, career-minded Claudette's priorities. When Nina came to the phone and heard the news, she said: "You're lucky to be in Europe now. It'll be easy to find a nanny here to take care of your kid when it comes. My Kenny is a handful."

"Ninochka, I'm so anxious to see you. When can we expect you here, in Heidelberg?" Vickie asked, hoping her tone of voice did not reveal doubt.

After a moment's hesitation, Nina replied: "I haven't made up my mind yet, but I thought I'd like to stay in Paris another week or so. I'll let you know."

"Who's taking care of Kenny while you are gone?"

"Papa takes care of Kenny while Mother is working, and Ross has him all weekend."

"Oh, please, come soon. Now that you're in Europe, I can't wait to see you." No use insisting any more, or her hot-headed sister might decide not to come at all.

"Please let me know soon when you're coming. It will be so good to have you here with us," she said and rang off.

*   *   *

Ten days later Nina arrived by train looking tired and thinner than Vickie remembered. On the way to the house, Nina talked about Paris, about Claudette's elegant apartment, about her friend's stylish clothes. Vickie listened in silence, happy to see Nina, yet aware of her sister's affected chatter.

That evening, after dinner, they moved to the living room—Vickie with a cup of coffee, and Nina cupping a brandy snifter in her hands. Brian followed, looking from one to the other with an indulgent smile.

"Well, sister-in-law, what do you think about Kenny having a cousin soon?" he asked.

"I'm delighted. Join the sleepless club." Nina's voice lacked enthusiasm. Brian raised his brows and said with a perplexed smile: "I'm afraid I don't understand."

"Wait till you're awakened every four hours for feeding time."

Brian laughed. "Small price to pay for fatherhood. How is Kenny, anyway?"

For the first time since her arrival, Nina's face glowed. "He's a cutie. Full of dimples, walking, and into everything."

Brian rose, kissed Vickie on the cheek and smiled at Nina. "I have some work to do in my study, so I'll leave you to visit." At the door he hesitated. "Hon, are you sure you don't want anything else to eat? Can I bring you a glass of milk, or a cup of hot chocolate?"

"If I accepted every one of your offers, darling," Vickie said smiling, "I'd be twenty pounds overweight already. The doctor said I must be careful not to gain more than I should."

Brian spread his arms in an apologetic gesture. "I'm sorry. I guess I'm an eager-beaver father-to-be. Nina watched him leave the room. Her face seemed hardened and showed signs of strain. She pressed her lips into a determined line, the way she had when she was a child and was refusing to apologize for something she had done. Vickie's glance travelled to Nina's hands holding the brandy snifter. She was clutching the glass too hard, concentrating on the amber liquid too intently. Suddenly, Vickie felt like wrapping her arms around Nina, comforting her. Instead, she put down her coffee cup and asked quietly: "Ninochka, what happened?"

"I just couldn't stand it any longer, Sis. Had to get away." Nina raised her head and looked at Vickie with a crooked smile. "We're not only sisters but also reluctant friends, aren't we? So I'll tell you. Do you know what it's like to have a constant, twenty-four hour responsibility for another human being? An active boy who is totally dependent on you for everything? And I mean, everything."

"I can see where it can become trying, but you sound almost…almost resentful."

"I'm not resentful. I adore him. That's just the point. I'm scared to death he'll hurt himself if I leave him alone. And don't tell me to get babysitters. I already told you how I feel about that. I have this thing about babysitters. I can't explain it, but I don't trust a stranger with Kenny. And so, I'm worn out watching him every second."

How strange, Vickie thought, why doesn't she want to have anyone around? What's really behind this?

"The other day," Nina went on, "I thought Kenny was safe in the playpen in another room. Well, the next thing I knew, there was this terrible shriek. I ran in and there he was, half squeezed under the playpen, his fat bottom sticking out, his bare legs kicking up a storm and howling for all his worth. How he got out of the pen I'll never know, but he's a year old now and is always into some mischeif."

"Every child that age needs watching."

"My neighbor talks on the phone while her two-year old sits on the floor in another room, and she doesn't worry. Anyway, I finally reached a point where I had to get away or lose my mind."

"Getting away for a while is one thing, but telling your husband that you're leaving him is another. Every mother has to go through this phase and that's no reason to leave your husband."

"So, Ross complained to you. I didn't come here to listen to your preaching. I broke away to keep my sanity intact."

Vickie pointed to her brandy. "And that's not the way to do it."

"I can control it. That's the way I cope with my boredom, so leave me alone."

"Do Mama and Papa know about this?"

"There's nothing to know. I don't drink when they're around. And speaking of Mama, she's very much involved in the White Russian community affairs. She plans to take a vacation in a few months and come over. Come to think of it, it'll be just about the time your baby is due."

"Yes, she mentioned it in one of her letters." Vickie hesitated, then asked: "What kind of activity is Mama involved in?"

Nina shrugged. "I don't know exactly. Something to do with keeping the patriotic spirit alive. The old Imperial flag, dreams of restoring the monarchy, that kind of stuff, if you can believe it. Thank God, I'll never be a Russian refugee again. That dirty word."

"Why, Nina! Why are you ashamed of being Russian? Does Mama know how you feel?"

"I don't tell her. I want nothing to do with the Russians, and the less I'm reminded of them, the better. Some of them—" Nina shook her head, "live in the past and shove it down their children's throats with the result that the young people don't know where their loyalty lies."

"Nina, I'm sure there aren't many of those. The majority of the White Russians are proud to be Americans and place their two loyalties where they belong. Why, Ross's parents were a perfect example of that. Of course we must be loyal to America first, but by the same token, we shouldn't be ashamed of our culture and heritage."

"I don't feel that way at all. It irritates me no end to see Papa completely submerged in Imperial Russia. He reads only the old classics and listens exclusively to Russian music. He lives with his memories. He's aged and is slumped over like an old man. Mama says he only perks up in the church where they defer to him as His Excellency, the Prince. It's unhealthy. What good is it to be a prince in exile?"

Vickie sighed. Nina was right, of course, but evidently Kiril's past was what sustained him now, and to take away that illusion would be cruel.

"We can't change him, Ninochka. Let's talk about something else. Tell me more about Claudette."

Nina brightened. "My time with her in Paris was pure heaven. I didn't have to say much. We've been so close in Shanghai that after all this time I could talk to her and she understood. She listened. She's kind and cheerful, and full of excitement. We're still close. It was so refreshing to be with her, to discover there's more to life than having a man in bed making babies, or being stuck in the house changing diapers all day."

"I'd think that sweet Kenny would be ample compensation for what you imagine you're missing out of life. Just think, you're about to become a citizen, acquire a wonderful country, and all the benefits that go with your marriage and security. And last but not least, you have a fine man for a husband."

Nina put down her brandy glass and turned to face Vickie. "He turns me off," she hissed. "I can't bear for him to touch me."

"My God! Why? You must have liked him when you married him. Ross is so good-looking, so charming and loving. What's the trouble?"

"It wouldn't be so bad, if he took his satisfaction and left me alone, but no, he takes forever trying to arouse me and then looks crestfallen when I don't react. I tried to tell him that it doesn't matter, but I guess his male ego smarts and he won't give up."

"That's enough, Nina. I don't want to hear any more."

"Don't you understand? I can't achieve what he wants me to achieve in bed."

"Then you can pretend, damn it!"

Nina sneered. "Voice of experience, sister?"

Shocked, Vickie sat back. What was she doing? She could certainly understand her sister's problem, yet here she was telling Nina to do what she loathed doing herself—pretending that made her feel such shame…

"Be grateful that Ross is trying to satisfy you," she said, thinking of Brian and how he took it for granted that she had had her satisfaction. Suddenly, Henri's image intruded, making her catch her breath. "You'd be surprised to find out what you're missing."

Nina gave Vickie a sly smile. "I've already found out, sister. In Paris. I thought I was frigid, that I was one of those unfortunate women who were destined never to reach an orgasm. I was wrong."

"What are you telling me?"

"That I had the most fulfilling, the most exquisite experience of my life. I was shown that love has many faces."

"In such a short time? Who's the man?"

"Man? There was no man. Why do you think Claudette hasn't married? She's taken me to the heights of such ecstasy, I never knew existed."

Vickie stared at her sister. "Claudette?…You mean…"

Nina's mouth twitched with a smug smile. "Yes. And you, dear sister, don't know what you're missing."

Appalled, Vickie whispered, "Oh…my…God! How could Claudette…"

"She could and she did!" Nina's voice rose. "What's more, I don't regret one moment of it."

"I'm shocked. I didn't expect this…this…" Vickie shook her head and let the sentence hang.

"Are you being righteous or jealous, big sister? And who are you to sit in judgment? We both went into our marriages while loving another."

Vickie bit her lip. That part was true. She of all people had no right to shame Nina. But resentment? For what? For always being second best to her sister? The thought stunned her and deep in her soul, a shocking truth stirred. But she had promised herself to take care of Nina, not resent her.

For a few moments she sat still, then took Nina's hand and squeezed it. "I'm sorry. I love you, Ninochka, and I just don't want you to be hurt. Think what would happen if Ross found out about...about you and Claudette."

"I don't intend to move in with her. This was only an interlude that I...I..." Nina's face crumpled and she began to cry, handkerchief pressed against her mouth.

Vickie stroked Nina's hair. The same luxurious red hair, the same beautiful face as she sat there trying to stifle her sobs. She looked vulnerable and pathetic. Vickie moved closer and put her arm around her. "Stop crying, Ninochka. I love you, my little sister," she said softly.

Nina freed herself, moved away, and wiped her tears. Without looking at Vickie, she took a sip of the brandy, then said: "You can't imagine how stifled I feel, living with a man I don't love. My whole life is a mess, and I blame Papa for it. I shouldn't have listened to him. I should have married Joseph and gone with him to Australia. I loved him. I still do. I know, I know! Don't look at me like that. I went into it with my eyes open, but I had no idea what it was going to be like."

Nina put down her brandy snifter and clasped her hands. "That awful day when Sara died will haunt me forever."

Vickie leaned forward. "Tell me about it."

"Papa brainwashed me about Joseph being Jewish. He kept saying that I shouldn't give him false hope, but I didn't think Joseph was that serious about me. When he proposed that afternoon, I stumbled over words but he guessed the real reason. Vickie, I'll never forget the expression on his face when it finally sank in. He turned and ran away from me.

"What I didn't know was what happened that night. Evidently Joseph was so distraught by my refusal, he left the tent and went for a walk in the jungle. When the typhoon hit, Sara ran after him. Mama wrote to you how Sara died. It was terrible. They found her with a piece of metal roof imbedded in her back."

Vickie put her hands on her ears. "Please, Ninochka, no more!"

Nina went on. "I'm sure Mama didn't tell you what happened the next day."

Vickie shook her head.

"Papa went over to their tent with some food Mama prepared. Our tents were side by side, so I heard the whole conversation between Papa and Jacob. Papa said that he felt indirectly responsible for Sara's death and Jacob yelled at him that Papa was directly responsible. He called Papa a hypocrite. I can still hear his words. He said: 'Did you ever stop to think that Jesus Christ, your God, was a Jew? You pray to a Jew, yet you brainwashed your daughter not to marry one of His people. And then you tell me that you're not prejudiced.' Papa tried to protest, but Jacob interrupted him and shouted: 'You and your kind say: 'He's a friend of mine even though he's Jewish.' And when Papa didn't say anything, Jacob repeated: 'How does it sound to you? 'Even though he's Jewish?'

"Papa tried to calm him down but Jacob ordered him out of his tent. Papa's face was flaming red when he came back into our tent. Everyone in the neighborhood heard the argument. I'm sure people were snickering behind his back that a Jewish doctor told the prince off and threw him out of his tent. Vickie, I felt sorry for Papa at that moment but I felt he had it coming to him. To this day I blame him for influencing me and mad at myself for not being strong enough to defy him at the time."

Vickie took both Nina's hands in hers. "Don't be bitter about the past, Ninochka. You don't really know how your life with Joseph would have turned out. You have much to be grateful for now."

Words poured out easily enough, but deep inside Vickie was shocked. Poor Sara. Poor orphaned Rosen men. What a tragedy. Papa *was* responsible for what happened. Indirectly, true, but responsible nonetheless. Vickie sighed and hugged her sister without words.

The next morning, after Brian left for work, the sisters lingered over coffee. Nina stirred the sugar in her cup absent-mindedly. "Being with Claudette in Paris was like being let out of prison," she said, "and I don't know but that given a chance again…"

"Don't say it. Don't even think it," Vickie said, and when Nina didn't answer, she took her sister's face between her hands and turned it toward her.

"Ninochka? Please!"

"I never intended to leave Ross for good," Nina said. "I'm not stupid. Without a profession and college, I wouldn't go very far with a child on my hands. I'm not about to give up my security and my new country." She seemed tired and defeated, her face red with blotches.

"I'm sorry, Ninochka, that things haven't worked out for you, but please, give Ross a chance."

"I know. I have trouble keeping my mouth shut. I'm sorry I upset you. I promise to try and make things right between Ross and me. Good enough?"

Vickie nodded, still worried about her sister's frame of mind. "Just keep reminding yourself how much Ross loves you and how fortunate all of us are now."

*   *   *

Lydia's letters gave no hint of whether she had been aware of Nina's troubled marriage. She wrote about her daily life, about Kiril who was content to stay home and give Russian lessons, about her own satisfying job at the bank, her anticipation of a second grandchild, and her visit to Germany. Of her involvement in the Russian community, she wrote in vague terms.

It's a gratifying work we're doing, Vickie, she wrote in one of her last letters, both Papa and I feel useful and needed and we are involved in a truly worthy cause.

Then, in her last letter, she wrote: I'm worried about Nina. I discovered that she's drinking too much. One doesn't do that unless there's a problem. Is it Ross? I wonder…

Vickie slapped the sheet of paper against her thigh. How like her mother to blame someone else for her younger daughter's problem. Nina could do no wrong in her mother's eyes. She would have to have a heart-to-heart talk with her mother when she arrived in Heidelberg.

CHAPTER TWENTY-THREE

Winter covered the Heidelberg hills with glittering snow. Now and then in the bright sun, heavy clumps slipped off the weighted branches, powdering the cleared roads below with sparkling snowflakes. The crisp air was so still, voices floated down the river in a cadence of fading echoes. Nothing disturbed nature's serenity here, Vickie reflected as she sat by the window of her upstairs bedroom. Wars were fought, young men died, and the vicissitudes of life affected only human beings. How sad it was to hear early in February that King George VI had died in faraway England. He was only fifty-six. His pretty daughter ascended the throne as Queen Elizabeth II. The responsibilities weighing on the young queen! How would it be to have so much on one's shoulders? Thank God WWII was long over and the Korean War was a limited one and would surely end soon. Vickie sighed. When her baby came, God willing, the world would be at peace.

She shifted in her seat. No more wars. Except the Cold War. Why couldn't the Soviets get along with the West? Simplistic wish, that, but what a thorn it was in her side to hear people say: "Those Russians…"

The baby kicked and she moved her hand over her abdomen. She had developed that habit during the last three months when the baby let her know of its presence. She was due in March. Another month and she would hold her child in her arms. My own baby. She savored the words in her mouth. Mine. And Brian's.

Her thoughts were fragmented as she looked down at the street. Two women, bundled in heavy coats with fur collars, woollen stockings and heavy boots trudged uphill on the street below, carrying packages, daily groceries, no doubt. A cream-colored Opel rolled in the opposite direction. Vickie watched its progress along the road. The same model as the one Henri had owned. How was he? Had he fallen in love with America yet, had he changed? A squeezing ache settled in her chest whenever the longing for him surfaced. Would it ever leave?

Somewhere in Washington he waited. If she were to meet him again, accidentally of course, what would she do? What would she say? Somehow she had to stop loving a man who yearned to live in the Soviet Union. She had to think of the future because it belonged to Brian and their child. Henri and their love had to become the past.

Her translation work was a Godsend. It helped to forget things. But at moments like these, when the work was done and Brian had not yet returned from the office, her mind travelled into unwelcome territory.

Her mother was going to arrive a few days before the baby was due. Too bad she hadn't been there to attend the baby shower Betty Campbell had given her. She smiled, remembering. She had never been to a baby shower, and when Betty called to invite her to an afternoon tea, Vickie, cumbersome with her heavy figure, demurred. To her surprise, Brian, who never interfered in her women's club activities, urged her to go.

She went. There were ten women, all wives of the officers with whom Brian worked. When Betty wheeled in a baby buggy overflowing with presents and parked it by Vickie's chair, everyone smiled and looked at her expectantly. Vickie smiled back and glanced at the gifts, all gaily wrapped in pink and blue paper printed with chubby babies, umbrellas, and rain showers.

"Thank you! It is such a surprise. I never had anything like this happen to me before. I mean—" she fumbled for words, "we don't have this custom where I came from. Thank you."

She didn't know what else to say and knew there was something she was supposed to do, but what? Finally, Betty picked up one of the gifts and said: "May I help you unwrap this?"

So that was it. What a strange custom. She had been taught as a child never to open a gift in front of the giver. "You don't show your curiosity by opening it right away," her nanny, Lisa, used to say.

Vickie unwrapped each gift and read the accompanying card, following Betty's example. Then she passed it around the room for everyone to see. In the end, she decided it was a delightful custom. Americans were uninhibited and no one thought her curious or ungracious. Too bad that no one in her family had known to do the same for Nina when she was expecting Kenny. For once, Brian's mother should have said something, but she never mentioned it.

Vickie thought of her mother. A few more weeks of peace and then Lydia would arrive. Brian's mother would follow.

> I don't want to impose on you while Lydia is there, Jane had written, but I do want to come after the baby is born and see my first grandcild. I won't be staying with you as I know you will be busy with the baby and your extra room will be occupied by a new nanny. I invited Louise Chambers to keep me company and the travel bureau reserved rooms for us at the Ritter Hotel.

Jane and the nosy Louise, Vickie thought. She was grateful that Jane had opted for a hotel. Perhaps Jane's first grandchild would mellow her and even Louise might refrain from needling.

*   *   *

March heralded the advent of spring with its dripping icicles and slush, leaving scattered patches of dirty snow on the ground. One Wednesday, a couple of weeks before Vickie was due to deliver, she felt the walls were closing in on her and she wanted to get out of the house. She decided to go shopping on the Hauptstrasse. It was the housekeeper's day off and Brian's afternoon home.

"Is there something specific you want?" Brian asked from his study, "I'll be glad to drive you there."

"No, thanks. I need this time to be by myself." She chuckled to soften what she had said. "Who knows, this may be the last time I'll be able to get out for a while."

"Well, be careful. How long do you think you'll be gone?"

"I really don't know. I have nothing specific in mind, just a stroll up and down the main street, window shop, and maybe stop at a café for a cup of chocolate. I'll probably be gone a couple of hours or more."

She parked the car in a side alley and walked along the Hauptstrasse, stopping occasionally to look in the display windows. In the narrow street, streetcars lumbered noisily past, cars honked and after an hour of idle walking, she walked into a gift shop to escape the grating sounds outside.

On the counter, she found linen placemats with the Florentine turquoise Wedgewood pattern that matched her china set. Surprised to find it in a German store, and pleased by the discovery, she picked out eight placemats. While the woman went to wrap them, Vickie opened her bag to retrieve her wallet. She pulled out her compact and handkerchief, but the wallet was missing. With her hand still inside the purse, she paused and realized what had happened. In a hurry to get out of the house, she had taken the wrong bag. A sinking feeling clutched at her stomach. She had no money with her and worst of all, she had been driving without a license.

Using her hands to help her halting German, she conveyed her problem to the saleslady and asked her to keep the placemats until she returned. She pointed to her wristwatch and said: "*In eine uhr.*"

She drove home resisting the impulse to hurry and watched carefully for pedestrians and other cars. The wife of an American army officer driving in Germany without a license. She felt the perspiration in the palms of her hands. She took her hands off the steering wheel one at a time and wiped them on her coat.

The traffic thinned as she drove along the river and she relaxed. When she reached the house, she was surprised to see a strange car parked in front of the entrance. It had a U.S. military license plate. Who was visiting? She didn't recognize the car.

No one was in the living room. Must be Brian's colleague in the study. Laboriously she climbed the next flight of stairs to the bedroom. Thank God she remembered exactly where she had left her other purse. In her dresser. The bedroom door was closed, and as she approached it, she heard sounds from within. Not words, but...sounds. Puzzled, she frowned and slowly opened the door.

The shades were drawn and in the semi-darkness the white skin shone. She had never seen the look of such ecstasy on Brian's face before. He was half-reclining in an armchair, his head far back, eyes half-closed, mouth open, legs spread apart.

And he was naked.

Kneeling before him, and also naked, was another man, his head between Brian's legs moving rhythmically up and down.

Vickie made a sound. She could not remember afterwards whether it was a gasp or a groan, but the two men sprang up and faced her, horror on Brian's face.

Numb with shock, she started backing away toward the stairs. Knees buckling from under her, she missed the first step and the last thing she saw was Brian's glistening erection and then, oblivion.

*   *   *

She came to at the 130th Station Hospital to the distant sounds of a nurse's voice: "Mrs. Hamilton, Mrs. Hamilton, can you hear me?"

She slowly opened her eyes, and the first face she saw bending over her was not the nurse's but Brian's terrified, anguished face. When full consciousness returned and she focused her eyes on Brian, he turned to the nurse.

"Thank you, nurse. Please leave us alone for a minute."

The nurse raised her brows. "But, Colonel, I must take her blood pressure and pulse, and—"

"Yes, I know, but give us these few moments before you do that. Please?"

Something in his voice was so urgent, that the nurse looked at him curiously, then shrugged and walked out of the room.

"Vickie," Brian said, trying to take her hand but she jerked it away, hid it under the blanket and pressed her elbows against her body to keep from shivering.

"Vickie, please listen to me. I'm sorry. Oh, so sorry you had to find out this way. But please, I beg you, don't tell anyone about this. I told the doctor that you were overtired from shopping and fainted after climbing the stairs. You hit your head on the railing as you fell down to the landing below. I couldn't bring you around. God, I was so scared! The doctor wants to keep you overnight for observation and then I'll take you home. We'll talk then. Please! My whole career is at stake!"

Vickie, who had turned her face away, now looked at him in anger. "Your career? That's all you care about?"

Brian's lips tightened. "I said we'll discuss it at home. Think of our child. All I ask is that you say nothing until we have a chance to talk."

The next day they drove home in silence. Vickie couldn't bear to look at Brian and when they got home, she climbed the stairs without his help. She stood in the bedroom shivering, repelled by the armchair she could see out of the corner of her eye.

"Please, Vickie, sit down. We have to talk."

Brian touched her arm and Vickie threw it off. "Don't touch me! Get away from me!"

"O.K! O.K! I will! But we must talk."

Vickie turned her back toward the chair, sat on the edge of the bed, and buried her face in her hands. "Why? Why did you marry me?"

Brian grabbed her wrists and forced her hands away from her face. "Look at me! I'm still the same man who loves you. I wanted to have a wife and a family. Is that so wrong?"

"It's what you are!" Vickie screamed. "That's what's wrong!"

"Lower your voice. You don't want the housekeeper to hear you."

"I don't care who hears me! Take your hands off me!"

She fought him, then wept, beating the bedspread with her fists.

Brian backed off. "Please, please, I beg you, listen to me! I fought this thing. God knows I've tried to conquer it, but it's not as simple as you'd think. It's only recently that I came to terms with myself. I was born that way, Vickie. Think of the great men like da Vinci, and your own Tchaikovsky."

"Don't try to justify yourself, it's disgusting!"

"I'm not trying to glamorize myself. I'm only saying that there are other men like me and it doesn't interfere with their ability to lead productive lives. Haven't I been a good husband to you? And considerate son-in-law to your parents?"

"Leave my parents out of it. I want a divorce. How can you say you love me after…after…" Vickie choked on the words.

"I could have married any number of American girls if it were just for appearances sake, but I fell for you. Why do you think I took such a chance, marrying you over there, knowing so little about you? Believe it or not, I do love you. Maybe not in the way you expect, and God knows how I wish I could. But we had a good marriage, didn't we? It would have worked if not for yesterday."

Vickie averted her eyes from his pleading face. She thought: I tried to have a good marriage, but it was all a delusion. What now? "I want a divorce," she said, gasping, "I won't ruin your career, I promise. No one will know. Irreconcilable differences, is that what they say to avoid a scandal?"

"There would be a scandal just the same. How do you think it will look for us to divorce right after the baby is born? What explanation could you give to your parents, to my mother? No. No divorce."

She saw a firm line around his mouth, a tightening of his jaw. "What do you mean, no divorce?"

"Just what I said. We stay married. Do you really want to raise your child alone?"

"What kind of father can you be?"

"I am going to be a devoted father, I promise you."

Instinctively, Vickie wrapped her arms around her belly. She had hoped that the baby would be Brian's. Now she wished fiercely, protectively, that it would be Henri's.

"No. I can't bear the thought of what you really are," she said. "After the baby is born, I'll go back home."

"I won't let you. You can't deny me watching my child grow. That other thing has nothing to do with my being a good father. Besides, you'd be punishing our child by depriving it of a loving father."

For a few moments Vickie was silent, then she glanced at him and quickly looked away. "Can you promise that from now on you'll never have sex with a man?"

Brian sighed. "No. That's the one thing I can't promise. I can't change what I am, but what I can promise, is that you will never know about it, never see or hear anything."

In spite of her revulsion, Vickie felt pity for him. "At least you have the integrity to be honest about it. But oh, God, I can't forget what I've seen."

Now she looked at him straight in the eye and saw such utter humiliation that the words strangled in her throat.

"I'll do anything you ask," he pleaded, "never touch you again, give you complete freedom to do as you please, to lead your own life as discreetly as I will. But don't break up our marriage, I beg you."

Vickie rose. No. She could never let him touch her. But lead her own discreet life? She had to love a man before she could go to bed with him. And the man she loved was gone.

Eyes blurred by tears, she tried to pass Brian, but he blocked her way. "At least give yourself some time. Think of the alternatives. Please!" Gently, he pushed her into the armchair.

Instantly, the picture of Brian's naked body flashed before her and her stomach heaved. Pushing his arms away, she rushed to the bathroom.

As she emptied her stomach, she felt a gush between her legs. Shaking, she wiped her face on the towel, then walked slowly out of the bathroom, holding onto the wall.

"Brian! My water has broken. Call the ambulance!"

*   *   *

Through the blur of anesthesia, Vickie heard snatches of conversation, isolated words, but could not grasp their meaning. One moment she thought she saw Brian's smiling face bending over her, and the next, an unfamiliar male voice floated somewhere above her: "You have a boy Mrs. Hamilton." She heard her own tired voice: "A healthy one?"

"You've got it!" came the reply. She felt her mouth spread into a happy smile and then fell asleep.

A long time seemed to elapse before she opened her eyes again. Fully awake now, she saw that she was in a hospital room with an empty bed next to her. She felt rested and nothing hurt. Out of habit, she ran her hand over her abdomen. It was flat. Instantly, memory returned. She had a son! A little boy! Where was he? Anxious, she rang for the nurse, and when she entered, smiling, Vickie raised herself on the elbow. "May I see my baby?"

The nurse nodded. "Of course. But you can't nurse him yet. It takes about twenty-four hours before your breasts fill with milk. I'll bring him to you. A cute fellow."

Dear God, please God, let him be Henri's. Please!

When the nurse returned and placed the little bundle in the crook of her arm, Vickie bent over the infant and stared at his sleeping face. The shape of the jaw, the little mouth with a curved lower lip, the forehead…A miniature of *his* face. There was no mistake.

She sank back on her pillows, weak and trembling. His legacy to her. His hold on her. She wanted to break with the past, but the past pursued.

The baby moved. A warm, sweet-smelling living creature, hers and Henri's. But mostly hers. Yes, she carried him for nine months, she labored to bring him into the world. Suddenly a fierce love surged through her, a fierce, possessive, selfish love. She moved her son closer to her body, leaned over and kissed the moist, pulsating top of the baby's head. "We'll christen you Gregory, American for the Russian Grigory," she whispered, "and call you Grisha. My sweet, darling Grisha. My own."

Brian beamed, telling her how many cigars he gave out at the office and saying that he thought his son was the most perfectly shaped baby in the world. He presented Vickie with a two-karat emerald ring surrounded by tiny diamonds and kissed her on the forehead.

She pushed the jewel box away, her lips quivering. "Don't! Don't do this!"

"Please! That's to say thank you for my son."

Her face burned. She thought: Oh God, not *your* son, not *yours*! But when the nurse brought the baby in and let Brian hold him, Vickie saw his tender smile as tears flowed unabashedly down his cheeks.

"Such a perfect baby," he said but his look, searching Vickie's face, spoke of other things. Anguish, supplication, hope, they were all there.

Ever so gently, he pressed his lips to the baby's forehead, then reluctantly handed him back to the nurse. She took the infant and smiled at Vickie. "Such an adoring father," then looked at the child. "A lucky baby."

Left alone, Vickie saw other young men pass her room to visit their wives and newborns; listened to their laughter, their thrilled voices, their plans for the future.

The future.

Was she really prepared to raise her son alone, conceal the truth from her family, and cause such heartache to Brian? There was no avoiding the truth. She was never truly in love with him, though she desperately wanted to, tried and failed. Who was she to act righteous after her own deceit? The discovery of his homosexuality was more an insult to her pride as a woman than a personal heartbreak. The more she thought about it, the more compassion she felt for him. In some ways they were not so different, she and Brian, both with their obsessive loves.

And so, she went home with the baby and told Brian that they must never speak of *it* again. She insisted on replacing their queen-sized bed with the twin beds from the guestroom and moved the offending armchair out of the master bedroom.

Brian's gratitude was abject. He showered her with gifts and attention but made his presence scarce when he sensed that she needed to be alone.

Lydia arrived two weeks after Grisha was born, and had immediately taken over the running of the house in spite of Vickie's objections.

"You shouldn't be climbing all those stairs so soon after childbirth," Lydia said. "Whoever thought up such a highrise house? This is not San Francisco where land is at a premium. You should rest part of the day and let me take care of the chores. You look peaked."

Helga, the German housekeeper pouted. "*Frau Hamilton,*" she said firmly, "*Die Küche ist meine! Ihre Mutter...*" she didn't finish her sentence and went back in the kitchen, banging the door behind her.

Vickie's stomach tightened. "Mama, please, stay out of the kitchen."

Lydia fumed. "Who's the mistress here? Are you allowing this woman to run your house?"

Vickie wanted to scream and run but instead, she said with an effort: "No, Mama. Only the kitchen, and I'll thank you to leave her alone."

And so it went. She envied Brian's ability to tune out friction that sparked in the house, or hadn't he noticed it at all?

From the very day Lydia arrived, they started off on the wrong foot. Vickie had asked her mother why she thought that Nina's drinking was Ross's fault.

"Why else would Nina drink?" Lydia said. "She's obviously unhappy or she wouldn't need to look for an escape. Maybe she found out that Ross was seeing another woman. It happens, you know, when the wife is housebound with a newborn child and is too tired at night. That's when the husband can stray."

"Mama, I don't think it's like that at all. Have you at least talked to Nina about her drinking?"

"Of course I did. I was stunned when I dropped in unannounced one afternoon and found her staggering in the kitchen." Lydia shuddered. "I'm glad Kiril wasn't with me, it would have been such a shock for him. Anyway, her excuse was that she was bored at home, and when I asked if she talked it over with Ross, she quickly changed the subject. Something is wrong, Vickie, I can sense it."

Vickie bit her tongue. The temptation to tell the truth was great, but who knows what Lydia would advise her darling daughter to do then. Aloud she said: "Mama, you have no right to accuse Ross of straying. He's such a homebody, always working with his hands, fixing things around the house, helping anyone who needs him. Sooner or later, you have to face the fact that Nina is headstrong and spoiled. She needs to be talked to firmly before her drinking gets out of hand. We'll have an alcoholic in the family."

"Now *you're* jumping to conclusions. Alcoholic, no less. I'll see to it that it never happens."

Vickie put her hand on Lydia's arm. "Mama, it's up to Ross to do something about it. Don't interfere, for heaven's sake."

*   *   *

Lydia continued to fuss over Vickie, urging her to rest, and Vickie suspected that her mother only wanted an excuse to handle Grisha. Lydia showed her how to diaper the baby, how to hold the bottle when her breasts were emptied and Grisha was still hungry.

"Mama, now you have to divide your love between Kenny and Grisha," Vickie teased.

Lydia looked surprised. "What do you mean, divide? Not divide, but multiply."

For the first few days, Vickie didn't mind Lydia's overbearing presence, but when she regained her strength, she began to chafe at her mother's meddling behavior. Brian sensed it too.

"When would you like to hire a nanny, hon?" he asked. He wore an ecstatic smile on his face whenever the conversation centered around his son.

Gratefully, Vickie smiled. "As soon as Mama leaves, I'll appreciate some help."

"And when is that going to be?"

"Soon, I think." She almost said 'I hope' but caught herself in time. But Lydia didn't seem in a hurry to leave. She played with her grandchild and enjoyed being waited on by the German housekeeper. Helga was pacified now that Lydia's attention was diverted to guiding Vickie through her first steps as a new mother.

Brian was a tender, indulgent father. Every night when he returned from work, he kissed Vickie on the cheek, then rushed to the living room to pick up Grisha, who had already been fed and bathed, and was lying on a blanket on the floor, cooing happily. This was peace time, play time, and Vickie saw to it that it was never disrupted. But Lydia disapproved. "You should let Brian feed Grisha and change his diaper once in a while, like Ross did with Kenny. It would make him appreciate what a mother has to do while the father is away from home."

"Mama, I don't believe in it. Brian works hard all day, he is the breadwinner in the house, and the least I can do is have the baby ready for him to play with, instead of having him change Grisha's diapers." Vickie paused, reluctant to admit even to herself, the real reason behind it. This was *Henri's* baby...

In a moment, she smiled. "Listen!"

Delightful gurgles came from the living room where she had put Grisha shortly before Brian came home. They went in. Brian was on his hands and knees making faces at the baby, who was kicking his legs and arms and staring at his father, bubbles coming out of his pink mouth.

"I thought newborns didn't smile this early," Lydia said watching them.

"Whether it is a smile or a grimace, we don't know, but they both are enjoying themselves."

"I guess I can't convince you otherwise. Suddenly, you know so much about being a parent. Nina was delighted to let me handle Kenny after he was born. It wouldn't hurt to listen to your mother once in a while."

"It isn't once in a while, Mama, that you find fault with the way I handle Grisha. It is all the time."

"That's the new generation for you, sharp-tongued. I'd never dare to talk back to *my* mother like that."

Vickie sighed. No use starting another argument. No matter how hard she tried, she could never please her mother. But the next day, something hardened inside her. Vickie went down to the dining room while Lydia was finishing her cup of coffee, and without sitting down, said: "Mama, I think it's time for you to go home. I'm sure Papa misses you very much and it isn't fair of you to be away from him this long. I'm perfectly capable now of getting along by myself, especially since we're going to hire a nanny."

Lydia wiped her mouth with the napkin. "I see. I'm not needed anymore, so you're ordering me out of the house."

"Mama, don't make it difficult for me. I'm simply saying that Papa needs you more than I do."

*   *   *

A year had gone by and another autumn tinted the Neckar hills with a profusion of gold and rust foliage. It had been a busy year. For months afterward, Vickie regretted that her mother had left in anger. But no sooner was she gone and a German nurse hired for Grisha, than Brian's mother and Louise Chambers arrived. Vickie sighed whenever she remembered those stressful few days when Jane filled the house with her presence. At least Lydia showed genuine affection for Grisha, but it was different with Jane. She held her first grandchild gingerly in her lap for a minute or two, then gave him back to Brian, and smoothed her silk skirt. "He is heavy, isn't he?" she said, and proceeded to unwrap all the gifts she brought for the baby: a hand-embroidered silk christening dress, matching booties, delicately knit blue sweaters, a silver brush and baby cup, and a set of sleepers and baby blankets. Louise Chambers gushed over the baby but never touched him.

Later, when Brian was out of the room, Jane leaned over the crib, studied Grisha for a while, then straightened. "He is darker than Brian," she said looking at Vickie, and when Vickie held her gaze, she added with a shrug: "Although newborns are frequently that way. Maybe his hair will lighten up later on."

"It may not," Vickie said, trying to keep her voice casual. "After all, my hair is dark, and Grisha may have taken after me."

"It was quite a wonderful surprise," Jane went on, "to learn that you were pregnant, darling. I'm sure Brian told you that there were complications after he had mumps as a youngster. Our family physician was not too optimistic about his ability to father a child." She brushed a fleck off Vickie's shoulder. "I'm delighted to have a grandchild, after all. Take good care of him. Who knows? He may be the only one you'll ever have."

So that's why Jane told her not to hurry with pregnancy that time in San Francisco, and that's why Brian was annoyed after she had gone to see a doctor and suggested that he too have a checkup. Why hadn't he told her this himself? Male pride. And all those years she had worried that she was the one who was barren.

After Jane left and time went by, Vickie resigned to her life. The year was coming to a close and she knew that Brian's assignment in Europe would soon end. She watched the events at home closely. The year before, a polio epidemic had killed over three thousand people and crippled thousands more, but now, with the Salk vaccine being tested, they would surely be safe. Grisha was a toddler, twenty-one months old and already constructing sentences. A bright boy, that one. His hair remained dark, and his eyes were blue-green but Brian never mentioned it.

There was much to be thankful for, and although she was ready to return to the States, there were things back home she worried about: Senator McCarthy's communist witch-hunt for one, and when last January the federal jury in New York had convicted thirteen communists for conspiring to overthrow the U.S.Government, and the Rosenbergs were electrocuted as spies in June, she had been shocked and frightened. What was Henri doing in Washington now? Was he careful? When at last the Korean armistice was signed in July, she was reassured. Maybe the national paranoia would ease and President Eisenhower would see to it that Senator McCarthy was censured. But there were good things that happened too. Vickie never dreamed she would be glad at anyone's death, but when Stalin died in March and Bcria was shot, she was relieved. New leaders, fresh hope.

In the summer of '53, she and Brian went to London, Rome, Vienna, leaving Grisha in the capable hands of his nanny, Ursula. A trained nurse and a spinster at thirty-two, she was young and robust, and fond of American music, making Grisha laugh and repeat 'Arf, arf' when she sang to him *Doggie in the Window*. She adored Grisha, and Vickie was able to travel without concern.

Vickie would have preferred to travel with another army wife instead, but Brian worried about appearances. "How would it look if we never traveled together?" he had said the first time she mentioned it. "At home we have plenty to keep us busy, but there are times when we must get away by ourselves." He looked at her pointedly. "We need to remain friends, Vickie, for both our sakes. Try harder."

And Vickie tried. Counted her blessings, wrote them down on a piece of paper, read them every day, and gradually became used to living with the secret that hung heavily between them. The tension eased, and they never quarrelled anymore, were polite to each other and behaved like civilized friends living under the same roof.

When they visited Paris, she resisted the temptation to visit the House of Christian Dior, so influential now in haute couture. Was Claudette still there? She didn't want to see her. The graceful city, the spoken French around her, tested and teased. At times, walking along the Left Bank, stopping at sidewalk cafés for an omelette and a glass of wine, she thought she heard *his* voice. On several occasions, she turned around startled, only to catch Brian's quizzical look.

Three years in Germany. Long enough. She hadn't seen her stepfather all those years, and Lydia wrote that Kiril was having heart problems. Ross had written a short, noncommittal note thanking her for all that she had done, and because he said nothing else, she knew that things had not improved.

Grisha waddled into the room, whimpering, followed by Ursula. "Mrs. Hamilton," she said in her careful English, "I am worried. Grisha's tummy is running. I fed him rice water and oatmeal, but nothing helps. He also has a little fever."

Vickie rose and picked up her son. He was pale and cranky. "We'll have to take him to the doctor tomorrow morning if he doesn't feel better," she said, feeling the little boy's head. It was warm.

During the night, Vickie took turns with Ursula watching Grisha. By morning, it was clear that the boy was very sick. Brian rushed him to the hospital.

For several days the doctors fought to control Grisha's diarrhea, but the child was apathetic and weak. For hours Vickie sat in the hospital room hoping for improvement. "I don't understand it," she kept saying to Brian when he joined her after office hours, "he was born so healthy." The anxiety in her was fierce and bitter. Surely there was something that could be done. There were all those antibiotics…She felt so helpless.

In keeping a vigil by Grisha's bed, they held hands tightly, and spoke little. Only once, did Brian lose control. "What's the matter with our doctors?" he raged. "Can't they cure a simple diarrhea in a child? Hell, this is the twentieth century!"

At some point, Vickie leaned on Brian's shoulder, and accepted the comfort of his embrace.

At the end of the week, the pediatrician at the 130th Station Hospital said to them: "We've done all we can, but Grisha isn't responding to treatment. We are getting ahead of the infection, but his diarrhea has weakened him and he won't take any food from the nurses. I don't know what else we can do. I'm so sorry…"

He patted Vickie on the arm and started to walk away. Vickie grabbed his sleeve. "Can't you think of anything? Anything at all that would make him eat?"

The doctor hesitated. "You may try feeding him yourself," he said. "Sometimes a child will take food from his mother when he won't from a stranger. It's a long shot, but the way he's used to being fed by you, the familiar hold…" The doctor spread his arms and shrugged.

Vickie hung onto his last words. "How often should I feed him?" she asked.

"I'm afraid four times a day, because his stomach can't hold too much at a time."

Grisha's emaciated little body, strapped and connected to intravenous tubes, looked so pathetic, Vickie didn't try to hold back tears.

She picked him up, pulled his spindly right arm under her armpit as she used to do when he was an infant, and talking softly, spooned a half-a-teaspoon of farina into his mouth. For a moment it stayed there, leaking out the side, and then, as his blue eyes focused on her, she coaxed him, scooping the overflow back into his mouth. Grisha moved his lips tentatively once, twice, then swallowed the mush and formed his mouth into a tiny 'O' to receive more. What joy! From then on, she drove the ten miles to the hospital four times day, and the hardest thing was to resist overfeeding him.

Two weeks later, Brian and Vickie were allowed to take Grisha home, still a little wobbly, but a smiling and active child. Vickie sat down on the living room couch and let out a flood of tears. Little Grisha. Her baby.

Brian put his hand on her arm and for the first time she noticed how pale and drawn his face had become.

"Oh Brian, Brian, thank God it's over!"

"You saved our child. Literally. How can I ever make it up to you? If not for you…" his voice broke and he turned away.

Vickie pulled his arm toward her, touched his face. "You look so tired."

Brian took her hand, then dug into his pocket and pulled out the jewel box. Without looking at Vickie, he put the emerald ring on her finger and kissed her hand. "Thank you for everything, hon," he said in a choked voice.

This time, Vickie admired the ring. "It's beautiful, Brian. Thank you," she said simply.

"It's all over, thank God," Brian said with a smile, "and now we can enjoy our last few months in Germany."

Vickie drew back. "What? Are we going home?"

"Not exactly home to San Francisco, but home to the States."

"Where?"

Brian took her hand and kissed it. "I have a little surprise for you. I requested a refresher course in Russian, hoping that one day I may be assigned to the embassy in Moscow. You'd like that, wouldn't you? I have orders to Washington, D.C. because one of the language schools is near there, and later, I'll stay for an assignment at the Pentagon."

PART IV

UNITED STATES AND RUSSIA

1954-1959

CHAPTER TWENTY-FOUR

Washington, D.C.

Grisha at four, was active and bright. The 'why Mummy?' was a daily occurrence, and Vickie coped with her inquisitive son the best she could. Today was no exception as he scrambled up the steps to where she was readying the bedrooms for Nina, Ross and Kenny.

"Auntie Nina is coming. Cousin Kenny is coming," he chimed from time to time, tugging at his mother's skirt. "Mama, I want to show Kenny my toys," he said lifting up his metal fire truck. Clear blue-green eyes shone with excitement and Vickie lifted her son up and twirled him around the room.

"Yes, they'll be here soon, isn't it wonderful?" she said kissing him on both cheeks and nuzzling his plump, baby neck. Then she put him down. "Now run to your room like a good boy and stay there, so Mummy can finish fixing the flowers for your auntie."

She arranged pink carnations in a Chinese vase she'd brought with her from Shanghai. Winter or summer, Vickie kept the house full of flowers, sometimes buying floral arrangements at the florist when cut flowers from the garden were hard to come by. Thank God, Brian didn't mind this extravagance, and today was a special occasion: Ross said in his letter that his transfer to Washington D.C. was a promotion. She could hardly wait to hug her sister and welcome her family to Washington.

When she and Brian had returned from Germany and visited San Francisco, there had been too much excitement, too many friends to enjoy. Kenny and Grisha getting acquainted; Lydia, the beaming grandmother; Kiril, the reserved grandfather trying to hide his pride in the two little boys. And then there was Jane...poor Jane who had never learned how to allow family love to enter her programmed heart. And now that heart had stopped.

She had had a massive heart attack and died a year ago. Brian's grief had been deep. The day he learned of his mother's death his hand had shaken as he'd fumbled for his handkerchief. When Vickie saw his face crumple, she put her arms around him. "I'm so sorry. It's such a shock. At least it was fast and she didn't linger. Mims was a proud lady and she would have hated to be bedridden."

Brian held her in his arms for a moment. "Death is so final. So unexpected. It was different when my father died. We were never close. But my mother..." His voice broke and he released Vickie. "I must fly to San Francisco right away."

"Would you like me to go with you?"

"No, thank you. I'd rather you stayed home with Grisha." He kissed her on the forehead. "Thank you, thank you for everything," he whispered.

Vickie didn't press. It was not the time to make him realize just how over-protective he was of Grisha. She felt sorry for Brian. The last parental tie had been severed. There, but for the grace of God...She shuddered.

Brian flew to San Francisco for the funeral. As the sole heir to Jane's estate, Brian inherited his mother's home and a fortune in securities. That, coupled with his private income from his father's legacy, made them wealthy. He sold the house in San Francisco, and didn't hesitate to look for a larger one in Washington. He and Vickie chose a brick home on wide Sixteenth Street among tall, shady trees. Upstairs had four bedrooms, three baths, and a separate dressing area adjoining the master suite; downstairs, it had a living room with a glassed-in porch, a separate dining room with beamed ceiling, wood-panelled library, kitchen with a pantry, and maid's room. Large brick fireplaces added warmth to the twelve-foot ceilings.

Vickie was pleased to find all four bedrooms wall-papered in colonial motif. She loved it. The house was so American and looked lived in, something she had always missed in Jane's house with its studied elegance. The only thing Vickie changed was the wallpaper in Grisha's room. She found a pattern with train engines and fire trucks in bright reds and blues on an off-white background.

She hung framed drawings of Williamsburg street scenes in the living room and bought Couristan wool rugs for the wood floors. The effect was one of subdued gentility and yet there was warmth in the rooms in spite of their large size.

Such a big house called for a housekeeper, and this time Brian didn't object when Vickie hired a woman to come in during the day. He still wouldn't let her have live-in help. "It won't sit well with our army friends," he said. Vickie thought it foolish for him to feel that way, but she was grateful for what she now had, remembering what a long way she had come from the rooming house in Shanghai.

She phoned and wrote detailed letters to her parents, urging them to visit. "We have plenty of room," she said, and although she suspected that they couldn't afford the trip, she didn't know how to offer to pay for their air fare without hurting her stepfather's pride. Still, she wanted them to see her lovely home and dreamed that someday soon she might find a way to bring them to Washington.

Lydia's letters centered entirely around Kenny's progress with scant mention of Nina or Ross, and none at all of her own activities. When she mentioned the day of her naturalization only briefly, Vickie worried. Her parents were so much on her mind that she lapsed into long silences in Brian's presence trying to hide her concern.

One night after dinner as she and Brian sat in their wood panelled library filled with books and records, Vickie said: "I wonder what my parents are doing in their spare time. Mama writes nothing about their activities. She knows that I don't like their involvement with the Russian community to the exclusion of everything else."

Brian raised his head from the *Life* magazine he was reading. "Will you please stop worrying? I've been watching you brood night after night. Your parents are American citizens now, so let them be. I don't want to hear about it anymore. It's tiresome." He closed the magazine and put it down on the small coffee table in front of him. "Why don't you get more involved in our own lives? It would take your mind off your parents. You have yet to serve on the board of the Officers' Wives Club. You may find it rewarding."

"You don't understand!" she cried out. "The Wives' Club serves a worthy purpose, but for me—how can I explain it to you? Itt's my mind that goes hungry."

"Why can't you Russians count your blessings and just be satisfied with what you have?"

"I don't like the way you say 'you Russians', Brian. I know that my membership in the Wives Club is important to you, but I want to use my languages, to be doing something more than attending luncheons. You and I speak English, but we might as well be talking Arabic to each other."

Startled, Brian said: "You mean you want to speak Russian to me? Why didn't you say so before? I'm all for it. It's good for me. A home refresher course!"

"That's not what I meant."

His eyes narrowed. "So that's it. You want to work again."

Vickie avoided a direct answer. "There's the Voice Of America for instance that needs people who speak a foreign language like a native, and the State Department that can use escort-interpreters."

"Why do you have to be so different from other army wives?"

"Because I *am* different," Vickie said. "Because I am Russian and my skills could be of use here in Washington."

Brian threw his arms up in the air. "What do you want from me, for heaven's sake? You worry about your parents' involvement with the Russian community, yet you tell me that you are Russian." He studied her for a moment, then said: "Tell me something. If Russia were to become democratic, where would your loyalties be?"

"That's not fair! Above all, I'm a loyal American. You know that. It's only my soul that speaks Russian."

"What the hell do you mean?"

"You'll never understand."

"Maybe not. I'm just a simple American and I don't understand your emotional outbursts."

Vickie slammed shut the book she had been reading and rose. "Oh, what's the use!"

Brian raised his brows. "Jesus! This Russian soul has a temper. O.K. Let's compromise: Stop brooding about your parents and I'll drop a hint in the right places that my wife is eager to use her languages as a freelancer. I'll check out the embassies and the State Department, but not VOA. That's a full time job. And who knows?—" Brian winked at her, "President Eisenhower is a former army man, so we may even get invited to the White House."

Embassies. The word made her heartbeat quicken. She had long stopped looking over her shoulder expecting any moment to run into *him*. She had even braved the thought that if she saw him, she would handle it well.

*　　　*　　　*

While she waited for something to turn up, she resigned herself to attending monthly Officers' Wives luncheons where she met several friendly women but none she could get close to. Then at one of the gatherings she met Sue Brennan again. The short, plucky Sue hadn't changed in the years since they parted in San Francisco. The same freckled, cheerful face, the same reddish hair and plump figure. They picked up where they had left off.

"This is the good part of the military service," Sue said giving Vickie a warm hug. "Sooner or later, you run into old friends. Now bring me up to date on where you've been and what you've been doing."

The two friends chatted through the luncheon and Vickie learned that Sue's husband had been assigned to the Pentagon and they had bought a small house in Arlington.

"That's the bad part," she said with a smile. "You're in Washington, and we're in Arlington, but there's always the phone and the car."

In the ensuing months, the two couples rarely got together because of the distances involved, and because the men hardly knew each other. Vickie and Sue, however, were on the phone almost daily, and frequently met downtown for lunch. Vickie no longer felt isolated in a world of strangers and when she learned that Nina and her family were moving to Washington, Sue was the first she called.

"I'm so excited, Sue! Can't wait to see them. It will be so good for Grisha to have his cousin to play with. Kenny is such a darling boy. Nina is beautiful and vivacious, and Ross is such a sweet fellow. I hope you'll like them."

"How great for you, Vickie. I'll look forward to meeting them all," Sue said. "Just don't forget your friend here!"

*   *   *

"Mummy, Mummy! They're here! They're here!"

Grisha's excited voice startled Vickie. Brian had gone to pick the family up at National Airport and she hadn't expected him back so soon. She ran out to greet them. After a round of hugs and kisses, everyone settled in the living room, talking at once. Grisha, gregarious as usual, pulled Kenny by the hand and the boys disappeared into his room.

Vickie couldn't help but notice how thin and drawn Nina looked, and that night, after everyone had gone to bed, she lay next to Brian, unable to sleep. Is Nina drinking more? she wondered. How is Ross handling it? How can I help Ross to convince Nina that she must join AA? Over and over her mind labored to find the answers. None came.

*   *   *

Ross and Nina bought a house in Silver Spring, not far from Vickie and Brian, and the two families saw each other often. One night, Kenny and Grisha had lined up their wooden soldiers in one corner of the Antonov's living room and were at work staging a battle.

"They don't look like cousins at all," Nina commented, pouring another cup of coffee from a china set—a wedding gift from Vickie and Brian.

Vickie tensed whenever Grisha's appearance was mentioned. "That's hardly surprising," she said, twisting her wedding band. "You forget that both your parents are fair. My father was dark and so am I. They say that brown eyes are dominant and Grisha's blue-green eyes are a compromise between mine and Brian's."

She knew she was doing too much explaining. Had anyone noticed?

"Kenny looks so much like Papa," Vickie commented. "Such a beautiful child."

"Yes, and because of that resemblance, Mama all but took over while we lived in San Francisco," Nina said. "Another year or two and Kenny would have become more Russian than American."

"Your living room is cozy, Nina," Vickie said, hoping to change the subject.

"Thanks, Vickie. It's not as elegant as yours, but that's all we could afford at the moment, and it's close to Ross's office."

"Why, it's a nice house," Brian said. "You have three bedrooms upstairs and plenty of room downstairs."

Vickie glanced at Ross. He wasn't smiling as he turned to Nina. "It's certainly larger than the house we had in San Francisco," he said.

His was no longer the relaxed, friendly face Vickie had remembered. He looked tense, preoccupied. Why was it that Nina always put everyone on the defensive?

Grisha came up with a toy soldier in his hand. "Mummy, I want one like this!"

Vickie took the soldier out of his hands and studied it. "Why don't you ask your Daddy to get you one?" she said giving the toy back to her son and ruffling his hair. Brian laughed. "Me too, syndrome."

Kenny brought over two soldiers on the palm of his hand. "Aunt Vickie, I have one of each, an American and a Russian." His round blue eyes rimmed with long lashes, looked at Vickie with candor. So much like his grandfather's. But what was not like Kiril's were the dark circles under those beautiful eyes.

"And do these soldiers fight each other?" Vickie asked, examining the toys and stroking his hair.

"No. They fight together, not each other, Babbie says. They are the Tsar's soldiers and they are friends."

Nina nodded knowingly. "See what I mean?"

Ross picked up the newspaper from the coffee table. "There's a good movie playing in town. Why don't we get a babysitter and go to the show?"

"Why get a babysitter?" Vickie said quickly. "Let's take the children to our house tomorrow and I'll ask Mrs. Stewart, our housekeeper to watch them…she often does that for us. What's the movie?"

"*Anastasia* with Ingrid Bergman and Yul Brynner."

Nina pursed her lips. "Not that again. I'm sick and tired of hearing about the pseudo-Grand Duchesses surfacing all over the world. I'd rather see *Around the World in 80 Days*. Much more fun."

"Nina, *I* would like to see *Anastasia*. Just once, can you do it for me?" Ross said, an edge to his voice.

"Actually, Ross," Brian said, cutting in before Nina had a chance to answer, "I'm not too interested in *Anastasia,* either. I vote with Nina on *Around the World in 80 Days.*"

Some stubborn streak surfaced, and Vickie said firmly: "And I have to side with Ross. What shall we do, draw lots?" Ross turned to Vickie. "No. If Brian doesn't mind, why don't we split up? I'll take you to see *Anastasia,* and I'll trust Brian to behave with Nina at the other movie."

Vickie thought bitterly: *Don't worry, Ross, Nina is completely safe with Brian.*

"How about, it, Brian?" Ross said.

Brian laughed. "Why not? Are you game, Nina?"

"Sure!"

*   *   *

The next evening, when Ross and Vickie drove up to the house after the movie, Brian and Nina had not yet returned. Vickie dismissed the housekeeper, fixed two cups of coffee, and sat down at the kitchen table opposite Ross.

"Well, what do you think, is this Anna Anderson really Anastasia?" Ross asked.

"I don't know. I went to the movie with the idea that she was yet another fraud, but after seeing it—" she shrugged, "she appears genuine enough. What a tragedy if itt's true."

Ross added a spoonful of sugar to his coffee, then stirred it pensively. "You know," he said, "my father had conflicting emotions about the Tsar and the aristocracy in general. He kept telling me how lucky we were to live in America where there were no titles, but at the same time he revered the pictures of the Tsar and was quite in awe of the gentry."

"And how do *you* feel about it?"

"I feel like you do. I have no problem with being born an American and loving my Russian background. Nina is a riddle. Why is she so ashamed of being Russian?"

"I don't think it's so much being Russian that she is ashamed of, as having been born without a country. In her eyes, she was an outcast."

"You were born without a country too, but you're not ashamed. Quite the contrary, I would say."

"You have no idea how I envied anyone who had a citizenship. But I understood that being stateless and being Russian is not necessarily synonymous. Too bad, Nina doesn't see it that way."

"Of course the Cold War doesn't help."

"That's right. I find myself always on the defensive, trying to make people understand the difference between the Russians and the Soviets. Oh, Ross, it's so complex, and no one can truly empathize unless they themselves have gone through it."

Ross wiped his mouth with a napkin and put his hand over Vickie's. "I can," he said. "I've never been stateless myself, but through my parents, I sensed what it must be like. Fortunately for me, they never felt inferior. Of course that may be because they came here from Russia as immigrants and not as refugees."

"You've blended the two cultures admirably, Ross. Do you miss the Russian traditions you were used to while your parents were alive?"

"Yes, I do, and I always enjoy being invited to a Russian home, or going to church on holidays. This is why it's so difficult for me to understand Nina's attitude. I've lost a lot of my Russian friends since my marriage."

Vickie poured another cup of coffee for herself and for Ross. "Funny, I find myself in somewhat the same situation with Brian, only in reverse. I try very hard to become fully Americanized, but there are times when my Russian side surfaces and when I talk about it, he acts bored or angry." She paused, then went on. "I guess Brian would have been better off married to someone like Nina who is anxious to forget that she's Russian."

Ross sighed. "Perhaps we are both married to the wrong people," he said.

After a moment, Vickie averted her eyes and checked his cup. "More coffee?" "No thanks. Brian and Nina should be home any minute."

"Is Nina still drinking?" Vickie asked.

Ross hesitated, then nodded. "I'd like to put a lock on the liquor cabinet, but according to AA, that won't make any difference. Nina has to give it up herself. I feel so helpless just watching her."

There was such pain on his face, such pain! Vickie put down her cup and hugged him. "Oh, Ross! I'm so sorry."

Ross stiffened, but after a moment his arms circled her waist and he buried his face in her neck. "Oh, Vickie, Vickie!"

She felt his warm, quickened breath on her skin. Something leaped inside her. Her face aflame, she pulled herself away with an effort. "I wish I knew how to help you. My talking to Nina in the past only antagonized her."

Ross picked up her hand and kissed it. "Thank you. I know you would help if you could. I've tried to encourage her to join AA, but she won't admit that she needs help. I worry about Kenny and what this is doing to him. The boy is six now and he feels the tension in the house."

"In a way, I'm sorry you're not near Kenny's grandmother. Does he miss his grandparents?"

"Very much. There again, Nina fought Lydia when Kenny went to Russian church and stayed after the services to play with other children. At least that friction is removed."

"I'll try to do what I can, Ross. I've been reading Russian fairy tales to Grisha, and I can do the same for Kenny."

"Would you? I'd be so grateful."

Vickie rose, collected the empty cups and went to the sink. Ross followed, bringing the cream and sugar, then picked up the towel and waited for her to wash the dishes.

"It was good to talk to you, Ross," she said. "I don't remember when I had such a heart-to-heart talk without having to explain or defend myself. You—" she searched for the right words, "share my feelings. You understand exactly what I mean."

"I do. You see the world in the right perspective," he said, picking up the rinsed cup and drying it. "You're a warm, intelligent woman, Vickie."

Vickie looked at him and their eyes locked.

"Are you happy with Brian?" he asked.

She was taken aback. "Why do you ask?"

"I don't know. Just a feeling I have."

Suddenly the desire to unburden herself, to tell him about Brian and what a sham of a marriage she had, was so compelling, she blurted out: "Are you psychic or something?" Ross grabbed her by the shoulders and pulled her close to him.

"What is it Vickie? Share it with me."

His glance, so full of concern searched her face.

"I was kidding of course. Nothing's wrong," she said with a forced laugh, and hated herself for the lie.

"I'll always be here for you," he said softly.

Reluctantly, she pulled away. Ross was her sister's husband. She mustn't forget that. Time to pick up another dish out of the sink and rinse it.

"Tell me," she said, "whatever happened to that project you had in mind when we first met? The one for the cardiac patient?"

"I had to set it aside. Right now, it's filed away in my cabinet. I'm too busy at work, and I can't concentrate at home with Nina the way she is. If she ever admits that she needs help, then I may return to it. I haven't given up."

CHAPTER TWENTY-FIVE

The State Department reception room was so packed with people that Vickie and Brian moved sideways as they worked their way to the refreshment table. There was a sprinkling of foreign uniforms, but by far the majority of people were in civilian clothes and in such a crowd it was impossible to tell the Americans from the foreigners. The chatter, the laughter, the clicking of champagne glasses reverberated in Vickie's ears. So this was one of those sophisticated cocktail parties she had read about in society columns and had wondered what it would be like to attend. Army receptions were far smaller and more intimate.

Still, it was a heady experience to know that they were invited to this reception not because of Brian's position at the Pentagon, but because she now worked for the State Department as a free-lance interpreter. Brian had kept his word, and she had been invited to take a test which she passed easily.

The invitation had been addressed to her, and to her surprise, Brian had been good-natured about it.

"Well, well, what do you know, I'm invited as Victoria Hamilton's husband!"

"Does that bother you?"

"Not really. I'm still not crazy about your working, but since it's on a freelance basis, you can always turn it down."

As they stood by the table laden with food, Brian kept close to her. "I don't want to lose you in this crowd," he whispered, picking up a smoked salmon canapé and looking around the room for a familiar face. No luck. So, it was up to him to break into one of a number of conversations going on around them.

Introductions followed and although Vickie tried to listen, she could not catch the names.

"Have you been in Washington long?"Someone asked, and—"we came from our embassy in Greece…You must be new here…Have you seen the new exhibit at the Smithsonian?…What do you think of our beautiful city?…" The disembodied words bounced without waiting for an answer, a well-rehearsed exchange of pleasantries and current news. How disappointing. But then what did she expect…instant recognition of her skills? How naïve. There must be dozens like her in the room.

She looked for her examiners who had been so impressed by her knowledge of Russian, but couldn't find them. Her gaze floated over the crowd, then froze.

He was standing by the table, talking to someone.

Although she could only see his profile, the thick dark hair, the firm outline of the jaw and cheekbone were unmistakable. He turned and looked straight at her. Her heart skipped. She put her hand on the table to steady herself, for she could not take her eyes away. He had stopped talking to a blond woman and stood still, holding her gaze.

He looked the same—handsome, elegant, and so painfully dear.

He was the first to lower his eyes. Then he turned, threaded his way toward the opposite end of the room, and lost himself in the crowd.

Spared? Relieved? She should have been. Instead, she felt a dreadful sense of loss.

He recognized her, she had no doubt of that. The look in his eyes—that enigmatic, intense look. Oh, he knew her! Across the room full of people, he knew her.

"Hon, what's the matter? You're so pale."

Brian's voice sounded alarmed.

"It's…it's so stuffy in here. I feel faint. How soon can we leave?"

"No one will miss us in this mob. Let's go."

*   *   *

The next day the phone rang in mid-morning. Vickie picked up the receiver. "Hello?"

"I have an apartment on Constitution Avenue. I'll be waiting for you tomorrow afternoon." He gave his address and hung up before she could say anything. As she replaced the receiver, she wondered if the hammering of her heart could have been heard at the other end.

Ever since her arrival in Washington, she had avoided looking him up in the phone book, but now with those few words, spoken with such confidence, he'd demolished her resistance. She stood there in her bedroom, wrapped in joy by the intoxicating thought that he hadn't walked away from her after all.

The following afternoon, she stood before him in his apartment, hands clasped together in an effort to hide her trembling. How was it possible to feel such joy and such pain at the same time? Unable to take her eyes off his beloved face, she said: "You turned away from me at the reception. I thought…I…"

He smiled. "You thought what, my love? Did you really think I could have come up to you, casually kissed your hand and exchanged banalities with your husband? When I saw you together, I was so blinded by jealousy, I *had* to turn away."

Vickie closed her eyes and inhaled deeply. "Don't…Don't be jealous."

He crushed her to him. "You're here. You love me still. That's all that matters now."

They had soothed the frenzy of their bodies, and lay in each other's arms in the abundant light of the afternoon sun. In that hour after love-making, gentle words, like soft caresses, stroked her soul.

When he asked if she had children, she said she had a son and tried to change the subject, but he kept on: "How old is he?"

"He's—hee's three," she lied, and thought: Will he count the years?

"And what is his name?"

"Grisha."

"What does he look like?"

She stirred, moved out of his arms to hide the sudden knocking of her heart. He tried to hold her back but she pulled away. "I feel strange talking about my son while I'm with you, Henri. My other life intrudes. Please, let's talk about something else. Is Claudette still in Paris?"

"She'll never leave France. Can you imagine, my little sister extremely successful and rich in her own right? She has an apartment near the Bois de Boulogne and a house in Cannes."

"Still not married?"

Now it was Henri's turn to move restlessly. "No. I don't think she'll ever marry. She seems happy as she is."

"And your father?"

"He's well and lives in Fontainebleau. I visit him from time to time."

"And your work? Do you like it?" That was all she intended to say, but the words slipped out: "What about Igor Sevich?"

"Nothing has changed there, Vickie. I realize now that I can't make you accept things that go against your nature. So let's not talk about it anymore."

"Are you a spy, Henri?"

Instead of answering, he kissed her again. Her heart was lost in the kiss and the question fell away unanswered.

*　　　　*　　　　*

They met every week for a stolen hour or two in the afternoons. This time there was no inner struggle because she had finally faced the truth that Henri was a part of her, that he was in her heart and in her blood forever. During their time in Europe, she had thought she would conquer her love, but now that she knew about Brian, the old guilts were gone.

Henri no longer mentioned marriage, and an undeclared truce was established. No questions about his secret work were traded for no questions about her life with Brian. The past and the future had no place in their present, where his apartment had become their accomplice erasing the world around them until nothing existed but the joy of being together.

Often they listened to music and read Pushkin or Lermontov to each other. Once, lying on the carpet propped up by cushions near the fireplace, they listened to the whole of Beethoven's seventh symphony. When the last notes died down, they did not move. Vickie stirred first. "I love that piece of music. It's passionate, vibrant, and for me, rebellious."

"Is that how you think of yourself, too?"

Vickie sat up, pulled her knees under her chin and, wrapping her arms around her legs, stared into the fire. "I don't know. But that's how I'd like to be."

"Well, you are. All of these." He pulled her down into the crook of his arm and kissed her deeply on the mouth. When he released her, his eyes shone. "Yes. You're passionate and vibrant, and for sure, rebellious. How else could I have made you come here?"

"I don't think of myself as rebellious," she said. "I've always told myself that life is full of little pleasures if one only looks for them. Now I have this pleasure, being with you again."

"Oh? Am I only a *little* pleasure?"

She laughed. "Of course not, my darling. You're a big pleasure in a little space of time which makes it that much more intense."

"And I call it luxury. An intense fulfillment of senses." He pulled himself into a sitting position. "All six of them," he added with a twinkle in his eye.

"Six of them? Please enlighten me."

He rose to his knees and with his hand over his heart, made a mock bow. "To hear you laugh and want to smile. To see your face and want to touch it. To watch your mouth and want to taste it. To stroke your hair and feel its silkiness. To bury my face in your neck and smell your scent. And then the sixth, the ultimate sense: To possess your body and soul and know the world is now mine. That's *my* luxury. Nothing else matters."

"There's a poet in you, darling. I'm surprised you've never written any poetry."

"I can't write it. I just feel it."

He took her in his arms again. "I love you, my *golubka.*"

Time flowed undisturbed by the muffled sounds of traffic outside. Within the walls of the apartment, the sounds were soft, a gentle moan, a pleasing laugh, a murmur.

*   *   *

She was not in control of this love, it controlled her, and Vickie realized that she was caught in a conflict, for she could no more give up Henri than she could abandon Brian. So she had to come to terms with her situation and prayed that Brian would never find out. Even though he had told her that she could lead her own life discreetly, she knew that in this case, he would object to her affair with Henri.

When the famous Washington cherry trees bloomed, Vickie sent plane tickets to her parents. She realized that a check, no matter how well-intentioned, would offend her stepfather. The tickets she offered in-lieu of a birthday gift to him. She knew that if she sent them to Lydia, Kiril would be humiliated. She could hear him saying: "Does Vickie think I can't afford to give you such a present?" But he could hardly refuse a gift to himself without being ungracious.

She was right. They arrived for a two-week visit laden with toys for the grandchildren, thrilled to be in the capital. In spite of their smiles and excitement, Vickie was shocked to see her elegant, handsome stepfather so frail and short of breath.

"What does your doctor say, Mama?" she asked when Kiril was out of earshot.

Lydia busied herself with unpacking. "He says that Papa has to take it easy. There's nothing else to do, so I try to protect him from undue stress. I'm glad he's not in medical practice. Teaching Russian is much less strenuous and he enjoys the children. And speaking of children, let's go down and watch Grisha unpack his presents."

Grisha, who had been standing at the foot of the stairs, solemnly watching his father carry the bundles and the suitcases up the stairs, put his thumb in his mouth and followed his grandmother's movements with pensive eyes. When Lydia sat down, she placed some packages at her feet and beckoned to Grisha.

The little boy took his thumb out of his mouth and said: "Babbie, are you old?"

Startled, Lydia smiled. "I guess so."

"Are you going to heaven soon?"

Lydia raised her brows. "I will when the good Lord calls me."

Grisha turned to Vickie and tugged at her skirt. "Mommy, I don't want Daddy to take Babbie's suitcases to heaven."

Vickie stroked his hair and whispered: "Don't worry, Grisha, he won't." She looked at her mother and rolled her eyes. "Smart kid!"

Lydia laughed and handed Grisha one of the packages. "Here, open it. This is a present for you."

That night, when the whole family gathered together and the two boys were asleep, the adults sat in the spacious living room sipping tea and coffee and catching up on the last two years. Vickie watched her family over the rim of her cup. Brian and Ross sat on the loveseat apart from the rest, engrossed in their discussion of the cease-fire that United Nations Secretary-General, Dag Hammarskjold, had arranged in April between Israel and Jordan.

Ross sat relaxed, legs crossed, one arm over the back of the loveseat as he listened to Brian who was leaning forward, gesticulating to prove his point. She hadn't seen Brian as animated in a long time, and was pleased that he found Ross so much to his liking.

"You what?" Nina's angry voice startled Vickie. Her sister had lost more weight than was becoming, sharpening her features and robbing her of that soft beauty that had earned her so many compliments in the past.

"You what?" Nina repeated staring at her mother.

"You needn't raise your voice. I hear you," Lydia replied calmly. "I said that I support a Russian scout organization, and as soon as Kenny is a little older you should find out if the Russian community in Washington has one. Don't forget, he's the grandson of a prince and should be taught to revere Imperial Russia."

"Are you out of your mind, Mama? No son of mine is going to join any Russian scouts. Kenny was born an American citizen and he'll join the *American* cub scouts. He's an American, do you hear? How can you be so disloyal to your new country? You and Papa are citizens now."

Nina rose abruptly and went over to the sideboard to pour herself another brandy. Unstable on her feet, she staggered a little and bumped into a chair. Vickie caught Kiril's shocked glance as it followed his daughter across the room.

Lydia sighed. "It is you who are disloyal to your past. The Russian scout organization is not going to teach your son to be disloyal to America. The two flags stand side-by-side. Don't forget that your father and I were refugees from our country not by choice, but through necessity. We appreciate the sanctuary that America has given us, but our first loyalty belongs to our *Rodina*."

"But you pledged allegiance to the United States and renounced all others! What you're saying is treason."

Lydia glanced at Kiril and then back at Nina. "I'm a citizen, Nina, and I wouldn't betray America, but if communism is overthrown during our lifetime, we shall return to Russia."

"How can you be such a hypocrite? You're either Russian or American. Not both."

"Life is full of compromises, my dear. I pity those who are ashamed of being Russian."

"And what do you think would happen in America if all immigrants sided with their ethnic countries?"

"Don't exaggerate."

"I'm not. The Russians were always fighting among themselves, always divided. Remember the Decembrists of 1825? What a revolt that was, ha! They couldn't agree on the changes they wanted and ended up on the gallows. And even here, in America, our Orthodox Church is divided, not on religious grounds, mind you, but on political." Vickie leaned forward. "Papa, how do *you* feel about this dual loyalty?"

Kiril joined his fingertips to form a pyramid and squinting at Vickie, said: "I feel very much like your mother does, dear. Actually, more so, because I never took out American citizenship."

Vickie suppressed a gasp. Brian and Ross stopped talking, and the room became quiet.

"Why not, Papa?" she asked.

Kiril raised his head and sat up straight. "Because I am a titled prince of Russia, and I take an oath of allegiance only once in my life."

Brian walked over to his father-in-law "Are you going to live here as an alien for the rest of your life?"

"I have to be true to myself," Kiril replied stiffly.

"A-ha!" Nina cried, waving her right hand with the brandy glass and spilling part of it on the carpet.

Vickie grabbed a napkin. "Nina, please, calm down!" she said, mopping up the spot on the floor.

Nina turned on her. "Papa and I may not agree but at least we take a stand. But you! Who *are* you?"

"I'm a loyal American citizen, Nina, but that doesn't prevent me from loving my Russian heritage."

"There! Compromising again, trying to please everyone. You can't have it both ways, dear sister. You're serving two masters at once."

Vickie noticed how Ross quietly appeared at Nina's side. "That's enough Nina. You're upsetting your parents. Don't you understand, that the two loyalties can coexist without betrayal of either?" He took the brandy glass out of her hand. "Now, say goodbye to everybody. It's time to go home."

After they left, Kiril rose slowly from his chair and faced Brian. "I apologize for my daughter's behavior, Brian," he said, his voice shaking with emotion. "I have never seen her drink so much."

Brian exchanged a quick glance with Vickie, then smiled at his father-in-law. "Forget it. It happens to all of us once in a while. Why don't we call it a day?"

Upstairs in their bedroom, Vickie thanked Brian for his tact. "Papa was upset hearing us argue, and God knows what would happen if he found out about Nina's drinking. He's sixty-eight, but looks ten years older."

Brian nodded and went to hang his clothes in the closet. Vickie sat on their bed, shoe in one hand. How could her stepfather keep clinging to his dream of the re-emergence of Imperial Russia? How could he not see that the past was over and would never return?

Brian came in. "Your stepfather is sure hard nosed about the 'good old days of Russia.'" He sat on his bed and took his shoes off. "But," he went on, "at least he's forthright about where his loyalties lie. And I have to say, I admire his honesty."

"You mean, of course, he's not like mother, becoming an American citizen but keeping her first allegiance to Russia."

"Well, you said it, not me."

"I know you resent their attitudes, and I'm sorry you had to hear all that. But in her defense I must say, there's a difference. She's more loyal to a memory than what's happening in Russia today."

"There you go again, making excuses for them. What I don't understand is why you're so defensive."

"That's not fair. I'm not! America is so different from anything they've ever known. It's not easy to adapt to change when you're an adult. Believe me, I know. I've tried hard these past nine years to learn all about this country and…and to understand you. It seems we aren't communicating at all."

"You've got that right. We live under the same roof, sleep in the same room, and if it weren't for Grisha—well, he seems to be all we have in common."

Indignant tears sprang to her eyes. "How can you say that? I think I've done pretty well by you considering our situation. You should understand when once in a while I cry out for something else."

His face hardened. "I'll never figure you out. I told you a long time ago that I wouldn't interfere in your private life. You can do what you want. I don't give a damn what you do."

When she didn't answer and wiped her eyes, he took her hand. "I'm sorry. I guess tonight just got to me. Your parents, your sister. Not fair to take it out on you. Of course you've done well by me, and I appreciate it."

Long after he fell asleep, Vickie stayed awake. He was right. How could he ever understand her stepfather, a man who clung to a passionate dream? Brian had no threat of love divided between two countries. He was not burdened by such passions. His was of a different kind, smugly hidden under the pretext of a wholesome family life. Vickie stirred under her blanket. She, too, knew the torment of divided loyalty. Henri and Brian…

*   *   *

The next day, Vickie had just brought her parents back from the tour of the National Gallery and was helping the housekeeper fix sandwiches when the phone rang. "I'll get it," she said wiping her hands on her apron and picking up the receiver.

"I need to see you right away. Don't go to my apartment or anywhere near Constitution Avenue. Take Sheridan or Tuckerman Street to Georgia Avenue. Meet me at the Deli there in half an hour."

Vickie gripped the receiver. "I can't right now. I'm serving lunch to my parents."

"This is an emergency. Find an excuse." He hung up before she could argue further.

There was such urgency in his voice. What happened?

Lydia watched her. "What's the matter, Vickie? Your face is flushed."

With an enormous effort she kept her voice calm. "A friend of mine needs me right away. She sounded upset. Please excuse me, I'll have to leave. I won't be gone long."

"Don't worry about us," Kiril said. "Take your time. As a matter of fact, I'd like to take a walk after lunch. Your street is so shady and beautiful, I'll enjoy it."

Vickie grabbed her purse and rushed out of the house.

What had happened to Henri? She knew he would never have called while her parents were there if it weren't a real emergency.

CHAPTER TWENTY-SIX

Vickie found him sitting in the farthest booth in a small, dark deli that was filled with people gulping their coffees and sandwiches on forty-five minute lunch breaks. A most unlikely place for them to meet.

"I don't have much time," Henri said in a low voice. "My colleague, René Duval, received word from his contact that the authorities are closing in on him. This could mean me as well. I was ordered not to return to my apartment, but to go directly to the Soviet Embassy and wait there for my flight to Moscow." He smiled ruefully. "My wish is about to come true at last, but at what price! I have to leave without you."

Her heart stood still. "Maybe they haven't connected you to this Duval man. Can't you wait?"

"No. This is my chance to immigrate. In Russia I'll be greeted as a hero, while here..." He frowned. "Here, I'd be tried as a traitor to France." He smiled a bitter, sardonic smile. "But, my darling, traitor or hero is in the eye of the beholder, isn't it? Your own George Washington would have been labeled a traitor if the Americans had lost the Revolutionary war."

"Then you're leaving right away?"

He leaned forward and took her hands in his. "Yes."

She tried to pull away, but he held tight. "Vickie, you must come to Russia. Just think, we'd be together at last. What do we have here? A few stolen hours—nothing more than crumbs of love. Come with me to the

Soviet Embassy and put in your request for immigration. You don't love your husband. How can you stay with him for the rest of your life?"

Vickie withdrew her hands abruptly. "I won't go to Russia. You know that."

"Do you want me to stay in the west and risk going to prison?"

"Of course not. But even if I wanted to join you, I couldn't leave my son behind."

"I want him too. You must take him with you."

"I can't do this to Brian. How can I take his son away from him?"

Henri narrowed his eyes. "He'll manage. I saw Grisha on the street. You lied to me. He's older than three." He looked at her intently, then took her hand and kissed it. "He's *our* son."

When Vickie shook her head, he raised his hand. "Don't deny it, darling. I saw him close from my parked car as he walked by. Grisha is mine. The color of his eyes, the shape of his face—everything about him is mine. II'm surprised your husband doesn't see it. Grisha is *my* son, and I want you both with me in Russia."

Tears cramped her throat. The three of them together…How would it be? Dear God, she couldn't think that!

"When did you see him?" she managed to whisper.

"Yesterday. It was quite a shock. I wanted to leap out of the car and scoop my child up in my arms, but he was walking with your mother and of course, I couldn't do it."

"America is now part of me, Henri."

"Don't deceive yourself, it's not. You're more Russian than American and always will be."

"Not your Russia, Henri. I love America."

"Vickie, my love, you're in my blood. How can I survive knowing that I'll never see you again?"

"We've parted before, and thought it was final."

"No. I always knew I'd find you again. I can't live without hope, and once I'm in Russia…Don't you understand? While I lived here, I dreamed that sooner or later you'd leave Brian, and now that I have a son—" he grasped her hands, "You both belong to me!"

Vickie freed her hands. "Oh, God! Our love is such a burden."

"Do you really think I can say a final goodbye right here? Our souls are one. Don't you see what you're doing to us? Separated, our love will destroy us."

The rest of her life without him. A lifelong winter without him.

"No, Henri. We're both strong. We'll survive."

"You're robbing me of yourself *and* my son. How can you be so cruel?"

"Your son will grow up in a free world, cared for and protected by his legal father."

"Don't take my hope away. Let me dream that one day you'll come to me."

When she didn't answer, his eyes filled. Slowly, he pulled a jade ring off his finger and handed it to Vickie. "When my son is old enough give him this ring. He may never know about me, but at least *I'll* know that he's wearing something of mine."

When Vickie hesitated, he closed her opened hand. "Please?"

Reluctantly, she nodded.

*   *   *

Two days later, Henri's and René Duval's pictures appeared in the newspaper with the story of their defection to the Soviet Union. Henri was described as the accessory to René Duval's covert activities, and although the French Embassy had been embarrassed by the incident, the damage to the West was not deemed catastrophic, according to the embassy's spokesman.

An early riser, Lydia read the paper before Kiril came down for breakfast. Vickie saw her mother's face and thanked God that Brian had already left for work. The paper shook in Lydia's hands, making a rustling sound in the room.

"My God!" she said. "Katya's son…a traitor! How could he?" Propped by her elbows on the table, Lydia lowered her forehead against her interlaced fingers and shook her head from side to side. "Do you suppose Katya knew?"

Suddenly, it all poured out: the whole story about Henri's involvement with Igor Sevich, his decision to immigrate to Russia, his mother's influence on him, and her subsequent death at the hands of the Chinese mob.

Telling it, Vickie was dried-eyed and spoke in a detached voice. When she finished, Lydia sighed and wiped a tear. "My oldest friend, Katya! We grew up together. I never once suspected." She fell silent for a moment, then said: "Is this, then, why you broke your engagement in Shanghai?" and when Vickie nodded, Lydia looked at her with admiration. "How strong you are. And loyal. You didn't betray him. You've seen him since, of course, or you wouldn't have known about Katya's death."

Vickie nodded. "Brian and I saw him at the army reception in Heidelberg. He was with the French Consulate in Frankfurt at the time."

She dared not look at her mother. God, what was she going to say?

Lydia did not keep her guessing long. "I often wondered why Grisha was much darker than Brian."

Vickie held her breath for a second, then asked as casually as she could: "What are you talking about, Mama?"

"He's Henri's, isn't he?"

"Of course not! You're jumping to conclusions, Mama. Grisha is a Hamilton. He is dark because I'm dark, or have you forgotten my real father's coloring?"

"Forgotten? I shall never forget. But don't worry. Your secret is safe with me. You obviously still love Henri or you wouldn't have had his child." She sighed. "Believe me, no one can understand your anguish better than I."

Vickie frowned. "What do you mean, Mama?"

"Sit down. I've never told you this, but when Peter Sokolov left me, I found out that he was having an affair with his secretary, and wanted out of our marriage. He *wanted* to believe that you were not his child. So, as I said, your secret is safe with me. No one must know the truth about Grisha."

"So that's why Peter Sokolov was so cruel when he threw me out of his office." Vickie shook her head slowly. "I was only four years old then, but I still remember it. But how tragic for you, Mamochka. You were so wronged."

"No. You're the one who was wronged. But I did try to be a conscientious mother to you."

"You've used the right word, Mama, 'conscientious', but you can't fool a child. I knew you loved Nina more."

"Oh, don't say that, Vickie. I do love you. But I found my love in Kiril and because Nina is our daughter, it may have seemed to you that I loved her more." Lydia coughed. "We've both been hurt, and now you have another heartache, this time of your own doing. I ache for you."

"I have a good life, Mama. I care about what this country can give to my son," she said.

"You did the right thing, Vickie, in staying with Brian. The only thing."

"Henri is gone from my life forever," Vickie said, then added after a pause: "What I haven't been able to do myself, has been done for me."

For a few moments they were both silent, then Vickie rose. "I'll be right back, Mama." She ran upstairs and returned a few minutes later with the jade brooch. Without looking at her mother, she handed it to her. "Henri gave it to me in Shanghai. I've never worn it since…since our breakup. I want you to have it."

Lydia examined it. "What a beautiful piece. Thank you, my dear. I'll enjoy it."

When Kiril came down for breakfast and read the article, he said: "I'm glad now, that you didn't marry him, Vickie. What shame upon his parents' head."

Vickie told him that she and Brian—she was careful to include Brian—met Henri in Europe. He'd told them that Katya was dead. "How sad," Kiril said. "But at least his mother was spared this disgrace."

Vickie exchanged glances with her mother, and Lydia gave her a warning look. No use, it said, telling Kiril more than was necessary. At that moment, Vickie felt closer to Lydia than ever before. All her life she had tried to please her mother, to win her affection, and how ironic that it took a common sin to bring them closer together.

Surprisingly, it was Brian's reaction that evening that upset her the most. As if his subconscious mind suspected something, he reacted to the newspaper article with derision. "What do you know, the man turned out to be a spy. And to think that I invited him to visit us in Heidelberg. Good thing he didn't take me up on it, or we would have had the FBI on our doorstep. You know how those things work. The slightest connection and I would have been suspect."

Vickie picked up the dishes, carried them out to the kitchen and started washing them. Squeeze the soapy sponge, watch the bubbles slide down the china plate, then rinse with clear water and drain. A task that required no thought.

Lydia came in, took a towel to dry the dishes. "Try to ignore what people say in the next few days, Vickie," she said quietly. "Brace yourself for some nasty remarks."

"I will, Mama. From now on there will be no more temptation, no more tearing of my heart in two. As far as I'm concerned, he's dead. Do you understand that, Mama?"

Lydia caught her gaze, held it for a few moments, then lowered her eyes without saying anything. But even as Vickie uttered these words, she knew that she would never be free of him. Somewhere inside her she would always see his face and hear his voice, feel his touch, and endure forever the unremitting pain of loss.

*   *   *

Three days before Kiril and Lydia's vacation was over, they started out for their daily walk along Sixteenth Street.

"Why don't I drive you to Rock Creek Park?" Vickie asked. "You'll enjoy it more than walking on the street."

"No thank you, dear, we enjoy this beautiful area and I love looking at the old brick mansions, they remind me of my youth. Kiril and I don't see many of these in the west."

While they were out of the house, Vickie busied herself with daily chores: instructions to be given to the housekeeper, a grocery list made out, Grisha bathed. This morning, she enjoyed the child's chatter, and was about to read him a story when Ross called.

"I'm sorry to bother you, Vickie, but I don't know where else to turn. I don't suppose you can do anything about it either, but I have to talk to someone and it seems you're always the one."

"What's the matter, Ross?"

"Nina again. This time she has gone too far. I hid the liquor, but she got around it by having a taxi driver buy vodka for her. Can you imagine her stooping to that?"

"My God! Why doesn't she go herself?"

"I took the car keys away from her." There was a slight pause and then Ross's voice shook with poorly concealed anger: "She's let herself go, looks sloppy at home, and I suppose she's too proud to be seen outdoors. Her mind is in a fog so much, I'm afraid to leave her alone too long with Kenny. I worry about those hours after school before I get home. Why is she drinking? I don't understand."

"Ross, I think it's time to tell my parents and confront Nina, but without you. Maybe if we face her in your absence, she may not be so defiant, and we can make her realize that she needs help."

"But don't you think I should be there, too?"

"No. Nina would be too stubborn to listen while you're there. We'll try to convince her that she needs professional help. At this point I don't think AA is enough. Let me talk to my parents and maybe we'll go over this afternoon."

*   *   *

They rang the doorbell several times before Kenny opened it. His tear-stained face lit up when he saw his aunt and grandparents.

"What's the matter, darling?" Lydia said, kissing him and wiping his face. The child didn't answer.

"Where's your mother, Kenny?" Vickie asked, putting her hand on his shoulder. Kenny's lips quivered. He pointed upstairs. "In her bedroom," he said. "Aunt Vickie, she…she's lying down on her bed."

"Babbie and I will go upstairs, Kenny. We'll wake her up if she's asleep, O.K.?"

Vickie and her mother climbed the stairs closely followed by Kenny, and turned toward the master bedroom. Nina must have heard them, for she opened the door and leaned against the molding, one foot inside a high heeled shoe, the other bare. Her eyes roamed unfocused, and as Vickie came near her, the stale smell of vodka was unmistakable.

Lydia put her arm around Kenny and looked at her daughter. "Nina. You need help. Professional help."

"It's none of your business, Mama. Don't meddle in my life. Why the hell do you think we moved away?" Nina's speech was slurred and she held onto the doorknob.

"And look where it got you," Lydia said indignantly. "You're an alcoholic. Why? I never expected this of you. Look at poor Kenny. Look at him!" Lydia lifted the boy's chin and pointed to the dark circles under his eyes. "Think of your husband and child. What do you think this is doing to them? Now pull yourself together and come downstairs. Maybe Papa can talk some sense into you."

"Leave me alone!" Nina screamed suddenly. "All of you! Don't you tell me what to do!"

Kiril climbed the stairs and stared at Nina. "How dare you scream at your mother! Look at yourself. One shoe on, the other off. Your dress is wrinkled, your hair's a mess. By the right of your birth, you're still a princess. So behave like one. You're a disgrace to the Muravin name, not to mention your husband's."

Nina's lips curled. "Don't worry about *him*. He's not an aristocrat, remember? Let me remind you…" she paused blinking, her tongue thick, then tried again, "remind you that he's from a merchant class."

Kiril raised his voice. "Don't be insolent. I'm your father and I demand your respect and—"

"And telling me what's not—not good enough for a princess? Well, let me…let me tell you something. I made a mistake listening to you. You know what?" Nina took a step forward, her voice rising, her finger pointing at her father. "I should—should have married Joseph! Yeah, Joseph Rosen. I loved him! But you brainwashed me, didn't you?" She pursed her lips mimicking her father: "Princess Muravina couldn't marry a Jewish boy. God forbid. Right?"

"Nina!" Lydia raised her voice. "How dare you speak to your father like that?"

"I'll tell you how. I'm sick and tired of being Russian, and a princess at that. I mean…I thought I'd marry Ross and be through with this nonsense, but no! Underneath that all-American image, he—he's still Russian, *very* Russian. And he likes it. He makes me sick!"

"I'll overlook what you've said," Kiril said, his face so pale, Vickie took a step toward him. "Clean yourself up and come downstairs. Then we'll talk about getting help for you. If not for Ross, you must do it for your son." With that, he turned and went downstairs.

Kenny leaned against Lydia's waist and pressed his face against her. Lydia stroked his head. "Now Kenny, your mama is upset, but she'll be fine. I'm going to find out tomorrow if there's a Russian scout organization here and sign you up. Would you like that?"

Nina staggered toward her mother and wrenched Kenny away from her. "You're not going to start that again. I won't let you fill his head with that…that Imperial Russian crap!"

Lydia gasped. "Watch your language, Nina!"

"I'll say what I damn well please."

Kenny looked up at his mother, eyes full of tears. "Mommy, I don't want the scouts. I have my friends at school."

Vickie moved toward Nina, but Nina backed away, holding Kenny against her.

"Nina, don't you see what you're doing to Kenny?" Vickie said, gently taking Kenny by the arm. "Please! We love you! All we want is to help you."

"What do you mean, 'help me'? Are you preaching again? 'All we want is to help you'—" Nina mimicked. "Just like Ross. You're always on my husband's side, aren't you? Always siding with him against me." She lunged forward. "Let go of my son!" She grabbed Kenny by the shoulders and pulled him away from Vickie.

Vickie took a step toward Nina, but Lydia came between them. "Stop it, you two, this instant!" she cried, spreading her arms to keep them apart.

Nina loosened her hold on Kenny and tried to push her mother aside. The boy wrenched himself free and dashed past the stairs to his room. Nina went after him. "Kenny!"

The heel of the one shoe she was wearing caught in the shag rug as she reached the top of the stairs. She tried to regain her balance, tottered for a moment and then with a single cry, fell head first down the stairs.

A sickening series of thumps and then…silence.

One endless scream came from the top of the stairs. It was Lydia. Kenny ran out of his room but Vickie rushed to him, pressed his head to her chest and held it tight against his struggle.

Moments later, Kiril's voice: "My God. Oh, my God! Vickie! Lydia!"

Vickie pushed Kenny and Lydia into the bedroom. "Keep him in until I come for you, do you hear?"

Lydia nodded, her face ashen. Vickie closed the door and ran down.

At the bottom of the stairs, Kiril was cradling his daughter in his arms and rocking from side to side. Vickie bent over them.

"How is she? Shall I get cold water?"

Kiril shook his head. "She's dead, Victoria. Her neck is broken."

*   *   *

Her parents left for San Francisco after the funeral and Vickie worried that the combination of stress and the long plane ride might be too much for her stepfather, but she could not persuade them to stay longer.

"My vacation time is over, Vickie," Lydia said, "and it's the best thing for both of us to go back to work."

And so they left, Kiril helping Lydia up the steps at the National Airport as Vickie watched her parents—suddenly stooped and aged, disappear inside the plane. She held tight to Grisha's soft little hand, her vision blurred by tears that ran down her cheeks. The plane's door closed, the aircraft taxied down the runway, but Vickie did not move until she saw the plane take off in the distance.

Two days later, Kiril died from a massive heart attack. Lydia's hysterical voice shrilled over the phone. "Why am I still alive? Death has forgotten me!"

*   *   *

For weeks afterward, Vickie was haunted by the memory of the two funerals, so painful, so close together. Her stepfather who had always been so good, so loving to her, and whom she loved deeply, was no more. A part of her childhood and adolescence died with him. A loving, tender bond had been broken. And how sad that he had died in his self-imposed exile, without giving up his dream of an Imperial Russia. The last time she saw him at the airport—did she hug him well? Did she kiss him? She couldn't remember, and those details tortured her. And her sister…her spunky childhood companion. Her beautiful, defiant sister. She never realized how much she loved Nina when she was alive.

During the day, this layered residue of memories pursued her. It hurt so much. If only they hadn't quarrelled. If only…but all the 'if onlys' wouldn't bring Nina back.

There was something else. She hadn't tried to help her sister more with her problem; she had been more disgusted by her alcoholism than she had been compassionate and understanding. And…she had felt sorrier for Ross than for her sister. This made it harder for Nina.

How awful to admit that.

In the ensuing months the shock wore off, sharpening the pain of loss.

Ross kept saying that if Nina hadn't been drinking, this would not have happened. "I should have been more forceful with her," he said. "I didn't do enough. I should have put her in a hospital."

Vickie put her hand on his. "Ross, my dear, did it occur to you that even if you had done that, it might not have worked anyway?" She paused and held his look for a few seconds, then added softly: "I knew my sister better than you."

He stared at Vickie for a long moment, then slumped in his chair and sighed. "God, these last few months have been hell."

Kenny's nightmares gradually became less and less frequent and eventually disappeared altogether, but almost a year passed before he stopped asking about his mother. At seven, he was a quiet child with thoughts and questions serious beyond his age. But one day he raised his trusting eyes to Vickie and said: "Aunt Vickie, Dad says that my mother went to live in heaven because she was very sick. Does this mean that in heaven she is not sick anymore?"

Vickie pulled him into her arms, stroked his hair and kissed him. "Yes, Kenny. Your mother is well in heaven. I'm sure she would want you to be a happy little boy and not worry about her."

"I think so too." And with that Kenny turned and walked out of the kitchen looking for Grisha.

Vickie put down her cup of tea on the kitchen table and let her gaze drift into the distance. How wrenching it was to see Kenny left motherless, and watch Ross-so stunned and bewildered.

And what of her mother? She was the one Vickie worried over the most. She had written her a letter.

Dear Mama, I worry about you constantly and I have a hard time understanding why you don't leave San Francisco for good and move to Washington. Your whole family is here, your grandchildren would enjoy you, and all of us would be relieved to have you nearby. I can appreciate your reluctance to live with us permanently. Your independence is too great for that, and I am not arguing that point. But you could live near enough for us to keep an eye on you and see you often. As for work, you'd have no problem here. Your age is no factor. They're crying for people like you with your knowledge of Russian and a good command of English. A few days ago I was approached by an engineering company asking if I knew of anyone who could take a job translating research papers. Evidently, they need technical articles translated into English. With an appropriate dictionary to assist you, it wouldn't be hard. Do think about it.

Lydia wrote back immediately: Vickie, dear, don't think me ungrateful, for I deeply appreciate your concern, but it is difficult for me to uproot myself and start all over in another city. First of all, you have no guarantee that you and Brian will be in Washington for a long time. It's not a permanent residence for you, and once you leave, I'd have no one there except Ross and Kenny. After almost eight years in America, my roots are here in San Francisco. I like my work, my colleagues, and I have a wide circle of Russian friends whom we met through Church activities. I have our apartment where Kiril and I were happy together, and there are his students, whose parents haven't forgotten me and occasionally invite me for dinner. Even Jane's friend, Louise Chambers, keeps in touch and takes me out to lunch. All these things connect me to Kiril. He's buried here and when I visit the cemetery, I talk to him and feel his presence.

What would I do in Washington, that huge, sprawling city? I would have to meet new people and make friends all over again. San Francisco is small, it's easy to get around and most of my friends live in the Richmond district within a short distance of one another.

No, dear girl, I want to stay here. As long as my health holds out, and I have no reason to think otherwise, I'll be able to visit you all and enjoy my grandsons. You see, I want to think that I'm still young enough to be independent and not lean on my children.

"She shouldn't live in the past, it isn't healthy," Vickie said to Brian, after she had read the letter. "Here, in Washington, she'd have all her family around her. She would make a fresh start and find Russian friends in no time at all."

Brian listened, then said: "Sounds like Lydia has her life well in hand. What makes you think that a fresh start would be good for her? I remember my mother saying once how traumatic it would be for her to uproot herself and move away from San Francisco. It may be that this link with Kiril is exactly what your mother needs to keep her going. I know you're upset, hon, but your obligation toward her is getting to you. Sometimes the hardest thing to do is to let go of our loved ones."

"I wish I had your practical approach to life, Brian. I envy your knack of forgetting you had a problem once you've come up with an answer."

"Oh, I don't know about that. I may keep some of my worries to myself while you're able to get them off your chest. Your way may be healthier in the long run."

Vickie laughed. "Your only obvious concern is over Grisha. You're afraid to let him run free even in our fenced garden. You hover over him constantly. We must be careful not to spoil him more than he is already. He's becoming quite a handful, or haven't you noticed?"

"Well, he's my only child, and he's quite a kid. I don't think you can spoil anyone with love."

"I'm not talking about love. He's my child, too, remember? But I try not to give in to him like you do."

"Well, hon, I indulge him, and you discipline him. What are mothers for? Let's not quarrel over our Grisha, shall we? Ross and Kenny are coming over tomorrow night, and while Ross gives me another lesson in chess, you can discipline the boys."

"Thanks a lot!" Vickie cried in mock anger, but Brian had already left the room.

*   *   *

Ross and his son had become frequent visitors to the house on Sixteenth Street, where they were welcomed with open arms. Brian enjoyed Ross, who was a good listener, who appreciated and responded to his sense of humor. For her part, Vickie was glad to mother Kenny and have a playmate for Grisha. The two cousins complemented each other well, for Grisha at five was a constant chatterbox, precocious and curious about everything.

The next afternoon Ross and Kenny arrived before Brian returned from work. "Are we too early?" Ross asked, giving Vickie a peck on the cheek.

"Not at all," Vickie said, hugging Kenny. "You're right on time. Brian called a few minutes ago and said he'd be a little late. Why don't you be the man of the house and pour me a drink?"

Ross smiled. "I'd love nothing better."

Vickie took the boys by the hands and led them into the kitchen, where the housekeeper was making a casserole. "If you boys are good tonight, Mrs. Stewart will give you some popcorn while we wait for dinner."

Grisha clapped his hands. "Goodie, goodie!"

Kenny nodded eagerly. "I'd like that too. Will we have butter on the popcorn?"

Mrs. Stewart, a short and rotund woman, well over fifty, shook her finger at him. "And what do you think? What kind of popcorn is it without butter? Of course it has butter!" and when Kenny blushed, she chuckled. "You'll have two big bowls, because my dinner won't be ready for some time yet. Now run along both of you and be good."

Vickie took the bowls and beckoned the boys to follow her to the stairs, where she placed the popcorn in their hands and said: "Now go to Grisha's room and don't drop too much on the floor."

The boys scrambled up, leaving a trail of scattered popcorn on the stairs. Vickie sighed, and rejoined Ross in the living room. He handed her the bourbon and coke, then sat down in an armchair and put his scotch and soda on the coffee table.

"Boys will be boys," he said, leaning back. "You have no idea, Vickie, how fortunate I feel to have you all in Washington. Especially this last year…" he coughed, then went on, "I don't know how I would have managed alone. You're so good to Kenny. I know that if not for you, Kenny would still have nightmares."

"You're giving me too much credit, Ross. You're a loving father and Kenny senses it. You can't fool children."

Ross took a sip of his drink. "For a while there I thought the world had stopped for me. It was so hard to go on." He paused, looked at his glass, then lifted it in a toast. "But thanks to you, I'm better now. Guess what, I'm even thinking about starting a new project."

"What about that cardiac machine you were going to work on?"

Ross shrugged. "I waited too long. Someone else thought of it already. When things settle down a bit, I may come up with another idea to work on."

"I'm sorry."

"Don't be. After Nina died, nothing mattered except Kenny. Losing the idea to someone else was a small price to pay to insure Kenny's emotional health. And I still say, I have you to thank for it. But what about you? Have you completely given up working for the State Department?"

"Brian objects, and I'm no longer that eager to work there now that I have two boys to care for. What I'd really like to do, is broadcast for the VOA. That would be a real challenge, but I admit Brian has a point. I'd have a problem keeping a schedule that could include night shifts as well."

"I have to side with Brian on that one, Vickie. Kenny and Grisha are lucky to have you at home."

"Anybody home?" Brian's cheerful voice sounded in the hallway and moments later he burst into the living room, all smiles. "Boy, do I have news for you!" he said, hugging Vickie and whirling her around the room.

The boys scrambled down the stairs and Grisha rushed at Brian. "Daddy, Daddy," he cried, "Look! Kenny and I had popcorn! There's one left for you. I saved it."

"Well, how generous of you, son," Brian said, popping the lonely kernel into his mouth. "And what about you, Kenny, did you eat all of yours?"

Kenny shook his head and silently offered him his bowl. A few kernels were on the bottom. "That's for you, Uncle Brian. You can have them all."

Brian took one and gave the bowl back to Kenny. "You eat the rest, like Grisha did, O.K.?"

"What's the good news? I can't wait!" Vickie said.

Brian sat down on the couch. "How would you like to live in Moscow for a while, hon?"

"Moscow??"

Brian grinned at Ross and then looked at Vickie. "Yes! I've been assigned to our embassy there!"

Vickie blinked several times, then added quickly, "Why, that's great!" hoping that her voice sounded enthusiastic. A moment later she rose. "I have to get something in the bedroom. Will you two excuse me for a moment?"

She ran upstairs and locked herself in the bathroom, the only place she had ever felt safe from prying eyes.

She leaned against the door and breathed deeply.

Moscow. Russia. Henri.

She had thought she would never see him again, but fate was leading her close to him once more. Was he in Moscow?

Claudette could tell her. And if he lived in Moscow, how would she be able to keep herself from looking him up?

She glanced at herself in the mirror and pressed a wet washcloth to her flaming cheeks. Brian had been promoted to full colonel a year ago. She should have expected a transfer, expected that Brian could be assigned to Moscow, but she had never permitted her random thoughts to dwell on that possibility or to open the airtight urn of hidden memories.

She closed her eyes and sighed. Russia. Her parents' *rodina,* their homeland. At last she would see it....

They were waiting for her in the living room. She had to go and rejoin them. Quickly, she brushed a curl off her forehead and went downstairs.

CHAPTER TWENTY-SEVEN

Moscow and Leningrad
Summer of 1957

On their way to Moscow, the Hamiltons stopped over in Paris. Lydia had asked Vickie to see Claudette as a gesture of kindness to the daughter of her old friend. When Vickie hesitated over the phone, Lydia added: "After all, Claudette was not responsible for her brother's actions."

When Brian said that he had other things to do in Paris, Vickie took Grisha with her to see Claudette.

They met at a small restaurant off the Champs Elysées, where Claudette, svelte and chic in a tailored blue suit and matching pillbox hat, knelt before Grisha, shook his hand solemnly, then hugged and kissed him. As she stood up, she kept looking at the little boy, then slowly, with a knowing smile, raised her eyes to Vickie.

"What an exquisite child," she said, ignoring Vickie's hand and clasping her in her arms. "I'm so grateful you brought him along."

Vickie stiffened at her touch. "Mama asked that I be sure to see you for old times sake." She wanted her voice to sound cordial, but it came out flat.

Claudette pulled back, her hands on Vickie's shoulders. "Thank you," she said, then added, "For many reasons." She then turned back to Grisha, and lifted him up on a chair beside her. "You can call me Aunt

Claudette," she said to him in Russian, and little Grisha, never one to hold his thoughts in check, said: "Aunt Covette, you smell good!"

The tension eased and both women smiled. After they ordered lunch, Claudette said: "Vickie, you look wonderful, and I'm so glad to see you."

"Thank you. You look well too. Paris must agree with you."

"Yes, it does. I love it here." Claudette lit a cigarette, inhaled deeply, then leaned forward. "I was so shocked by Nina's death. Your mother wrote that Nina fell down the stairs. How did it happen?"

Vickie hesitated. She couldn't talk about Nina's alcoholism. She didn't want to hear pity in Claudette's voice or listen to the platitudes about a young life so tragically snuffed out. She laced her fingers under the table and squeezed hard.

"She caught a heel of her dress shoe on the shag rug," she said.

Claudette waited for further details and when none came, she touched Vickie's arm. "Must have been terrible for you all. What a waste." Her voice broke. "Nina was such a dear friend."

Her voice quavered and Vickie saw that she was trying to blink away tears.

"I loved her," Claudette added, and Vickie saw genuine grief in her eyes and a flash of some deep, hidden emotion. It occurred to her that it was Claudette who had awakened Nina sexually, Claudette who had given her something she would not have otherwise experienced before her death.

She leaned forward and put her hand on Claudette's arm.

"It was a dreadful shock," she heard herself say. "And then, right after Nina's death, my stepfather died."

"Yes, I know. It was good of your mother to write me. I know what it means to lose a parent. I cried for a long time when Mama died."

Vickie was glad for a change of subject. "What about your father? Where is he now?"

"He still lives in Fontainebleau. I visit him regularly."

"You must be a great comfort to him, Claudette. You were always his favorite."

Claudette shook her head. "He's disappointed in me because I haven't married. Frankly, I don't want to dash his hopes, but I doubt that I shall ever marry. I'm too involved in my career. Besides, I don't want to change my way of life."

How sad for Jacques Jobert, Vickie thought, especially if he suspected the truth about his daughter. Aloud she said: "I'm glad you're near enough to visit him often."

"Yes, I am too. Now Papa and I have another tragedy to cope with. Such a shame for our family. How could Henri have done such a thing?" She narrowed eyes. "Did you know about his work with the Soviets?"

Vickie avoided Claudette's eyes. "He told me he wanted to immigrate to Russia when we were still in Shanghai. That's why I wouldn't marry him."

"I can't excuse what he has done, but he is my brother and I worry about him. His letters are pathetic because they say so little. The fact that he doesn't rave about his life there, tells me a lot."

"Then what does he say?"

"He says that he teaches French at an elementary school and receives a good stipend from the government. He has an adequate apartment in Leningrad and has a housekeeper. Although I don't know what he means by 'adequate'. Oh, Vickie, he must be so lonely!"

Vickie's heart lurched. He was in Leningrad. He lived in Leningrad. She would be visiting the great city. And he would be there.

"What makes you say that he's lonely?" She placed her words carefully between the thumps of her heart. "He speaks Russian as well as you and I do, and he always dreamed of living in the Soviet Union. Why don't you visit him?"

Claudette shook her head vigorously. "Oh no! I can't!"

"Why?"

"I'm afraid of what I'd find."

"What about your father? How is he taking this?"

"Papà can't forgive. He's so ashamed, he won't even come to Paris for fear he'll meet somebody who knew Henri. I told him that you were going to Russia, and hoped that he'd ask you to see Henri, but he never said a word. So, I'm the one who is asking you now to see my brother. Perhaps it will be awkward for you, considering everything..." She glanced at Vickie, averted her eyes and took a deep draw on her cigarette. "But please! Write me how he is! Maybe he needs something from the west but is too proud to ask?"

She opened her purse and pulled out a piece of paper. "Here's his address." When she saw Vickie hesitate, she said softly, "Please?"

Vickie stared at the piece of paper. "I—I can't promise. I may not be alone in Leningrad, or there might not be time."

Claudette put her hand over Vickie's. "Please, I beg you!" she said. "Surely you'll be able to find an hour to slip away and see him?" There was such pleading in Claudette's eyes. How could she refuse to see him? She reached for the address and put it in her purse. "I'll see what I can do."

Claudette squeezed her hand. "Thank you."

Grisha tugged at Vickie's sleeve. "Mama, I don't want to eat this fish. Why can't I have a hamburger?"

"He's going to have a hard time getting a hamburger in Russia, isn't he?" Claudette said, tickling Grisha under his chin.

Vickie laughed. "I'll have to get him used to our Russian *kotlety*. After all, it's almost the same thing, only shaped differently."

Claudette bent over, smoothed Grisha's hair and kissed him on both cheeks. Then, looking at Vickie with a slow smile, she said: "A beautiful boy! Will you let me see him again when you come back to Paris?"

✳   ✳   ✳

In Moscow, Brian and Vickie were assigned an apartment in the embassy compound on Tchaikovsky Street. The two-bedroom affair came with a sulky Russian housekeeper—no doubt cleared by the Soviets and instructed to report on their activities. It was a far cry from their spacious home in Washington, which they had leased before leaving the States. Vickie was prepared to adapt, however, to the inconveniences, and was vastly amused when in their initial briefing they were told that since their apartment would be bugged, they were to go outdoors for any private conversations or arguments they might have.

"It works very well," the official said with a chuckle. "By the time the angry couples take the elevator down past security guards, they're either too embarrassed to quarrel or else had time to cool off. More often than not, they smile sheepishly and return to their apartments."

Very quickly, Brian and Vickie were swept up in the merry-go-round of diplomatic receptions where Vickie was in demand as an interpreter. She set aside Claudette's request with various excuses: she was living in Moscow and had to wait for a suitable opportunity before she could go north. What possible reason could she give Brian so soon after their arrival without arousing his suspicions?

*   *   *

Moscow in the summer with its still and tired air, did nothing to cheer up the somber faces of forever hurrying pedestrians. Over the centuries, the warm sun had bleached the gaudy colors of St. Basil's Cathedral on Red Square. Vickie marvelled at the intricate design of the church's cupolas and wondered how many people who admired the cathedral knew about the torture at its completion when, to keep the edifice unique, Tsar Ivan the Terrible ordered that the architects, the Yakovlev brothers, be blinded.

Across the square, however, the golden domes of the Kremlin cathedrals still sparkled, rising majestically into the sky. What a thrill it was for Vickie to see the places she had studied about in history books: The Kremlin's churches, the Armory museum, the huge Tsar-Bell that was so heavy it had dropped and cracked as it was being hoisted up centuries ago.

For the first few weeks in Moscow, she couldn't get enough of sightseeing. She went to the Novodevichy Monastery and saw the cloister where Peter the Great had incarcerated his rebellious half-sister Sophia. In the adjacent cemetery, Vickie visited Gogol's and Chekhov's graves, where loving hands had left fresh bouquets of flowers. Flowers everywhere!

She steeped herself in this Russian past, avoiding the showplaces of Soviet achievements. She stood in the Tretyakov Gallery before Shishkin's famous painting, *Morning in the Pine Forest,* and felt as if she were back in her childhood. She wanted to reach up and touch the three cubs and mama bear as she had done so many times to the reproduction that hung in their home in Harbin.

As she left the gallery and walked to the bus stop, she passed a long line of people waiting to get into a tiny store on the corner. Vickie stopped.

"What are you waiting for?" she asked a woman at the end of the line. The woman glanced around her suspiciously, then closed the book she was reading and said: "I don't know." When she saw Vickie's surprised look, she added: "If I go to the front and ask, I'll lose my place. Whatever they're selling, I can use."

Vickie walked on. Near the entrance to an apartment building, an old woman was sweeping the sidewalk with a long besom of twigs. As Vickie passed by, the woman paused, leaned on the broom and watched her with wary eyes.

Vickie sighed. Mother Russia. What has happened to you? She rode the bus back to the embassy in a daze. This Russia was not as familiar as she had expected it to be. Although everything around her was written and spoken in Russian, the whole atmosphere was heavy with suspicion. Her soul wept for the people. Stalin's purges, Hitler's war. The strength it took under such odds! She had once said to Brian that her soul cried out in Russian and she felt a foreigner in America; well, she was in Russia now, and she felt more a foreigner here than back in the United States. A Russian saying came to mind: 'Neither fully detached from *us*, nor fully attached to *them*'.

Was she going to mourn a Russia that no longer existed? Her parents had believed that it would return, but did *she* believe it? Of course not. She had long claimed America as her own. This country she had learned to love as a child through her parents was her heritage, and as such, must be stored away in the attic of her mind.

At their apartment, Grisha greeted her with hugs. "Mama, mama! Papa promised to ask Santa Claus to bring me a tricycle for Christmas!"

"Yes, I'm going to do just that," Brian said. "Going for a walk with you on the streets of Moscow is a real challenge, young man."

Vickie raised her brows. "Why here, in Moscow?"

"Too many people on the sidewalks. He'd let go of my hand and I had a terrible time keeping an eye on him. Crossing the street was something else. It's amazing that the militia doesn't arrest anyone for jay walking. It seems like the pedestrians play a game: if the traffic is still a fair distance away, they rush against the red light."

He looked at Vickie. "By the way, I was told today that a group of embassy wives are planning a tour to Leningrad and you're included if you want to go."

*   *   *

Of course she went. How could she not want to go? Leningrad. Peter the Great's city. Immortalized by Pushkin when he wrote: 'I love you, Peter's creation, I love your stern, graceful look…'

How often had she read about it, heard about it, dreamed of it? Peter the Great wanted it to be a window on Europe, Pushkin said, and indeed it was. Not at all like Moscow with its medieval Byzantine Kremlin. This one had been enhanced by Italian architects, Rossi and Rastrelli who had brought their talents to the city during the reign of Peter's daughter, Elizabeth, and dressed the Neva River's shores with palaces in pinks and yellows and blues and greens. The result was an elegance few cities could match.

But the pastels had faded over the years, and the rusted, gaping drainpipes now wept with muddy rain water. In the back, hidden in the bowels of the city, soot and slime-covered courtyards with unlit stairwells still exhuded their foul breath.

She had gone on a city tour that took her to the Peter and Paul Fortress, where she saw a row of identical white marble sarcophagi of the Tsars, whose opulent and sometimes turbulent lives were so equalled in death; she was overwhelmed by the pink marble and sheer magnificence of the malachite and lapis lazuli columns inside the St.Isaac's Cathedral, where the Tsars' ghosts still worshipped at the silenced inner sanctum; she had broken away from the conducted tour to go to the Moika Canal and visit the house where Pushkin lived and died. There, the sight of the dark leather couch on which he lay in mortal agony—the victim of a senseless duel—filled her with sorrow. She took a taxi to the Alexander Nevsky Cemetery and stood in awe before the two black marble angels, their wings spread over Tchaikovsky's grave, guarding the immortal music of the mortal man.

During the whole time, the thought of *him* would not leave her. Somewhere in this city, he was going about the business of living, unaware that she was in town. What had happened to her resolve to see him? Why the fear, the avoidance? She had promised Claudette. So, finally, the morning the other wives were going to the Hermitage to see the Impressionist art, she told them she didn't feel well and would not go along.

She would see him today. Quick, before her courage failed her! Her hands shook as she studied the directions to his street she got from the concierge downstairs. It was within walking distance of the Hotel Astoria. She took a western edition of collected poems of Anna Akhmatova out of her locked suitcase and leafed through the pages. Akhmatova—a great Russian poet of the twentieth century who had been alternately held in esteem and disgrace ever since the revolution. Henri loved her work. Vickie wrapped the book. She would give it to him if she made it all the way to his apartment without turning back.

On the street, the refreshing breeze from the Gulf of Finland cooled her flaming face. She walked slowly, and was amused by two young men who passed her and commented on her good looks, unaware that she understood Russian. She paused at the bridges, watched the hydrofoils skim the surface of the Neva, followed the progress of a dried leaf bobbing on the river's current. Her feet kept moving, carrying her closer and closer to her destination. And then, she found herself standing on the sidewalk across from his apartment house. An old building, it had an air of exhaustion with its paint faded, its corroded drainpipes leaking remnants of yesterday's rain in a rusty rivulet across the sidewalk.

What if he walked out and saw her there. What would he think? That she had finally given in, or that she was just curious? She mustn't let this happen. It would be cruel. But hadn't she suffered too? The anger, the frustration, the appalling sense of loss. Her heart knocked in her ears. She rubbed her temple, brushed her hair back, and, clutching the book to her chest, crossed the street and rang the bell.

A young, dark-haired woman in a print dress opened the door and stood wiping her hands on her apron. With one quick glance she took in Vickie's clothes and shoes and then said cautiously: "*Vam kovo nado?*—Whom do you want to see?"

"Is Henri Jobert in?" Vickie asked.

The woman turned her head to the side and called: "Henri, we have a visitor!" then, stepping aside, let Vickie walk into a spacious room furnished in modern blond furniture and oriental rugs.

The woman pointed to a straight chair at the dining table and said: "Sit down, please," but Vickie remained standing. The woman looked up the carpeted stairs, and called again: "Henri! There's a woman to see you."

She used the familiar 'thou' and Vickie took a second look. She was a little plump and rather pretty with dark eyes and short curly hair. Her lips were red and full, and although she wore no makeup, her face had a healthy glow. *Young and pretty.*

Vickie straightened and tensed.

"Where are you from?" the woman asked, looking at Vickie with suspicion.

"I live in Moscow," and when the woman raised her brows, Vickie hastened to explain, "my husband is with the American embassy. I knew Henri when we lived in China."

There was a hint of relief in the woman's face, and a first tiny smile touched her lips as she offered her hand.

"My name is Irina Volkova." Her palm was rough and the handshake firm.

"And I'm Victoria Hamilton."

At a slight sound behind her, Vickie turned to see that Henri had come down and stood at the bottom of the stairs, holding on to the banister. All color had drained from his face as he stared at her. His face was drawn, there were deep lines around his eyes and mouth. He had lost weight and his slacks and open-collared shirt hung loosely about his frame. All the anger she had felt on the street evaporated and gave way to an overwhelming surge of love and compassion.

Aware that Irina was watching them, Vickie moved quickly, offering him her hand. "*Bonjour,* Henri. Brian is now with the embassy in Moscow," she said, her words racing forward. "When we stopped over in Paris, Claudette asked me to see you."

Henri didn't say a word. It was obvious that he was making an enormous effort to control himself.

"You never told me about Madame Hamilton," Irina Volkova said, accusation clear in her voice.

Slowly, Henri pulled his eyes away from Vickie and glanced at Irina. "Please leave us alone," he said, his voice hoarse.

Irina looked from one to the other, then turned on her heel and stalked out of the room, banging the door.

So, the woman cared enough to be jealous.

"Who is she?" Vickie asked nodding after her.

"My watchdog, assigned to me by the government. She's also my housekeeper and—and sometime companion."

Companion! She sensed embarrassment in his voice and felt her face grow warm with resentment. She had never stopped to think how she would react if another woman came between them. God, what right did she have to…

They sat down across the table from each other. The room was quiet. She was used to hearing cars and trucks rumbling past the embassy compound in Moscow but here, there was no traffic. Homey sounds came from the kitchen: a whistling kettle, a clanking of pots, a scraping of a chair on the floor.

After a short pause, Henri said: "Would you like a cup of tea?"

"No, thank you. I can't stay long. How are you?"

Henri shrugged. "I'm alive."

Vickie looked at him closely. "You're different."

"Forgive me if I'm slow, but it was such a shock to see you. For just a moment, I thought that—" he shook his head dismissing the thought…

She touched his hand. "Tell me about yourself. Are you happy to be in Russia?"

"I made a terrible mistake." He gave her a small, sad smile. "After I sacrificed so much…It wasn't easy to admit that I was wrong. Wherever I turned, the truth stared me in the face." He chewed on his lip. "The devil of it is, there's no escape. Can you believe that? No escape. That's the worst of it."

"You can't leave Russia?"

"I've tried. God, how I've tried! No one wants a traitor. I'm no longer a man with a dream. And even if—as I've dreamed you'd have come to stay—I'd have sent you away. At least there is that much decency left in me."

"Don't crucify yourself. You followed your conscience," she said with compassion. "You followed your conscience," she repeated. "People live here, work, enjoy themselves. You…you could get married, have a family, have friends."

"Yes, there are good people in Russia, and one day there will be someone with a vision to change things, but now…" Henri hesitated, then went on, "I can't relate to anyone. I live among strangers. We speak a different language."

She had said that often enough herself. The air between them was heavy.

"If there's no way out, you must adjust, Henri."

"And have *you* done that?"

"Yes, I have. America is where I belong. But you are here, and you must ignore things that bother you."

He nodded toward the kitchen. "She's the only one I can talk to."

"But you teach French, you're with students and colleagues during the day. What about them?"

"I'm ignored by most. To them I'm a man from the west. And they were taught since childhood to mistrust foreigners."

He paused, then burst out: "Oh, why did you have to come here?" There was such pain and love in his eyes. "I had reached a point where I wasn't thinking of you every day, and now—" He grasped her hands. "You look wonderful, so vibrant, so luminous. You wear life with such grace. Tell me, how's Grisha? My little Grisha?"

Vickie pulled her hands away. "He's fine. Active and curious about everything."

"Did you bring a picture for me?"

"No. I thought it best not to."

Henri sighed. "You were right. It would hurt more."

Vickie tried to steer the conversation to safer ground. "What do you do with your free time?"

"I read. I have enough money to buy lots of books. I stand in line when new ones come out and buy all I can. I reread Jack London recently. He said that the proper function of man is to live, not to exist.

And I'm existing, Vickie, not living."

"You should marry, Henri. Have someone to care for you," she said and was surprised by her own words. Love still shone in them but she realized that the nature of her love had changed, for the desire had burnt itself out. There had been too much pain, too many partings. And he realized it too, for she saw that particular sorrow in his eyes—the deep, grieving sorrow...

"It's too late. Everything is too late."

"Count the good things. I've heard of communal apartments, and you know what that means. You have a whole apartment to yourself, and a very nice one. Be thankful for that!"

"It's all over for me. I'm trapped here and it's all of my own making. That's the worst torture."

The back of Vickie's neck crawled. She wanted to leave, yet lingered, yearning for the old Henri to surface if only for a second, so she would have that memory to take away with her.

The kitchen door flew open and Irina walked into the room, her arms propped at her sides. "Do you want some tea or coffee?" she asked, hostility frank in her voice.

Vickie rose. "No, thank you. I must leave now." She turned to Henri. "I have to join the rest of the tour group I'm travelling with. What shall I tell Claudette?"

"That I'm alive."

She gave Henri the book of poems, and shook hands with him. At his touch, a wave of such burning raced up her arm that she withdrew her hand quickly, and turned to Irina. A sometime companion, he had said. This dark-haired woman and Henri...Vickie clutched her purse. She must leave. Now.

But at the door, she paused. Irina cared for him, probably loved him, and without her, Henri would be far worse.

Blinking the tears away, she turned to Irina. "Will you please come outside for a minute?"

Out on the sidewalk, Vickie searched Irina's face. "I don't know how you feel about Henri, but I suspect you do care. Stay with him. Don't leave him!"

Irina's eyes flashed. "He hardly looks at me. He sits all day with a book or listens to records. I have to drag him out to go to a concert or even for a walk. He—hee's so sullen."

"Don't give up. Be patient. Please!"

Irina raised her chin. "I have my pride. Do you think we're not human here? We too have feelings."

"That's why I'm asking you to stay with him. Henri needs to know that someone cares for him in Russia, don't you see?"

Irina looked at Vickie for a while, then turned and ran back into the house.

Vickie stumbled blindly along the street, turned the corner, and hurried toward her hotel. Pedestrians crowded the streets, bumped into her and rushed on without apologizing. She slowed down when she reached the Dvortzovy Quay on the Neva. At the railing, she leaned over, her stomach heaving, teeth clenched so hard her jaws ached.

Someone touched her shoulder. "Are you sick?"

She raised her head to face a fat woman in a blue dress, holding an *avoska*, a net bag full of groceries. The stem of a turnip protruded through the net and a large onion next to it smelled so strong, it sent a wave of nausea through Vickie again.

"No, just a little dizzy," she managed to say.

The woman looked her over—they all looked her over before speaking—and asked: "Do you want me to lead you to a taxi stand? It's only one block from here."

"No, thank you." And then, not wanting to sound rude, she added: "I'll be all right. I need some fresh air."

She wanted peace, a quiet time without people, just the trees and the grass and the sky. She went to the Summer Garden. Inside the filigreed iron gate, she walked along the sandy path, flanked by shrubbery, leafy elms and lindens. Scattered among the lilac bushes were mythological statues, a reminder that this was the famous Summer Garden, another remnant of the golden era of St.Petersburg, where ladies in batiste dresses with lace-trimmed parasols walked on the arms of their escorts, and children frolicked under careful supervision of their nannies.

The garden had a natural setting, not studied like the grounds in Jessfield Park, where she and Henri had walked together along those well-kept pathways. Strangely, it evoked a soothing sense of sadness, a pocket of pleasant memories that she did not want to throw away. Those were the memories she would treasure.

She sat down on a bench, listening to the birds and the distant sounds of human life. An ant scurried across the path seeking the sanctuary of the grass. She made circles in the sandy earth with the toe of her shoe. Round and round, like the spiral of life's journey.

A breeze rustled the leaves of an elm, whined somewhere above her head, then vanished around the statue of Krylov and the animals from his fables. How she loved those fables as a child! Now, the statue towered over her—a link between the treasured past and the modern Russia.

She had said her final goodbye to Henri in Washington. She thought she would never see him again. Still, somewhere in her subconscious she had been hiding a dream: Brian had taken a Russian refresher course and one day he could be sent to Moscow. Then maybe...

Now, though, she would not see Henri again by her own choice. He had that doomed look about him. If she had found him happy in Russia, if he had told her that he had realized his dream, perhaps she could have made peace with herself. Perhaps, at long last she could have accepted the chasm between them, and the finality of a love lost. And then, she could have succeeded in tearing him out of her system...maybe. But not this. Not the wrenching pity she felt seeing that his dream, which had cost them their happiness together, had betrayed him.

"Why are you crying, *tyotya*?"

Vickie started. A little boy, no bigger than Grisha, stood before her, licking an ice cream cone and staring at her with serious brown eyes. His mother came up. "Don't bother the lady, Slavik," she said taking his arm and pulling him away.

Vickie rose. She had to write to Claudette, tell her about Henri in softly couched words. Why upset her? Things always seemed so much worse when one was far away. She hurried back to the hotel. The other women in her group would be waiting and she would have to pull herself together, listen to their excited talk about what they had seen and what she had missed. She wanted nothing more than to be back in Moscow with Brian and Grisha.

Two blocks from the hotel, she paused before a window display of sausages and cuts of meat which, she saw on closer scrutiny, were made of plastic. Vickie looked through the window. Several shoppers stood in line while three unsmiling women took their time waiting on them. Next to the shop, a gaping archway led into an inner courtyard. She peered in. A few mud puddles glistened in the sun, but the ground was well swept showing uneven streaks from a stiff besom. A whiff of urine sent her scurrying ahead. She increased her pace, anxious to be inside the red-carpeted hotel.

Once in her room, she took off her shoes, poured herself a glass of *Borzhom* mineral water and sat down in a red plush armchair. It was an old hotel, built in Tsarist times and furnished with Empire furniture, its dark woods polished to a soft gleam. The room was made to look like a parlor, the single bed curtained off in an alcove by a brocaded curtain. She drank the mineral water, waiting for the other women in her tour to knock on her door. Another day and she would be on her way to Moscow. She longed to hold Grisha in her arms. Her precious little boy. She closed her eyes, imagining Brian and Grisha waiting for her in Moscow, two people whose life she shared, and who would be so happy to see her.

Brian was such a good father. On weekends she must see to it that they did things together, just the three of them. They must go to Gorky Park where there would be other children for Grisha to play with.

Her Grisha. *That* joy no one could take away from her.

                *   *   *

Two embassy officials were waiting at the apartment when she got back to Moscow.

"There's been an accident, Mrs. Hamilton," the older of the two men said gently.

"Accident?"

The question echoed, hung in the room that had suddenly gone cold. The Russian housekeeper, Masha, stood just within the kitchen door, watching.

"My husband?"

"His leg is crushed. He's in the hospital, but it's—"

"What happened?"

"Your son. He ran out into the street and Col. Hamilton tried to stop him." The man's face worked hard. "The truck. It had no time to stop. It was very quick. Grisha didn't feel anything."

The younger man nodded. "Yes. He didn't feel anything. It was instant."

Something black and bottomless opened at her feet, and she fell into it. She heard a scream. Over and over it tore at the air.

Her own voice and it wouldn't stop.

CHAPTER TWENTY-EIGHT

Washington, D.C.

Brian had been evacuated first to the U.S.Military hospital in Wiesbaden, Germany, and then to Walter Reed Army Hospital in Washington. He was sedated most of the time, but in moments of lucidity, kept sobbing: "I failed! I failed! I couldn't stop him…Grisha! My Grisha!"

Vickie couldn't bear to look into his tortured eyes. The flight home was a blurr. Anger, blind, unreasonable anger choked her. Tight-mouthed, dry-eyed, she hugged herself and waited in the hospital until he was placed in a private room, then fled down the long corridor and out on the street.

Their house was still rented, so she looked for an apartment in Silver Spring and rented the first one she found near Walter Reed Hospital.

*   *   *

After the initial searing pain, came the long, bleak nights. Her grief was private. No one she knew had lost an only child and no one knew the truth about Grisha. Lydia knew, but she had never been close to her mother and it was too late now.

Sara Rosen would have understood. Sara would have found words of comfort to ease the pain. Oh, Sara, why does God take the good ones? She couldn't cry. She remembered that Henri couldn't either when he'd learned of his mother's death. Oh Henri, we've lost our child! Pain again. White hot. She yearned for sleep. Peaceful sleep. But peace wouldn't come. Grisha, Brian, Henri, Leningrad. Round and round the thoughts went, caught in a whirlpool. They chased sleep away and sucked her into herself. She drowned in her guilt, real and imaginary. The rational thought that she would have had no reason to keep Brian from taking Grisha for a walk even had she been in Moscow, had no power to erase the guilt that she'd lost Grisha because of her absence.

Was that her punishment for loving another man? Was this God's way of telling her that she must break her tie to Henri once and for all? But how does one make the heart heed the mind? She had already decided never to see him again. Hadn't God trusted her to keep her word?

She remembered Grisha's crestfallen face when she had left for Leningrad, his clinging to her skirt, her last hug and the hurried kiss on his cheek. She wanted to stop time, turn the clock back and hold him once more.

In the dark, early hours of the morning, she would doze and dream seeing Grisha stretching his little arms to her. She struggled over invisible obstacles to reach him as his terrified screams faded in the distance. She would wake gasping with a bruise on her soul, yet grateful that it was just a dream, only to come fully awake moments later to the real life nightmare.

Her apartment was small, two bedrooms, a living-dining room combination, a tiny kitchen. Yet she was glad their big house was still occupied. She didn't think she could bear seeing Grisha's room with its cheerful wallpaper that she had selected with such love and joy.

Once, she looked out the apartment window but all she saw was an unkempt back yard with a battered garbage can, where an alley cat scraped at the paper cups strewn on the ground, and meowed, shrinking into a corner at each sound of human steps. Thinking was hard.

Moving was hard. Her grief, having turned inward, fed itself on her strength, making every physical effort an enormous chore.

Sue Brennan came to see her, put her arms around Vickie. "I'll say it only once," she said. "I'm so sorry about everything that happened, sweetie. If you want to talk about it, fine, if not, it's O.K. too. I'll understand."

Vickie didn't answer. She sat at the kitchen table, still in her morning robe, half-full cup of cold coffee before her.

She couldn't talk. She was afraid to allow herself to speak for fear she'd go to pieces. Sue helped her dress, cleaned up the kitchen, promised to come back, and kept her promise. On the days when she couldn't come, Sue phoned in the mornings to ask if Vickie had had anything to eat, and when Vickie said yes, she pressed her to tell what she had eaten.

Slowly, Vickie forced herself to keep busy with chores. The hardest thing was to remember not to look at coloring books in a drugstore, or to stop at the grocery shelf for Grisha's favorite chocolate chip cookies. She avoided looking at children on the street.

Her beautiful boy was gone, brought home and cremated, so that there would be no grave to keep the pain alive. Ross had been wonderful. He had made all the necessary arrangements, and never once brought Kenny over.

She had to be strong. Brian's leg was not healing well, and he was growing more and more depressed. The doctors had warned her that he might lose his leg. Then came the day when they called her in and told her that it would have to be amputated below the knee. The surgeon assured her that with the knee intact, it would be much easier to use the prosthesis. "Go talk to him. You need time together," he said.

But what the doctor didn't know was that Vickie hadn't been able to mourn with Brian. All she had been able to do was to endure his guilt and his agony as she sat frozen, shrinking inside. When he stretched his hand seeking comfort, she could not give it to him.

And now his leg had to be amputated.

She went to his room but found him sedated and asleep. She glanced down at his legs outlined under the thin hospital blanket. A great surge of pity overwhelmed her, and she sat down on a chair beside his bed. Ever so gently, she stroked his leg, rubbed her face over his limp hand, then kissed it and tiptoed out of the room.

Brian was in great pain and sedated now, but later, as an amputee, he would be medically discharged from the army. How would he cope with the reality that his army career was over? Worried and distraught, she wanted to see Ross, to talk to him, to feel his strength and support. And suddenly she longed to hold her nephew in her arms. She called Ross and he said they'd be there in an hour.

They arrived at her door with large bouquets of roses and carnations, and, as Ross stepped into the hallway, Kenny rushed past him, circled Vickie's waist, and pressed his head against her chest. "Aunt Vickie, I missed you! I love you."

Seeing his upturned face, those round blue eyes, Vickie sank to her knees and hugged her nephew. "And I love you too. Very much." In the child's warm, soft embrace, she broke down at last.

"Aunt Vickie, please don't cry. Grisha isn't lonely. My mother is taking care of him in heaven. I know she is."

Vickie kissed him on the cheek, held his face between her hands. "Yes, Kenny, yes, she is."

Ross put his hand on his son's shoulder. "Kenny, would you like some cookies? I'll talk to Aunt Vickie while you go get them in the kitchen, O.K.?"

When Kenny was out of the room, Ross took Vickie's hand and stroked it while she wept.

"Ross, thank you for not saying anything," she managed to say, struggling to check her tears. "I can't stand any more words of sympathy."

"I know. I'm here whenever you need me."

The days were not as bad as the nights, she told him. There were errands to do and there was Brian.

"I'm so worried," she said. "What's he going to do after he's healed?"

"He'll make it. There are quite a few government agencies in Washington that could use him. Whatever he finds will keep him busy and that's the important thing."

He paused, then kissed her hand. "You're strong, Vickie. Brian needs you, but you need healing too. Think of yourself. Don't try to solve everything at once."

✶   ✶   ✶

As the doctors had predicted, the amputation went well, and Brian would be sent home to wait for the stump to heal before he was fitted for a prosthesis.

The day he was released, the surgeon talked to Vickie. "Mrs. Hamilton," he said with compassion, "your husband's depression has deepened. I'm afraid he may need treatment."

"What treatment are you talking about, doctor?" Vickie said, sitting up straight in her chair.

"Methods vary. There's psychotherapy for one, and drugs we could try."

Vickie had trouble breathing. "Doctor, my husband blames himself for our son's death. And the loss of his leg…I don't understand why you're talking about psychiatric treatment."

"Just a suggestion, Mrs. Hamilton."

Vickie rose. "Thank you, doctor. Let me bring him home and see how he does, before we do anything else."

The doctor nodded. "If he doesn't improve, I recommend you contact Col.Stevens. He's chief of our psychiatric department."

Vickie took Brian to the apartment. All he needed was to be home. It wouldn't be easy for him to find work, and he certainly didn't need psychiatric treatment on his record as well.

After she had settled him on the living room couch and covered his leg with a blanket, Brian appeared so weak, so pale and vulnerable, that she dropped down to her knees, put her arms around him and wept.

"Oh, Brian, I had such anger inside me. I'm sorry. So very sorry. But soon you'll be well. I'll help you. We'll help each other."

Brian tensed. "Damn it, Vickie, the guilt isn't eating at *you*."

But it is. It is!

Aloud, she said: "It wasn't your fault."

She tiptoed around his anguish, smoothing his hair and stroking his hand. "Don't blame yourself. Please."

Days passed in which he spent hours curled up on the living room couch, eyes closed, a deep scowl on his face.

Vickie went to a bookstore, bought every book on depression she could find and spent her evenings studying them.

"Don't push, but try to encourage your husband not to stay in bed," the doctor had said. What a dichotomy. Brian did not stay in bed, but wasn't lying all day on the couch the same thing? Night after night, she sat in the living room and watched him curl up into a fetal position, hiding from the world, from the very air they shared. He rose for meals, rolling himself in a wheelchair to the table, head bowed over the plate, frowning. He picked at his food, ate little, then returned to the couch.

She tried to rouse him. "Brian, please get up. Sit in a chair, talk to me. Or at least, read, watch television…*Anything* but what you're doing."

"It's too hard to get up," Brian mumbled. He mumbled a lot lately. "Leave me here for a little while." And that 'little while' stretched into hours.

One day, she borrowed Ross' record player and put on a record with the tunes they had listened to during their courting days in Shanghai: *As Time Goes By, Sentimental Journey, I've Got You Under My Skin*. Then she smoothed the blanket over his legs, took his hand and squeezed it. "Remember how we laughed in Shanghai about the trouble I had with American idioms? I didn't even know what 'kidding' meant. I thought it was a kid, a child."

But Brian did not respond. She replaced the record in its jacket and sat down in an armchair at the other end of the room, folding her arms tightly to control a rising panic. The man she had married, with his cheerful disposition and light touch, was gone now. Even the expression on his face had changed as if another entity inhabited his body. A melancholy presence moved about the room, permeated the atmosphere, strangled her.

Isolated from the world outside, suffocating in the presence of his depression, she endured another few days, and then went to see the psychiatrist.

Dr. Stevens listened sympathetically. "Mrs. Hamilton," he said, "your husband needs therapy. There are several drugs we can try, but you'll have to be patient as it may take a while to find the right one for him. If, however, a therapeutic dose becomes necessary, then he'll have to be hospitalized in the psychiatric ward."

"Why?"

"Because he has to be monitored carefully."

It would destroy Brian, Vickie thought.

"Depression caused by a traumatic experience," the doctor went on, "usully takes its course and disappears with time, but if it persists, it can cause chemical changes in the brain and that requires medication. There are several new drugs on the market, but it may take a few weeks before your husband shows improvement, so watch for any difference in his behavior. I'll follow him weekly." He wrote out a prescription and handed it to her.

Vickie twisted and untwisted the strap of her purse. "Dr. Stevens," she said, forcing the words out, "I need help too. His depression is suffocating me."

"Let me give you something that will help you sleep at night," Dr. Stevens said. He scribbled another prescription and handed it to her. "Don't be afraid to use it. You may be strong, but living with a depressed person takes its toll and affects even the strongest. Don't overestimate yourself. Take this medicine when the going gets rough."

He rose and patted her shoulder. "Do yourself a favor and don't hide your husband's illness from others. Remember, it *is* an illness. Find a friend to talk to. It'll be a lot easier on you."

Over the next few days, she tried the medicine, but it made her listless and weepy. In the quiet rooms, even the silence seemed to weep. Discouraged, she flushed the pills down the toilet.

It was easy for the doctor to advise her to confide in a friend. She just couldn't bring herself to complain about her husband. Being silent about Brian's problems had become a habit. There was Ross, of course, but she couldn't impose on him too often. She had no right, family or no family.

She didn't talk about Grisha and in her ironclad grief, threw herself into caring for Brian with a fury that had allowed her no time for healing. She cooked his favorite meals, practically force-fed him his breakfast, telling him over and over how important was the first meal of the day, helped him settle in his wheelchair in the living room, combed his hair, and saw to it that he had fresh pajamas every night.

But the medicine Dr. Stevens prescribed had strange side effects on Brian. Ordinarily a quiet sleeper, he jerked and thrashed at night, and his breathing was spasmodic. During the day, his hands trembled, and beads of perspiration glistened on his forehead. One morning, sitting opposite her at the kitchen table, he said: "I'm blocked. I can't think straight. What can I do now? I'm not prepared for civilian life. I'm finished."

Terrified to see the once-strong, self-assured man losing confidence in himself, she pleaded with Dr. Stevens to try another medicine.

So he started him on another drug, but the high dosage calmed Brian so much he acted like a zombie.

Desperate for company, she finally called Ross at work. He came in the evening, bringing Kenny with him. Vickie insisted they stay for supper. "I have leftover curried spaghetti. Enough for all of us. Brian doesn't eat much these days."

Ross held her face between his hands. "You're thin, Vickie. I worry about you. Try to eat more, you have to stay well."

"I know, but food sticks in my throat." She led them into the living room, where Brian was sitting in his wheelchair, staring at a book that she had placed in his lap earlier.

"Hi, Uncle Brian," Kenny said, leaning over to kiss him. Brian raised his head, his gaze focusing slowly on the boy's face.

Ross smiled at his brother-in-law. "Hello, Brian. How are you doing?"

"O.K." Brian said without looking up.

"I hear your leg is healing well. I guess you'll be ready for the prosthesis soon."

"Yes, but what good will that do?"

"Plenty. You'll be able to walk without crutches."

"Yes, but what kind of work can I do?"

"A lot. For one, you know Russian. There are companies who need translators."

"Yes, but my Russian isn't all that good."

"There you go again, 'yes, but.' Stop it!" Vickie cried. "It's the third time you've said it in the last few minutes." She glanced at Ross, threw her hands up, and went into the kitchen, closely followed by Kenny.

She turned to him. "The spaghetti will be ready soon. You like my spaghetti, don't you, honey?"

Kenny nodded, his huge eyes watching his aunt's every move. "What's wrong with Uncle Brian, Aunt Vickie? He looks funny."

"He's sad, Kenny. But I hope he'll be well soon."

"Is he sad because of his leg?"

"Yes, and other things too."

"I know. He's sad about Grisha, isn't he?"

Vickie busied herself with the casserole.

"Aunt Vickie," persisted the boy, "maybe if we told Uncle Brian that Grisha is happy in heaven, he'd feel better?"

Vickie put the casserole in the oven, and turned to Kenny. Lifting his chin up, she kissed him on the cheek, then stroked his hair and face. "Darling Kenny, I don't think we should talk about Grisha to Uncle Brian right now."

Ross came in. "Vickie, the medication is really affecting Brian. What does the doctor say?"

"He's changed the drugs. The first one wasn't the right one, and now he's—" she spread her arms in a helpless gesture, "I don't know what to do. I'm afraid to complain again, because the doctor said that the next step would be to hospitalize him in a psychiatric ward."

"Oh, Vickie! I wish—" Ross checked himself as Vickie's eyes filled. "Good Lord, how much more can you stand?"

Vickie bit her lip and didn't answer. He slapped his hand on the table. "You're taking too much upon yourself. You can't help him. If the psychiatrist wants to put Brian in the hospital, do it. He'll be better off in professional hands. You can't compete with professionals. Besides, you have to have time for your own grieving." He paused, then asked: "Is there another reason why you don't want him in the hospital?"

The buzzer sounded on the oven. Vickie put on padded mitts and pulled out the casserole. "We mustn't let this get cold. Will you get the salad from the refrigerator? We can eat in the kitchen."

"I won't wheel Brian in until you answer my question. God, I'm so worried about you!"

She sat down on the kitchen chair, propping her forehead with her hand. "Oh, Ross, I can't bear the thought of him in the hospital. It will destroy what pride he has left. I worry about his future. Who will hire someone who has been in a psychiatric ward?"

He sat down next to her and placed his hand over hers. "Aren't you mixing up your priorities?"

She glanced at him. "What do you mean?"

"I mean that you have to decide what's more important, his pride or his health."

She was silent for a few seconds, then sighed. "I guess you're right. That's what the doctor implied too. I'll talk to him tomorrow."

After dinner Ross said: "Brian, why don't we go to the movies? It'll do you good to get out of the house."

"No. You all go. I'm tired."

For a couple of hours Vickie was able to lose herself in a Disney movie, and listen to Kenny's happy laughter. It was good to be with them, to walk in the unburdened air outside, and she understood now what Dr. Stevens meant about the effect depression had on healthy people.

Back in the apartment, after she'd said goodbye to Ross and Kenny, she felt her throat tighten again. It was quiet and she found Brian asleep in the living room. A glass of water and a bottle of pills were on the coffee table beside the couch. She bent over to straighten the pillow under his head. Another bottle fell out spilling colored pills over the carpet. Vickie recognized Nembutal and Seconal capsules as well as other less potent sleeping pills.

The anger that for days had been crouching inside her, now exploded, pounding her head. She picked up a handful of pills and shook Brian. "Brian! Wake up! Do you hear me? Wake up!"

Brian opened his eyes and frowned. "Yes?"

She opened her fist. "What's this?"

He turned his face toward the wall. "I'm a noose around your neck."

"You're hiding behind your depression. Do you hear me?" She grabbed his shoulders but he freed himself. "I don't want to live anymore. I can't cope."

"What makes you think you have a monopoly on grief? Don't you think I suffer too? But I'm not hiding from the world."

"You're stronger than I am. I'm a failure."

"You know something? Your weakness is your own brand of strength. You're feeding on me! Well, I'm sick of it, do you hear?"

His face had a stony expression. "It's all my fault," he said in a flat voice. "I failed as a father and I failed as a husband."

"Stop pitying yourself! You've been a good father and a good man."

He looked at her with piteous, clouded eyes. "A good man? Not me. Not me!"

"Why not?"

He averted his eyes. "You know…that…other thing."

"I know, I know, but you've kept your side of the bargain and you've been good about it."

"Who needs a gay cripple for a husband? Find yourself another man."

Vickie straightened and took a step back. *What if he knew about me and Henri?* "Don't be foolish. All I want is for you to get well."

On an impulse, she moved toward him and took his hand. "Brian, would you like for a friend of yours to come and see you? A—a friend you care for…" She was digging for words in the dark pockets of her mind but they eluded her. "I—I mean someone like that Keith in San Francisco. Would he come if I phoned him?"

There! The name was out, the desperate, last ditch effort to help.

Brian's voice rose. "No!" Then he lowered his head. "I don't deserve you. Oh God! Our child, and I couldn't save him."

"Stop it! I miss him too!"

He grabbed his head in his hands. "It'd be better for me if Grisha had never been born."

Vickie advanced on him. "Whaaat?"

"You're the one who wanted a child." His voice was petulant.

"How dare you!"

He swayed from side to side. "Can't you understand? My very own…and I lost him! My own flesh and blood…I wish we'd never had him!"

Vickie went mad. She rushed at him and pounded his shoulders with her fists. "Oh, you miserable wretch!" she screamed. "Grisha was mine, not yours! Do you hear? Not yours!"

Brian caught one of her wrists. "What do you mean, not mine?"

Vickie gasped, clamped her hand over her mouth and tried to free her wrist but he held it. "What do you mean?"

She slumped and began to cry. "He was not your son. You were not…not his father."

Brian sat motionless for a few moments, then released her wrist and rearranged his hands on his lap. "The Frenchman." Vickie stiffened as he went on, "In Germany. Of course."

"Brian, please! Don't!"

But he went on as if he hadn't heard her. "How dumb to think that I would father only one child." His shoulders began to shake as he covered his face with his hands and broke into sobs.

Oh, God, how did she blurt this out? She knelt beside him, put her arms around his neck and cried with him. "Oh my dear, I'm sorry. So sorry! I never meant to—I mean, I was so mad. So mad at—at your depression."

She rose, wiped her tears with the back of her hand, and ran to the kitchen. There she leaned over the sink, trying to stem the flow of tears. She wiped her face with tissue, then saw the dinner dishes. Ross had helped her rinse and stack them, but now they had to be washed and dried. Methodically, she went about her work, hanging the wet towel on the oven handle, putting dishes and glasses away in the cupboard. But her hands trembled and one glass slipped out and fell to the floor, shattering into small pieces. She took a broom from the utility closet and swept the shards into a dust pan. Then she returned to the living room, knelt beside the couch and put her arms around Brian.

"My dear, I didn't mean to hurt you! You were a good father to Grisha. You were his only father. He loved you. What happened was my fault. Please! We're both distraught, let's grieve together, work through this terrible time together!"

He freed himself from her embrace, moved away. "You never really loved me," he muttered, then reached out his hand. "Just give me back those pills, will you?"

"You don't mean that," she said, her voice breaking. "You're passing your guilt on to me."

When he continued to keep his palm up, she rose. "I give up. Dr. Stevens was right…you should have been in the hospital all along."

"Dr. Stevens? I can't go on the psychiatric ward! It will be on my record when I'm discharged from the army. You can't do this to me! It will destroy me!"

Vickie steeled herself against his pleading voice. She turned and walked out of the room closing the door behind her. He was right of course. It would always be on his record. But what was the alternative? This time she had found the pills, but what of another time?

The next day, Vickie took him to the hospital and left him in Dr. Stevens' care.

"For the first week, Mrs. Hamilton, it would be a good idea if you didn't come to see your husband," the doctor said. "He uses you as a whipping boy, and it impedes his therapy."

A whipping boy? She finally realized that her listening to Brian all those days hadn't helped. All those psychology books she read…

She had a week. A week to gather strength for the next onslaught, for the doctor had warned her that the recovery was going to be slow and difficult.

The weather was turning cool, the fall colors were in full splendor and Vickie inhaled deeply the fresh, fragrant air. Maybe she would call Sue Brennan and meet her for lunch somewhere. She would have Ross and Kenny over for a family supper, another movie, or a quiet talk.

Anything to keep busy.

She would try to grapple with the long nights and the torment of waking up in the mornings. And yes, she would even try to think of Grisha with less pain or anger.

CHAPTER TWENTY-NINE

Vickie realized now what a tremendous burden she had been carrying, trying to care for Brian herself. What an enormous relief not to keep constant vigilance, to know that a professional was taking care of him.

She was able to sleep longer in the mornings. Alone in the apartment, the atmosphere shimmered with light, clear air, and quiet of her own choosing.

After the first week, Dr. Stevens called and said it would be best if she didn't visit Brian at all until he felt better.

"But he'd expect to see me!" Vickie cried into the phone.

After a small pause, the doctor said: "It would be painful for you and would serve no purpose. He—he doesn't *want* to see anyone."

Vickie didn't argue. She was relieved not to have to visit him and ashamed of that relief at the same time.

Starved for affection, she asked Ross and Kenny to come over every day, and when they missed an evening, she called to hear their voices over the phone. Ross breathed vigorous, athletic health. He spent a lot of time with Kenny and saw to it that the child was never left alone. Such a good and caring father.

He loved working with his hands and one day brought over the model airplanes he helped Kenny build. Dressed in jeans and sweat shirt and leaning over his father's shoulder, Kenny looked like an all-American boy. Vickie's heart turned over. Grisha too had looked like an all-American boy. Her impish, happy boy. She had had so many plans for her American-born son, who would never have suffered the handicap of being stateless, who would have had every opportunity his country had to offer. Tears welled in her eyes and she quickly blinked them away.

"I'm so glad you're here in Washington...So glad," Ross repeated, warmth shining in his eyes. Then he smiled sheepishly. "I must confess, it's a selfish feeling."

Vickie put her hand on his arm. "If you only knew how good it is to have you here. Before Brian's illness, I never realized how important it is to have a normal dialogue between two people."

He gave her a soft look. "I always enjoy talking to you."

*   *   *

There came a day when she felt like having a luncheon date with Sue Brennan. They shopped and ate at a small café, and through it all, Vickie couldn't help smiling. It had been a long time since she had been out with Sue on a shopping spree. She had forgotten how good it felt.

It was already late afternoon when she came home. She closed the door and leaned against it. Count the little pleasures, Victoria, she told herself, as she did during the bleak days in Shanghai.

It took almost five weeks to get Brian through the crisis. At the end of four weeks, the doctor let her visit him.

"I'm much better, thank you," Brian said with an arctic chill in his smile. "The doctor said I could be released in about a week."

"I'm so glad," was all Vickie could muster, hurt by his aloofness.

She stayed a few minutes then told him she'd be back the next day.

"Not tomorrow," Brian called after her. Vickie paused, but didn't turn around. "Come in a few days," Brian went on, "when I am about ready to be discharged. I don't want to see you here, in the psychiatric ward. We'll do the talking at home."

Her legs trembled, her whole body trembled as she carried herself out of the ward, out of the hospital and to her car. At home she was haunted by the sight of him sitting in a wheelchair by the hospital bed, remote, unsmiling. She dreamt all night, fragmented, fog-smothered scenes and couldn't translate any of them into any semblance of rational sense.

But the next day, lured back by duty and pity and yes, affection, she went to see him again. Brian was sitting in the wheelchair in the same spot as the day before, but this time a startling metamorphosis had taken place in his appearance. A sparkle in his eye and a contented smile greeted her as soon as she entered the room.

"I knew it! I knew you'd be back today, so I made a decision. Sit down, Vickie. Since you've come, we might as well talk here."

Vickie sat down, dazed and disoriented. "What happened to you since yesterday, Brian? You were distant and—and unsmiling, and now you look as if a miracle has happened."

"You guessed it," he said with a broadening smile, then grew serious. "I had a lot of time to think while I was in here. I decided that this is the right time to make a change in my life. I'll get an honorable discharge from the army, and once out, I won't be subject to army regulations. In short, Vickie, I want to live in San Francisco."

Their eyes locked and she saw a defiance in his, an arrogance even, and an indifference toward her that was more hurtful than anger, more chilling than hate, as if a stranger was sizing her up with cool detachment.

He leaned forward and said in measured tone: "Do you understand?"

A tide of choking bile rose to Vickie's throat. She forced the words out. "You—you phoned Keith."

His mouth stretched into a satisfied smile. "Yes, I did. I want a divorce, Vickie. Right after I'm out of the army. I won't have to hide what I am anymore."

Her eyes stung with tears of humiliation. Brian's face swam distorted like a fish in raging waters, his smile curved out of shape. She blinked the tears away and asked: "You don't mind if everyone knows?"

He laughed out loud, and it shocked her even more than his words. "Mind? Mind you say? You have no idea how relieved I am not to live a lie anymore."

"But you loved being in the army!"

"Yes,I did, but all those years I had to pretend being someone I was not. And now, fate has stepped in, hasn't it? My disability is a high price to pay for my freedom, but nothing worth having comes cheap." He paused, as if remembering some unfinished business. "Don't worry, I'll always take care of you. You stuck by me when I needed you. You'll never want for anything. I owe you that much. But be honest, you were never happy with me, certainly not since you found out about me. After all, you wanted a divorce then, and now you should appreciate your freedom. You deserve a straight man who can give you another child and— "

Vickie raised her hands and winced. "Stop! I don't want to hear any-more." She rose and rushed out of the room.

She didn't sleep that night. The longest hours. Five o'clock. Seven. She went to the kitchen, tried to make coffee, abandoned the effort.

She made her bed, got dressed, applied her makeup. In the walk-in closet, she hung her nightgown, careful to avoid glancing to Brian's side. But her head turned, her eyes riveted to his uniforms and civilian clothes, hanging on the hangers, half on, half off. Automatically, she reached to straighten them, but her arms stiffened. She went to the living room and paced the floor, rubbing and rubbing her hands.

Time crawled. In the little powder room, she leaned forward and studied herself in the mirror. Who was she now?

A fool. A woman who kept her husband's secret and lived in a sexless marriage. A woman who was discarded when her husband chose to reveal himself. Filled with rage, she ran back to the bedroom closet, grabbed Brian's shirts off the rack, threw them on the floor and stomped on them.

The rage died away. In some small way she was relieved to be out of this farce of a marriage, yet her stomach churned. She was now a woman alone.

Panic. Total, paralyzing panic. The fear. The shame. She knew the feeling. As a four-year old she knew it, when Peter Sokolov rejected her. Hunched over, she clasped her upper arms, returned to the living room and resumed pacing.

Suddenly, she stopped. Peter Sokolov was not her father. So, even that rejection was based on a lie. She stared at the phone, then at her watch. It was eight o'clock. For a few moments, she hugged herself. Then she picked up the receiver and dialed Ross' number.

The doorbell rang half an hour later and the instant she opened the door, she threw her arms around Ross's neck.

He held her head against his shoulder, guided her to the couch and sat her down.

"What is it, Vickie?" he said, genuine concern in his voice.

She was suffocating. She needed room. She pushed him away and jumped up.

"Brian wants a divorce."

Ross threw his hands up. "Now that's a misguided sacrifice. When he gets his prosthesis, he won't even know that—"

"No! That's not it at all!"

"Why then?"

The last ounce of energy seeped out of her. She dropped into the armchair and lowered her head. "It's—it's so hard to tell you."

"Try me."

"He wants to move back to San Francisco and live there with..." her lips trembled, "with a man." She could barely whisper the last word, but Ross heard it, and groaned. Vickie raised her head blinking. Sunshine favored the room, showering gold dust on the dark mahogany coffee table. The air glittered and sang a dirge in mock silence. She couldn't meet Ross's glance.

"How long have you known?" He asked.

"Since Grisha's birth."

"Good God! Why didn't you divorce him then?"

"He begged me to stay. He was afraid there would be a scandal if I left right after Grisha's birth. And then he argued that it would be hard for me to raise a boy alone, and I'd be depriving Grisha of a father. He also said that it would ruin his army career if I walked out on him at any time."

Ross listened, his face tensed by a moving jaw muscle. Through clenched teeth, he sucked in his breath. "The bastard! And all these years, you lived without—"

"Please don't!" Vickie pleaded blushing. "I can't talk about it. But you'd know sooner or later, and I hated to lie to you now."

She wrung her hands. "Oh, Ross, I am so alone!"

"What do you mean? You have Kenny and me. You also have your mother. We all love you."

Vickie stared at him. "Oh, Ross, you're so good to me."

He took her hand. "It's hard for you, Vickie, but surely you know that it's for the best. What possible future could you have had with him? I'll do all I can to help you find yourself. Remember, you're in Washington, you have talents that are needed by our government. You can have an exciting career. Think of it."

He paused, then gave a little shudder. "As for Brian, I can't condemn him for what he is. It must have been hell for him to live a lie all these years. But I can't forgive him for what he has done to you."

"Part of it was my fault too, Ross. I could have left him then and there but his arguments were so convincing that after the shock wore off, I realized that I *was* afraid to be alone with a baby. So I stayed and tried—"

"Yes," Ross interrupted heatedly, "and wasted five years of your life!"

"No, no! He was good to Grisha, he was a good father and for that I am grateful." She paused and thought: and grateful for my citizenship, and grateful for bringing my family to this great country. Aloud she said: "We were friends, I did care for him."

Ross was about to say something else but changed his mind and shook his head.

After a moment, Vickie said quietly: "Thank you, Ross, for your support."

"I need to get back home right now," he said, "and make sure Kenny has his breakfast. But I want you to know…" his breath quickened, then he paused, recovered his composure and added: "I'll always be here for you."

Vickie hugged him, kissed him on the cheek and saw him to the door.

Outside, the wind was blowing whistles, quarreling with the trees. The leaves fretted, thrusting a rippling protest into the room. She closed the door and took several deep breaths. Thank God for Ross…

*   *   *

She couldn't get out of the rented apartment fast enough. She wanted to buy a condominium right away, but Ross begged her to wait.

"I've got to get out of this apartment!" she cried, pressing her fists into her thighs. "Don't you understand? I have to!"

"Then rent another," Ross insisted, "but don't buy anything right away. You have to pull yourself together first."

She gave in to reason and rented a small apartment in the city.

Lydia, no longer entirely dependent on her job because of the trust Brian had established for her after Kiril died, wanted to take time off and come to Washington. But Vickie had never received any solace from her mother, and Lydia's presence in Washington would have made it that much harder to cope.

"No, Mama," Vickie told her on the phone. "That's not necessary. I have Ross and Kenny."

"I see," Lydia said and did not insist.

Had her mother guessed that she was unwelcome? "As soon as I can," Vickie hurried on, "I'll come to San Francisco to see you."

After a small pause, Lydia said: "It may surprise you, Vickie, but I can't condemn Brian for marrying you. He loved the army and tried to fit in. He can't help what he is. He was good to all of us. Try not to be bitter."

The first few weeks were hell. Vickie hated to admit it, but she missed Brian. He had been her guide and stability for so long, she hadn't realized how much she had depended on him to make major decisions. She tossed at night regretting her confession about Grisha. In the mornings, she looked at the racks in her closet with only her own clothes hanging there. The awful emptiness. Tears came easily now. She cried every time she cooked a meal for herself. She cried when she turned on the television and happened to tune in on one of Brian's favorite programs.

She bought fresh flowers every few days, and one sunny day went to the park. The day was brilliant, the sky without a cloud, the sun gentle on the grass. Here, the air was fresh, the neighborhood serene with a welcome intrusion—a busy finch chirping its way from branch to branch. Vickie felt isolated, no longer a part of this universe that dared to glow today in all its splendor. She wanted sullen clouds to mourn with her, she wanted pouring rain to weep her tears. Her subconscious sent signals that her heart understood but her reason could not define.

At home, she held the family album on her lap, and although she knew she shouldn't, some hidden masochistic streak pushed her to leaf through the pages to find Grisha's and Brian's smiling faces even though she could hardly focus on them.

One evening Ross caught her weeping over the snapshots. Gently but firmly, he took the album out of her hands and put it back in the drawer. "Promise me that you won't do this again, until you're able to cope with it. Crying is a healthy release, but not this way."

Vickie sniffled and said: "I keep thinking...where did I fail?"

"You didn't fail. When Nina died, I thought I had failed too. I thought I should have tried harder to make her change. But I finally realized that Nina herself would have had to make that decision." He reached over and tilted her chin. "Neither Brian nor Nina wanted to. So stop blaming yourself. I did."

She was silent for a few moments, then sighed. "There are times when I want to tell him something that happened during the day, share a joke, laugh a little. I miss his humor, his easy-going ways."

Ross smiled a warm, sad smile. "It's all in the sharing," he said, took her hand and kissed it. "But you and I are luckier than most people who lost their spouses..." He hesitated, then said very softly: "We have each other."

Vickie withdrew her hand. "It's warm in here. Can I get you something to drink?"

*   *   *

In a few weeks she renewed her contract with the State Department and found herself interpreting for Soviet delegations. Every time she faced a Soviet citizen, Henri's face floated before her. And behind Henri—Grisha's angelic face. Dull pain prowled in her chest.

Phoning Ross when the going got tough, became routine. Always patient, always kind, he listened.

"I was a fool to start working for the State Department."

"Why?"

She thought quickly. "I don't want to deal with the Soviets, that's all," she said, aware of a petulant tone in her voice. "I should have gone to VOA right away. That's what I'll do. I'll broadcast to the Soviets, without having to see them."

She resigned from the State Department and went to VOA. The work turned out to be absorbing and gratifying, leaving her no time to brood, for her days were filled with translating articles into Russian, then broadcasting them in a soundproof booth to the invisible audiences across the Atlantic.

Her superiors were pleased with her easy delivery.

"What a find you are for us, Victoria Kirilovna," one of them said, and she smiled at hearing the unaccustomed use of her patronymic.

*   *   *

Five months had passed since Brian left, and winter had set in with a thin layer of snow. Vickie hadn't bought a condominium yet. Every decision seemed like a giant hurdle. The tenants in the big house still had a few months before the lease expired and then she would put it on the market. She wanted no reminders.

Aside from a few brief notes from Brian's army associates, many of whom had been transferred out of Washington, she had been left to her own devices by their army friends. She had no desire to develop new ones, turning down invitations from her VOA colleagues, and if not for Ross and Kenny who came often to spend an evening with her, or Sue Brennan who called almost every day and whom she met once a week for lunch, she would have been entirely alone.

When spring came and the cherry blossoms graced the city, Ross took her and Kenny downtown for a walk. In the company of the two people who were so close and dear to her now, Vickie enjoyed seeing the Jefferson and Lincoln Memorials again and, holding Kenny's hand, walked along the flowering Basin inhaling the fragrant air.

At some point, Vickie noticed that Ross was watching her from the corner of his eye. "Your cheeks are showing color again," he said, "and I see an occasional sparkle in your eyes." He touched her arm. "Why don't you take a few days off and go visit your mother? It will do you good to get out of Washington for a while."

Vickie stopped, aware that a fugue of emotions was playing across her face. "I haven't thought about it yet, but now that you mentioned it...I guess I should."

Although she had not been with the VOA long enough to earn a vacation, she decided that she would ask for leave without pay. One of the benefits of having no financial worries. She bought a ticket to San Francisco and prepared to leave.

Ten days before she was to leave, Mrs. Greer, the tenant of the big house, called her.

"Oh, Mrs. Hamilton, I don't know how to tell you this, but I'm so ashamed!" she gushed. "In the last few days I've been doing some spring cleaning and started clearing my husband's desk. I found this letter addressed to you that we received last Fall. I remember giving it to my husband, thinking that he would re-address it to you, but he must have put it with his other papers and forgot about it. I'm so sorry!"

"Who is it from? Is there a return address, Mrs. Greer?"

"It's from France, Mrs. Hamilton. From a Claudette Jobert. I hope it isn't something terribly important?"

Vickie tightened her hold on the receiver. "No, Mrs. Greer. I'm sure I know what it is. I'll have to go to work this morning, but I'll ask my brother-in-law to pick it up late this afternoon, if you don't mind."

She called Ross. Yes, he would be glad to pick it up on his way to her house that evening. As a matter of fact, he had hired a babysitter, hoping to take her out to a movie.

A letter from Claudette. She must have written it after receiving mine from Leningrad, Vickie thought. Probably thanking me for the information. I don't want to read it.

Ross came in at six o'clock. "How about going out to dinner before we take in a movie?"

He handed her the envelope and then, looking at her steadily, added, "This is an old letter. Maybe you'd like to read it before we go."

Vickie took the letter. "No. It's nothing important, I'm sure. I'll read it later."

Ross's eyes narrowed. "Vickie," he said quietly, "open it. It's from Henri's sister, isn't it?"

Vickie avoided his gaze.

"You're surprised I know about Henri, aren't you?"

"It was in the papers." She hoped her voice sounded casual.

"I didn't mean his defection. I meant you and Henri."

"You mean our engagement in Shanghai? That was a long time ago."

"More than that. I guessed about Grisha, too."

Vickie's breath caught in her throat. "How?"

Ross sighed. "Nina. One night when she was drinking, she told me what a good time she had had with her friend, Claudette, in Paris, and then said that you were once engaged to her brother, Henri. She also told me that he was stationed in Frankfurt while you were in Heidelberg. When Henri defected and I saw his picture in the paper I wondered why he seemed vaguely familiar. The next time I saw Grisha—" Ross spread his arms, "I put two and two together. Brian never suspected, did he?"

Vickie lowered herself on the couch, burying her face in her hands. "What you must think of me!"

Ross sat down beside her. "I'm not judging you. You must have loved the man. I admire you for being so good to Brian, for doing so much for him. Nina didn't even try to make me happy."

"But I cared for him too."

"You don't need to explain." He took the letter from the table where she dropped it. "Read it, Vickie, don't be afraid to see what Claudette has to say."

Vickie rose, fists clenched. "No. I'll read it in due time."

"Vickie! Read it now!"

"Don't you order me! Why are you insisting?"

Ross's face turned pale. "Because—because—" His mouth worked nervously, "Damn it!" He pulled her roughly toward him and took her in his arms. "Because I love you. Do you understand? I...love...you!"

She raised her head and saw in his eyes a man's love for a woman...there was no mistake...saw his desire and his longing.

He came down hard on her mouth and she went weak in his arms. For one long, delicious moment she responded hungrily to his kiss. Her body throbbed with the sensations she hadn't ever felt with Brian, sensations she hadn't felt since—since—

Oh, my God! What is happening?

Shaken, she pushed him away. "Oh, Ross!"

As Ross looked at her she felt her face burn.

"We mustn't let Nina stand between us," he said. "We have our lives to live."

Vickie buried her face in her hands. "I'm stunned!…Please!…"

Ross threw his arms up in the air. "Oh, what's the use!"

He grabbed his raincoat. "I'll call you tomorrow," he muttered and stalked out of the house.

Vickie watched him leave, then sat down, trying to sort out her thoughts. Her husband was gone, her child was dead, and she was alone. Is that why she had been leaning on Ross so heavily?

But that kiss…not brotherly, but passionate and possessive and…wonderful. A powerful yearning stirred within her, and the shock of recognition of something she had been refusing to admit, made her pulse race.

She stared at the letter on the coffee table. She'd read it tomorrow after work. Right now she needed a drink. She went to the liquor cabinet and, her hands shaking, poured herself a glass of wine. Then, passing the table, she paused and reached for the letter. It was dated a month after she had written to Claudette from Leningrad. She opened it and read:

Dear Vickie, Henri is gone from Leningrad, resettled to Siberia. Those dreadful bureaucrats…"

A piteous whimper escaped Vickie's throat. She dropped the letter and doubled over, making small, whining noises. As she sank to her knees, she saw the letter on the floor, reached for it, and read on:

…Those dreadful bureaucrats won't tell me where he is. They won't even answer my letters. Can you imagine that? The news came from the woman who lived with him. Forgive me if I sound bitter, but I would like to know just why my brother fell out of favor. The woman claims that he has a good apartment in Siberia, but I have a hard time believing he wouldn't have written a few words to me—his sister…"

Claudette went on to describe how she broke the news to her father, and how he made her feel worse by saying that he had expected something like that to happen to his traitor son.

Vickie put down the letter with a shaking hand. She was convinced that her visit to Henri in Leningrad caused his exile to Siberia. The authorities knew of his efforts to get out of Russia, and must have been suspicious of a foreign visitor.

She rushed to her desk, found Henri's picture she kept hidden among her papers. She studied it, traced the outline of his face with her finger. Slowly, she tore the picture in two and threw the pieces back in the drawer. But as she slammed it shut, something clattered against the wood. She opened the drawer and saw the jade ring that Henri had given her for Grisha. She picked it up and studied it for a while. It would have been Grisha's. *Was* Grisha's. *That* she would keep. Lovingly, she wrapped it in tissue paper, went to the bedroom, and put it in her jewel box.

After a few minutes, she reread the letter and sat staring into space for a long time. Then she picked up the receiver and dialed Ross' number.

"Ross? Henri was exiled to Siberia."

"How tragic," Ross said.

"Ross, can you please come over?" she asked in a small voice.

"I'm sorry, Vickie, I can't."

"Why not? I need you! Please come."

A small pause, then: "I let the babysitter go."

"Oh, I forgot. My mind isn't working straight."

"I see." There was an odd note in his voice. "You never got over him, did you?"

"How can you say that? I've just had a bad shock, that's all!"

"I'm sorry, but you'll have to cope with this one without me. As I said, the babysitter is gone and under the circumstances, it wouldn't be right to bring Kenny along."

Vickie replaced the receiver slowly, picked up her sweater, hung it in the closet. Ross. His strong, warm face. Did she think she owned him? But he had always been there when she needed him and she had never stopped to think…

*   *   *

Sometimes she thought her memory served her false when only Henri's drawn and pained face appeared before her mind's eye. She tried to recreate the other times, the beautiful times but they eluded her in a shadowy procession of blurred images obscured by grief and time.

During the day she held herself together by sheer force of will, broadcasting at the VOA in a steady measured voice, discipline of deadlines forcing her to concentrate on her work and keep the private demons at bay.

But at night, burrowing her face into the pillow, she tried to blot out the hollow silence in the apartment. Ever since Brian left, there was a different quality to the silence. This silence had the weight of permanence. It hummed with the sounds of Grisha's giggles and Brian's laughter and distant whispers of Henri's voice. She yearned for her piano to play her favorite pieces but even that pleasure was denied her because the piano was in the big house and the tenants were still there.

And so she wept when no one could hear her. She wept for Grisha, her beautiful boy, and for Henri, her first love; she wept for her stepfather, and his misguided loyalty; she wept for Nina, and her tragic death; she wept for Brian and her failed marriage; and she wept for herself and her uncertain future; All the grief that she had suppressed during Brian's illness poured out now in soul-cleansing tears.

Gradually, good memories emerged. She relived the happy days with Henri in Shanghai; the stolen moments in Germany; the glorious few days in Salzburg; the hours together in Washington. And she thought of Grisha, their love child, and the happy childhood he had had with all the love she and Brian had given him. And as she sat there, remembering, the enormous weight of guilt and torment lifted, and she knew that she could finally forgive herself and begin to heal.

The day before she left for San Francisco, she called Ross and Kenny and said goodbye. She wanted to get away. She *needed* to get away. She checked her purse, pulled out the plane ticket.

Tomorrow she would be in California.

CHAPTER THIRTY

"Let's have lunch downtown, at the St. Francis Hotel," Lydia said the first morning after Vickie arrived in San Francisco.

Downtown was Union Square. The big stores crowded around it like elegant siblings vying for attention. How many times had she gone shopping there alone or with Brian's mother? Now, in retrospect, even Jane's barbs seemed innocuous, and in their own way, helpful. After all, Jane didn't have to teach her American ways, could have let her make the blunders and pointed out to Brian what a mistake he had made in marrying a foreign girl.

Brian. Should she call him to say hello? They had parted amicably enough, but then why stir up old wounds? Besides, he may be embarrassed by her call. Why take a chance? It would achieve nothing and make it awkward for both of them.

San Francisco had a special charm she had not seen anywhere else: a sophisticated, cosmopolitan city in a relatively small area. She remembered her surprise on arrival in America to see how old-fashioned the city's buildings were compared to the modern apartment houses in Shanghai. Now she appreciated the appeal of the Victorian houses—narrow and tall, standing side-by-side on twenty-five foot lots, yet each distinct from the other in its color and design—friendly together, never alone. A charm unique to San Francisco…

Suddenly, Vickie wanted to prolong her visit. What if she bought a house and moved here? She would look after her mother, could bring back the happiness she had known before leaving San Francisco…make new friends, start her life over. In Washington, there were constant reminders of sadness and tragedies.

She sighed. What about Kenny? And…Ross.

Lydia touched her arm. "Vickie, you're miles away."

"I was thinking how much I missed San Francisco. It's still the same and doesn't seem to change."

"How long will I have you with me?"

Vickie played with her fork. "I haven't decided yet. I don't have any definite commitments."

"What about your job?"

"I took a leave of absence and told them I'd let them know when I'd come back."

*　　　　*　　　　*

Back in Lydia's apartment, Vickie looked around the living room. The scatter pillows she had bought for her parents before they arrived from Tubabao were still in place, and in the kitchen Lydia was still using the same pots and pans.

With a cup of tea in her hands, Vickie stirred the sugar thoughtfully. "Mama," she said, "Does the extra income give you enough to indulge yourself once in a while?"

Lydia's eyes filled. "It's more than enough."

"Tell me," Vickie said after a pause, "have you thought of—of another man?"

"There is a gentleman who takes me to the Russian parties and to the movies," Lydia said with a shrug. "I'm glad to have an escort, but I'll never marry again."

"Why not? Companionship—"

"Companionship, bah! I have my friends, my work, and at night I can do what I want. To think that I'd have to get used to another man's habits, darn his socks, and take care of his ailments! Never!"

Vickie laughed. "I'm glad you have your life pretty well settled. What about your work with the Russian community?"

Lydia reached over and spooned some black currant jam into her tea. "I've dropped some of my friends and acquired new ones. The longer I live in America, the more I think that poor Papa was wrong to cling so hard to the past. Old Russia is gone forever, and even if there were to be a democratic government, it wouldn't be the same. I'm now convinced that any changes, if there are to be any, must come from within, and not by pressure from without. I help when our church members send clothing and parcels to the needy in Russia and to the few unfortunate Russians left in Harbin."

Vickie hugged her mother. "Oh, Mama, I'm glad to hear that. What made you change your mind?"

"A Soviet girl who married an American businessman and now lives here, warned me that the propaganda material my friends were sending to Russia could cause real trouble for the people, and achieve little. She also said that after talking to us old Russians, as she put it, she found less in common with us than with native-born Americans. That's what started me thinking."

"You know, Mamochka," Vickie said, "after coming here and seeing you, I feel very much at home. I've been toying with the idea of moving back to San Francisco. Wait! Don't shake your head, hear me out. I wouldn't live with you, I know that wouldn't work. But it feels so good to be here."

Lydia put down her cup, folded her hands on her lap and studied Vickie with narrowed eyes. "Stop fooling yourself. What in the world would you do in San Francisco—be a secretary? Or worse—with your wealth, become a social butterfly? Remember, your army friends are no longer at the Presidio, and you'd have to make new ones.

That wouldn't be so bad, since you're still young, but what else would you have? You'd be wasting your talents. What about your work at the Voice of America?"

"There are other agencies in Washington—I could do translating work by correspondence. As for VOA, I cann't cling to that one reason."

"Rather an important reason, seems to me. All of a sudden, you're ready to throw it all to the winds. What's behind all this?"

"I have too many awful memories in Washington, Mama, and I should live near you."

"So you're running away from bad memories. What you don't realize my dear girl, is that those memories will follow you here. I have my sad memories too, but I didn't run away from them, I coped with them and they don't keep me awake anymore. I'd hate to think that you'd move here not only to escape from bad memories, but because of me. Let me set you straight: get rid of the misguided illusion that it's your duty to be near me."

Lydia paused, then went on. "I'm fully aware what a wonderful daughter I have. I enjoy you, Vickie. I can talk to you in a way I never could to Nina. You and I understand each other, don't we? But that doesn't mean I want you to live here. We can both afford to visit each other. Besides, I want you to keep an eye on my grandchild."

Lydia rose and went to the kitchen

Her mother's reasoning was valid, Vickie thought, and it was obvious that she was really independent and self-sufficient. Vickie remembered those two times when her mother had offered to come to Washington, one after Grisha's death, and the other when she learned about Brian, and how, after Vickie declined her offer, Lydia hadn't insisted on coming, and probably had been relieved. And now, Vickie thought, with all Mama's friends around her, she most likely won't miss me after I leave. Thinking about it, it was not the idea that her mother hadn't insisted on her staying that surprised her, but her own reaction to it. She should be hurt but it no longer mattered.

After all the years she had tried to earn her mother's love and approval, she had only won her appreciation. She remembered her Christmas parties in Harbin, when Lydia had taken meticulous care to make each one different, hiding the children's presents and making them hunt for them, or creating a ship out of colored paper on the dining table and hiding the presents inside. She remembered other times, when Lydia explained to her that Father Frost gave out presents with his gloves on, so his hands wouldn't melt. She smiled and put down the teaspoon she was playing with. Yes, she understood her mother now. Lydia had done the best she could by her, had given her what she had been capable of giving, and it was unrealistic to expect anything beyond that, because Lydia's deep maternal love had gone to Nina.

The amazing thing was that it neither pained nor angered her. Actually, the only time she had been totally happy in her life was when she had disobeyed her mother's rules and become Henri's lover, and later, when Grisha was born.

She was filled with relief and a sense of freedom and ease, like a person who had finally shed the burden of a long illness and was now free to enjoy good health.

Perhaps now, at long last, they could be friends.

When Lydia came back with a fresh pot of tea, Vickie waited until she refilled their cups, then said: "I can see that you're comfortable and content with your friends and don't need me all that much."

"All I'm saying," Lydia said, "is that you don't need to worry about me."

Sounds of long ago conversations, subtle hurts, sharp retorts, proud silences, hovered between them. Vickie glanced at her mother and, seeing her eyes blinking to hide her tears, knew that Lydia was remembering too.

Vickie leaned over and took her mother's hand between hers. "Oh, Mamochka, I'm so glad we had this talk. I love you."

Lydia cleared her throat, then said: "I love you too, but you haven't mentioned Ross yet. How is he?"

"Fine. He's been of great help to me during the past few months."

"What is he doing with himself? Besides helping you, I mean?"

Vickie blew on the cup to cool the tea. "I don't know."

Lydia looked at Vickie steadily. "What do you mean, you don't know?"

Vickie took a sip from her cup and burnt her tongue. "Just what I said, Mama. He and Kenny spend a lot of time with me, but what he does on his own, I don't know."

"Oh-oh! You little fool."

Lydia's voice was so soft, Vickie was startled. "What did you say, Mama?"

"I said, you fool. You must be totally blind. I've seen how he admired you, even before Nina died."

Vickie felt her neck grow hot. "That's not true! He's family to me, Mama."

"You pack up your suitcases, young lady, and go back to Washington. You have a promising career at the VOA, don't forget that. And be good to Ross. He's Kenny's father and part of our family!"

"Yes, Mama," Vickie said quietly, and at that moment she longed to see him with an intensity that was a sudden revelation.

"It doesn't matter, is or was," Lydia said, raising her voice, "just be good to him!"

During the night, Vickie tossed in bed. All her life she felt a distance from her mother and maybe that was another reason why she had leaned on Brian during her marriage. But since the divorce, she had been able to realize her ambition of helping her adoptive country. And now, she hadn't allowed herself to think about her work at the VOA. How could she have thought of giving it up? She remembered Henri telling her once that Russia was the country of his heart. Well, America was the country of *her* heart.

Of course she had to return to Washington. That was the right thing to do. She would cope with unwanted memories and build a future for herself. She would still keep in touch with her mother but lead her own life without needing Lydia's approval, now that she no longer expected the impossible from her. And she'd be near Kenny and Ross.

It was all a matter of loyalties, wasn't it? Divided loyalties. Over the years, she had had to make a choice—a wrenching choice that hunted her down in China, in Germany, in America. Some people choose their destiny once in a lifetime but she had been put to the test three times, and three times she made the same choice. There could have been no other. Of that she was certain…

Over and over her thoughts returned to Ross. She couldn't stop thinking about him. She hadn't been honest with herself. She had run away from that one thrilling moment.

In the dark of the night, she stretched and smiled, reaching out to the future. As if the light was turned on in the dark corridor of her life, and Vickie saw a door opening ahead.

*   *   *

When she returned to her apartment in Washington, she turned on all the lights in the living room, put down her suitcases and went to the phone. She dialed and waited three rings before Kenny's voice came over the wire.

"Hello?"

"Kenny, honey, Aunt Vickie is back."

"Oh, Auntie, Daddy is sick. Very sick!"

"What's wrong with him?"

"The doctor said it's the flu. Oh, Auntie, can you come over?"

"I'll be right there."

She pushed the suitcases out of the way, grabbed her car keys and rushed out.

Kenny opened the door and wrapped his arms around her. Oh, how good it was to feel the child's hug! The little face was pinched and the big blue eyes frightened.

"Where's Daddy?" Vickie asked, kissing Kenny and stroking his hair.

"In the bedroom, Auntie. He's been in bed for two days."

Ross was asleep when Vickie entered the bedroom. His breathing was erratic and beads of perspiration stood out on his forehead. Vickie tiptoed to the bathroom, wrung out a cloth and came back into the room. She knelt beside the bed and gently wiped his forehead.

Ross started and opened his eyes. They were clouded with fever. He tried to raise himself.

"Vickie! When did you get back?" He touched his chin. "I— I haven't shaved in a couple of days, I'm sorry."

Vickie pushed him back on the pillows. "Lie down, you have fever. What does the doctor say?"

Ross groaned and tossed about. "It's the flu. I've got to stay in bed and take aspirin until I stop hurting so damn much."

"Where does it hurt, Ross?"

"All over. I've never had anything like it. Especially my back."

"Can I get you something to eat?"

"No, thanks. But Kenny must be hungry. I haven't been able to get out of bed since yesterday. There should be something in the kitchen."

"I'll see to it."

She leaned over and kissed him. Her lips lingered on his cheek. Her heart knocked against her chest wanting to leap out and shout: *I love you!* She tried to smooth his hair off his forehead, but he turned his face away.

"Don't come too close. I don't want you to catch it. I'm.—I'm so thirsty. Would you see if there's any juice in the refrigerator?"

Vickie went to the kitchen. A couple of empty cans of Campbell's soup stood by the sink and a loaf of bread with peanut butter and jelly jars were on the kitchen table. Kenny followed on her heels.

"Is that what you were eating, Kenny?" she asked. The child nodded solemnly. "I tried to make Daddy eat, but he wouldn't. I'm hungry, Auntie. You're not going to go away again, are you?"

The large eyes looked at her anxiously. A lump lodged in Vickie's throat. She swallowed. "No, I'm not going away again. Tell me, did anyone come over to help from Daddy's office? Or any of his friends?"

Kenny shook his head. "Daddy didn't want anyone to come over. He said he'd be well soon. A lady called from the office and then brought that soup." He pointed to a pot on the stove and made a face. "It's bean soup. I hate it!"

"Why don't you put the plates on the table while I fix us something to eat? But first, I'll get some juice for Daddy."

Vickie took a glass of orange juice to Ross. He was dozing again, but she slipped her hand under his neck and lifted his head. "Here, drink this."

He drank the juice obediently. "Thank you, Vickie. I guess I won't be up and around as soon as I thought. I…would you call my office and ask if they know anyone who would come in and cook for Kenny? Or maybe your cleaning lady knows someone?"

Vickie straightened his blanket, took the empty glass out of his hand. "I'm moving in here, Ross. I'll feed Kenny, then go home to pick up a few things. I'll stay here until you're well."

Ross tried to say something, but she put her finger to her lips. "I don't want to hear anything from you, do you hear? You rest now, and I'll check on you a little later."

After she and Kenny ate in the kitchen and she gave Ross a cup of hot bouillon, she went home, repacked hurriedly, and drove back. Kenny was waiting for her with his assignment book, and she settled in the living room to listen to him read. Later, the boy followed her around the house tapping her arm to ask a question, offering to help make her bed in the guest room, showing his homework.

As she tucked him in for the night, up went his arms around her neck in a surprisingly strong hug for an eight-year old.

"Auntie," he whispered in her ear, "I wish you lived with us."

"Don't worry, honey, I'll stay here until Daddy gets well."

"Why don't you marry Daddy and then we'll be a family forever?"

"You go to sleep now, young man. We'll talk tomorrow."

Throughout the night Vickie heard Ross moaning in his sleep in the adjoining bedroom. Several times she went in and changed his pajamas top and wiped his face with a washcloth. Once, in the dim light of the night lamp, he raised his eyes glazed with pain, then caught her hand in midair and brought it to his lips. "Oh, Vickie, Vickie!…How I missed you!"

"I'll be here. Go to sleep now," she whispered, as he fell back on the pillow half asleep. Vickie smoothed his hair, tucked in his blanket and returned to her room, leaving the door ajar so she could hear him and Kenny.

$$*\qquad\qquad *\qquad\qquad *$$

She stayed with them for three more days and on the fifth, when Ross felt better, she went home to unpack and see that everything was in order in her apartment.

After she had put her clothes away, dusted and cleaned up, she stood in the middle of the living room listening. There was a dense quality to the silence this time. Whoever said that silence couldn't be heard or that it wasn't alive? Dread crawled up her back, filled the room. The sounds coming from the street below were muffled, and she opened the window to let them in. A woman's voice calling her child; the purr of an idling engine; and a man's carefree laughter.

But here, in the apartment, the silence prevailed. She stood stiffly, certain that at night old ghosts would return in a procession of time warp scenes, the dead come back to life to haunt her. Abruptly, she turned and went to the kitchen to fix a cup of tea. Waiting for it to cool, she watched the dust motes whirling in a narrow shaft of sunlight. How many times as a child had she watched them floating in the air? She glanced out the kitchen window that opened on a small garden. The dead leaves of last Fall had been swept away a long time ago, the snow had melted, and with the changing seasons, the grounds were now brilliant with petunias and impatiens. A hummingbird was drinking the nectar from a fuchsia blossom outside, flashing its iridescent green and magenta colors in the shimmering air.

She hurried to the living room, reached under a pile of books stored away on the top shelf and pulled out an old album with snapshots taken in Harbin and Shanghai. She sat down on the couch and leafed through the pages of her youth. Some pictures had begun to fade, but most were still clear. Someday she would take time to sort them out and see if the poor ones could be restored. This time she shed no tears. With a sigh, she put the album down. For a few moments she stood over it, then picked it up and replaced it on the top bookshelf. An idea struck her. She went to her jewel box in the bedroom and took out Henri's jade ring that she had been keeping for Grisha.

Back in the kitchen, she sat still, overcome by a sense of peace. She closed her eyes, savoring the sweetness of the moment, then admired the ring. Grisha was gone, but Kenny—her nephew, her sister's flesh and blood—was alive and he loved Grisha. She would give the ring to him. And she had to see Ross.

She smiled and reached for the phone. Ross answered.

"Ross! I'm glad you're out of bed."

"I feel much better today, Vickie, thanks to you." He chuckled. "I guess that hot bouillon you've been feeding me did the trick."

"I'm so glad. I called to say that I'm on my way and should be there in a few minutes."

A brief pause, then: "I think I'll be able to manage from now on. We've imposed on you already, but…it'll be good to have you here for a while longer."

Fifteen minutes later, she opened the door with the key that Kenny had given her and walked into the living room. Ross, in his dark blue velour robe, rose from the chair and took a step forward, then stopped and looked at her. It was a long look, a waiting look. She stood a few paces away and stared at him. Such a strong, handsome face. She realized that she had never really *seen* him this way. The collar of his pajamas was open and she had a wild desire to press her mouth over the fast pulsating vein on his neck.

A wave of something hot and thrilling surged through her. She threw down her purse on the chair, then turned to him.

"Ross, I've been such a fool. Do you—" she stumbled over the words, "do you still want me?"

He grasped her hands, pulled her to him. "Do I want you? My God, I'd almost given up hoping!"

Through the loose folds of his robe she could feel his tensed, aroused body. She buried her face in his neck. "I love you, Ross."

He silenced her with a deep, probing kiss, and she responded with a fire that flared through her with a stunning force.

He moved back. "Do you want a formal proposal?" he said with a twinkle in his eyes.

Vickie regained her equilibrium with difficulty and smiled. "Your son took care of that three days ago when he asked me why don't I marry his Daddy."

He tilted her chin. "I have to ask you this…is your heart free of—of ghosts?"

She slipped down to her knees, wrapped her arms around his thighs and throwing her head way back, looked him full in the face. "Free! Free of ghosts at last."

*   *   *

A year later, a nurse at Georgetown University Hospital walked down the hall carrying a newborn in her arms. She entered room 102 and smiled.

"Mrs. Antonova, feeding time." She placed the baby in the mother's arms. "I'll be back in a few minutes."

Vickie looked down at the howling little face in the crook of her arm. "Don't be so impatient, Miss Lydia Antonova. You'll get your milk in plenty of time before your daddy and your brother come to see you again."

As the baby suckled, grunting with pleasure, Vickie played with the tiny hand, admiring the perfect little fingers. The baby had emptied her breast and was pulling on the nipple. She changed her to the other side, then settled back on the pillows, squinting at the sunlight that had burst through the window, touched her face, and dazzled her with its radiance.

She closed her eyes, overcome by a sense of great happiness, her mind dwelling on the sweetness of the past year, the wondrous passion of her new, consuming love, and the exquisite moment when a new life stirred inside her. At last everything had come together. Her love *was* her husband and his *rodina* was her homeland as well. No more divisions of heart and soul and body.

She listened to the sounds outside her door. Doctors giving orders, nurses answering phones, visitors asking directions to their loved one's room.

People died, people were born. In the ever-changing human seasons, she would count the pleasures. Always. She smiled at the baby, sated now and asleep. Gently, she tickled her cheek.

Her little girl…A woman of tomorrow.

THE END

ABOUT THE AUTHOR

Alla Crone was born in the White Russian culture of Harbin, Manchuria. She lived there during the Japanese occupation and eventually moved to Shanghai, where she married an American physician. She now resides in California. Her articles have appeared in The Michigan Quarterly Review, The Christian Science Monitor and other magazines. She is the author of four historical novels.